Cool Water

Dianne Warren
Cool Water

A PHYLLIS BRUCE BOOK
HARPERCOLLINS PUBLISHERS LTD

HarperCollins Publishers Ltd
2 Bloor Street East, 20th Floor
Toronto, Ontario
M4W 1A8

www.harpercollins.ca

Library and Archives Canada Cataloguing in Publication

Warren, Dianne, 1950–
Cool water : a novel / Dianne Warren.

ISBN 978-1-55468-558-5

I. Title.

PS8595.A778C66 2009   C813'.54   C2009-905717-4

Printed in the United States
Text design by Sharon Kish

RRD 9 8 7 6 5 4 3 2 1

In memory of
Harriet and Milford Taylor

The Distance

It was the end of August, before the Perry Land and Cattle Company's fall gather, and the ranch cowboys had too much time on their hands. They were standing around the dusty yard doing nothing more than watch the horses swat flies with their tails when the young buck, Ivan Dodge, somehow managed to convince one of the old veteran cowboys—Henry Merchant was his name—to meet his challenge of a hundred-mile horse race through the dunes and the grasslands of the Little Snake Hills. It wasn't like Henry to act so impulsively, but Ivan Dodge was getting on his nerves with his restless strut and his mouth that never stopped yapping, even in his sleep. Henry figured he could beat him. He figured Ivan Dodge was a rabbit, fast all right, but not smart enough to win. You needed strategy to win a hundred-mile race.

The Perry cowhands got enthusiastically involved in the pre-race planning, as did the ranch manager, who saw an opportunity to build relations between the ranch and the burgeoning community of homesteaders. They decided on five in the morning as a start time and agreed on the buffalo rubbing stone just north of the settlement of Juliet as the start and finish of the race. This was close to the ranch headquarters, but also close enough to town to create some excitement and attract the local gamblers. The cowboys would each ride four horses—the first- and fourth-leg horses their own, and the middle-leg mounts selected from the ranch remuda—switching every twenty-five miles in the corners of a hundred-mile square. They each put up fifty dollars, a lot of money in those days. The challenge became known and race day settled into the consciousness of everyone for miles around Juliet. Word spread like chicken pox.

Popular support went to the elder. That was because Ivan Dodge was arrogant and needed to be brought down a peg or two. It was *right* that Henry Merchant win the race, and so the cowboys and the townspeople and the settlers alike bet their money on the veteran, believing in life lessons and confident that Ivan Dodge would be taught one. Only a few of the more serious gamblers bet on Ivan, suspecting that youth might just skunk experience.

The ranch cowboys and a few men from town (the ones who had bet the largest sums of money) showed up to see the riders off in the early morning, rubbing their hands to warm themselves in the cool air, building a fire in the hollow next to the buffalo rubbing stone to boil coffee in an old pot. The first-leg horses stamped and snorted, sensing excitement and ready to go, while the gamblers examined them closely for clues as to which would carry its rider to an early lead—the young cowboy's prancy bay gelding with his wide nostrils, clean throatlatch and distinctive white markings, or the old cowboy's leggy sorrel mare, who looked as if she might have the reach of a racehorse.

Ivan and Henry discussed the route, and Henry said, "I've got people in the corners to make sure you ride the whole hundred, so don't go taking no shortcuts," which made Ivan smirk and say, "I wouldn't be worrying about me, old man. I doubt those rickety bones can even sit a horse for a hundred miles." The two cowboys said, *Ha, we'll just see,* back and forth, *we'll see about that, won't we.* Ivan Dodge was wearing a new pair of fringed leather chaps with silver conchas and the old cowboy couldn't help but make fun of his fancy outfit. When they mounted up and loped off as their pocket watches marked five, they were still exchanging barbs about the young cowboy's sense of direction (famously bad) and the old cowboy's bones (famously stiff), which added to the entertainment. The gamblers were in high spirits, and they told and retold the best retorts to newcomers as they arrived wanting details about the start of the race.

The day took on the atmosphere of a summer fair. Spectators congregated at the three change stations, but by far the largest crowd gathered at the buffalo stone, which was the finish as well as the start of the race. Town families walked the short distance to the stone, and farmers and their wives and children came horseback or in wagons from all directions, by road or cross-country. They brought picnics. A fiddler showed up—no one seemed to know him—and he played jigs and folk songs to entertain the women and children. The local newspaperman took pictures, although he wasn't much interested in the farmers and their families and wished he could ride with the two cowboys and capture the race as it unfolded. Like the gamblers, all he could do was wait for the finish.

The two riders went north from the stone, past the Torgeson homestead, past the Swan Valley Cemetery with its one lonely marker for Herbert Swan, the first settler in the area to die. Then along a soft dirt road for twenty miles, all the way to the Lindstrom place and the new schoolhouse, the first change station. A good well in the schoolyard, but no time for much of a break. West into the sand hills, the sun just beginning to climb in the eastern sky. Up the first big dune to the top, sharp-edged ridges breaking away like crusted snow, rivers of sand cascading down. To the west, a wilderness, endless miles of sand and grass.

No fences, no farms at all until you come to the Varga homestead, the second change station, where the Varga brothers and their families have begun construction of a Catholic church so the visiting priest will have a proper place to conduct the mass. Fresh horses waiting by the newly laid stone foundation, a drink from another good well, the warm smell of sweat and leather, and then south again into the heat of the day. No active dunes now, just low rolling hills, August brown and stabbed with the blue-green of sage, muted colours sliding by under the horses' long-trotting strides, the mercury at its peak for the day, the air so hot it's hard to breathe, heat waves blurring the land ahead.

Then relief. Down a sandy cutbank into a coulee, deer scattering, a doe and her twins separated in the excitement. At the bottom, a spring-fed creek, an oasis of sorts shaded by willow and poplar trees. Such respite from the sun, the temptation strong to wait here until later in the day, but after a brief stop, back up into the heat and a stretch of good flat land. Farms cropping up again on this stretch, small clapboard houses and newly erected pasture fences, newly patented wire gates to open and close, and then the east-west rail line where someone has planted a Union Jack and people are waiting for the last change of horses.

Twenty-five miles to go in the blistering sun, straight east through open grassland. Soft rolling hills, an endless graveyard of bleached cattle bones, sober reminders of the previous winter storms. The rise and fall of landscape, the monotony of up and down, twenty-five miles going on and on and feeling like the whole hundred all over again. Until finally, the creek that winds toward Juliet. Water for man and horse, then up out of the draw, the pace quickening with the sense that the finish line is not far now. The horse's head high, a trot turning into a lope and then a hard gallop for the buffalo rubbing stone and the waiting crowd of onlookers.

Most of whom quit cheering when they saw it was the young buck galloping toward them, whooping and waving his hat, his horse lathered and foaming. They'd bet on the wrong cowboy.

And then their jaws truly dropped when they saw he was riding the same bay horse that he'd set out on.

Impossible, they said.

The horsemen among the spectators looked carefully for signs that this was, in fact, a different horse. As the young cowboy cooled him out, they examined his markings—a star, a snip and one white foot—and concluded that he certainly *looked* like Ivan's first-leg horse. Then one of the spectators from the first change station rode in and verified Ivan's claim that, after giving the bay a brief rest, the young cowboy had carried on, leaving his fresh horse behind. This spectator also brought the news that Henry Merchant's first horse had thrown a shoe and with it a piece of his hoof a fair distance short of the change station, and Henry had lost precious time walking.

The gamblers gave the win to Ivan Dodge and accepted their loss. The newspaperman made his notes about the race (*won in a time of 12 hours and 32 minutes*), the weather (*seasonably hot*) and the young cowboy's sensational mount (*purchased from Mister Herbert Legere of Medicine Hat and said to have Arab blood*), and took a front-page photograph of Ivan and his horse, prancing as though he was ready for another twenty-five miles, which was good, because they still had to get home to the ranch headquarters five miles to the southwest.

The ranch hands were mostly disgusted and tired of spending the day among farm families with noisy children and plow dirt under their fingernails, and they drifted into town in search of new excitement. Most of the townspeople—the implement dealers and hotel owners and railroad men—went home for supper, except for the few serious gamblers who had won money and were now happy to stick around and shoot the breeze with Ivan Dodge, who was telling the story of his heroic race over and over, and couldn't wait for Henry Merchant to come into view so he could rub the old cowboy's nose in his loss. A couple of the men had flasks with them and when the farm women noticed, they moved their picnics and their families away from the buffalo stone and the bad influence of the gamblers. They knew that their husbands had bet good money too, but they pretended not to know.

The children were tired and cranky at the end of a long hot day. The fiddler was still there and he was trying to play for them, but his tunes had taken a sad turn, as though he were lamenting something lost—his homeland perhaps. When one little boy put his hands over his ears and began to cry, the young but forthright Mrs. Sigurd Torgeson handed the fiddler a pie plate of cold chicken and boiled eggs and dill pickles, and firmly tried to say in a mix of Norwegian and newly acquired English that everyone had heard enough fiddle music for one day. She noticed that the fiddler's hair was unkempt and his clothes were not all that clean, and she wondered why she hadn't noticed that earlier, and why the mothers had let him near their children in the first place.

A malaise settled over the farm families, one that they didn't quite understand. They weren't sure why they were waiting. They ate their picnics quietly, feeling strangely depressed about Henry Merchant's absence. They kept looking to the west, watching for a horse and rider to come into view. They wanted to see Henry Merchant cross the finish line, as though doing so would punctuate a disappointing day with something good. After they'd finished eating and he still hadn't arrived, they concluded that he'd given up and gone home to the ranch, that there was nothing to do but pack their picnic things and leave. They said their goodbyes and headed off in various directions to homesteads that suddenly felt lonely and tentative. They were, all of them, sombre, not because of money lost, but because they'd been *so certain*. This was a determined lot who wanted badly to believe in the future. It was disconcerting to be wrong.

Eventually, it became known that the old cowboy's race was pretty much a lost cause from the time his first horse threw the shoe. He'd failed to make up the time on the second and third legs, and on the fourth his best horse, pushed beyond what his usually sensible rider knew was wise, quit on him. When the horse stretched out and released a stream of urine the colour of coffee, the old hand knew the race was over.

Into the evening, the young cowboy sat on the buffalo rubbing stone and smoked cigarettes and talked to the few people who remained—the newspaperman and the three or four others who were still there—and finally he said, "Well, boys, I don't suppose there's any point waiting much longer. It's past old Merchant's bedtime and I imagine he's sound asleep somewhere. Either that, or he's up and died." He guffawed in a way that annoyed even his new fans, and then he mounted his horse and rode back the way he'd come. His own body felt a little worse for wear when he climbed into the saddle, but of course he kept that to himself. He felt let down that he hadn't had the chance to rib Henry Merchant in public; that had been the whole point. He thought about riding into town to find the other ranch hands and then realized he didn't want to see them. He tried to reason why that was and grew dejected when he figured out it was because they really hadn't wanted him to win.

Just as he was about to turn south and head for home, he saw Henry's bow-legged hobble coming toward him in the dusky light. The young cowboy waited, having planned something smart to say, but thrown off guard because Henry was without his horse.

"Tied up on me" is all Henry said when they met.

The two of them turned south toward the Perry ranch, the excitement over and the challenge won or lost, depending on whose perspective you were looking from.

By now it was almost dark. The two cowboys walked together for a ways without talking, young Ivan still horseback, not thinking that Henry might want to change places with him after his long walk, and then Ivan grew impatient with the slow pace and said he was going to ride on ahead.

"Well, I guess I won," he said. He couldn't help himself.

The old cowboy stopped and took off his worn Stetson hat and shook sand from the brim and then gave his head a good scratch before putting the hat back on.

"I guess you did at that," Henry said.

"I won good."

"You did."

"Fair and square."

"I wouldn't go that far," said Henry. "Fair's got nothing to do with it."

"How's that?"

"You needed to be taught a lesson and you weren't."

"Who's the one with a million-dollar horse?" asked Ivan. Then he added, as though the idea had just come to him, "I could make money with this horse."

"He's got distance," said the old hand, "I'll give you that. But he's about as cowy as a housecat."

The young cowboy moved his horse out and tried to urge him into a lope, but this time the horse wasn't anxious to pick up his pace. He balked, and when Ivan hit him with a spur, he gave a good buck, straight up, all four feet off the ground, and Ivan wasn't expecting that and was just plain lucky that he managed to stick. When the horse finally moved out, Ivan called back, "I'll tell you who needed to be taught a lesson and it wasn't me."

Henry let it go. He dearly would have loved to see Ivan and his fancy new chaps in the dirt, to at least have that bit of victory, but he was exhausted, and he thought maybe he *had* learned a lesson, although he didn't want to admit it. A hundred miles is a long way to ride in one day, even for a man who made his living horseback, and he was feeling his age, and wondering why he'd been so stupid as to rise to Ivan's challenge. Worst of all, he had pushed a good animal too hard and had risked losing him. Now here he was walking as the last of the daylight disappeared, alone, his feet and his hip joints killing him, the insides of his calves raw as skinned rabbits, his savings fifty dollars leaner, and it served him right, or at least this is what he thought as he limped home, not knowing whether his horse would be dead or alive when he rode back to get him and his saddle, or maybe just his saddle, in the morning.

To add to the humiliation, when Henry went to strike a match and check the time on his pocket watch a half-hour later, he found the watch was missing. He couldn't remember where he'd last looked at it, somewhere along the trail. Well, he'd just have to accept that loss too, even though the watch had cost him a week's wages.

When he finally reached the Perry ranch yard he headed straight for the barn and lay down in an empty box stall. He was thirsty but too tired to risk running into anyone, too mad at himself to tell the story of what happened, not wanting to see Ivan Dodge again until he'd had a good sleep. Ivan Dodge, who was bound to be lying in his bunk waiting with one more irritating remark. Tomorrow would be soon enough to hear it.

But even though he was bone tired, Henry couldn't sleep. His throat was dry and he didn't feel right. His body felt heavy. He was lying in a deep bed of straw, but he could still feel the ground underneath him, like a hard clay pallet. And although the night was dark as pitch, he could see pictures drifting by in front of his eyes. The whole country moving, as though he were watching it through the window of a slow-moving train. He could hear sounds in his head. A train whistle. The repetitive clacking of steel wheels on the railway tracks. And off in the distance another sound, the pounding of thousands upon thousands of hooves. The buffalo. He'd wished many times that he'd seen the buffalo. He'd witnessed the prairie before crops and barbed-wire fences and towns like Juliet, before it was divided into townships and sections and quarter-sections for men with one-way plows and wives who tended vegetable gardens, but he'd been too late for the great woolly herds that migrated through the grassy expanse. He listened to the thundering of their hooves and it turned the pictures in his head into rolling black clouds that seemed too big to fit within the contours of his skull. They pushed outward against the bone, colliding with one another and changing direction, rolling and bumping until they slowed and flattened out into blackness and, finally, the night was still. The sounds that emerged were quiet, comforting sounds. The breeze whispering through the sage and buck brush. The rustle of poplar leaves. A fiddler's sad tune, barely audible. Fine grains of sand spilling to the ground off the brim of a hat.

A cat descended from the hayloft above Henry and curled up beside him in the straw and began to purr in his ear. The cat's domestic purring was the most comforting sound of all and Henry considered something he had never considered before: that a prospect besides death might be out there waiting for him beyond the boundaries of his life as a ranch hand. There was talk that the Perry Land and Cattle Company would soon close its northern operation, give up on the harsh Canadian winters and let the government parcel off the grazing land for cultivation. Henry thought about the homesteaders who had congregated at the buffalo stone and the other three corners of the hundred-mile square. He'd hardly given them a glance twenty-four hours ago, but now he began to envy them their self-contained lives and the privacy of the homes they'd built to return to at the end of the day. He pictured one of the houses that now dotted the landscape—a simple, two-room wooden structure with a single-pitch roof, like a chicken shack. He saw his dusty boots on the doorstep, a white curtain blowing through an open window, a houseplant in a coffee can on the windowsill. A good deep well nearby, the first furrows of cultivation and planting. Although it was travesty for a cowboy, he imagined himself stealing away from his ranch hand's life into a new one, on a piece of land with his name on the deed, not here, so close to the Perry ranch, but north maybe, or east along the rail line. He could leave the ranch quietly and just disappear. He liked the idea of that, disappearing without a nod to anyone.

As his departure became a certainty, his heart slowed and his body lightened, and the straw beneath him became as soft as a feather bed. In the hot barn, tomorrow was cool and clear, like water on his tongue.

With the cat purring next to his head, Henry Merchant fell asleep.

By morning, he was gone.

Soon forgotten.

Night Travel

Ancestors

Just east of Juliet, there's a little campground known to the locals as Ghost Creek, even though there has never been a ghost sighting that anyone can recall. Perhaps it once had an Indian name that translates as Ghost Creek—the evidence of an encampment lies in the half-dozen teepee rings in a nearby pasture—but if the place was named by the Cree or the Blackfoot, that's not common knowledge.

The campground is usually a peaceful spot. The highway traffic sounds at night are muted and the noisiest neighbours are the coyotes, whose eerie falsetto voices carry like sirens in the darkness. The town kids might drive through and rev their engines or spin their tires, but it's not a place they're much interested in. It's too quiet for them.

On this particular August night, though, there *is* one loud tenant in the campground: a horse making a racket inside a steel horse trailer while his owner sleeps soundly in a pup tent. Bored with standing around in the trailer, the horse plays with the dangling end of the lead rope that secures him, biting and tugging with his teeth, loosening the carelessly tied knot. When he backs up, the rope pulls free, and when he leans his weight against the trailer door he's surprised that it swings wide, allowing him to make an escape. Moonlight glints off his white coat as he ambles around the side of the trailer, sniffing at the spot on the ground where he'd earlier had a good feed of hay and picking with his lips at the bits he left behind. Then he walks over to the tent and gives it a good snort before heading toward a fence and the grass that grows tall beneath the strands of wire. He grazes his way west along the fence line, lifting his head periodically to listen to the night sounds.

Until he stops suddenly. Stamps with his front feet, whinnies softly. He takes a few tentative steps and breaks into a trot, head and tail high, into a lope, floating in the moonlight. When another fence line blocks his way, he turns south until the fence ends and he can once again move west through a field of dry stubble, in the direction of Juliet.

When the horse reaches the edge of town, he turns north and jogs along the soft shoulder of the grid road. Ahead he sees the outline of a parked vehicle, and the movement of a man in the ditch. The horse slows, walks cautiously forward, keeping his eye on the dark shapes. As he comes parallel with the man, he turns his head toward him, snorting, both ears pricked forward. He swings his hip outward, still tracking north, almost past, when the man makes a drunken lunge for the dangling lead rope. The horse spins away and breaks into a gallop up the road while the man (who had stopped to piss on his way home from the bar in the Juliet Hotel) stumbles into a badger hole and, cursing loudly, rolls down into the ditch again.

The horse hears the shout behind him and his senses tell him to run, go faster, flee, until he's well away from danger. Then he slows once more. Stops. In the ditch beside him, thin grass that no one has bothered to cut and bale. Clumps of clover. The horse forgets about the danger behind him and steps down into the ditch to graze. A dog barks in a nearby farmyard but the horse ignores this sound, rips the clover with his teeth.

The barking dog belongs to Lee Torgeson, a black-and-white mutt he calls Cracker. He was a stray when Lee took him in, a dog dropped off in the country by city owners who didn't want him any more. When he first wandered into the yard he had no manners and expected to be invited into the house, but he turned out to be a good farm dog. Now Lee appreciates the job Cracker does standing guard against intruders.

The dog barks once again before giving up on whatever is out there. Lee listens from his bedroom in the two-storey farmhouse, still not used to the fact of the house being his, not used to the idea of Lester and Astrid being gone like their ancestors before them. Their deaths were not unexpected; they had both been well up in years when they passed on. But their deaths within four years of each other had left Lee alone sooner than expected, and responsible for eleven quarter-sections of mixed farm land: the original homestead, and the others that were acquired over the years, one quarter at a time, the way a wise investor slowly and steadily builds a portfolio.

At the age of twenty-six, Lee knows he is capable, in theory at least, of managing the land he's inherited. The knowledge of his legacy is one he grew up with, and Lester prepared him well. But as darkness falls each night and bedtime looms, uneasiness settles over him, grows stronger as he climbs the stairs to the second storey where the bedrooms are. Astrid and Lester's room across the hall from his, their clothing removed from the dresser drawers with the help of neighbour women but their possessions still ordered with care on the closet shelves. The photographs still on the walls. The bed neatly made as though Astrid herself had tucked the sheets. Their bedroom reminds him more than any other part of the house that he's alone.

He wonders if he will always be alone here. He can't imagine the person who might share his bed and help fill the rooms. He has no prospects, at least not at the moment, and the girls his age from Juliet are already married or long gone. His high school girlfriend went off to university without him, not happy that he turned down a scholarship to stay home and farm. Lee had argued that Lester was old and couldn't do it on his own, but she didn't want to be a farmer's wife. They'd drifted apart, and he hasn't had a serious girlfriend since.

Without Lester snoring in the room across the hall and Astrid puttering, always the last one to bed, the house is unnaturally quiet. So quiet that some nights Lee can hear sounds he knows aren't real, like the mysterious pounding of horses' hooves far off in the distance. Whenever he hears this sound he thinks of Rip and Tom, who were always called Young Rip and Old Tom, even though there weren't many years between them. Somewhere among all the family photographs, there's a picture of Lee as a baby, perhaps a year old, sitting on Old Tom's wide back with a grin on his face. There's an arm in the photograph, the hand not quite touching Lee, ready to grab him if he loses his balance or if Old Tom decides to walk off. The arm belongs to Lester. It's covered with a cotton sleeve—Lester never bared his arms, even on the hottest summer days, of which this is probably one because Lee is wearing only a light overall and a peaked cap. He's leaning forward with his hands buried in Old Tom's ample mane, and Lee swears he can remember the moment—the heat of the day, the warmth of Tom's back, the sureness he felt that the horse would look after him and that a quick response from Lester would not be needed to keep him from falling that long way to the ground. Of course, he can't really remember this. The memory is constructed from what he later came to know—that Old Tom *was* a kind horse (whatever falls Lee took from his back were in spite of Tom's best efforts to keep him there) and that Lester's strong arm was a constant, and never far away should it be needed.

Astrid was, as always, behind the camera. When Lee looks at the photo he imagines that he sat like that on Tom's back for a long time, but whenever Astrid came across the picture she shook her head and said that she'd snapped it as quickly as she could and then lifted Lee down, even though Lester wanted her to take another in case the first didn't turn out. She said this as though she were apologizing for co-operating with Lester in putting the baby in harm's way. Still, the photograph is clear—no shaky finger on the trigger—but then Astrid did everything with sureness or she didn't do it at all. The old-timers used to tell Lee that Lester had found a wife just like his mother, Sigurd, who was as formidable as she was kind-hearted. They used to tease Lee that, although he might *think* he was the apple of Astrid's eye, he'd better do exactly what she said because if he ever crossed her, boy oh boy, watch out. Lee remembers (again, impossible) the feel of Astrid's hands as she lifted him down and then held him so he could run his own baby hands over the patient Tom's face.

Old Tom was a good honest horse, Lee thinks. He had learned to ride on Tom—bareback, since no saddle Lester owned would fit—and Tom taught him balance and kept him safe until he had the skills to handle Rip, who was more playful and liked to jump sideways and out from under an inexperienced rider. Rip was cagey and hard to catch, too—you had to halter Tom and pretend you didn't care if Rip came along, and then he'd follow, believing that it was his own idea. The two of them were descended from generations of working horses that pulled plows and hay wagons and stoneboats. They were not graceful, and not in possession of any special equine beauty or athleticism, but when something unusual was in the air—an uneasy wind, perhaps—they'd race around the pasture guided by an instinctive fear, galloping side by side with Old Tom ahead by a nose, running straight for a fence and then stopping just in time, spinning and starting up again, their hoof beats carrying into the growing darkness. Although normally calm and content with their state of domestication, the two old horses on such evenings ran with the wildness of mustangs, and after they died, Young Rip first at the age of twenty-four and Old Tom not long after, Lee missed the sound of their hooves at dusk transforming the Torgesons' ordinary farm into a strange and primal place.

There are no longer horses in the pasture. Now, when Lee hears the sound of hoof beats he knows he is hearing spirit horses. He knows also that the spirit voices of Astrid and Lester will follow. Astrid will say, *When company comes, Lee, use the silver tea service.* He's always tempted to ask why, just so he can prod Astrid into telling the story of his arrival once again, but he knows there is no conversation in these voices. When Lester says, *Get yourself a good map,* Lee recognizes this too from the story, but there's definitely no point asking Lester for an explanation. When he was alive he was a man of few words and not even Astrid knew why he attributed such importance to a map when he hardly ever went anywhere, except to town, and he could have driven that distance blindfolded. Lester's advice hangs there unexplained, just as it was in the story.

Lee can't help but wish he still had Lester's wise counsel, not about maps but on the more important matter of running a farm business. As Lee lies awake at night, he feels like the two old horses did when the wind was coming from the wrong direction: uneasy, fearful. But what is he afraid of? Disappointing Lester and Astrid? They're not here to notice. Still, worry keeps him awake, listening to the sound of phantom hooves and cryptic bits of advice about tea services and navigation. His head is a reverberating drum.

He rolls onto his stomach, and closes his eyes and tries to change his heart's rhythm to match the hoof beats. Some nights, this works to put him to sleep, but tonight it doesn't. He is too aware of the blood pumping through his veins. Even without the sheet covering him, he's too hot. Perhaps he has a fever. He flops onto his back again and puts his hand on his forehead the way Astrid used to. Nothing unusual. For some reason, he remembers a song he sang at the Co-op camp he went to one summer, at Astrid's insistence: *fire's burning, fire's burning, draw nearer, draw nearer.* He can remember only those words, and they begin to circle in an endless loop in his head, making sleep even more impossible although it's now well after midnight.

He gets out of bed and stands at the wide-open window, trying to catch a bit of breeze. He can hear mosquitoes humming on the other side of the screen. The air is close, almost humid, although this country hasn't seen rain in months. There's a full moon and in its light Lee surveys the yard—the dark shapes of bins and machinery, the Quonset and the shop, and the barn, built when Lee was thirteen, after the old one burned down in a spectacular fire. Who says horses won't leave a burning barn? Old Tom and Young Rip were saved thanks to Lester's quick response to the dog's barking, and the two horses had bolted for the door as soon as they were loosed from their tie stalls. Shortly after that the whole barn went up, and a cow and her new calf, the first one of the season, brought inside away from the heavy spring snow, were lost, along with a litter of kittens. (Lee hadn't known where the kittens were hidden, but he knew they were gone because of the frantic mewing of the mother cat for days after.) It took less than an hour for the fire to level the barn, but it was almost morning before Lester was sure the fire wasn't going to spread to other buildings or ignite one of the nearby stacks. The yard was full of neighbours who had spent the night throwing water on the roofs of outbuildings, slapping at spot fires with blankets and wet gunny sacks.

After the neighbours left, Lester had turned his attention to Lee. How, he wanted to know, had the fire started? He looked at Lee as if he should have the answer, as though he must somehow have been the cause because he was the only one there of an age to be irresponsible enough to start a fire, even though it was Lester who had earlier rigged up a heat lamp for the shivering newborn calf. Lee could not think how he had started the fire and he said so, and then went into the pasture to search for the two panicked old horses. He found them pacing along the fence line in the snow, but he couldn't get near them, so he left them there to calm themselves down.

When Lee got back to the yard, Lester asked him again how the fire started. Again, Lee said he didn't know, and then he said, because he was wet and cold and upset about the cow and the new calf, "If you don't want me here, say so. I know I'm just some relative you got stuck with." He'd never said, or even thought, anything remotely like that before. He'd never imagined himself saying words out loud that sounded so ungrateful, and he gave them, as did Lester, much more weight than they deserved.

They turned away from each other after Lee's childish reply to Lester's childish accusation. They went to the house and sat at the table with Astrid and drank tea and ate toast, and then they all went back to bed for a few hours. Lester said nothing to Astrid (who could have provided relief with her common sense) for fear of worrying her, and Lee lay awake wondering why he'd said what he had, convincing himself that there was something wrong with him, that he was not deserving, and worrying that maybe he'd inherited a mean streak from someone in a line of unknown relatives, instead of seeing that his little outburst was exactly like Lester's.

In the weeks that followed, Lee and Lester rebuilt the barn. They took great pains with each other. Lester was on his best

behaviour and said not one harsh word throughout the entire
construction, even when the trusses fell like dominoes before
they could get them anchored in place, and they had to untan-
gle the mess and start again. And Lee worked like he'd never
worked before to be Lester's hand, and he held his thirteen-year-
old tongue even when he wanted to complain, even as he wondered why Lester couldn't just hire contractors like everyone else.
The barn became known as the new barn, despite there being no
other to distinguish it from.

As Lee stands in the bedroom window looking down on his
holdings, the new barn among them, he hears a coyote yip and
another answer from somewhere close by. Cracker joins in, not
very successfully.

The hoof beats have stopped but Lee is still wide awake and
now there's no point even trying to sleep. His jeans are lying on
the floor where he left them the night before. In the dark, he
grabs them and pulls them on, then reaches for a work shirt from
the pile of clean clothes he has stacked on a wooden chair. The
shirt is wrinkled; he doesn't need a light to know that. When
Astrid was alive, he never wore a wrinkled shirt, even a work
shirt, but ironing is something Lee can't generate much enthusi-
asm for, although he would make an effort on a special occasion,
if one arose. In the bathroom, he studies his face in the mirror.
Astrid was right when she said he had a baby face. On the rare
occasion that he goes into a strange bar and orders a beer, he still
half expects to be asked for proof of his age. He's reminded that
Lester's father was only nineteen years old and knew barely a
word of English when he came to Saskatchewan from Norway
and staked his claim to the homestead.

Lee goes downstairs, buttoning and tucking in his shirt, and
finds his boots by the door. The night air, although warm, is a
relief from the heat of the day before, still trapped in the house.

Cracker can't believe his luck—company at this unusual hour—
and he follows Lee out into the pasture, toward the sounds of
the cattle. Lee's small herd of cows watch with curiosity as he
approaches. Many of them are lying down and they rise and
turn toward him. Cracker keeps looking at Lee for clues as to
why they're here, what's expected of him, but apparently nothing is. Lee walks quietly so as not to get things stirred up, keeping an eye on the one cow in his herd that he doesn't trust, that
just might choose to take a run at him. Although she's young,
he's already made the decision to cull her after this year's calf
is weaned. He's got several cows that he wants to cull now that
cattle are moving again and he's facing a hay shortage. *I should
have a horse,* he thinks.

Lester wasn't really a horseman in spite of his attachment to
Rip and Tom. His interest in horses was left over from his father's
need for four-legged horsepower (a need made redundant by the
tractor), and his cattle, kept close to home, were not wild range
cattle. When Rip and Tom died, they weren't replaced. Lester
did buy one horse for next to nothing at a sale, but he turned
out to be lame and Lester sold him again right away to keep Lee
from getting attached to an unsound horse that couldn't earn
his keep. Lee had asked if they'd be getting another horse, but
Lester said they didn't really need one any more, and that he was
glad not to have the extra work. One horse, he'd said, is more
trouble than a herd of cows.

If Lee had asked a few more times, told Lester how much
he wanted a horse, one that he could rope calves off and ride
for miles in the hills, Lester probably would have bought one
for him, but Lee, conscious since the barn fire of his self-
proclaimed status as a mere relative, didn't ask for things. Now,
as he surveys his herd on foot, he thinks he should have bought
that Hancock-bred mare Blaine Dolson was selling a while

back. He'd bid on her at Blaine's sale but the bids kept going up and Lee still couldn't bring himself to spend money in a way that Lester would not have.

Lee approaches the water trough in the dark and checks the hose. His dugouts are dry, but this home pasture has a spring, and a pump keeps a trough full as long as the hose stays put and doesn't get knocked loose by the cows. Once he's ascertained that all is working, he takes the long way back toward the farmyard so he can check the fence. He knows there's a bad spot in the northeast corner where a couple of the posts have rotted out and are pretty much held upright by the strands of wire. It wouldn't take much for a cow to walk right through. When he gets there, the fence is still standing but he makes a note to get a couple of posts out here and do a proper repair.

About halfway back to the yard Lee realizes his feet hurt and wishes he'd worn running shoes instead of boots. He's tired now, although the dog doesn't seem to be and looks at Lee full of anticipation that more of an unusual nature is in the offing. When they get home, Lee disappoints Cracker and walks toward the house, weary and ready for at least a few good hours of sleep.

"Sorry, pooch," he says. "If you want more excitement, you're going to have to find it on your own."

Cracker obliges and heads across the yard, and as Lee is about to step into the porch he hears him barking at something near the barn. Lee hopes it's not another porcupine. The dog is fearless when it comes to porcupines and having had a nose full of quills on more than one occasion has not deterred him.

In the kitchen, Lee gets himself a glass of water and his eye lands on the silver tea service behind the glass doors of Astrid's oak cabinet. It's looking tarnished and he doesn't know what to do about it. His wrinkled shirt, spots on the water glass in his hand, rings of blackened grease around the burners on the stove.

To Lee, these are domestic mysteries. So too is the stack of mail on the counter by the phone, solicitations from credit card companies and charities and politicians. Astrid always knew which envelopes could be recycled without being opened. Lee lets them pile up until there's no more room and then he burns the whole works. There was a phone message from Mrs. Bulin at the post office earlier in the day: "Give me a call, Lee. There's something I need to discuss with you." Maybe he'd burned a letter that he shouldn't have, the yearly bill for his mailbox perhaps. He'd erased Mrs. Bulin's message without writing down her number. He dislikes her. She knows too much, sees his mail every day and he's sure that she takes note of exactly where it's coming from. He's annoyed that she called him at home. She can easily catch him in the post office if she needs to talk to him.

Lee places his glass in the sink, turns out the kitchen light, climbs the stairs and lies on his bed without undressing.

The dog is still barking. Not from the direction of the barn but right under Lee's window, and the hoof beats start up again, only now they're close by and clear, and not the distant muffled beats of his restless imagination. Lee gets up to look out the window, and in the moonlight he sees a grey horse loping a wide circle in the yard below, his head high, a lead shank trailing from his halter. Lee recognizes the fine, dished face and arching tail of an Arabian. Cracker is sitting at the edge of the circle, watching. His head moves with the arc of the horse's path. The horse lopes a few times around in one direction, then stops, reverses, and goes the other way, trotting a few steps and then breaking into a lope again.

Lee calls down from the open window. "Yo, Cracker," he says.

The dog looks up at him and whines, then turns his attention back to the horse. He looks puzzled, as if he doesn't know what to think of this four-legged stranger. The horse stops momentarily at the sound of Lee's voice, and then resumes circling.

By the time Lee gets outside, pulling on a light jacket now that the air has finally cooled, the grey horse is casually grazing in the moonlight on Astrid's now overgrown lawn. Lee approaches the horse's shoulder, talking softly, picks up the lead, and gives him a rub along the crest of his neck. He notes that the horse is a gelding, and assumes from the combination of brown flecks in his coat and faded dapples on his rump that he's in between young and old. He's well fed, free of scars. His feet are trimmed. Lee can't imagine that this horse came to be here the same way that Cracker did. Someone will be looking for this horse.

"You're a handsome devil," he says. "Where did you come from?"

Cracker watches with interest, waiting for direction from Lee as to how he should proceed. The horse continues to graze, paying not much attention at all to either Lee or the dog, even as Lee runs his hands down a front leg and picks up a foot. He leans his face into the animal's side, closes his eyes and sucks in the sweet, familiar smell—the blend of dust and grass and warm sweat. The smell of the horse takes him back to when Rip and Tom were there in the pasture, when he was a boy on another hot summer night, when the fences of the farm encompassed his world and he knew every inch of it as well as he knew his own skin.

He is startled when he hears a choking sob coming from his throat, which is tight, he realizes, aching even. *What is this about?* He steps back in surprise from the horse, who has swung his head around to stare at him. Cracker is staring too. Lee tries to stop the sobs, but he can't. Another, and another. *It's because I'm tired, I've been up all night.* But it's not just that. He's missing the two old horses, as stupid as that might seem, and he's missing his childhood, not because it was easier, but because there were people in it. Astrid and Lester, and in this moment he's missing them in a way he hasn't allowed himself to miss them. Cracker whines and paws at Lee's leg. Lee pushes him away with his foot, almost cruelly, and then immediately regrets it and reaches down to give the dog's head a pat. He can hardly see Cracker, his eyes are so watery, and then the emotion passes as quickly as it came upon him.

He takes a deep breath, gives his head a shake and wipes his face on the sleeve of his shirt. He can't remember the last time he cried. It frightens him, the way this feeling, whatever it was, snuck up. It's not as simple as sadness. This was much more physical in the way it took hold of his body. It's left him feeling exposed, although only a horse and a dog are watching.

Lee takes the horse's lead, and the co-operative animal follows him to the pen on the south side of the barn. When Lee hangs a water bucket from a fence rail and fills it, the horse sniffs, splashes with his nose, and drinks. Lee forks some hay off one of his new round bales and throws it over the rails of the pen. The horse accepts the feed readily.

In the moonlight, Lee sits on the top rail and watches the horse shove the hay around with his nose, looking for the choicest bits. He would love to get on the back of this horse. There are still a couple of saddles in the barn. He could try them for fit, ride the horse in the pen, see how broke he is. Lee knows he's not a rodeo cowboy, but he spent a lot of hours on the wily Rip and can ride well enough to help his neighbours out when they need a crew.

"What do you think, Cracker?" he says.

The dog wags his tail.

Lee gives up completely on the idea of sleep. He gets down from the fence, crosses the pen and gives the sliding barn door a shove with his shoulder. He enters the dark interior and heads for the corner stall at the back, where Lester hung the saddles from a beam after he sold the lame horse, saying, "Don't imagine we'll be needing these." Until he died, Lester had taken them down every spring and cleaned them up with Murphy's oil soap. Several springs have now passed without Lester, and Lee is reminded that the saddles are no longer getting their yearly cleaning. He will do this, he thinks, once he's had his ride around the pen on the horse, maybe a loop around the yard. He'll do right by Lester, clean off the dust with Murphy's and polish the leather to a rich shine and then hang the saddles once again in the barn.

As Lee lowers the smaller of the two saddles in the dark, he hears a barn owl swoop from its perch in the hayloft above and fly out the open loft window, his wings flapping with effort. An owl has lived in the barn, first the old barn and now this one, for as long as Lee can remember. The current occupant screeches as it flies through the yard and lands in its favourite old poplar tree by the house.

Lee dusts off the saddle and looks around for a saddle pad and headgear. Rip's old bridle is too big and anyway the leather is dry and cracked, but Lee finds one made of nylon hanging on a nail, the bridle that Lester bought for the lame horse, its hardware a bit rusty but it will do. With the pad and bridle in one hand and the saddle in the other, he makes his way to the pen. The owl screeches in the night as Lee approaches the horse with the saddle pad, and the horse makes no fuss at all when Lee throws it on his back. He swings the saddle up and still no protest. The horse takes the bit easily, gets a little anxious when Lee steps up and settles his weight in the saddle, but Lee watches the horse's ears and sees nothing to be concerned about. The moon shines on the Arab's white coat. Lee reaches down to rub the horse's neck.

"Good buddy," Lee says aloud.

He hears himself, his own voice, and it's a voice from the past, and he's a boy again talking to Rip.

He can sense the two old horses watching him.

It's that kind of night, rife with the presence of ghosts.

The Desert Drive-in

To the west, the faintest hint of a horizon line separates the dark earth and the blue-black sky. The yardlights in this expanse of open country glow softly. A hundred square miles of farms and ranches, pasture and cultivated fields, sand and coulees. Rail lines, some of them abandoned, a network of grid roads and dirt tracks and cattle trails, and the more recent tracks of gas and oil company trucks cutting erratically into the hills.

Open windows encourage air to circulate, curtains barely moving in what can't quite be called a breeze. Air conditioners and overhead fans, bedsprings and pillow-top mattresses shifting under the weight of sleepless bodies, radios tuned to American all-night talk stations. A rooster crowing, confused about the time of day. The yip of coyotes, cattle bawling, tires spinning on gravel. The ping of a bullet ricocheting off a metal highway sign. A match rasping across a rough surface. The sound of laughter, a whispered *shhhhh.*

Lee is not the only one who is restless, awake.

Several miles to the south of the Torgeson farm a great horned owl calls in the night. Not with a barn owl's screech, but with a wise and deep *who who whooo* that carries like a radio signal from the dark bones of the Desert Drive-in movie theatre—one of the last of its kind—owned and operated by Willard Shoenfeld. The summer Lee turned fourteen (Astrid had designated the date of Lee's arrival as his birthdate) he and a couple of friends rigged up an elaborate system of ropes and pulleys and climbed to the top of the projection screen, newly rebuilt after a twister had blown down the old one. If Willard's late brother Ed had caught the trio messing with the brand-new construction, it's hard to say what would have happened, but he didn't. The dog he owned at the time (for a very short time) could be bribed, and while the dog feasted on homegrown beef from Astrid's freezer, Lee and his friends climbed upward and sprayed WE WERE HERE in bright orange paint in the top left-hand corner of the screen, like a return address on a giant white envelope. The sun has since faded it but you can still make out the hint of orange.

A hundred yards south of the movie screen, toward the highway, is the house in which Willard and his sister-in-law Marian live—a modest, prefab bungalow constructed in 1960 by Willard and Ed to replace the trailer they'd lived in for so many years, and to provide an incentive for the woman, as yet undiscovered, whom Ed planned to marry. Its original lap siding has been replaced in recent years with beige-coloured, no-paint vinyl, purchased from a travelling salesman who sold the exact same siding to half the homeowners in the district and then disappeared. There's an old barn on the property that had once housed the brothers' chick hatchery, and then a hog operation (unpopular with the Juliet town council because of the smell), and then a chainsaw and snowmobile sales-and-service shop, and, finally, a camel named Antoinette. Since Antoinette, the barn's been empty except for the odds and ends it stores and the shelter it provides for Willard's vehicles, which include a shiny new Silverado crew cab, a twenty-year-old Ford Taurus (driven to town twice a week by Marian), and a Massey Ferguson tractor that doesn't like to start on a cold, blizzardy day when you need it most. There are the remains of an old shed that Willard knows he should tear down, and of course the drive-in ticket booth and concession stand plastered on all sides with layers of movie listings and Coca-Cola posters. At night, the white face of the movie screen looms over the sandy lot, a giant relic from a different world. And beyond the fence that is designed to keep out those who don't want to pay, the sand hills roll northward. On a windy day the surface of the land rises, and grains of sand hit the back of the movie screen like buckshot.

Willard's current German shepherd dog (this one can't be bribed) has a number of favourite spots in the yard, but tonight he lies among the movie screen's elaborate supports, unconcerned, pricking up his ears with only mild interest when the owl hoots above him, or a coyote yips in the hills, or a small nocturnal animal, a skunk perhaps, rustles in the bushes. These sounds are familiar; they tell him that nothing unusual is happening here. No vehicles stopping where they shouldn't. No kids trying to climb the fence just because it's there, to do damage for the sake of getting away with it.

Inside the house, Willard is awakened, not by anything he hears outside the window, but by Marian in the hall. Through the crack beneath his door he sees a light go on, and then she closes the bathroom door and opens it again a few minutes later, and the light goes off. He hears her footsteps in the hallway once more and they stop, as they have been stopping every night for the last month, outside his door.

Although Willard was initially perplexed by Marian's lingering every night in the hallway, he now has it figured out. She wants to tell him something, and he's concluded after several weeks of mulling that she's made the decision, finally, to pack up her things and move on. He's been expecting Marian to leave ever since Ed's death nine years ago. It's a wonder, he reasons, that she's stayed this long.

He checks the digital numbers on his bedside clock: 3 a.m., about the usual time. The minutes pass. The night is as still as a church. He imagines he can hear her breathing. Five minutes. Six. Seven. Seven minutes is the record, but tonight he counts eight and she's still there. What makes her hesitate? he wonders.

Perhaps he should speak up, put aside his own trepidation about her departure. It might make things easier for her, he thinks, if he were to jump-start the conversation. But he's by nature a quiet person, and so he says nothing.

In the months after Ed's death, Willard fully expected Marian to leave. Why would she want to stay with Ed gone? He supposed that she would move into Juliet, or to Swift Current, or back to Manitoba and her own people, but when she didn't say anything and time passed, Willard thought about it less and less and became merely grateful that she'd decided to stay on for a while longer, although he had never come to believe that she was staying for good.

He assumed people in town talked about the two of them living together in the house but he decided he didn't care about gossip if Marian wasn't bothered by it. In the long hours of winter, Willard grew to prefer Marian's company to his own, although he had never really lived with just his own company. Ed and Marian had married late in life (or at least late in Ed's life; he was a good ten years her senior) and before her arrival the two brothers had lived, always, together. Ed, the cantankerous older brother who once joined the Communist Party of Canada and talked at great length to whoever would listen about the benefits of living in Mother Russia, and Willard, the eccentric younger brother who never joined any questionable political movements but provided plenty to talk about anyway.

Willard's most famous exploit was buying Antoinette the camel so he could sell camel rides to tourists passing through on the Number One Highway. He came up with the idea after he heard the provincial minister of tourism talk about the uniqueness of the Saskatchewan landscape and about how Americans were generally better than Canadians at recognizing potential gold mines in the tourist industry. Willard looked around. He saw sand. He bought a camel from a wild animal park in Alberta and painted a huge sign in the shape of a cactus, saying, SNAKE HILLS CAMEL RIDES: SEE THE DESERT THE WAY GOD MEANT YOU TO. The sign, which Willard stuck in the ditch by the approach to the drive-in, drove Ed crazy because he was an atheist. It also irritated Ed that, in the spring when the ditch was full of runoff, the cactus appeared to be growing not in the desert, but in standing water.

When Willard came home with Antoinette, the people of Juliet were well entertained. They said Willard bought the camel because Ed had kicked him out of their double bed when he married Marian. They referred to Marian and Antoinette as the Shoenfeld women. Much of the teasing about the camel was to Willard's face and he took it good-naturedly, as was his character. He had Antoinette for three years and, even though she was as ornery as Ed and didn't work out as a tourist attraction, he became attached to her. He found out that Canadians don't stop for the Canadian version of American trends, assuming (probably correctly) that they won't be as good as the American counterparts. And the Americans, who did stop because they were used to such things, expressed their disappointment by saying, "One camel? You've got just the one?"

Despite the fact that Antoinette was not a roaring financial success, Willard kept her and fed her, and when she appeared to be sick he called the vet, who was not a camel expert but did his best. Ed didn't think Antoinette was worth the vet bill and didn't hide the fact that he hoped she would die on Willard. He hated it when neighbours who had guests from other parts of the country would bring them to see the camel, especially if they had children visiting. Sometimes Willard would give them free camel rides just so he could enjoy Ed's predictable irritation.

One morning after Willard had had Antoinette for three years, he woke up and she was gone. He picked up her tracks north of the drive-in, but immediately lost them again. He thought because she was a camel she'd probably headed for the sand hills, so he borrowed an old horse from Lester Torgeson and spent several days riding through the grasslands and dunes searching for signs of Antoinette. He found the odd track, but nothing more. He couldn't believe she could disappear. The Little Snake Hills, after all, were not as expansive as a desert like the Sahara or the Gobi. Willard got numerous anonymous tips telling him Antoinette had been spotted masquerading as the rodeo queen in Maple Creek, or Antoinette had fallen in love with a camel in a travelling circus and was now following it from town to town in a love-sick fever. Harmless jokes, and Willard accepted them in good spirit even though he missed his camel.

In a way, Antoinette figured into Ed's death. A good number of years had passed since Antoinette's disappearance, and Willard's cactus sign was still standing in the ditch, annoying Ed. One spring day Willard found Ed in his hip waders, standing in the ditch with a crowbar, and they had a brotherly quarrel. Willard argued that the cactus was a monument to Antoinette and a bit of a local curiosity, a landmark that would be missed if Ed destroyed it, but he knew this was a fight he wasn't going to win, so he went to town for the mail. When Willard came home and saw the sign still up, he knew something was wrong. As he drove alongside the sign, he saw Ed face down in the ditch. He'd had a heart attack while trying to pry the sign out of the still-frozen mud under the spring runoff.

After Ed was buried, people wondered, like Willard, what Marian would do. She kept to herself as she always had, but sometimes in the summer that followed Ed's death she sold tickets or drinks at the drive-in. Because Willard was liked, people who knew him hoped that a love affair would develop between him and Marian, but it never had. Willard kept the cactus sign and changed the words to read, DESERT DRIVE-IN: SEE THE MOVIES THE WAY GOD MEANT YOU TO. One Christmas he'd gotten the idea to decorate the cactus with Christmas lights. He did an elaborate job, stringing the green lights so they followed exactly the contour of the cactus, and using white lights to represent the cactus needles, and he even created a pink cactus flower. Most people in the district now look forward to the night when Willard hangs the lights and illuminates the cactus. It marks the onset of the Christmas season more so than the decorating of the Christmas tree in the small foyer of the United church. It gives Willard pleasure that people, especially the kids, like his cactus. After he decorates it, he lies in bed at night and imagines a whole ditch full of cacti, but he never gets around to building and decorating more than the one, just like he'd never got around to buying more than one camel. And apparently Marian likes the decorated cactus even though it was the immediate cause of her husband's death. She told Willard once, "I do like your Christmas cactus. Much easier to bring into bloom than a real one."

Those had been a lot of words for Marian. One of the things Willard appreciated about Marian right from the start was her apparent lack of any need to chatter, and her ability to communicate without talking. Her gestures, her expressions, even the attitude in her walk, all made sense to Willard. Within days of her moving into the house, they exchanged their first glance at Ed's expense, which they continued to do over the years for their own pleasure, without Ed having the slightest clue. Ed was their common denominator, and Willard's and Marian's glances implied both tolerance and affection for a man who could summon passion when not much was at stake, but wouldn't know how to give a compliment to save his life. They both understood Ed even though, to this day, they haven't really talked about him.

Willard hears a creak outside his door and realizes that Marian is still there. He sits up and checks the clock: 3:20. She's never before stood there for twenty minutes. But perhaps he's mistaken. Perhaps she slipped back to her bedroom just as the dog barked and he missed the padded footsteps. He decides she isn't there after all, and is about to lie down again when he hears another creak and Marian pushes the door and it swings slowly open. In the moonlight Willard can see her in the doorway. She's like a ghost in her long nightgown. He swallows and prepares himself for what she's sure to say: *I'm sorry, Willard, the time has come . . .* But then she pulls the door closed again without speaking, and Willard hears the footsteps padding back down the hallway.

So she's put it off for one more night. He doesn't know whether to hope she'll keep putting it off or to wish she would just get it over with. The latter, he concludes. Always best to get things over with. He'll try to bring it up tomorrow at breakfast. Perhaps she's worried about him, about leaving him on his own, and he'll try his best to let her off the hook. He'll be attentive when it's her turn to speak—*Yes, Willard, you're right, I feel the need to carry on with my life*—and to look like a man who can accept bad news.

It doesn't occur to Willard that his explanation for Marian's odd behaviour is entirely wrong, that he's not understanding the new language she's added to her quiet repertoire. And that, in nine years of living with Willard, of his constant companionship, she has grown to love him. Romantic love is not a topic Willard has spent any time at all on, in spite of being the proprietor of a business that thrives on the anticipation of love in its various forms—silly, tragic, dangerous, young, old, true, dispassionate. He's seen it all, but never once felt that he was watching a movie that had the remotest thing to do with him. And all that love in the front seats and back seats of cars, or on the hoods of cars on summer nights when it's too hot to sit inside them, or next to cars on blankets in the sand—love for teenagers, Willard believes. Willard has never been in love, not even once. Or at least not that he knows.

He's feeling something now, though, as he tries to go back to sleep. He's feeling the loss of Marian. It's a feeling of dread, an ache in an unknown place. Just to prepare himself, to get used to the idea of her being gone, he tries to picture her walking out the door with her suitcases. He can't remember her having had suitcases, although she must have, when she arrived to be Ed's wife. Willard tosses and turns and throws his pillow to the floor, and then retrieves it when the bed feels too hard and flat under his head, and when he finally falls asleep again, he dreams he has the most awful toothache. He is jolted awake by a rhythmic throbbing in his jaw, and then he realizes that the throbbing is an owl—*who who whooo*—and the sound has gotten right inside him like the bit of a dentist's drill.

Sleep now is impossible, so Willard rises and pulls on his clothes and walks out into the night air. He stands in the middle of his drive-in lot with its miniature hills of sand, ordered to position the cars with their windshields at the right angle for movie watching. He rolls himself a cigarette and looks up at the blank screen, and then he turns a slow circle, puffing on his smoke and looking at the yardlights in the distance, thinking about all the people in Juliet and in the farmhouses around him, and how people come and go, they grow up or die or go broke and move away, and the ones who are left carry on, that's just the way it is. He'll carry on without Marian in the same way the two of them continued without Ed after his death. When Willard's circle points him in the direction of the house, he thinks about the way she sits in the picture window—Ed's window—invisible in the dark and watches the movies. He stares at the window, perplexed by his own feelings, without knowing that Marian is staring back.

Watching this man. Wishing she could speak up, wondering if she ever will. And where would she go if she were to speak up and ruin things, frighten Willard half to death and drown the two of them in awkwardness? Her life would be over if she had to leave. She follows Willard's dark shadow as he turns another circle like a man who has lost his way and is trying to remember the tricks of navigation. She watches the firefly light of his cigarette, disappearing and then appearing again as he turns, turns in the darkness.

Crash

The Dolsons' yardlight is one of the ones that Willard can see north of town. The Dolson house—which of course Willard can't see—has the same vinyl siding as his own house. It had galled old Mrs. Dolson to no end when she realized she'd been taken in by a confidence man with coloured brochures and a promise of siding longevity. As the siding began to lift and snap in the wind and her calls to the sales company remained unanswered and finally they wouldn't go through at all because the phone had been disconnected, Mrs. Dolson's disappointment at her own gullibility caused her finally to agree to her husband's retirement plan, and the old couple moved to the West Coast a dozen years ago and left the farming operation to their son, Blaine, and his wife, Vicki. And no sooner had the senior Dolsons settled in a condominium complex in Nanaimo than Mr. Dolson died, and now Mrs. Dolson lives near Blaine's sister in Vancouver and shows no interest in returning to her former home, even for a visit, because she *just can't bear* to see what has become of it in Vicki's care. It's convenient to blame Vicki for the siding mistake.

The Dolsons' three-bedroom bungalow was built about the same time as Willard's to replace the original farmhouse that was old and small and did not reflect the prosperity of the times. The new house (not so new any more) sits three hundred yards off the grid road, surrounded on three sides by trees lovingly planted by Blaine's mother: poplars, Manitoba maples, even a weeping birch that has somehow survived the arid conditions of this part of the country. The house faces the road and from the living room window you can see the barn that is now pretty much unused, a rail corral, and a half-acre pen that is home to Blaine's horse, the only one he has left. In front of the house is a miraculous plum tree, of which Blaine's mother was exceedingly proud. South of the house is the vegetable garden, enclosed by chicken wire to protect it from the deer. The fact that it is still bountiful is perhaps more miraculous than the plum tree, since the gardens throughout the district are sparse, even non-existent, thanks to drought and grasshoppers. Vicki's garden is rich with produce. No one can figure it out. She plants in the spring and then forgets to water and never has time to weed. And the grasshoppers seem to have passed Vicki's garden by as they devoured everyone else's. Her own theory is that grasshoppers don't like weeds. They've cruised the country looking for the weed-free gardens, she tells Blaine, which is why it's a good idea not to weed a garden. "Ha ha," she says. "It's a joke." Blaine—who remembers the neat garden his mother was famous for—doesn't laugh.

Blaine's parents had three children and the house was a perfect size for their family, but it's a tight fit for Blaine and Vicki, who have six kids. Until today, the boys shared one bedroom and the girls the other. What's different about today (or technically, yesterday) is that Shiloh, the oldest and almost a teenager, has been allowed to "build" his own bedroom downstairs. Blaine didn't see the need for it, but Vicki tried to be more understanding of

Shiloh's growing desire for privacy. She and Shiloh decided on the southwest corner as the driest and brightest spot in a mostly dark unfinished basement. Although she didn't really have time (the garden's bounty was waiting for her attention) Vicki helped Shiloh build a low wooden platform out of scrap lumber to keep the bed up off the cement floor. They carried a worn area rug down the basement steps and laid it on the platform, and they hung two old bedspreads from the ceiling to create walls, or at least the illusion of walls. Then they took Shiloh's bed apart and reassembled it in the new room, and Vicki found a floor lamp and a couple of plastic storage tubs for Shiloh to use for his clothes, and she made him some shelves out of boards and bricks for his CD player and other personal things.

Vicki noticed that Shiloh was sullen the whole time they were creating the room and moving him into it, but she didn't say anything. She assumed it was his age and adolescent hormones, and she promised to get him a desk as soon as they had a bit of extra money, and even a computer if they could afford it. She ignored him when he said, "I guess that won't happen anytime soon"— he was getting so like his father—and she said cheerfully, "Well, maybe not, but you never know, I might win the lottery." She left him to his decorating then, and he covered the two cement walls with pictures of hockey players cut from *Sports Illustrated* and a poster from the national rodeo finals in Edmonton that Lynn Trass had let him take from the window of the Oasis Café.

Shiloh Dolson, just shy of his thirteenth birthday, likes his new room even if he doesn't show it. He doesn't care that it's dark and it doesn't have real walls and he's already had to squash a couple of sowbugs. There is one problem though, which he discovers on this, his first night in the basement. The problem is a heating duct that runs along the floor joists above his head. He wakes up at three in the morning, and through the duct he can hear his parents arguing. The fact that they argue is nothing new. Shiloh's heard them a hundred times before. What's problematic is that he can now hear what they're arguing about. He'd always assumed money, being fully aware of the situation his parents are in. He knows the farm is mostly gone, all but the home quarter, although Vicki keeps trying to reassure him that things will get better and that Blaine will get the land back, or at least be in a position to rent before too long. It's happened to people before, she tells Shiloh, and they bounce back. It's not your father's fault, she says, it's the times, it's like people running out of fish on the East Coast, not their fault, but things will change. Wait until people in Ottawa and Toronto have to pay five dollars for a loaf of bread, she says, then the politicians will come to their senses.

Shiloh doesn't know what to think. He doesn't know what the cost of a loaf of bread in Toronto has to do with anything and, except for Vicki's reassurances, what he hears, he hears on the TV news like everyone else in the country. Maybe there's too much wheat in the world and Blaine hasn't figured that out, although Shiloh does remember him growing canary seed a few years ago and swearing he'd never do it again because of the full-body protection he'd had to wear to harvest the damned stuff, complaining to Vicki about the itching and chafing he'd had to put up with to grow feed for canaries in New York City. But maybe the canary-seed experiment failed because Blaine is a bad farmer. Maybe it *is* all Blaine's fault.

There's another possibility. Maybe, and this is what Shiloh would rather believe, it's Vicki's fault. Vicki who, according to Blaine, is "bloody useless" on a farm. Sometimes Blaine calls her this in a teasing way, as though her scatter-brained nature is endearing, but if he's desperate for another set of hands and sends one of the kids to the house for Vicki and then she sends a wrench clanging through the frame of a piece of machinery or lays a bolt on the ground to get lost forever, or fails to hold her ground and lets a yearling calf escape through an open gate, he'll say something like, "For Christ sake, you grew up on a farm, how can you be so bloody useless?" and the way he says "bloody useless" in these circumstances leads Shiloh to believe that his mother actually is. Vicki never gets mad in return, or defends herself, and Shiloh takes this to mean she knows Blaine is right. Shiloh is too young to understand Vicki's brand of diplomacy, which involves keeping your mouth shut until things blow over. Of course the need for Vicki's help on the farm is now a thing of the past because there's no farming left to do, but Blaine still finds the odd occasion when the word *useless* seems appropriate, or at least easy.

On this first night in his new room, Shiloh wakes up, and Blaine and Vicki are not arguing about land or cattle or money. At three in the morning, they're fighting about green beans. Shiloh thinks he must be hearing things, he must have it wrong, but Blaine says, quite clearly, "When I get home from work tomorrow I want those beans in the freezer, Vicki."

"I'm planning to do the beans tomorrow, I told you that. Or do you want me to do them now? Would that make you feel better, if I clattered around the kitchen right now and woke everybody up? Come on, Blaine. Be reasonable."

Shiloh hears Blaine's footsteps on the floor above. Back and forth.

"I don't want the only thing we grow on this place to end up moulding in the basement."

The beans in question, Shiloh knows, are in plastic tubs in the cold room, which is a misnomer at this time of year. He helped pick them two days ago.

"They aren't moulding," he hears his mother say. "There's plenty of time. But tomorrow. I promise."

"And I know how much that promise is worth," Blaine says. "You'll wake up with a big plan to get them done, but you'll be off to town before you've got a pot of water boiling. You'll be gone for the day, and I'll get home and you won't have done a damned thing and the beans will look like a compost heap."

"That's not fair," Vicki says, "that part about me not doing a damned thing. We have six kids. It takes a lot of time, looking after six kids."

Shiloh is resentful that he's included in the category of "kids." He doesn't need looking after. He tosses back the covers and swings his feet over the side of the bed, thinking he might get up and throw his two cents in. He knows Blaine will agree with him. There are only five kids who need looking after. He wants to say this, and be on Blaine's side.

"My mother raised three kids and grew a garden and worked like a man on top of that," Blaine says.

"I know about your mother," Vicki says. "She was amazing. I'm not. I don't want to fight." Then she says, as though she's just remembered, "Shiloh is right underneath us. Let's not wake him."

Shiloh is just about to part the bedspread curtains and head for the stairs when he hears Blaine say, "If it weren't for that bedroom idea—another one of your big plans—you could have had the beans done."

Vicki says something Shiloh can't hear, and then Blaine says, "To hell with Shiloh."

Shiloh stops. *To hell with Shiloh?* Did he hear correctly?

"Blaine," Vicki says.

"Don't Blaine me."

There's a long silence, and then Shiloh hears Vicki's footsteps going down the hall, and a few minutes later Blaine follows.

Once they're in their bedroom Shiloh can't hear what they're saying. Nothing, he thinks. He doesn't know that when Vicki asks

Blaine what he meant by "To hell with Shiloh," Blaine seems exhausted and answers that he didn't mean anything, he just said it. Shiloh doesn't hear Vicki swear to do the beans and not let them go to waste, and Blaine say, "Well, we both know it's not the beans that are stuck in my craw." Shiloh doesn't know that in spite of the arguing, his parents get into bed together and Blaine says, "How can you wear flannelette in the summer?" and Vicki says, "You never mind my flannelette."

Shiloh lies there most of the night, worrying. He's twelve years old and he's worrying about things he can't understand, not the least of which is why the words "To hell with Shiloh" slipped so easily from his father's tongue, just as easily as "bloody useless." He wants to cry, but he won't, he's too old to cry, and he reaches over and turns on the lamp, and the light falls on the cowboy in the rodeo poster, a bull rider wearing purple chaps with gold fringes. His hand is wrapped tight into his bull rope and the fringes on his chaps are suspended as he gets set for the bull's next jarring contact with the earth. Shiloh wonders if he could be a bull rider, and then remembers that the steers he could practise on are gone.

Who should he blame? Maybe, somehow, this is his fault, and that's why his father said what he did. Or maybe not his fault alone, but the six kids, too many, and the name Shiloh came out first because he's the oldest. He wonders how much money it costs to feed and clothe six kids. It must cost a lot. He wonders how they could save money, and makes a pact with himself not to ask for Big Gulps or rented movies. Or school things. When the teacher gives them notes about money for field trips or extra-curricular activities, he'll tear them up and not even show them to his mother. He won't ask for new running shoes or jeans or T-shirts. He won't, he vows, ask for anything, and his father will notice this and realize that he isn't a kid any more, and when he needs a hand he'll ask for Shiloh and leave Vicki alone because she's bloody useless anyway.

Shiloh lies awake and thinks of all the ways he can save money and not be like the younger kids, who are asleep upstairs and don't even know what's going on. He thinks and worries and tries to solve problems that his parents haven't been able to solve, and eventually he falls asleep, the light still on, the bull rider still suspended, waiting for the buzzer that will tell him he lasted the eight seconds and he can now begin the perilous task of getting off.

Upstairs, his mother—way too hot in her flannelette nightie—hears the droning sound of a small plane overhead, the same plane that she has dreamed about again and again since childhood. In her dream, the drone turns to a sputter, then a stall, and she witnesses the plane's death spiral from sky to earth, its disappearance behind trees or buildings, after which she reluctantly and never successfully searches for the wreckage. In variations of the dream she strikes out, always alone, down a blacktop highway, or a country road, or a path of nothing more than tire tracks through a field. Once, she got into a canoe (she'd never in real life been in one) and paddled across an open lake. In the way of dreams, her anxious journey turned into a pleasant, although confusing, paddle.

When Vicki hears the plane hiccup and then drone its way to earth, she thinks she is still awake. She sits up in bed, then stands and feels the floor beneath her bare feet.

"Blaine," she says.

He groans in his sleep and rolls over, away from her.

She can still hear the plane. The sound is real, she's sure of it. She grabs a pair of jeans off the floor and pulls them on under her nightie, but then the sound of the plane stops. No crash. She listens. Nothing. A dream. So she wasn't awake. She just thought she was awake.

She gets back into bed, still in her jeans, and pulls the sheet up even though she doesn't need it. She rolls against Blaine's warm back, but he mumbles "too hot" and pushes her away. She rolls to her own side of the bed and drops off to sleep.

No falling planes in her dreams this time. Just one endless, obsessive dream about shelling bright green peas and sweating in the hot, hot sun.

Home Invasion

There's barely a breeze but it doesn't take much to get a creak out of the ancient, probably half-dead, and therefore unstable, evergreen tree outside of Norval and Lila Birch's bedroom window in Juliet. As Norval half listens to his wife recite what she expects him to do the next day, he resolves, once again, to cut the tree down before it falls through the roof of their split-level house and lands right on top of them. Thinking about the tree leads him to think about his lawn, and then the hardware store and the new lawn mower he's been eyeing. It's not a riding mower, but it is a shiny green electric with many special features. Norval gets great pleasure from the act of mowing grass, which he's been unable to do since his old gas mower died on him a few weeks ago. It bothers him when he gets home from work and sees that his grass is too long, but he just hasn't had the time to stop at the hardware store. You'd think the overgrown lawn would bother his house-proud wife too, but it doesn't seem to.

From two blocks away, he hears Mrs. Baxter's rooster. The rooster has a defective *cock-a-doodle-doo* that makes him more irritating than a fully functioning rooster would be. He's not even useful as an alarm clock because he has no sense of night and day. His feeble half-crow reminds Norval of the imperfections in everything.

"I'd like to kill that rooster," he says. "A rooster that doesn't know the difference between night and day deserves to die."

His wife says, "You're not listening to me, Norval," and he turns his attention back to *the list*. All of the items on it have something to do with renovations to the church, which Lila sees as necessary for the wedding she is planning for their only daughter, Rachelle. Lila seems to have forgotten altogether their daughter's age (eighteen), along with the fact that she's just graduated from high school and has no plans to get an education that will be of use in earning her a decent living, and since she's marrying Kyle Hoffert, she really ought to have a backup plan. The Hofferts earned their living until recently off their contract to collect pregnant mares' urine for the hormone-replacement industry. Those contracts were cancelled when science decided the practice of replacing women's hormones was not such a good idea after all, and the farms quickly became a thing of the past. The Hofferts run a few hundred head of cattle and are trying to maintain their horse-breeding program, but the mares' urine had been a lot more valuable than either the cattle or the horses are now.

And in addition to the worry about Rachelle's financial security, there's the notable fact that the bride is pregnant. Lila has decided to ignore this detail until after the wedding, at which time she'll make an announcement as though it's news, when everyone in Juliet already knows, and if they don't they will when they see Rachelle in her wedding dress.

"Can't you take care of some of these things?" Norval asks in the dark.

"I have my own list," Lila says. "One person can't plan a wedding."

"What about the blushing bride?" Norval asks. "Perhaps there are one or two things she might do to help out."

"Don't be sarcastic," Lila says. "She has a job. She's busy. Anyway, you know how tired she is. Or maybe you don't. Maybe you have to be a woman to know just how tired pregnancy can make you."

"I thought we were ignoring her 'condition,'" Norval says.

"We're not ignoring it within these walls. Don't be ridiculous."

"Well, she didn't seem that tired yesterday," Norval says. "I walked by the swimming pool and there she was, prancing around in a string bikini, her little belly on display. Don't they have rules of conduct for lifeguards? A dress code of some kind?"

"They're not called string bikinis any more," Lila says. "You're so old-fashioned. Anyway, she's not showing yet. She has no 'little belly,' as you put it."

"You're in denial, Lila. One look and a blind man could tell."

Without realizing he's doing it, Norval pulls the sheet up to his chin. It has something to do with the idea of his daughter *showing*. "So what about Kyle's mother?" he asks. "Can't she lend a hand?"

"Mrs. Hoffert is lovely, but this is the bride's family's responsibility. You can't weasel out that way, Norval."

Lila's acting like this wedding is the most important event in the history of the town, Norval thinks, when in fact he sees it, well, not so much as a disaster, nothing is final these days, but as a mistake that will be evident before the guests have eaten their good-luck slivers of wedding cake. He wants to suggest again that the marriage take place cheaply and quietly, and that they spend the money to celebrate in a year's time if the future looks promising then. When he suggested this the first time, his wife and daughter in unison called him a tightwad and dismissed the idea without consideration.

Norval sighs audibly, tucking the sheet around his neck as though he's in a body bag with his head sticking out.

"In case you hadn't noticed," he says, "I too have a job. I too have a list, and a rather long one." He tries to picture his desk calendar, the one he's refused to replace with a PDA, and wonders who will be the first to enter his office at the bank in the morning playing a sympathy card and asking for more money or more time. And he's pretty sure he has school board business sometime after lunch, the interview of the only qualified applicant for the job of Home Economics teacher. Waiting in the wings is the righteous Mrs. Baxter, owner of Norval's favourite rooster, who has been trying to get her hands on the job for the last ten years even though she doesn't have a teaching certificate. He can only hope the qualified applicant isn't covered in tattoos. If she's at all acceptable, they'll have to hire her or face the teachers' union.

Lila says, "I want you to talk to someone at the church. The foyer absolutely must be redecorated, and I don't just mean a coat of paint. They'll listen to you, Norval. You're an important person in the community and, besides, you're a man."

Important, hah, Norval thinks to himself. Important, when his job description includes foreclosure on properties that have been in the family for close to a hundred years. Tolling the death knell for people like Blaine Dolson—who has found work on the road crew, thank God for that, he has a half-dozen kids to support.

What would happen, Norval wonders, if he just stayed in bed, didn't go to the bank on Main Street, just pulled the sheets over his head and stayed in bed until noon, and then got up in his pyjamas and watched whatever was on TV, whatever appeared on the screen when he hit the Power button on the remote—music videos, football or golf, some reality show about redecorating houses or ballroom dancing—and when the day was over he'd go back to bed and sleep with a free conscience. He wonders whether this is possible, if he could ever, at his age, close enough to retirement that the word has entered his vocabulary, quit his job?

And then he reminds himself that he's considering just the thing that he fears for his daughter—poverty resulting from a rash act—and he knows that if it gets too bad he'll apply for a transfer to another town and he'll start all over with new clients who will trust him, or give him the benefit of the doubt, for a few years at least.

Lila sits up in bed. "Did you hear that?" she asks.

"The wind?" Norval asks.

"Not the wind," she says. "There is no wind. I think it was the front door."

Now Norval hears something too. Footsteps.

"Rachelle's been home all night," says Lila. "I'm sure of it."

"I wouldn't bet your life savings," Norval says, throwing the covers aside and stepping onto the plush wall-to-wall carpet.

"Be careful," his wife whispers. "You hear stories. It could be a home invasion."

"It's not a home invasion," says Norval, reaching for his pants, which Lila has neatly folded over the back of a chair. "Rachelle," he calls, "where the hell have you been?"

No answer.

Norval pulls his pants on over his cotton pyjama bottoms and steps into the hallway. He descends the four carpeted steps to the landing, another six to the main level of the house, and finds Rachelle in the kitchen, her head in the fridge. She's wearing cut-off shorts and what they call a "tank top," which means to Norval that she's only half dressed, or more to the point, she's half naked.

"Where the hell have you been?" he asks again.

"Out," says Rachelle.

"With Kyle," says Norval.

"With the girls," she says, closing the fridge door and turning to face him.

Her eyes are bloodshot and he's pretty sure she's been drinking. He tries to keep his eyes from her belly but they keep drifting there. Maybe Lila is right. You can't yet tell.

"We went to the drive-in. That annoying Willard Shoenfeld checked the trunk of the car again. He has no right. I'm pretty sure about that. You can't just search cars without a warrant."

"For booze," says Norval.

"For people trying to sneak in," says Rachelle. "I suppose you're implying we were driving around with booze in the car. We're not stupid, you know."

"Rachelle," Norval says. "You're pregnant. Think about it."

"I may be pregnant but my life isn't over."

Norval pauses and then takes the opportunity to say, one last time, "Tell me honestly. Don't you wish, even just a little, that you were going away to school with Haley and Kristen?"

Rachelle looks him square in the eye. "No," she says. "Why would I want to do that? I'm getting married."

She tosses her long blonde hair away from her face, a move she's been practising since she was a small girl. There's not much Norval can say in response. He used to say, "Don't you shake your hair at me, young lady," but he learned long ago that his bland retort couldn't compete with Rachelle's dramatic gestures. She stomps away from him and up the carpeted stairs to her room, leaving him alone in front of the fridge with his pyjama bottoms bunched up under his pants. He stands in Lila's immaculate, glaringly modern kitchen and wonders if he should, after all, give Mrs. Baxter and her family values a shot at the Home Economics job. Maybe she could accomplish something that he and Lila apparently have not been able to, namely, keep teenagers from having babies. But he knows that Mrs. Baxter is not the answer. The best he can do now is wish the unsuspecting Kyle a whole lot of luck. Norval is quite sure that marriage to Rachelle will be a challenge to rival any he's encountered so far in life.

With the house once again silent and his sleep for the night ruined, Norval goes to the sunken living room off the kitchen and settles himself on the couch. Almost every time he sits on this couch he gets pleasure from the memory of how it was acquired. Lila had special-ordered not just any couch, she said, but an item of fine furniture, from some fancy company for half a fortune. When the couch arrived in Regina, she'd sent Norval to pick it up in a borrowed truck. She'd given him a photograph printed off the Internet to make sure they'd sent the right one. When he got as far as Swift Current, he drove by the local furniture store and saw the parking lot filled with row after row of couches and La-Z-Boys and bedroom suites. A portable sign on the sidewalk advertised a one-day-only pavement sale.

Norval got out and had a look and sure enough, there was Lila's couch, or one close enough to it that he couldn't tell the difference from the picture she'd given him. So he bought it for a third the price and called the Regina store and told them to send the fancy one back. Even when he paid the shipping and took the deposit into account, the parking lot couch was still almost two thousand dollars cheaper than Lila's special order. There was a manufacturer's tag on the back—the wrong one of course—but Norval figured if he could get the couch installed against the wall in the living room before Lila could look at the tag, he'd be home free. And he'd got away with it. Lila had never examined the couch closely enough to find the tag, and the manufacturer of the expensive couch had never phoned to ask why it had been returned. Norval had paid the credit card bill without Lila seeing it, and he'd saved himself some money and proven that even Lila couldn't really tell the difference between haute couture and the local offerings.

Norval flips through a variety of infomercials—cooking appliances, home gyms, skin care products—and finally settles, as usual, on the Weather Channel. Its forecasts are notoriously wrong, but he listens to the perky female announcer who tells him the day will be sunny, warm and windy, with a slight chance of a thunderstorm later in the day. Well, he thinks, you could probably make that prediction for southern Saskatchewan on any day in the summer and stand a pretty good chance of being correct, although the thunderstorm part of the forecast has been unusually absent for the past few summers. He stares at the television, which makes the same prediction every ten minutes, until his eyelids begin to feel heavy.

He's just about to lie down on the couch when he hears a truck pull up in front of the house. A door slams and footsteps sound, coming up the walk. Loud footsteps, unmistakeably Kyle's boots. Norval makes it to the door before Kyle can ring the bell.

"Well," Norval says to Kyle, who is teetering on the top step, one hand on the railing, trying hard to look sober for his future father-in-law but not succeeding. Norval notices that he's left his truck lights on.

"Good evening, Mr. Birch. Sir," Kyle says. He's trying to stand steady but gravity pulls him back down a step. It takes him a few seconds to regain his balance.

"It's hardly evening, Kyle," Norval says. "It's more like, well, the middle of the night would be more accurate."

"Sorry," Kyle says.

"What can I do for you, Kyle?" Norval asks. Of course he knows Kyle is here for Rachelle, but he makes him say it anyway.

"Can I talk to Rachelle?"

"I would imagine she's asleep," Norval says.

Kyle shifts from foot to foot, still holding the railing. A full minute passes. He seems to have forgotten where they are in their conversation, if it can be called that.

"I guess I should go," he finally says.

"I think that would be best," Norval says, feeling irresponsible for sending Kyle out on the road in the state he's in, but damned if he's going to let him into the house to climb the stairs and crawl into bed with his daughter. He has his limits.

He watches Kyle stumble down the walk, a cell phone in one back pocket of his Wranglers and a round tobacco tin in the other. Kyle's about to get in his truck—he's having trouble finding his keys—when Rachelle bounds down the stairs and pushes past Norval wearing some kind of gym pants now and a very worn and almost transparent T-shirt. She and Kyle throw their arms around each other right on the street, and then Lila calls from upstairs, "What in the world is going on down there?"

"Nothing," Norval calls back, and then he says to Rachelle, "Don't you dare get in that truck and drive anywhere."

"I won't," Rachelle says.

"I don't know how you can stay out late and then go to work in the morning. Don't you have to be alert? Wouldn't you say the state of being alert is an essential part of the job, Rachelle?"

"I don't have to work until eleven. Just go back in the house, Dad."

Norval doesn't go back in the house and instead finds himself staring at his lawn. Thanks to his careful watering it's the greenest lawn on the block, green as Ireland, he imagines. It needs mowing, yes, but it glistens in the light of the street lamp, a fine-looking crop, thick and even and free of a single weed, or blade of grass that was not planted by him.

"Dad," Rachelle says impatiently. "Have you gone to sleep or what?"

Norval says, "Promise me you won't go anywhere in that truck."

"I promise," Rachelle says.

Both she and Kyle stare at him, waiting for him to leave. Norval goes back inside and closes the door.

"Norval?" Lila calls. "Is something wrong? Should I come down?"

"No, Lila. Go back to sleep. I'll be up soon."

He goes to the fridge and finds a slice of leftover meat loaf. Lila would kill him, he thinks, if he were to carry it into the living room and eat it in front of the TV with no utensils and no plate to catch the bits he spills. He carries the cold slice to the couch that he secretly thinks of as *his* couch and sits down. It will be a great day on the Prairies, the perky TV weather lady says. She looks right at Norval when she says this, as though she is telling him to buck up and look on the bright side. Norval takes a reckless bite of meat loaf.

Horse Thief Moon

The horse jigs his way out of the yard with Lee holding him back until he can find a place where it's safe to lope him out. Cracker badly wants to come along, but Lee says, "Get to the house," and the dog immediately hangs his tail and obeys.

Lee rides in the ditch for a quarter-mile and then he sees in the darkness that the wire gate to Hank Trass's pasture is stretched out on the ground, which could mean kids from town have been drinking at the buffalo stone again, although it more likely means that Hank has moved his yearlings onto his north quarter. Lee heads for the opening in the fence and steers a course past the wire. He guides the horse toward the giant stone, amused once again by Hank's response to the Juliet high school grads' recent and much-discussed spray-painting exploits. The students had chosen the buffalo stone as the spot to record their year of graduation, and when the chair of the local historical committee got wind of the defacement, he'd printed a letter of protest in the paper and suggested that those responsible undertake a fundraising effort in order to invite an art restorer from Regina to come and give advice on how to remove the paint. Hank saw the letter in the paper and didn't want to have to deal with any so-called art restorer from the city, so he took a tin of paint remover and a wire brush and a half-dozen rags out to his pasture after dark and did his own restoration, or at least that's what he told Lee. After he was done the stone looked like the same old hunk of granite it had always been, Hank said, only cleaner, at least on the one side. When Hank was asked by the historical committee if he was responsible—apparently he'd done something wrong in removing the paint without the help of the art restorer—he denied any involvement. He let people think the graduates had had a change of heart.

The horse snorts when the stone's dark shadow looms and Lee expects him to shy sideways like Young Rip used to do, but he doesn't. Lee encourages the horse to walk around the stone and the depression that surrounds it, a reminder of centuries of shedding animals, first buffalo and now cattle, and in the moonlight he sees that it's been painted with new fluorescent markings— pink and green and yellow handprints. Hank must be getting sick of all this activity in his pasture, Lee thinks. Maybe the fancy art restorer will get a chance to come out after all.

He walks a wide path around the stone, holding the horse in check as he scans the moonlit ground for holes, and when he's satisfied that the footing is safe, he looses up on the reins and lets the horse go. The horse snorts and crow-hops a few times, then charges forward like a racehorse out of the gate. There's a moment when Lee thinks the horse is going to get away on him, but then he gets him going in a good circle around the stone, allowing him to set his own pace as long as he stays in the circle.

As the horse moves under him, Lee feels himself waking up— not just coming out of a sleepy state because it's the middle of the night, but *truly* waking up, as though every cell in his body is tingling. Here he is, out riding a mystery horse when he should be sleeping, in Hank's same old pasture with the same old buffalo stone, only nothing is quite the same because of the darkness. He loves the way darkness removes time and place. He could be a boy again, with Astrid and Lester asleep in their bed in the house across the road. He feels almost giddy.

When the horse begins to soften, Lee slows him back to a trot and they change directions and move into a lope again, this time at a more controlled pace. When the horse has relaxed and seems willing to go forward easily, Lee guides him out of the circle and they move off at a trot to the north, away from the stone, following the fence line in Hank's empty pasture.

Lee's plan is to ride the perimeter of the pasture, but it's hard to see the gopher holes, so when he comes to the north gate, he decides to dismount and open it so he can get into his own field of fresh summer fallow. He and the horse have an agreement now, that Lee is the boss and navigator. The horse stands quietly enough as Lee undoes the gate, and goes through obediently as Lee stands between the horse and the wire. Even though the pasture appears to be empty, he does the gate up again before he steps back into the saddle: leave closed what you find closed.

There's a trail to the west along the fence line, leading to a sandy section of Hank's pasture lease. Lee remembers—he *always* remembers when he looks down this road—the time he pedalled furiously on his bike with the evidence of a crime in his pocket, a watch that he'd taken from Lester's drawer and that is now forever buried in sand. To this day he feels bad about taking the watch because he never confessed and, worse, he lied when confronted. He wonders, if Astrid were here to ask him about the watch now, would he have the courage to tell her the truth?— the truth she already knew, he's sure of that, which would make coming clean all the harder. What had he been thinking when he threw the watch in the sand? He'd panicked because the crime of going into Lester's private things had seemed huge. Privacy was sacrosanct to Lester.

Lee looks down the sandy trail with its two tracks disappearing into the night, and then continues on to the north. He admires his clean black field in the moonlight, even though the practice of summer fallowing is no longer recommended by the agriculturalists because of the resulting moisture loss. But what are you going to do, Lester used to say, when you see the weeds coming up and don't want to pump more money into herbicides? Lee hadn't known what to do with the field either, so he'd done what Lester always had: turned the weeds under before they went to seed.

When he reaches the northern edge of the black field, he crosses into a field of stubble—a poor crop harvested early for feed. The horse moves under him, content enough now to be going somewhere. He settles into an easy jog and Lee gets the impression they could go forever like this. He's surprised at how smooth the horse is—he's heard that Arab horses are rough to ride.

North of the stubble field is a standing crop, so Lee rides the strip between the field and the ditch. Another crop, another quarter of old summer fallow, this one full of rocks and weeds and gopher holes. He lets the horse pick his way through and admires his ability to do so, the way he can place his feet so carefully and at the same time stay tuned in to any sound or movement around him, a perfectly adapted prey animal.

When they're through the summer fallow, they come to another standing crop, oats this time, ready for harvest from the look of it, and Lee is forced into the ditch. It's clean, with the grass cut and baled, and he rides there for another mile. With every new field ahead he considers turning around and going home, but only briefly because the tug is away from home and sleep and the next day waiting. When they reach the southern edge of the Swan Valley Community pasture, Lee almost turns back knowing that the pasture stretches for miles, but beyond it is the cemetery—where Astrid and Lester are buried. He makes the decision to keep going that far, to the graveyard, and the ground passes beneath him until he can see it up ahead, first the trees in the distance, and when he gets close enough the dark outlines of the headstones, most of them old and no longer perfectly upright. He slows the horse and they enter the cemetery under a wrought-iron archway, crafted years ago by a local blacksmith.

Not many people get buried here any more. The preference now is for the town cemetery where the lawn is watered and manicured, but Lee is glad Lester and Astrid chose this as their resting place. There's no church to clutter the landscape, no plastic flowers to fade and turn into refuse, just the tumbleweed blown up against the fence to catch on the barbed wire, and the remains of virgin prairie, blue grama and spear grass. He likes the wildness, the grass fighting against the threat of drifting sand.

Lee hasn't been to visit the graveyard since Astrid's funeral. He dismounts and leads the horse around the grave markers until he finds himself looking at the double headstone with both Astrid's and Lester's names carved in the marble. The stone—with its dates of death just four years apart—is one of only a few recent markers, and the mound of earth over Astrid's grave has not yet completely settled. Eventually, a concrete pad will cover her, a partner to the one that covers Lester. Even in the moonlight Lee can't quite read the inscriptions, but he knows what they say: LOVING WIFE AND MOTHER for Astrid, to mirror the LOVING HUSBAND

AND FATHER that she had selected for Lester. Lee had never called Lester "Father." Always Uncle Lester. Astrid had asked Lee if that would be all right, Loving Father, and he'd said of course, and understood immediately what Astrid wanted for herself.

The horse knickers and Lee lays his hand on his soft neck. "Just hang on a minute, buddy," he says. He's thinking, as he looks at the graves, that he is the only one—the only family, however dubious the blood relationship—who will ever make a trip to the cemetery just to pay respects to Astrid and Lester. Lester was an only child and Astrid's two sisters both died in infancy. There was no other family in this country, not that Lee knows of, anyway. He looks at the spot that will be his grave someday, if he so chooses. He tries to imagine the stone, separated from Astrid's and Lester's. What will it say? LEE TORGESON, GREAT-NEPHEW OF LESTER AND ASTRID TORGESON? But that might be confusing when Astrid and Lester are described as mother and father. He wonders why he hadn't been encouraged to call them Mother and Father. Perhaps because Astrid clung to the belief that Lee was related by blood and was not like other adopted children. The note he was found with made that claim, but really, he was like Cracker, left where someone knew, or at least hoped, he would be taken care of.

Although Lee doesn't know where he came from, he probably knows more about his own arrival into Astrid's and Lester's lives than most people know about their births. Astrid tried so hard to be open about his appearance in the porch that she turned the account into a bedtime story and told it often enough that Lee had it memorized. He would even correct her if she left out some detail or tried to rush the story for the sake of saving time. He can still hear her voice, the words, the first line always the same.

"The wind woke her," he says out loud to the horse, who is now grazing on the dry August grass, tugging at the reins, then the next line coming into Lee's head, and the one after that, still vivid even though he was just a child when he decided he was too old for Astrid to coax him to sleep with stories. He can see the luminous hands on Astrid's bedside clock as she checked the time and saw that it was just after three, can see her move from the bed to her armchair by the window, wrapping herself in the orange and brown crocheted afghan she kept there for just such a purpose.

She closed her eyes, hoping that she might nod off. Not much chance, she thought, with the wind blowing as it was. (*Listen,* she would say to him. *Can you hear the wind? That's just how it sounded.*) The bedroom window rattled in its frame. Tree branches groaned and cracked, and Astrid could hear the slapping of a canvas tarp in the yard. Sand hit the windowpane in gusts and she could well imagine its sting against your face if you were outside, unprotected. And a tom cat was making an awful noise under the window, likely the orange one from the Patterson place (Astrid always winked at Lee when she said this), who came in search of the Torgesons' barn cat and was responsible for the batches of orange and tortoiseshell kittens that Astrid was always trying to give away. The wind was howling like a banshee and she wondered why even a tomcat would venture out on such a night.

And Lester was talking in his sleep. This in itself was not unusual; he always talked in his sleep. What was unusual was that Astrid could understand what he was saying: *Never underestimate the value of a map.* It was clear as a bell, although she had no idea what it could mean. He spoke again, with great authority: *Never underestimate the value of a map.*

"What kind of map?" Astrid asked.

"A road map," Lester said.

"Lester," Astrid said, "what in the world are you talking about?"

He rolled away then (Astrid described the sound of the bed creaking over the racket outside) and the talking stopped.

She decided she might as well go downstairs and make herself a cup of tea. She wasn't sure where her terry-cloth robe was in the dark, so she went as she was, with the afghan around her shoulders. It wasn't cold—it was summer after all—but the wind made her think it *should* be cold.

She went to the kitchen and turned on a light. The first thing her eye landed on was Lester's mother's silver tea service in the oak cabinet across the room. It had come from Norway, so the story went, and Astrid could see that it needed a good polish. Well, she had nothing better to do at three in the morning. She plugged in the kettle and then got the tea service and placed it on the kitchen table. She was about to get the silver polish from under the sink when she heard the tomcat yowl again, making an ungodly sound like that of a baby in distress (sometimes she would throw in another wink here). It sounded as though the cat was in the porch off the kitchen. *How in the world could he have got in there?* she wondered, imagining the mess, a tomcat spraying everywhere.

"Git you," she said, opening the door to the porch and flipping the light on, a glass of water in her hand for encouragement should he refuse to go. But it wasn't the cat that was yowling. It was a baby (a *lovely* baby, she sometimes added—Lee liked the sound of that, and when he was playing alone with the new kittens in the barn he would repeat it to himself: *a lovely baby*), not a newborn, but not very old either, in a red plastic laundry basket. He'd been wrapped in a blanket but had kicked that off and was now wearing nothing but a diaper and a blue knit hat. A baby bottle and a half-dozen disposable diapers were tucked into the basket with him. The baby stopped crying and scrunched his eyes shut against the light.

Astrid stared. She didn't know what to do. "I didn't mean it," she said. "Git you. I didn't mean it. I thought you were a cat."

She came to her senses and set down the water glass and picked up the baby. She felt his hands and feet, expecting them to be cold, but they weren't.

Her first instinct was to call Lester, but then she thought, *What good will he be?* And she wasn't calling the RCMP, not yet anyway. She and Lester were far enough off the highway that no stranger was going to pick their farmyard at random, in the dark, as a good place to abandon a baby.

She sat down at the kitchen table with the baby, who now seemed content, and tried to come up with a logical explanation. He had been left sometime after Astrid and Lester went to bed. The yardlight switch was in the porch and there certainly had been no baby there when she'd turned the light off, as she always did, before they retired for the night. A calamity, perhaps. Someone from down the road had left the baby while she, the mother, dealt with whatever had come up. But that was ridiculous. Astrid and Lester never locked their doors. Someone desperate for help could have walked into the house and right into their bedroom if need be.

The kettle was boiling. Astrid moved the tea service from the table to the counter, and then she spread her afghan on the table and laid the baby down. She made tea in the silver pot, she wasn't sure why, perhaps just because it was handy. (*Or perhaps because we had special company*, she said to Lee in one telling of the story, and from then on Lee would say if she forgot, "Because you had special company, right?") She wondered if the baby was hungry, and retrieved the bottle and the pile of diapers from the porch. Although she'd never had a child of her own, she knew about caring for babies, having done quite a bit of that over the years for neighbour couples who'd been luckier than she and Lester. She placed the bottle in a pot of hot water and changed the baby's diaper. She took off the knitted hat so she could get a better look at him, and found a note tucked inside. It said, *Dear Uncle Lester, please take care of this child, you're own flesh and blood, as I can't.* That was it.

What in the world? Lester had no niece that they'd ever met.

"Oh my," Astrid said, and decided she had better, after all, call Lester.

She woke Lester and showed him the baby and the note. He sat down at the table and Astrid poured him some tea.

"This is impossible," he said.

That was about all she expected him to say. He talked more in his sleep than he did when he was awake.

"I know it's impossible," Astrid said. "But, Lester, somebody left this baby for us."

The baby, of course, was Lee. Astrid had told him the story so many times that he swears he can remember it—not the story, but his actual arrival—in the same way he believes he can remember, although he was only a toddler, the day he had his picture taken on Old Tom. He can, for instance, remember the sudden flash of the porch light when Astrid flicked it on, Astrid's face when she first bent over him, the tea service on the counter. These memories are picture-clear. The back porch is less clear, but he remembers himself wailing and the sound of the wind outside. Over the years, he's tried to go back just a little further, just minutes would be enough, to see a young woman hastily write a note in the dim light of a car's interior, step with him out of the car into the windy night, hold him with one arm as she carefully opens the door to Astrid and Lester's porch. To see her kiss him on the cheek as she lays him down, perhaps cry as she gives him one last look in the darkness. But he's unable to drag his memory back just that little bit so he can see his mother's face. To know who she was would be asking too much, he thought, but to know that she existed would require only a glimpse, just the briefest of memories.

Once, when Lee was seven or eight years old, he asked Astrid, Who do you think my mother is? and listened to her distress as she carefully tried to manoeuvre around the question she feared the most: *Why didn't she want me?* Astrid told him that his mother was a young woman—very young, far too young to look after a baby—but responsible enough to make a difficult decision, and didn't things turn out for the best because Astrid and Lester had for years wanted a baby of their own, and here he was and no one could love him more than they did.

And then later, when Lee was ten, more difficult questions. He came home one day and said, "This kid at school said I was really Lester's love child and so why do I call him Uncle Lester. But what does that mean? Love child?"

Astrid squirmed and turned red in the face, and then she gave Lee information that he didn't quite understand, about how he could not be Lester's son because, well, Astrid and Lester had no children of their own, and they had tried for many years to have a family, and it wasn't to be . . . *and so whatever you hear at school, Lee, don't you believe it, and if you have questions, you come right to me and ask them, just like you did today* . . . all of which was confusing and made him wish he hadn't said anything, and he still didn't know what *love child* meant.

But that evening Astrid sat him down again, this time with Lester there to help, and told him about the two theories of how Lee was related to Lester. "You pipe up, Lester, if I get something wrong," Astrid said, but Lester mostly looked down at his socks while Astrid talked.

The first theory involved a cousin with whom Lester's father had immigrated. The cousin had immediately left Canada and headed for California in search of warmer weather than the Canadian West had to offer. No one knew for sure what had happened to him but, through correspondence among relatives on both sides of the ocean, the rumour circulated that he had come to no good and was killed in a fight over a woman. The woman, it was rumoured, had been expecting a baby, so it was possible that Lee's mother was a descendant of that line of the family. How such a relative would track down Lester and Astrid . . . well, who knew, but it was possible.

The second theory was generated by Lester's cousin Olaf in Norway, and involved other relations in that country. Lester's grandmother on his mother's side had been the second wife of a man who had been widowed young, leaving two small children. The children were sent to live with the first wife's relatives until Lester's grandfather could find himself another bride and a suitable mother for the children. When he eventually remarried, the first wife's family refused to send the children back and the link with that line of blood was broken. When Astrid wrote to the relatives in Norway about finding Lee in the porch, Cousin Olaf proposed that one of the descendants of the two lost children had travelled to Canada to give back to Lester what had been taken from his grandfather. Lester looked up from his socks and interjected that Olaf was a watercolour painter and knitted sweaters for a hobby, so he no doubt had too much imagination.

"Lester," Astrid said. "Be serious. Lee is asking about his roots." So Lester got up and took a world atlas from his shelf of books and showed Lee exactly where in Norway his family had come from and where Olaf the watercolour painter lived, and then he patted Lee on the head and went to the barn.

"Well," Astrid said after Lester left. "He wasn't much help, was he." Then she told Lee that the RCMP had been unable to prove either theory, but blood tests presented evidence that Lee *could* be related to Lester, and custody of Lee was granted to them, and they were overjoyed. She told Lee that he was the greatest gift that she or anyone else, with the exception perhaps of Mary, had ever been given by God.

"Can I go to the barn now?" Lee remembers asking, and Astrid said of course, and off he went after Lester.

He'd had no idea that his simple question about what love child meant would precipitate his being given *so much* information, and in such a formal way, not like the bedtime story. And although he was reassured by what Astrid said, he was puzzled by her sudden reference to God. Astrid had never been much for church, although she did make Lester and Lee go with her at Christmas and Easter. From then on Lee kept his thoughts on the matter of his ancestry to himself, except for the time of the barn fire when he'd blurted out, regretfully, that he was just a shirt-tail relative.

Lee feels a tug on the reins. He blinks, brings the horse into focus, and wonders if he'd maybe dozed off on his feet for a few minutes. The horizon, he notes, is beginning to turn pink and his watch tells him that he should be getting out of bed in another two hours to prepare, as usual, for the day's work ahead. He leads the horse from the cemetery, back under the iron gate, and looks up the road to the Lindstrom place just south of the old Hundred Mile School. He calculates that he's covered nearly twenty-five miles. In the soft light of near-dawn it seems crazy to have set out the way he did in the middle of the night. Weary now, he remounts and heads up the road toward Lindstroms', not prepared to ride the whole distance over again. He'll get Tyler Lindstrom to trailer him back to his place.

As he approaches the farmyard he looks for signs that someone is about, but he sees no one. It's too early to arrive at the door. *The school then*, Lee thinks. Although the windows are now boarded up and it's been demoted into a grain bin, there's still a good well in the schoolyard. When they get there, he'll give the horse a drink and let him graze for a while before he sees if Tyler can spare the time to take him home.

The Lindstroms' collie dog comes to the end of the approach and barks once, then lies down with his head on his paws and watches in a bored way, as though it is not all that unusual to see a horse and rider across the road.

"Good boy," Lee says to the dog.

The horse's ears rotate as though he thinks Lee is talking to him.

"You're a good boy too," Lee says.

The sound of his own voice is disconcerting, jolting him back to the reality of who he is and what he does every day. Now that there's light in the sky everything seems normal again. He can hardly remember what possessed him just hours ago.

Happiness

The Cat

Hank Trass is dozing in the warm cab of his truck with his mouth wide open and his head jammed into the corner between the seatback and the window, which is rolled up against the mosquitoes. His cowboy hat is beside him on the seat, his takeout coffee spilled on the floor at his feet where he'd accidentally kicked it over. The day before, he'd travelled to a town just west of Winnipeg to pick up a used stock trailer he'd found on the Internet, but then he hadn't bought the trailer after all because it was covered in rust that suspiciously had not been evident in the pictures the owner had sent. Then Hank's truck had broken down and he'd waited several hours for a mechanic to get him on the road again, and he'd tried to make it home by driving all night but caught himself nodding off and ended up grabbing a few hours' sleep in the campground just east of Juliet. Hank knows from past experience that when he starts to fall asleep at the wheel, he'd better pull over, pronto. He rolled his truck once, trying to drive through a sleepy spell with the window down, gulping air to keep himself awake. It hadn't worked. He'd totalled the truck, but somehow emerged with only a few bruises.

When he pulled into the campground, he'd planned to sleep for only an hour or so, but the sun wakes him and when he looks at his watch he realizes he's slept for a good four hours. He can hear the steady sound of semi-trailers passing on the highway a quarter-mile to the south. His neck is so stiff he can hardly turn it. His wife Lynn is always trying to get him to do exercises—she herself does yoga that she learned from a DVD—and for once, in desperation, he thinks it might possibly do some good. He opens the truck door and wills his uncooperative body to unfold itself and step out into the early morning. The campground, pretty much empty, is just an open field with a half-dozen barbecue stands and picnic tables, a water tap and a pair of pit toilets. In the campsite next to his is a little red car with two mountain bikes on top. A young couple is sleeping in a pup tent with the front door unzipped and the top halves of their bodies out in the open air. Their hides must be tougher than his, Hank thinks, to sleep like that with a swarm of mosquitoes at them all night. Across the field next to the fence is a truck towing a small stock trailer just like the one he'd looked at in Manitoba only not as rusty, with several bales of hay in a rack on top. Another pup tent is pitched by a picnic table a few hundred feet from the rig. If there were a horse in the trailer he'd know why the tent was so far away from it, having spent more than a few nights next to a horse making a racket, but the door is wide open and there's no sign of a horse tied inside or out.

Hank visits the nearest toilet without checking to see if it says GENTS or LADIES on the door, then goes to the tap and splashes cold water on his face. The act of bending to the stream of water is painful, and then straightening up again is even worse, so he tries to picture some of the stretching exercises Lynn has shown him, thinking he can't get back in the truck until he's limbered up a little. There's one she calls the cat, he recalls, where she gets down on her hands and knees and arches her back and then lets it sink toward the floor. Well, he's not getting down on his hands and knees, he'd never make it up, so he improvises and does the exercise standing on his feet, bent forward at the waist. The stretch feels surprisingly good. He remembers Lynn doing something else, standing against the wall and sliding down and then up again, so he does this against the cab of the truck. The down part is easy enough, but to get back up he has to push himself with his hands on his thighs. Still, this one feels pretty good too. He won't let Lynn know, but maybe he'll find a way to do this once in a while when she's not looking. He closes his eyes, puts his hands on his hips and turns his head slowly, one way and then the other. Each time he manages to turn it a little farther. When he opens his eyes, he sees the girl in the pup tent watching him. He thinks he must make quite a picture to a young girl like that—a rickety old cowboy trying to stretch out his aching body, what hair he has left on his head sticking out all over. He reaches up to smooth it down and then gets his hat off the seat of the cab and puts it on. When he looks toward the tent again, the girl and her friend have moved inside. He sees the tent flaps being pulled together by a male hand with some kind of colourful woven bracelet on the wrist.

Hank's stomach growls and he checks the time once again. The early morning regulars will be arriving at the Oasis for breakfast just about now. Lynn will be there, baking the pies she's become famous for, serving her customers, keeping her sharp eye on the time so she can start phoning if whatever high school girl she's got working for her today doesn't show up when she's supposed to. Lynn has turned out to be a shrewd and successful business-woman. When she bought the restaurant six years ago Hank wasn't convinced it was a good idea, but he's convinced now. He's had to do without his best hand thanks to Lynn's entrepreneurial success, but he gets by with the help of neighbours like young Lee Torgeson, and when he has to, he hires a local kid to drive a tractor for him.

Just as Hank is about to get in his truck and hit the road, he sees a red-haired woman in bright pink pyjama bottoms, an oversized T-shirt and bright green running shoes walking into the campground along the access road. He watches her with interest as she approaches, wondering where in the world she might have come from. As she gets closer he sees that she is not young—approaching sixty if she's a day—and the red hair is definitely a bottle job.

"Morning," Hank says when she gets close enough to hear.

She stops and looks down at her pyjama bottoms.

"Don't worry," she says. "I haven't escaped from anywhere." She walks over to Hank's truck and asks, "You haven't by any chance seen a grey Arab horse?"

Hank looks over at the trailer with its open doors.

"Yeah," she says. "He's done a runner. I guess I forgot to latch the door. Idiot. Me, I mean, not the horse."

"I haven't seen a horse," says Hank. "It was dark when I pulled in, so I can't say whether there was one about then or not."

"He shows up pretty good in the moonlight."

Hank shakes his head. "Sorry," he says. "Where you from?" He's already noted the Manitoba plates on her rig.

"I'm not really from anywhere at the moment. Kind of between places. Damn it anyway. Should have pitched my tent closer but I wanted to get some sleep. He bangs around in there like a bull in a pipe factory. Well, I guess I'll talk to the locals. I can't think what else to do."

"Sounds like a plan," Hank says. "You could put in a call to the RCMP. And there's a restaurant up the road. The Oasis. Maybe tack a notice on the billboard."

"Damn it all to hell," she says.

"Arab horse, you say. You know we've got the sand hills to the west. Maybe he'll head thataway, hang out with the camels there."

When she doesn't respond, Hank says, "More likely he'll stick to where the grass is good."

He can tell she's not really listening to him. She's staring at the trailer, her mind on her problem, thinking about her horse making tracks and *how much trouble* this day is going to be.

"That horse has been nothing but a bother," she says. Then she points to the Coleman stove sitting on the picnic table by her tent. She asks Hank if he wants some coffee. She can make coffee in a hurry, she says.

He should get home, but a fresh coffee would really hit the spot. "Don't mind if I do," he says.

They walk across the campground, and Hank settles himself at her picnic table while she scoops coffee into the basket of a stainless steel percolator and fills the pot with water from a plastic jug. He can see from here that the crew cab of her truck is filled with household items (he can make out a lampshade) and the box is loaded with suitcases, plastic storage bins, a bicycle, and what could be a La-Z-Boy recliner wrapped in plastic. She's obviously not just out on a weekend horse-camping trip.

"So where're you off to?" he asks casually.

"I'm supposed to be moving to Peace River. Ever been there?"

"Nope," Hank says.

"Neither have I. My daughter lives there. She took her father's side in the divorce, decided she hated me and went to live with him. No contact at all. This was years ago. Then out of the blue she calls me and suggests we meet for the weekend in Edmonton, and now here I am, moving to Peace River. Funny how your life can change, just like that. Not sure how it will work out, but we'll see. She's got two kids I didn't know about. Both boys, just a year apart. My grandchildren. Hard to believe."

"That's quite a story," Hank says.

"Yeah. Just hope it works out. Nothing to lose, I guess. Other than the damned horse. I've got pictures." She rummages in her purse and pulls out an envelope with school pictures in it. Two smiling boys with missing front teeth.

"Good-looking little rascals," Hank says.

She nods and returns the pictures to her purse.

Hank finds himself scanning the horizon. It's possible the horse is close by, but more than likely he's spooked himself with his freedom and gone for a good run. Hank hopes he hasn't run into wire, or found a pile of grain in a field.

"The horse is going to Peace River with you?" he asks.

"Presumably," the woman says, "although it's all a bit of folly on my part. My daughter lives on a farm up there at Peace River, one of those hippie farms I imagine. I asked her if her kids had a pony, all kids want a pony, right, and she said, no, they don't have any animals except a budgie. She's a single parent, not much disposable income. So I'm on the highway passing the auction mart a few weeks ago and I see a sign that says HORSE AUCTION. So I stop, just to look. Just to see how much ponies cost. And there's a guy there buying up a whole bunch of horses and the man next to me tells me the guy's a meat buyer. The horse in the sale ring at the time was this pretty grey horse that had such a gentle look to it and the meat buyer started to bid and I couldn't stand it. Up went my hand. So that's it. I bought my grandkids a pony. Only I have no idea if he's a kids' horse. I've never ridden a horse in my life."

The coffee is percolating away on the Coleman and Hank thinks the woman is lucky she hasn't been hurt, hauling a horse around with no experience at all. And the daughter is likely not going to be all that happy when her mother shows up with a trailer full of horse trouble, not to mention a money pit, and once the kids see the horse it's going to be hard to say no, but Hank keeps quiet, none of his business.

"My status as a mother is still pretty tentative. You go a little crazy when you get a call from the daughter you thought was gone from your life forever. And grandchildren . . . well, whoever would have guessed?" She pauses, then says, "She needs help with the kids. She wouldn't have called me if she didn't need help."

The coffee is ready and she pours Hank a cup and hands him a tin of milk. "Hope you don't take sugar," she says. She gets a tray of doughnuts from her cooler but Hank turns them down. He knows Lynn will have something for him, and he should really drink up and be on his way. He takes a gulp of the coffee and burns his throat.

"Have you got kids?" she asks.

Hank nods. "Two daughters. Grown up and gone to the city. No grandkids. Working on their careers, I suppose."

"So you think I should get in touch with the RCMP about this horse, do you?"

"That's what I'd do," Hank says. "And talk to the locals, like you said. That can't hurt."

At that moment the girl from the pup tent crawls out pulling her jeans up over her tanned legs. The boy's hand reaches out and grabs her by the ankle and she shrieks and dances away. Hank turns his head, embarrassed. "Oh to be young, eh," he says.

"Younger and smarter," the woman says. "But those two things don't tend to go together."

Hank finishes his coffee and says he'd best be going. "I should have been home yesterday," he says. "I might find myself in the doghouse." He winks. He's not sure why. Old habit. The woman raises an eyebrow, but Hank doesn't elaborate. The story of his truck breakdown isn't as interesting as what she might be thinking. He asks if she's got a contact number just in case he sees or hears something, and she heads over to her truck for a piece of paper. He watches her comical pink rear end as she leans across the seat and rummages in the glove box. She writes on a scrap of paper and brings it back to him.

"My cell number," she says.

He glances at her name—Joni—and the number, and shoves the paper in his back pocket. He warns her that cell phone coverage comes and goes in this country, and then he wishes her luck with her move to Peace River, and luck finding her horse, and gets in his truck to make his way back to the highway.

It's another cloudless morning, the usual breeze from the west already hot, and he decides he'll pick up hay bales from the ditches today. There wasn't much to hay this year, but he'd been taught by his father to accept whatever nature offered because next year she might not offer anything at all. Maybe he'll call young Torgeson and see if he could use a hand. Hank hasn't checked on him in a while, and Lynn will have some baking she'll send with him. She has a soft spot for Lee, and they both figure the kid must get lonely there on his own. *He's not like you were at that age*, Lynn has pointed out to Hank a couple of times, still able to make him feel guilty after all these years.

Ten minutes later, he passes the bullet-riddled sign—WELCOME TO JULIET, POPULATION 1,011—and pulls onto the Oasis approach. He can just taste the slice of blueberry pie he'll have for breakfast, unless Lynn gets on a healthy rant and makes him have something else, like bran flakes or oatmeal. A Greyhound bus is in the parking lot, ready to pull out, and Hank notices that one of its cargo flaps is still open. He honks to the driver, trying to catch his attention, but it's too late. The bus pulls away and a cardboard box tumbles to the parking lot. It bursts as it hits the pavement, and paper—hundreds of small pieces of bright yellow paper—are caught by the bus's tailwind and blow outward and upward, all over the parking lot. One of them slaps itself to his windshield and he sees that it's a flyer. He can read what it says: *The end is near.* It gives a date, which is, indeed, just around the corner. He watches the Greyhound bus through the flurry of paper to see if anything else falls out, anything that he should retrieve and take inside for the next bus that comes through, but nothing does, so he parks and turns off the engine. He gets out and pulls the flyer from his windshield. He examines it for more information, but there is none. As far as Hank can tell, it's just an announcement, a headline. No advice on what to do.

"Huh," he says out loud. "'The end.' Well, that's a bugger."

He shoves the flyer in his pocket along with Joni's phone number and walks through the storm of paper to his wife's restaurant.

Sweetheart

Vicki Dolson always says of herself that she is not really capable of understanding great unhappiness. On the worst of days she sees, or at least tries to see, the best. With the exception of something having to do with the kids, like one of them getting childhood leukemia, she can't think of anything that would make her mope for longer than an hour or two. It's the way she was raised. So it's hard for her to understand Blaine and the dark lens through which he sees the world these days. Not that she doesn't understand the gravity of their situation and the extreme actions Blaine has been forced to take. He'd first sold off his herd of Charolais-Hereford cross cattle, and then the bank had insisted on the dispersal of his machinery, and then the sale of all his land except the home quarter. But Vicki's position is that they should be thankful they still have their house and they can rent out the pasture for a bit of income, every dollar helps. The bank did allow Blaine to keep an old stock trailer and one saddle horse—although not the good mare who would go all day for you, and Blaine claims the horse he kept requires an instruction manual to operate—so at least he can still drive up to Allan Tallman's place on a Sunday for a little team roping. There you go, Vicki says to Blaine on occasion, it's not all bad. Even as she knows this drives him crazy.

Most mornings, Blaine is up well before Vicki. This morning he sleeps right through the radio alarm and Vicki decides to let him rest for a few more minutes. She's lying there listening to a voice tell her that a heritage building in Regina is slated for demolition and there's a petition circulating, when she hears Blaine say, "My whole life has been slated for demolition and no one is organizing petitions about that."

She turns to him and says, "Good morning, you." She can see right away that she's annoyed him. He hates it when she talks to him as though he's one of the kids.

She throws back the covers and both she and Blaine notice that she's wearing jeans under her nightie.

"Oh," Vicki says, "that's odd." She has a sudden memory of the plane, how she thought she was going to have to go out and look for it.

"Did you hear me get up in the night?"

"No," Blaine says. "How the hell can you sleep with all those clothes on? It's still hot in here from yesterday, for Christ sake."

"I heard a plane," Vicki says. "It seemed pretty real but I guess it was the dream." She steps out of bed and slips her feet into her flip-flops.

Blaine gets up too, hurrying now. He prides himself on arriving at the job site ahead of most of the other men, including the foreman.

"Are you going to do those beans today?" he asks as he pulls on his jeans and tucks in a grey T-shirt.

Not the beans already, Vicki thinks, but she says, "Yes, Blaine. I'm going to do the beans. I've set aside the whole day."

"You're not planning to go into town, then?"

"Why? Did you want me to pick something up for you?" She's teasing, trying to turn Blaine's already-bad mood.

"No," Blaine says. "I want you to do the beans."

She goes to the kitchen, still in her nightie, to perk Blaine's coffee for his thermos. She discovers that there's hardly any coffee left—just enough for half a pot.

"Sorry, hon," she says when Blaine arrives in the kitchen a few minutes later. "We're all out of coffee. I forgot my list when I picked up groceries last week."

"Never mind," Blaine says. "I'll drink water."

As Vicki half fills the coffee pot, she can't keep her mind off the dreaded beans and what a pain in the neck a garden is. She makes a commitment to herself to get the beans done, if for no other reason than to get them out of her head. And Blaine is right, they won't keep long sitting in tubs in the basement, where they've been for the two days since she and Shiloh picked them off, sweating in the hot sun, because Blaine had said, "God dammit, Vicki, if you don't pick those beans today I'm taking away your car keys. We'll see how far you get without a car."

"We can at least wait for a cooler day," she'd protested. "Anyway, I'd be happy to give them away. I could put up a sign in the café."

Blaine had given her one of his looks and she'd felt instantly sorry for being flippant. She doesn't know what she has against the idea of preserving garden produce. Maybe it's the work, when it's so easy to buy frozen vegetables. Or maybe she's just trying to let Blaine know that she's not his mother and never will be. Whatever the reason, they go through this every year—Blaine harping about the garden and Vicki putting off the freezing and canning for as long as possible.

When she sees Blaine's lunchbox on the counter, she realizes she forgot to make his sandwiches the night before. There's no ham—Blaine's favourite—so she grabs a jar of jam and slaps together some sandwiches and pours the half pot of coffee into Blaine's thermos as the kids begin to wander into the kitchen for breakfast. Blaine grabs the lunch pail from her as soon as she closes the lid.

"I'm not kidding," he says as he heads for the door. "We can live on jam for a few days. Don't go getting any ideas. You get those beans done or else."

"Oh, for heaven's sake," Vicki says. "You're talking to me like I'm the hired help."

"Pretty bloody useless hired help," Blaine says.

She stands in the porch with the door open and watches Blaine cross the yard to his truck. It won't start. He gets out, fiddles with something under the hood, then slams the hood down. He gets back in the truck, starts it, then leans out the window and yells, "Don't you dare go to town today, Vicki."

She blows him a kiss. "And don't you take any wooden nickels," she calls, she doesn't even know why.

Seven-year-old Daisy has come to stand beside her. "What does that mean," Daisy wants to know, "'Don't take any wooden nickels'?"

"Nothing," Vicki says. "It's just a silly thing to say, like 'Don't let the bedbugs bite.'"

Blaine fishtails out of the yard, driving too fast, and Vicki and Daisy sit on the step and watch his trail of dust. The morning sky in front of them is pink.

"Look at that sky," Vicki says to Daisy. "Aren't we lucky to live where we can see that right out our door, every single morning if we want. It's better than a movie, don't you think?"

Daisy starts to list all the movies that it's not better than.

"Okay, okay," Vicki says. "I get it. But you have to admit, it's pretty."

"We should spray Bucko for flies," Daisy says.

"What do you mean?"

"Well, look at him."

Vicki looks. Blaine's horse is kicking at his belly as though he's got a horsefly biting him.

"You're right," she says. "After breakfast. You remind me." She can see the spray bottle hanging on the fence. "I guess we can't sit here all day, can we," she says. "We'd better get at those beans."

When she returns to the kitchen she finds four of her six kids sitting at the table eating jam on bread: nine-year-old Martin, little Lucille (the youngest, at three and a half), and the five-year-old twin boys, who look so much alike that even she has a hard time telling them apart. Shiloh isn't up yet. *He must be enjoying his new room*, Vicki thinks.

The children look at her.

"Daddy doesn't really like jam," Lucille says.

"Well, it's not his favourite, that's for sure," Vicki says. "But you can't always have your favourite, can you."

"Are we going to town for ham?" Daisy asks.

"Not today. We have a big job to get done."

"I need a fudge sundae," Daisy says.

"You don't *need* a fudge sundae," Vicki says. "You might want one but you don't need one. Anyway, they're too expensive."

"I heard Dad say we aren't supposed to go to town today," Martin says.

"That's right," Vicki says. "At least not until we get the beans done, and that's going to take all day."

"Fudge sundaes aren't that expensive," Daisy says. "Don't tell me we're so poor we can't even buy ice cream." She sticks her lip out and sniffles.

"Oh, stop it," Vicki says. "Those aren't even real tears. Those are crocodile tears if I ever saw them. You've been watching too much TV."

While the kids are finishing their breakfast, Vicki gets herself dressed and then, there's no way around it, she might as well get started. She kneels on the floor in front of her kitchen cupboards and fishes around for her two blanching pots. Pots and lids clatter as she drags them out and sets them on the floor. After the kids pile their breakfast dishes on the counter she decides she has to wash them up to make more room for the whole ordeal of doing the beans. Once that's done, she takes a final swipe with the tea towel at a few wet spots on the counter, and as she does so she notices just how white the towel is. It's amazing, like fresh snow in bright sunlight. The tea towel is like a pep talk, and as she looks at it she thinks, *I'm not such a bad homemaker, just look at how white that towel is.* She lays it on the counter and goes downstairs for the plastic tubs full of beans.

At first she tries to be quiet in the basement, but then she thinks Shiloh could be a help, so she crosses the cement floor to his new room and parts the curtains. She notices that the light is on, and she smiles to herself at the thought of her big boy Shiloh being afraid to sleep alone, in the dark. *He's not grown up yet,* she thinks as she switches off the light and says, "Wakey, wakey." When Shiloh opens his eyes she says, "So, Mr. Man. What did you think of your first night in the royal chamber?"

As soon as she's said it and sees the look that crosses his face, she knows she's made a mistake, just like when she said, *Good morning, you* to Blaine. Everything she says to either of them is wrong these days. She probably shouldn't have called Shiloh Mr. Man.

"You should knock before you come in," Shiloh says.

So that's it. The new room is to be private. Well, that makes sense. She'd wanted privacy when she was a teenager, although she'd never gotten it.

"You're right," she says. "Sorry." She steps back outside the bedspread curtains and says, "There's no place to knock." Then she stamps her feet on the cement floor. "Wakey, wakey," she says again.

Shiloh says, "If you weren't so useless you'd go away and leave me alone."

Vicki is shocked. Shiloh has been sullen lately, but he's never said anything like that to her. She isn't sure what to do. *Is this just typical teenage behaviour?* she wonders. She can't help but feel hurt by what he's said, but on the other hand she remembers saying a few rude things to her mother and then immediately feeling bad. She imagines Shiloh already regretting what he's said, but being unable to apologize because he doesn't know how. She decides to ignore the outburst. She leaves him in bed, gets a tub of beans and carries it upstairs to the kitchen. Then she retrieves the other two and sets them on the kitchen floor with the first tub.

She looks at the two little blanching pots and the three huge tubs of beans. She tries to imagine how many beans she will have to snap, how many times she will load the beans into the pots, time them, cool them in cold water, bag them, carry them down the basement steps to the freezer. The thought is unbearable. She prays that she'll be out of freezer bags, but, of course, when she looks in the cupboard, there are plenty. Years' worth. Every year she makes a special trip to town for more freezer bags. Her ability to maintain a positive attitude is being sorely challenged.

Vicki picks up a handful of beans, hoping there'll be something wrong with them, but there isn't. There's nothing to do but put them up. She looks at her stove. It has four burners. If she had two more blanchers she could cut in half the time she'll need to do the beans. She could borrow from a neighbour, but if she's going to load the kids in the car to go and borrow blanchers, she might as well drive to town and buy another two, and then she'll have them for next year. It will only take an hour or so.

"Come on, kids," she says. "We're going to make a quick trip to town. A quick one, mind you. In and out of the hardware store, that's it. And no fudge sundaes, Daisy. Don't even ask. And no crying about it, either. We're in too much of a hurry."

"But Dad said—" begins Martin.

"Never mind that," Vicki says. "Dad means well, but he doesn't know anything about freezing vegetables."

She calls down the stairs to Shiloh that they're going to town and to hurry up if he wants to come with them. Five minutes, she says, and within the five minutes he comes up the stairs with his hair all over the place. He doesn't say anything but makes a quick trip to the bathroom and then grabs a bag of Oreo cookies from the cupboard.

"That's not much of a breakfast," Vicki says. She almost adds "Mr. Man," but catches herself.

At the last minute she tells the kids to get their bathing suits, maybe there'll be time to stop for a quick swim at the pool since it's supposed to be such a hot day. She unzips a huge gym bag and they all shove their suits in, all but Shiloh. Vicki adds a half dozen old towels.

"Shiloh, don't you want to go for a swim?" she asks. "It's going to be hot."

He ignores the question and heads out to the car, jamming the cookie bag in his backpack. Vicki and the rest of the kids follow, and they all pile into her old Cutlass Supreme. Shiloh says, "Shotgun," and gets into the front seat, and none of the kids argues with him. Vicki is about to start the car when he says, "Wait," and he runs back into the house.

Vicki looks absently out the car window and sees Blaine's buckskin horse standing in the shade and is so thankful that they've been able to hang onto him even if no one but Blaine can ride him. The horse has his head around and is kicking at something on his flank, and Vicki remembers that she and Daisy were going to spray him. It would only take a minute, but then again, they'll be back home before the heat of day when the flies are at their worst and she can do it then. Anyway, Blaine never sprayed the horses when he had more than one. It was too expensive.

Shiloh comes back out with his hair combed, wearing a different T-shirt.

Daisy notices and says, "Shiloh's going to see a girl."

"Shut up, stupid," he says.

"No one in this family is stupid," Vicki says.

On the way to town, Lucille finds someone's lost ball of bubblegum on the floor in the back seat and chews it up and then sticks it in her hair. The twins watch her do it, and when Vicki hears them giggling she turns to look and sees the mess.

"I decorated it," Lucille says.

"Oh my God," Vicki says. "How am I ever going to get that out? We'll have to go and see Karla, and all I can say is, it's a good thing for you we had to go to town today." She tells Martin to keep an eye on Lucille and make sure she doesn't get gum all over the back seat. "You keep your hands away from your hair, Lucille," she says. "Or Martin will tell me and there'll be no candy for a week. Do you hear me?"

Vicki drives south along the grid road and just as they get to the railway tracks she sees at least forty head of yearling calves strung out to the west, grazing along the tracks. She assumes they're Hank Trass's calves and makes a note to call him from somewhere and let him know. She used to have a cell phone, but Blaine wouldn't let her renew her contract because of the money. She tried to argue that it was her way to get in touch with him in an emergency, but he said that if she'd stay home there wouldn't be any emergencies, and if there were she could use the perfectly good land line in the house.

She glances at Shiloh, who hasn't said anything the whole way to town. He's eating cookies and Vicki sees no sign of the teenage defiance she heard when she first called him to get up. *Their moods are all over the place,* she thinks, and then she notices with a sideways glance how much he looks like his father. She wonders how long it will be before he talks, and if she should say anything about the rude way he spoke to her earlier.

In the end, she doesn't have to. As they turn off the highway, Shiloh folds down the top of the cookie bag and zips up his backpack and says, "Well, anyway, you should have knocked."

She takes it as an apology. "You're right," she says.

She wonders where she should begin her search for blanchers and whether she should take the time to get a few groceries. These things are necessary, she thinks, just as necessary as, say, tractor parts. No farmer would consider frivolous a trip to town for parts. When there's a breakdown, a wife is expected to drop whatever she's doing and head to the dealership to collect some crucial pin or belt or drive chain that she's never heard of, and try to explain to the parts manager what she needs when she doesn't exactly know, and get home again as quickly as possible so the work can resume, and if she's lucky she won't have to make another trip because she's brought home the wrong part. A trip for blanchers and groceries is the same, inconvenient but necessary.

"Ha," she says out loud, congratulating herself for her brilliant logic. The kids all look at her. "Just part of the job, isn't it," she says.

Vicki turns up the street toward Karla Norman's house so she can get Lucille's hair fixed, the first of the quick stops.

There's lots of time in a day, she assures herself.

The Theatre

Norval opens his eyes to see Lila, hands on her hips, staring down at him. He can tell by the look on her face that he's done something wrong, but his head is fuzzy and he can't quite think what it is. As he slowly comes awake his misdemeanours begin to line up: he's on the couch (*Norval, why didn't you just come back to bed?*); the TV is still on (*How can you sleep with that sound blaring, for heaven's sake?*); the light is on in the kitchen (*The power bill keeps going up, I wonder why.*) And then there's the meat loaf, a crumb of which is lying in plain view on the white carpet. Norval watches as Lila bends to pick it up and examines it closely before giving him a glaring look of admonition. He watches her carry the crumb between two painted fingernails toward the kitchen, holding it out in front of her as though it's the most distasteful bit of evidence of Norval's domestic inadequacy.

"I am housebroken, you know," he says in his defence, although not really loud enough for Lila to hear him.

He sits up and switches off the weather lady with the remote control. Through the arched doorway to the kitchen he can see Lila obsessing with neatness, wiping the counter and the sink before anyone has even had a chance to mess them up, her green satin dressing gown swishing as she moves. He thinks of the TV commercial that makes fun of sea-foam green bridesmaid dresses and thinks, *Lila's dressing gown is sea-foam green.* What does that mean? he wonders. It can't mean that she has bad taste, for Lila is well known for her sense of style. Perhaps that her taste is of another era, although she wouldn't be pleased at the notion that she might be, heaven forbid, a fashion relic. Not that Norval has anything against Lila's style, which he has always appreciated as long as he doesn't have to be the other half of a matched set.

"Sometimes I just wonder," Lila says, and Norval thinks, *Sometimes I wonder too.* How he got into all this.

He and Lila met in the city when he was in the last semester of his commerce degree and she was beginning a degree in acting. Norval was working part time as a junior teller at the small bank where Lila had her account. It was in an older working-class neighbourhood, and not one in which university students generally lived. Lila was staying with relatives while she went to school, and she and Norval struck up a friendship over her careful managing of her money, which Norval couldn't help but notice. They ran into each other on campus one day, and Norval invited Lila to go for a beer in the campus pub. They played pool—Lila was surprisingly good and beat him in several games until coyness got the better of her and she backed off and let him win. As they played, she entertained him with stories about her adventures as a theatre student, making them sound more adventurous than they really were. In truth, Lila was a small-town girl who was having trouble fitting in with the trendy and sometimes ruthless theatre students who already had years of experience in high school productions and summer drama camps and improv competitions, none of which had been available to a student like Lila with her simple dream of being on stage.

At the end of the term, Norval went to see her in the theatre department's production of a Shakespearean play—he can't remember which one; he just remembers that he didn't have a clue what was going on and couldn't understand a word anyone was saying. Lila had a small part and was angry that the director hadn't selected her for one of the starring roles. Norval went backstage after the performance as Lila had directed him to do. There was to be a party, at which she would introduce him to the rest of the cast. But when he arrived in the green room after making his way down a dark, mouldy-smelling corridor in the bowels of the theatre building, she grabbed his arm and dragged him outside, still in her stage makeup, and when they were away from the building and on their way to his car, she burst into tears, because the cast were going to a party at someone's house and they hadn't invited her. She swore the slight was intentional. They didn't like her, she said, because she had talent and they didn't, and one of them in a mean fit had told her that she should try cosmetology for a career. It was a jab at the fact that Lila never went anywhere without *Cosmo*-girl lipstick and eye makeup, while the other theatre girls were experimenting with the Cleopatra look. Either that or going au naturel, blank slates to be made up as their roles demanded.

Norval held Lila in the parking lot, mascara running down her cheeks, his feathers all puffed up because it was clear that Lila needed him. She was quitting school, she said. She couldn't study theatre at this two-bit university, and she would work for a while and then go to a bigger university where they had a good theatre department and graduates got jobs in television commercials and even movies. Norval hadn't actually thought she was very good on stage, but that didn't matter because he believed studying theatre was pointless anyway and what was wrong with cosmetology, although he knew enough not to say this, at least not at that moment. Instead he suggested that they get married.

Lila quickly forgot about the tragedy of her theatre school experience, and became completely engrossed in getting married and the prospects of setting up house with Norval and following him wherever the bank sent him on his climb up through the corporation. Someday, she told him, they would live in, say, Calgary, and he would work at a big main branch, or perhaps head office, and they would build a new house in a new subdivision and their kids would play basketball and the violin, and they would have season tickets to the symphony and Lila would find an agent who would get her work at a real theatre. Norval wasn't sure about that whole scenario, but he was happy with the thought of marrying Lila. For one thing, there was the prospect of frequent sex (right now sex was not nearly frequent enough with Lila living with relatives and Norval sharing a two-bedroom apartment with three roommates). He admired her looks, and her taste in clothes, and she was outgoing and fun. He was happy to turn himself over to her certainty about how marriage should work, because he didn't have a clue.

Well, he knows how it works now. Lila's wish is pretty much his command. Not that he's complaining, not really. What is marriage in middle age but a living arrangement, a contract for comfort, and they have a comfortable home in Juliet, and a partnership with quite a lot of time and money invested in it. Investments of any kind Norval does not take or leave lightly.

This memory of Lila's past in theatre leads him to look at Rachelle's upcoming wedding in a new way. These demands for renovations to the church are really instructions for building a set. It all begins to look like a production in which Rachelle is the star and Lila is the director with a cameo as mother of the bride. And this leads Norval to feel just a little sorry for her, and to think that maybe he has failed her in some way by not being ambitious enough in his own career, by being satisfied with small-town banking, and by not aiming for jobs in progressively larger towns and cities. Norval knows himself well enough to admit that he hasn't really had the desire to be any more successful than he is. He makes a vow to participate more willingly, for Lila's sake, in the orchestration of her wedding production.

He lifts himself off the couch and makes his way to the kitchen, where Lila has his heart-smart breakfast waiting for him. Another reason he should be more generous in his feelings: if it weren't for Lila he'd fill up on bacon and put whipping cream in his coffee. Instead, he has a bowl of colourful fruit salad, followed by bran flakes with skim milk. He's learned to drink his coffee black. Lila eats only the fruit salad. She follows some kind of diet that doesn't allow you to eat anything but fruit before noon.

The two of them sit in the breakfast nook overlooking the backyard and just as Norval takes his first good sip of his morning coffee, Lila looks out the window and says, "Oh my God."

Norval looks. Under the maple tree is Kyle. Norval's resolve to change his attitude about the wedding quickly dissipates when he sees his daughter's fiancé sleeping or—more accurately— passed out, sprawled on his back on the lawn. Kyle's fly is undone and his pants are not quite as far up on his hips as they should be, as though he relieved himself in the bushes and then just keeled over backwards. Luckily, his boxers are all that Norval can see hanging out, although he's not sure that wouldn't change if he went outside and looked more closely.

"What should we do?" says Lila.

"What should we do," sighs Norval. "Well, we could bring him inside and lock him in the furnace room and keep him there without food or water until he promises to go away."

"I'm serious, Norval," Lila says. "We can't leave him there in broad daylight."

Norval has to agree.

"Go out and talk to him," Lila says.

"I have a better idea," Norval says.

He pushes himself away from the table and climbs the stairs to Rachelle's room. She can do the talking, he thinks, and besides, it wouldn't hurt for her to see her future husband in all his post-binge glory. Not that he expects Rachelle to be in much better shape, but at least she's had the sense to come in and not make a spectacle of herself in the backyard.

He knocks on Rachelle's door and gets no answer. When he pushes the door open he sees that she isn't there. The covers are thrown back on the bed, but no Rachelle. He checks the bathroom, but she isn't there either.

"Oh hell," he says to himself as he goes back downstairs. He'd dealt with the two of them last night with quite a lot of patience, he thinks, but he's about at the end of it.

"She's not there," he tells Lila.

He goes through the sun doors to the deck and down the steps and across the yard to where Kyle is sleeping. He pokes him with his bare foot.

"Wake up," he says, and when Kyle doesn't, he pokes him harder. You might even call it a kick.

Kyle opens his eyes and a look of almost-terror crosses his face when he realizes where he is, and that his fiancée's father is staring down at him. He jumps to his feet, grabbing at his pants when he realizes he's about to lose them. He turns his back to Norval as he zips himself up, and then he takes a deep breath and faces him again. His ball cap is lying on the lawn and he picks it up and adjusts it on his head.

"Don't say anything," Norval says, "unless you know where my daughter is."

Norval can see Kyle struggling to remember the night before. He opens his mouth to speak, then closes it again.

"In her room?" Kyle finally says, hopefully but without much confidence.

Norval shakes his head.

"Have you checked the truck?" Kyle asks.

"No," says Norval. "How about you make yourself useful and do that?"

He watches Kyle walk around the side of the house, and he waits for him to come back. When he does, Kyle stands at the corner of the house without coming all the way into the backyard and says, "She's not there," and then he says, "Actually, my truck's not there either."

"Oh for Christ sake," Norval says. He turns and goes back in the house, leaving Kyle outside. "You know this marriage is doomed to failure, don't you?" he says to Lila.

Lila looks as though she might cry. Norval doesn't care.

"I'm not kidding. Think about the baby. The poor kid doesn't have a chance."

She says, "I know they're young—"

Norval interrupts. "Some young people are responsible, Lila. Face it, these two aren't. Neither one of them. The baby would be better off raised by wolves."

Now Lila is angry. Norval can see he's gone too far.

"You listen here," she says. She aims one of her manicured fingernails in his direction to help make her point. "I know as well as you this is not a perfect situation. But that baby is our flesh and blood and I'm not going to let it go to be raised by strangers. Besides that, I read an article—in *Chatelaine*, Norval, that's a credible magazine—and girls who give up their babies almost always regret it later. So you'd better make the best of this, because they're getting married and Rachelle is giving the baby up over my dead body."

It dawns on Norval that Lila has had quite a bit to do with Rachelle's decision to get married, and not just so she can stage-manage a big production. He hadn't realized she felt so strongly about this. Maybe she's right. What does he know about these things?

"I'm going to work," he says.

"I hope you're planning to get dressed first."

Norval is surprised by the sarcasm. Lila hardly ever uses sarcasm—that's been his domain.

He goes upstairs and dresses (Lila has his clothes laid out, summer-weight khaki pants, a blue shirt, a tie and a lightweight sports jacket), and before he leaves he says to her, "You're probably right, Lila. I don't know anything about this business of teenage motherhood. But surely you can see why I'm worried."

"Of course I can," Lila says. "But you just let me take care of Rachelle. Here's what you can do." She hands Norval a piece of notepaper with cheerful-looking purple flowers across the top.

"What's this?" he asks.

"It's the list, Norval. The things we discussed last night, the church renovations. You just take care of the list and I'll handle the other. Rachelle is likely at Kristen's. I'll track her down and we'll have a talk."

Norval folds the notepaper in half and puts it in the pocket of his khaki pants.

"Aren't you going to read it?" Lila asks. "You might have questions. Points of clarification."

"Maybe Rachelle and Kyle could get some counselling," Norval says.

"They don't need counselling," Lila says. "They just need to grow up a little."

A little, Norval thinks, *will not do it*, but he's said all he can say.

He steps out the front door and finds Kyle sitting dejected on the top step. Kyle looks up and is about to say something, but Norval beats him to it and says, "Let me give you a bit of advice, Kyle. A wise man knows when to keep his mouth shut."

Norval heads down the sidewalk toward Main Street and the bank, resisting the temptation to look back. He knows that he would feel some sympathy for Kyle and God knows he doesn't want sympathy entering into this whole situation. Not unless it's for himself.

Small Talk

When morning finally comes, Willard Shoenfeld goes inside to the kitchen and Marian is there, as always, with the coffee perking on the stove and the frying pan ready for his eggs. He thinks back to the pre-Marian days when he and Ed ate cornflakes every morning and burned themselves a couple of pieces of toast.

"How do you want them this morning?" Marian asks, and Willard says, "Over easy, I guess."

The eggs are ready in minutes and Marian slides them onto a plate, adds two slices of perfectly browned toast, then hands Willard his breakfast. He's in a bit of a stupor. Marian asks if something is wrong.

Willard can't get the picture of her in her nightgown out of his mind, the way she opened his bedroom door, and he wonders if he should just say, *It's okay, you know. You do what's best for you.* But he can't; he's paralyzed. He says, "No, nothing," and he dips a corner of his toast in the deep yellow egg yolk. "You've eaten?" he asks, just as he asks every morning.

She nods, as always, in response to his question.

He takes a bite of his toast, expecting pain to shoot from a lower molar up into his face because of his toothache dream the night before, which still seems real. No pain, though. He savours the perfect over-easy eggs, eating one piece of toast with the eggs and saving one to slather with raspberry jam.

Marian is now standing at the sink with her back to him, leafing through a cookbook.

Perhaps if I start a conversation, Willard thinks. *About anything at all. Try,* he thinks. *Try to say something.*

"I do enjoy my breakfast," he says.

Marian turns to look at him. He fears he's said something stupid. "Do you?" she says. "So do I." Then she returns to her recipes.

Well, that's it. Willard can't think of anything else to say. He spreads some of Marian's homemade freezer jam on his remaining slice of toast and tries to plan his day. There's the new movie to pick up at the bus, and a few repairs he should make to the fence. Some kids tried to light fire to it one night a few weeks ago. They'd barely got the kindling organized and the match lit when the barking dog had awoken Willard. He'd looked out his bedroom window and seen just enough to know what was going on. He pulled on his pants and when he got to the living room he saw that Marian was already up, looking out the picture window.

"I think they've started a fire," she said. "The fence on the east side."

"Damn kids," Willard said.

He kept a fire extinguisher handy for times like this and he'd grabbed it while Marian flicked the yardlights on. The drive-in was flooded with light and, sure enough, about half a dozen kids jumped in a truck, some into the cab and some the box, and roared off down the access road. The dog was going crazy by now, running in circles and barking wildly in the middle of the sandy drive-in lot.

Willard hopped on his ATV and drove, the dog running along behind, to where the fire was trying hard to get started. When they got there, flames were licking up the sides of one fence panel, but they were quickly squelched when Willard turned the fire extinguisher on them. The fence was still standing, but he'd have to replace three or four boards. The dry grass was burned to the ground along the fence. This was the real danger, with section after section of dry grassy pastureland running to the north. "Damn stupid kids," Willard said again, and then he told the dog once more what a good dog he was. He'd gone back to the garage for a shovel, and then he'd spent an hour shovelling sand onto the grass along the fence to make sure the fire didn't flare up again.

When he returned to the house at three in the morning, Marian was still up, watching through the window. She wanted him to call the RCMP in Swift Current, but Willard figured that was pointless. The kids were long gone and he wouldn't be able to give any kind of useful description. Marian made a pot of tea and put a plate of cookies on the table. At three-thirty, they'd gone back to bed.

Willard is getting plenty tired of this nonsense. He's of the conviction that the kids of Juliet don't know the value of either work or money, and don't have enough to do, especially in the summer when school's out. He'd like to think the town kids are the main culprits because surely the country kids know the dangers of a prairie fire. The land is tinder dry and a small fire wouldn't stay small for long. It's not just the drive-in they'd be burning down. He's amazed by their stupidity, whoever it is that's doing this. Maybe it's drugs.

When Willard has finished his breakfast, he takes his plate to the sink. Marian is at the counter, assembling ingredients to bake something.

"Willard," she says.

He stops, his hand holding the plate in mid-air above the sink. *Here it comes*, he thinks.

Marian picks up a measuring cup and then puts it down again.

"I just want to say that I know for a fact you are a kind and generous man," she says.

Willard waits for more; that was the good news, now comes the bad. But Marian picks up the measuring cup again and dips it into a canister of flour, and then pours the flour into her big mixing bowl. She begins to hum. That appears to be all she's going to say, at least for now.

Willard carefully sets his plate among the cups and cutlery already in the sink.

"Well then," he says, and goes outside to begin his fence repairs.

Desert Dwellers

Drift

When Lee was a boy, he developed a passionate but not very scientific interest in deserts and oases and Lawrence of Arabia. Back then, the words *Gobi* and *Sahara* were enough to send him into an imaginary world where he lived in a nomad's tent with a desert moon overhead. Even the Mojave (not so far away, Lester told him, you could drive there in a few days if you wanted to) had exotic possibilities, with its scorpions and Joshua trees. The Little Snake Hills couldn't compete. They were simply a good place to pretend you were in a real desert.

As Lee lies on his back in the former schoolyard and watches the horse graze, he thinks about Lester's Ancient Lands anthropology books, a set of six written by an early twentieth-century English adventurer. The books—themselves now ancient—are still in a bookcase in the living room, along with several out-of-date atlases and *World Book* encyclopedias, collecting dust like everything else in the house since Astrid died. He recalls one favourite book on northern Africa and the Middle East that he'd read so often the pages started to fall out and Astrid had to bind them together again with tape and an elastic band. He'd been drawn to the book's hand-coloured photographs in pastel pinks and blues, accented by a brilliant red flower or a bit of gold jewellery. His favourite photograph depicted a Bedouin family sitting in a little courtyard in front of their open tent, smiling for the Englishman, with sand dunes rolling on to eternity behind them.

The text that accompanied the pictures was equally intriguing. Lee would copy the English explorer's dramatic pronouncements onto slips of paper and glue them into a scrapbook, along with pictures cut from magazines and articles photocopied from the library in Swift Current. Once he'd gone into a travel agency and asked for tourist brochures and the agent had given him a booklet on travel to Egypt. It contained several glossy photographs that he'd cut out and glued into the scrapbook, but the text in the brochure had been uninteresting. It couldn't compete with the mythical captions from Lester's books, which Lee memorized as though he were memorizing voice-over lines from a documentary movie: *The Arabs who inhabit these arid wastes are very different from the pale townsfolk. They are a hardy race, descendants of warriors.* Another favourite: *The desert wastes might be likened unto quicksand, for old civilizations, religions and cities have been engulfed by those fine tawny particles that trickle through one's fingers like water.* That one made him wonder what was buried in the sand hills down the road. Arrowheads maybe, the bones of domestic and wild animals, rusty old farm implements, nothing as exotic or colourful as artifacts from a buried Bedouin encampment.

Then there was the day when Lester came home with the news that Willard Shoenfeld had bought a real camel. That this desert creature existed in reality was remarkable enough, but that one now lived close to Lee, right here in Juliet, was astonishing. At every chance, he rode his bike to Willard's to see Antoinette, and he regularly spent his allowance on camel rides. Willard seemed happy to have a sidekick who appreciated Antoinette as much as he did, and Lee asked him endless questions: how she got her name (*after that fancy French queen*), how fast she could go (*about as fast as molasses on a warm day in March*), how long she can go without water (*won't know until I take that pack trip I've been planning*). Lee and Willard could barely contain themselves whenever Ed got too close to Antoinette and they heard the gurgle in her throat that meant she was preparing to spit at him.

When Antoinette disappeared, Lee shared Willard's distress. After she'd been missing for a week, Lee asked Willard again how long he thought she could go without water. Willard said, "Don't worry, there's lots of water out there for her." But Lee persisted—he even used the word *hypothetically*—and so Willard told him it was a myth that camels can go for weeks without water and that a camel will lie down and refuse to get up after only four or five days of thirst.

"Why do they refuse to get up?" Lee asked.

"They give up hope," Willard said. "They just lie down and decide to die and you can't talk them out of it. Of course some camels are special. The real athletes. They can go longer. Not the pampered camels, though."

Lee was thinking that they needed to find Antoinette right away because she was a pampered camel. He worried in bed at night that Antoinette might not be able to find a slough or a dugout, or that she might be afraid to go down into one of the coulees with a spring-fed creek running through it. He pored over library books looking for evidence of ordinary camels going longer than a week without water but he couldn't find anything that told him one way or another what to expect of Antoinette. *A camel is the life blood of those crossing the desert* was all he could find, *with its ability to go without water far surpassing that of the horse.* That had given him some hope.

Lee wonders if Willard ever thinks about Antoinette and what happened to her. No sign of her had ever been found despite the fact that CBC Radio had done a story on her disappearance.

Willard had eventually given up looking and decided she'd been stolen, but Lee thinks she must have died. He imagines Willard out there in the sand all by himself, looking for his camel. He wonders if Willard searched this far north where the dunes are the size of a two-storey house.

He wouldn't mind having a closer look at the dunes, now that he's here. They're just across the road. A quick look while he's waiting for the Lindstroms to stir wouldn't cut too much into his day.

"How about it, buddy?" he says to the horse, who lifts his head and then goes back to grazing. Lee tightens the cinch on his saddle, letting the horse know they're moving on. He offers the horse another drink from the pail that's hanging on the pump, and takes a long drink himself. Then he hoists himself into the saddle. He can feel the beginnings of saddle burns and bruises.

He cuts southwest across a Texas gate and onto Lindstroms' pasture lease, and almost immediately the grazing land is over-taken by sand. Huge dunes rise up out of the grass and sage, gen-tly sloping formations with sharp-edged shadowy ridges along the tops. He can't recall the last time he was here—high school probably, and the dunes would have shifted since then—but they look the same, the curving shapes, the way they roll as far to the west as he can see, sometimes connecting one to another. The sand surface is pristine except for the delicate wind patterns of ripples and waves. He looks back at the horse's tracks, which form a line of cavernous holes. He likes the way the tracks mark his trail, but at the same time he regrets that he's marring the perfect surface.

He remembers the time Lester brought him to the big dunes when he was five or six years old with an empty cardboard box, and he wouldn't tell Lee what it was for. When they got to the top of a dune Lester broke the box out into a big flat square and let Lee slide down on it, as though he were tobogganing down a hill in winter, as though the sand were snow. "So that's what I did when I was a boy," Lester said when they were on their way home.

Lee tries to picture Lester sliding down the dune, calling out in Norwegian to his father, who never did learn English. It's hard for Lee to imagine Lester doing anything as frivolous as sliding down a sand dune on a piece of cardboard.

Lee urges the horse to the top of the nearest dune and feels chunks of sand breaking away as the animal propels himself upward. From the crest, he can see the panorama of the Little Snake Hills. To the north and east, the miles and miles of rolling pasture. To the south and west, a patchwork of grass and sand. The tall metal frame of a gas well in the distance announces modernization when everything else looks more or less as it must have a hundred years ago.

There's a controversy brewing over the oil and gas interests. The ranchers fear that the rough access roads will break up the network of shallow roots holding the sand in place and cause the pasture grasses to lose way to the force of wind. Lee's been to several meetings in town, although he sat at the back of the room and didn't say anything because the government officials and environmentalists and representatives of the oil and gas companies were all terrifyingly good at talking. A few local ranchers had prepared statements about the importance of preserving their pastures and were brave enough to read them, and Lee was moved by their heartfelt presentations. He wished he'd had the confidence to present a statement himself, do Lester's memory proud.

Without really making a conscious decision to go farther west, Lee guides the horse down the western slope of the dune. The horse's ears are forward as though he's curious about what is ahead. The sun warms Lee's back and he notes the spectacular colour of the morning sky, the intricate designs everywhere around him in the sand. He feels the steady cadence of the horse moving under him and it seems right that he continue on, hardly gives it a thought.

"Atta boy," he says aloud for no reason other than to say something to the horse, who turns one ear in his direction.

As the day begins to heat up, Lee imagines the silhouette the two of them would make for anyone gazing east toward the sun—a man and a distinctively Arab-looking horse in a distinctively desert-like landscape. A photograph, he thinks, for his childhood scrapbook. He almost wishes someone were around to snap the picture, but then again not, because he likes the idea of being alone out here with only a horse for company. He just hopes that Lester isn't watching from above. Watching him waste time on a workday.

Scandal

When Vicki pulls up in front of Karla Norman's house she says, "Okay, kids, behave yourselves," and then all six of them pile out and head up the walk toward Karla's front door. They pass three polished and gleaming muscle cars lined up in the drive, all of them belonging to Karla's dad, whose name is Walter but he's known around town as TNT. He lives with Karla because he's had a stroke and is in a wheelchair. Karla is often seen in front of her house with the garden hose and chamois cloths and Turtle Wax as she shines the cars while her father watches from the shade. "And don't stare at Mr. Norman," Vicki says.

The rooster from next door is sitting on Karla's bottom step and he flaps out of the way and onto the lawn as they approach.

"Sorry to show up without an appointment," Vicki says when

Karla opens the door, "but I was wondering if you could give Lucille's hair a quick cut? She's got gum in it and she'll scream blue murder if I try to comb it out."

Karla holds the door for them to troop inside. "Someone's coming in half an hour for colour," she says, "but I should have time." She invites the kids to watch TV with her father, who sits small and crumpled-looking in an armchair facing the television. You'd never guess in a million years that he'd somehow earned his nickname. His wheelchair is beside the armchair and Daisy heads right for it and sits in it.

"Hi, mister," she says.

"That's Mr. Norman to you," Vicki says, "and you should ask him if you can sit in his chair. It's not a play toy, you know."

"Dad won't mind," Karla says. "Will you, Dad?"

Daisy is looking at him, waiting for an answer. He nods and she settles back, her small hands on the wheels as though she might wheel herself around the room. The other kids line up on the couch, all but Lucille, who has taken Karla's hand. Mr. Norman stares at the twins as though he thinks he might be seeing double.

"What's he watching?" Martin asks Karla.

"I'm not sure," Karla says. The channel appears to be set on a game show of some kind. "We can switch it maybe. Dad, can we find something the kids will like?"

Her father indicates with his shaky hand that the kids can have the remote control. Shiloh reaches over and picks it up from the arm of Mr. Norman's chair and finds a cartoon channel.

"Will that be all right?" Vicki asks.

"He doesn't really care what he watches," says Karla. "Except football. He loves football."

Karla takes Vicki and little Lucille down the hall to the bedroom that has been converted to her salon and lays a board across the arms of the chair for Lucille to sit on.

"Up you go," she says as she lifts the child onto the seat.

Vicki can see Karla is trying to find a place to start. Lucille is busy looking at herself in the big round mirror. She scrunches up her face and then sticks her tongue out.

"How short?" Karla asks Vicki.

"I think you'll have to go pretty short," Vicki says. "Maybe we should just shave her head."

"Oh, I don't think we'll have to go that far," Karla says. "Okay then, Lucille, what do you say we make you look like a pixie?"

Lucille nods.

As Karla begins to cut, she points out the goldfish bowl in front of the mirror to keep Lucille occupied. "How'd you do this, anyway?" she asks. "There's gum everywhere."

"I chewed it up first," says Lucille.

"Well, that makes sense, I guess," says Karla. "It always helps to have a plan."

She runs her fingers through Lucille's fine hair, trying to find all the bits of sticky gum.

"So who's up next?" Vicki asks just to make conversation. "Not that it's any of my business."

"Lila Birch," Karla says. "You know her daughter, Rachelle, is getting married? Lila wants me to do the wedding, which is good, I guess, a nice chunk of change, but I'm getting sick of hearing about it. You'd think it was a royal wedding. She wants me to come to the house for styling in the morning—or perhaps the girls will need to come here if they want colour, she's getting back to me on that—and then to the church for last-minute touch-ups before everyone walks down the aisle. And then she wants me to travel into Swift Current with the wedding party for the photo session. That will be at four o'clock, and then I might be needed before the dinner and dance as well, if the 'dos are getting tired. That's what she calls them—the 'dos. Anyway, not to complain. Like I said, nice chunk of cash. I'll have to hire someone to sit with Dad all day, though."

The phone rings. Karla ignores it, but after seven or eight rings Daisy appears in the doorway and says, "Your phone's ringing."

"I know," says Karla. "I'm ignoring it."

"But the man wants someone to answer it."

"Dad, you mean? Oh. Well, how would you like to answer it for me, then," says Karla. "Find out who it is and say I'll call back."

Daisy leaves, and then returns. "It's someone named Lou," she says. "You can't call her back because she's going out. She says she needs to talk to you *right now.*"

"She's going out. Wouldn't you know it. Sorry," Karla says to Vicki. "I'd better take it."

While Karla is out of the room, Vicki plays "I Spy" with Lucille to keep her in the chair. As Lucille argues with her that the goldfish must be yellow and not orange because gold is yellow, Vicki thinks about all the Norman family scandals. She shouldn't—Karla is really nice and good with the kids—but when you know things about a person you can't help it. Like when Karla's cousin Billy went crazy and stabbed his own mother and killed her. How can you not think about that? And Karla's father was an alcoholic and got his nickname TNT because of the time he was helping someone blow a granite boulder out of his new dugout and they blew out the side of the barn with the debris, lucky no one was killed. In spite of the picture of the barn demolition on the front page of the paper, people kept asking him for help with their blasting projects because he'd worked on the pipeline for years and actually knew what he was doing as long as he wasn't too drunk. Since the stroke, he couldn't drink any more, but this was after a lifetime of spending all his money on booze and cars and making life hard for his wife until her death several years ago. After he had the stroke,

Karla's older sister, Lou, refused to take him in with her, and Karla changed her plan to move to Calgary so that he wouldn't get sent to a nursing home in whatever small town had a bed for him because the one in Juliet had a two-year waiting list. Karla's planned move to Calgary had been to recover from being engaged to Dale Patterson three times—another scandal, or at least a subject for gossip. Vicki has heard that all the old ladies in town are secretly thankful for the stroke because they like the way Karla does their perms, and she'll even make house calls if they really need her to. And Vicki supposes that Karla's looking after her dad the way she does gives them hope that if they were to suffer a debilitating illness, someone would come out of the woodwork to care for them.

"I spy with my little eye something that is puce," Vicki says.

"What the heck is puce?" asks Lucille. That makes Vicki laugh.

She can now hear what Karla is saying on the phone because she's raised her voice. Vicki moves closer to the doorway so she can hear better.

"So a friggin' candle party is a priority for you, is it?" Karla says. Then after a pause, "That is not true. I hardly ever ask. I can't believe you said that." Karla slams the phone down so hard it crashes to the floor, and she says, "Pretend you didn't hear that, kids," and comes back up the hall to her salon.

"God damn that Lou," she says to Vicki, then, "Pretend you didn't hear that," to Lucille.

Lucille puts her hands over her ears.

"She's sharp as a tack, isn't she," Karla says.

"I can still hear you," says Lucille.

"I'd better watch my language, then," says Karla, picking up her scissors again. "So you know my sister, Lou," she says. Vicki nods. "Just once in a while—hardly ever—I ask her to watch Dad for a few hours so I can go out and have . . . you know . . . a

bit of fun, for God's sake, so I can convince myself I'm not living in an old folks' home. And every time—every friggin' time—
she gives me the third degree about where I'm going and who
with, as though I'm asking for something unreasonable. He's her
father too, like she's forgotten that. So today is my birthday—no
need for happy birthday, that's not why I'm telling you this—and
I thought she would call and offer to take Dad, but no, so I call
her, and she says she has to check something, and she calls me
back just now and says she can't take Dad because she's going to
Debbie Wells's candle party. Can you believe that? It's an obliga-
tion, she says. As though Dad isn't."

Karla finally stops talking and remembers that she's supposed
to be cutting Lucille's hair. Snip. A long lock of hair tumbles to
the floor. Now Lucille is short on one side and long on the other.
She studies herself intently in the mirror and when Karla goes to
snip the other side Lucille grabs the remaining locks of long hair
and squirms away from Karla's scissors.

"What?" Karla asks her. "You want to leave that side long?"

Lucille nods.

"Lucille," Vicki says, "don't be ridiculous."

"It's cool," Lucille says.

"Oh my God, she turned into a teenager while I was on the
phone," Karla says.

"Have you got the gum out?" Vicki asks.

"I think so. Honey, take your hand away so I can look for gum.
I won't cut. Promise."

Lucille takes her hand away and Karla does a quick check. "I
think we got it," she says. "Lucille, how about I snip that side off
and even it up. Remember the pixie? Don't you want to look like
a pixie?"

Lucille says no and grabs her hair again, all the while watching herself in the mirror.

Karla looks to Vicki for direction. "Never mind," Vicki says. "I can try to fix it myself later." She lifts Lucille down from the chair. "Okay, sweet pea," she says. "Good enough for now, I guess. Thanks, Karla." Then she says, "You know, I could sit with your dad sometime. I wouldn't mind."

"Absolutely not. Not when Lou is just down the block and this is her father too we're talking about. But thanks anyway. That's really nice of you to offer."

Vicki opens her purse so she can pay Karla and remembers that she has only a twenty and she'd better save that for the swimming pool and whatever else comes up over the course of the day. She'll have to write a cheque and hope it doesn't bounce like the last one did. That had been embarrassing but luckily Blaine had just been paid and she was able to give Karla cash before Blaine found out about the bounced cheque. Blaine thinks Vicki should just cut the kids' hair herself like his mother used to do, and she's had to set him straight on kids' expectations for trendy haircuts these days. "Get used to it, Blaine," she says. "When the girls get to high school, look out." Even Shiloh asked recently if he could get his hair dyed blond. Vicki didn't tell Blaine about that. Anyway, she thought Shiloh was just testing her since he hasn't mentioned it since.

She gets her cheque book out of her purse and says, "How much?" but Karla says, "That's okay. I didn't really do enough of a job to charge you."

"No really," Vicki says, her cheque book poised and ready. "How much?"

"You don't want to write a cheque for five bucks," she says. "How about I keep track and add it on next time you come?"

Vicki puts her cheque book back in her purse. "Okay," she says. "That's fair, I guess. As long as you remember."

"I'll write it down," Karla promises.

In the living room, everyone looks contented, sitting in front of the TV and watching cartoons, even Mr. Norman. Except for Shiloh, who has moved to the floor and isn't really watching. Maybe he's getting too old for cartoons, Vicki thinks. Maybe his thoughts have turned to a young man's thoughts.

"Do we have to go?" asks Daisy. "We're right in the middle."

"Of course we have to go," Vicki says. "Karla has other people coming for haircuts. Besides, we've got work to do, remember. Let's go. Toot sweet."

"What are you up to?" Karla asks as the kids line up behind their mother like a small brigade, all but Shiloh, who goes to the door and walks out without a word.

Vicki rolls her eyes at Karla, *See what I have to put up with*, trying not to look worried. Then she says, "What are we up to?" to the rest of the kids.

"Beans," they say in unison.

Karla laughs. "I can see you're full of beans, every one of you."

"Not that kind of beans," says Lucille, still playing with her lopsided hair. "Green beans."

"Oh, I see," says Karla, although she doesn't.

Just as they're about to file out the door, the phone rings again and Vicki hears Karla answer and say, "Oh, it's you," and then, "I said I would. Okay. Later." Then she hangs up.

When they get outside, Vicki sees Dale Patterson's red truck round the corner. Well, well, maybe that had been Dale on the phone, calling Karla from in front of her house. And maybe they're heading for a fourth engagement. She has no real opinion on Dale Patterson and Karla Norman. Well, actually, she does. She thinks Karla is too good for Dale, but then what does her opinion or anyone else's matter when it comes to love?

As they walk by the three shiny cars, she notices a scratch on the hood of the black one, the Trans Am, a fresh shiny scratch. The rooster is pecking at Mrs. Baxter's lawn nearby and Vicki wonders if he is responsible. She's pretty sure he would lose his head if he were caught in the act of damaging one of old TNT's prized possessions. Why in the world do they keep three cars? She's heard a story that Lou and Karla had a big fight over the cars, that Lou thought they should all be sold and the money used for their father's care, but then Karla said the cars were his only pleasure and she went out and sold her own car and now drives one of her father's when she needs a vehicle, a different one every time she goes out. Imagine the cost of keeping the three of them licensed, Vicki thinks. She looks down the walk to her own rusty old Cutlass, expecting to see Shiloh, but he isn't there.

"Shotgun," shouts one of the twins when he sees that Shiloh isn't in the car. He races to the street and yanks the passenger door open and gets in before his luck runs out and Shiloh appears to take control of the front seat. But then Martin says, "I'm older," and tells him to get out and in the back, and he dutifully does.

Vicki notices that Shiloh's backpack is not in the car where he left it.

"Darn him anyway," she says. "Well, get in, kids, I guess we have to go looking for your brother. Funny thing, when the oldest gets to be the most trouble."

"Will Shiloh catch heck?" Daisy asks.

"I'm not sure," Vicki says. "Probably not. He's likely walked over to Main Street. Although he should have said something."

They drive the few blocks to Main, and Vicki looks up and down but can't see Shiloh. She angle parks in front of the post office and tells the kids to stay in the car while she goes to collect the mail.

The mailboxes are open at the back to the inner workings of the post office, and as soon as Vicki has her box open, Mrs. Bulin, the postmistress, says, "Hi, Vicki. How's the day treating you so far?" She doesn't wait for an answer before she says, "I guess hell must be freezing over. They say it might rain."

"Where'd you hear that?" Vicki says. "Doesn't look much like rain." She can't see Mrs. Bulin, but she speaks to the voice. Mrs. Bulin talks to everyone who comes in for mail, but the whole town knows not to say too much back. Mrs. Bulin is approaching sixty-five and has expressed no interest in retiring. She likes her access to information too much, so the story goes.

When Vicki leaves the post office with a phone bill and a bank statement she doesn't care to open, she sees a middle-aged woman with red hair and green shoes talking to Martin through the car window.

"Hello," the woman says to Vicki when she sees her. "Your kids and I have been having quite the conversation here."

Just then they hear the sound of a ring-tone coming from the open window of a truck piled high with furniture and packing boxes, and towing a trailer.

"My phone," she says. "Best answer that." She gets in the truck and flips open her phone, but it looks as though she's missed the call. She waves at Vicki and the kids as she pulls away. "Keep your eyes open for a grey horse," she calls.

"Well, that was a funny business," Vicki says to Martin after the woman is gone. "What was she talking about?"

"She lost her horse," Martin says.

"Pretty stupid," Vicki says. "How do you lose a horse? And I don't know why she'd be telling you." She turns to look at the kids in the back seat and says, "What do you say we go buy Karla Norman a birthday cake?"

They all cross the street to the grocery store, where Vicki goes to the bakery section to check out the cakes. There's one devil's food cake but it looks as though it's been there for days. The chocolate icing is dry—the top of the cake resembles a bare field baked and cracking in the sun. She'd have to be desperate to buy Karla that cake, Vicki thinks, but then she sees it has a half-price sticker on it, so she buys it anyway. She pays with her debit card, holding her breath while the clerk rings in the sale, and it goes through. She should be getting her groceries and putting everything on one sale, but she has things to do and she doesn't want the groceries to sit in the car on such a hot day. Blaine's ham would be green by the time they got home.

"Hey," Daisy says when they get back outside. "There's Shiloh."

Vicki looks in the direction Daisy is pointing and sure enough, there he is at the end of the street, heading for the railway tracks.

"Good," says Vicki. She reaches through the open car window and gives the horn a couple of blasts, but Shiloh doesn't turn around and look. She hands the cake to Martin, who has positioned himself once again in the front seat.

"All right," she says. "Everyone in. We collect Shiloh, go for a quick swim, do our errands and drop off the cake. Then home again, home again."

She looks at her watch.

"What about Hank's calves?" Daisy asks.

"Oh my gosh, we forgot to tell someone about Hank's calves. Okay. One stop to make a phone call, and then the swimming pool, and then home."

"Toot sweet, right," says Lucille.

"That's right," says Vicki. Even though she knows it's getting a bit late for toot sweet.

Key Lime Pie

Lynn Trass has found a recipe for key lime pie on the Internet. She likes to try new things, and key lime pie is something she and Hank discovered on a trip to Florida last winter. They'd started out thinking they would go to a lot of casinos, but they'd ended up going to a lot of restaurants, looking for key lime pie for Hank. In between tasting sessions, they visited Disney World, an alligator farm and the Everglades swamp, which Hank was amazed to find resembles a tall-grass pasture, at least until you step in it and discover yourself knee-deep in swampy water. He'd been expecting a lush canopy of trees with huge trunks and moss hanging everywhere, but Lynn said he had Florida mixed up with Louisiana. He was also amazed at the tenacity of the mosquitoes, and concluded that maybe Saskatchewan in the winter isn't such a bad place after all because it's mosquito free.

When Hank comes into the restaurant he sees one of Lynn's high school girls, Haley Barker, waiting tables. She's wearing a skimpy little T-shirt that looks as though it shrunk in the wash, and has a gold ring in her navel, which she absently plays with all the time, turning it round and round. A man can't help but notice.

"Hey there, Haley," he says. "Getting ready for life in the big city?"

"Not really," Haley says.

A few locals and a couple of truckers are having breakfast. He can smell the bacon. Lynn won't let him eat bacon, for his own good, all the fat and nitrates.

"Well, don't get too smart to be useful up there in Saskatoon," Hank says.

He goes to the kitchen looking for Lynn, and finds her getting ready to cut one of a half-dozen key lime pies into slices.

"Is that what I think it is?" Hank asks.

Lynn hands him a slice. "Let me know what you think," she says. "Or rather, what your taste buds think. It's low-fat, but I probably shouldn't have told you that."

Hank takes the plate and sits on a chair in the kitchen so he can talk to Lynn while she works. Once he bites into the pie, though, he doesn't want to talk. He closes his eyes and rolls the custard around on his tongue before he swallows it.

"I guess it's a hit, then," Lynn says.

"You'd better give me another, just so I can be sure."

Lynn slides another piece of pie onto his plate while Hank admires its lovely green colour. In spite of his lack of sleep the night before he couldn't be happier, sitting here in Lynn's kitchen, the promise of a new day all but guaranteed by a counter full of sweet and tangy green custard.

"So what happened to you last night anyway?" she asks. "I thought you'd be home."

"Got as far as that campground just east," Hank says. "Couldn't quite make it the rest of the way."

Lynn knows he's referring to his habit of falling asleep at the wheel. She often does the driving when they're out late.

"Did you get your trailer at least?" she asks.

"Nope," Hank says. "Rusted right through above the wheel wells. Tried to tell me he thought I was asking about a different trailer when he sent the pictures. I was none too happy, but what are you going to do. Turned around and came home."

When Hank has finished the second slice, Lynn tells him that's all he can have, she wants to try it on someone other than him.

"You're the boss," Hank says, and heads back into the restaurant to see who else has come in for an early coffee or a late breakfast. As he's about to go through the swinging door he asks Lynn if she knows the end of the world is coming. He reaches into his pocket and pulls out the yellow flyer that had stuck to his windshield, and holds it out to her, telling her about the flurry of paper in the parking lot.

She gives it a quick read. "You know I don't have much patience with fanaticism," she says, and then wads it up and tosses it in the garbage. Haley comes through the door just then with an empty coffee pot and tells Hank he'd better get out of the way, she's coming back through with a tray of clean cups.

"Out of the kitchen," Lynn says to Hank, and he goes into the restaurant and lets the door swing closed, and Lynn picks up another piece of paper that fell out of Hank's pocket. The one that says *Joni* and gives a phone number.

As Lynn stares at the name and number, she feels as though she's having heart palpitations, or a stroke maybe. The big, loopy script and the little smiley face dotting the *i* jolt her back to a time—long ago now—when she spent hours of every day and night imagining Hank with girls who had flirty hair and makeup and names like Joni and Cindy and Louise. Hour upon hour with her imagination running away, picturing barrel racers and trick riders and girls who wouldn't know one end of a horse from the other; waitresses and hairdressers and elementary school teachers. Hours of every day, jealous and miserable with not knowing for sure, and then knowing, absolutely, and then not knowing again, back and forth, the truth as illusive as a poltergeist. The sudden memory is so intense she feels faint. She leans against the kitchen counter and thinks, *The past never leaves you.*

When she and Hank were first married, Hank had a hard time with the idea of "forsaking all others," mainly because several of his buddies were still living the bachelor life. When Lynn had become pregnant at twenty-two, she and Hank had a quick wedding, and not long after that, she'd heard the words from a distressed friend, *I don't want to tell you this, Lynn, but if it was me I'd want to know.* According to the friend, Hank had spent the weekend with someone he'd met at a rodeo dance north of the river while Lynn thought he was at a cattle auction in Alberta. It had almost been the end of them, but Hank had admitted to the dalliance and had sworn that it was the only time—*the only time, Lynn, I swear to God, and it meant nothing, it was just the stupid booze, an old habit.* When their daughter Leanne was born, and a second girl, Dana, a year later, he'd turned into a responsible husband and father. He continued with the amateur rodeo circuit, but he was now introduced by the announcer as a family man, and the farm and his girls took priority over going down the road. Everyone but Lynn knew that. She couldn't get the rodeo-dance girl out of her head. She'd never heard the girl's name, but for years after, she'd looked for evidence, a scrap of paper hidden in a pocket, a name written on a matchbook cover, and her obsession had almost driven her crazy. Her doctor had even given her a prescription for antidepressants at one point but she'd never filled it.

And now here the name was, all these years later, having slipped from its hiding place in Hank's pocket just as she had imagined it would. *Joni.* Lynn stares at the paper and feels the familiar old fear. Then she tells herself to smarten up, be realistic. Hank is no handsome young catch. He's a man old enough to have two kids grown and gone, and grey hair—what's left of it—and a bum hip. This is obviously the handwriting of a young woman, and what would a young woman be doing with Hank? She lets go of the counter and stands up straight. She folds the paper carefully, puts it in her apron pocket and picks up three plates of key lime pie.

"Coming through," she says, and pushes the kitchen doors open with her shoulder and an expert swing of her body. She slaps one of the plates down in front of Willard Shoenfeld, who is sitting with Hank, and the other two she hands to a couple of her regular truckers.

"On the house," she says. "I'm considering adding it to the menu. Let me know what you think."

She watches Willard, who looks like he's in heaven as he savours each bite.

"Not too bad, eh," Hank says.

"What do you call this?" Willard asks.

"Key lime pie," Lynn says. "After limes that grow in Florida. Keys are islands, like the Florida Keys."

"Pretty swanky," Willard says.

"I suppose," Lynn says. "For this place anyway."

As she stands there, her mind keeps wandering to the paper in her pocket, and the added fact that Hank had not come home with a trailer. Maybe he had never gone to look at one, the trailer was just a story. She forces herself to think about something else. Willard Shoenfeld. What kind of life do he and his sister-in-law have out there at the drive-in anyway? Such a strange arrangement. Marian is a nice enough woman, although she's quiet, like Willard, and keeps to herself. People used to say she was a communist when she first moved here, but Lynn always thought that was just silly gossip because Ed was always talking about Russia. A woman communist would have to be *serious*, like that Emma Goldman, and a serious communist would not bother with a place like Juliet.

Willard finishes his pie and lays his fork down.

"Delicious," he announces.

Lynn checks in with the truckers and they each give the pie two thumbs up.

"All right, then," she says. "Starting tomorrow, it's on the menu and you'll have to pay for it."

As she returns to the kitchen, Lynn is reminded that sometimes younger women are attracted to older men. She had worked with a girl named Lois when she was just out of high school. Lois always went for men old enough to be her father. One night Lois talked Lynn into going to a party with her in a neighbouring town, and everyone there was twice her age. The experience had given her some insight about Lois; she, being the youngest and prettiest at the party, had been the star as far as the men were concerned. She was rewriting high school, Lynn thought, with herself as the femme fatale. Lois eventually married one of her older men, an oil tycoon of some kind, and he died not long after and left her a lot of money. His family, especially his ex-wife, was furious.

When Lynn passes through the swinging door she sees that Haley is in the kitchen, fingering her belly ring and staring at the dirty coffee cups on the counter.

"They're not going to wash themselves," Lynn says.

"I guess not," Haley says. Still, she doesn't make a move to begin the ritual of rinsing and washing that Lynn is very strict about.

"Chop, chop," Lynn says, clapping her hands together, and Haley finally steps up to the sink and dons a pair of purple rubber gloves.

"God, these things are hideous," she says, looking at her gloved hands.

"Well, *Vogue* magazine isn't going to come through the door and snap any pictures, if that's what you're worried about."

The pies are cooled enough now to go into the fridge and Lynn gets out the plastic wrap. She says to Haley, "So what do you think of older men anyway?"

"Huh?" asks Haley.

"Older men. You know, Hank's age. Would you ever date a man that age?"

Haley turns to Lynn with a look of horror on her face. "As old as Hank?" she croaks.

"Oh, never mind," Lynn says. "Just get those dishes done before the coffee rush."

She wraps the pies and puts them in the cooler, tells Haley to speed things up and goes back into the restaurant, where she stands with her hands on her hips, staring at Hank and Willard. Then she says, "Excuse me."

Hank thinks this is a little odd—the way she said *excuse me* for no reason that he can see. "I guess so," he says. He watches Lynn leave the restaurant and go to the little vestibule that separates it from the Petro-Can station and the convenience store. It looks as though she's heading for the pay phone but he can't really see, and he soon goes back to his conversation with Willard about how the Internet is a mixed blessing, which is way over Willard's head since he's never been on the Internet in his life and doesn't plan to be.

Lynn rummages in her apron pocket for a quarter and the paper with the phone number on it. She turns her back to the glass door leading into the restaurant so no one can see her dial the number. She's not even sure why she's doing this. When a female voice says hello, she immediately hangs up. She stays by the phone for a minute, thinking, and then goes back into the restaurant.

Hank looks at her as she passes his table, but she ignores him and gives one of the swinging doors a good hard kick. It flies open and she steps through, and he hears her raise her voice with Haley, something about the dishes.

Hank has been planning to follow her into the kitchen to see if he can talk her into one more slice of pie before he goes to work, but he changes his mind. The phone by the till rings. Once, twice, Lynn's angry voice again, and Haley comes hurrying through the door to answer it, shedding the purple gloves to pick up the receiver. It's apparently for her because she says, "I can't talk now." She fiddles with her belly button ring as she listens to whoever is on the phone.

Lynn sticks her head through the door and sees Haley on the phone and says, "That had better not be a personal call."

"I have to go," Haley says, and hangs up. The kitchen door swings shut and immediately the phone rings again. Haley looks as if she's afraid to answer it and lets it ring, but then Lynn's voice comes from the kitchen, "Someone *please* answer the phone."

Haley picks up the receiver and listens, and then says, "Okay, I'll tell him," and hangs up once again. "Vicki Dolson," she says to Hank. "Your calves are out. They're along the railway tracks north of town."

"Damn it anyway," Hank says. He turns to Willard. "The damned kids keep leaving the gate open. There's a good fence in that pasture. I just checked it."

"Don't tell me about the damned kids," Willard says.

"I guess I know what I'm doing this morning," Hank says. He sticks his head in the kitchen door to tell Lynn where he's going, but then he has to get out of the way because she's coming back through with a fresh pot of coffee. He can see she doesn't want to stop and talk, so he leaves without saying anything more. She'll know he's gone to work.

Just as Hank's leaving the restaurant, Dale Patterson pulls in off the highway and gets out of his truck. Hank sees that Dale has one arm in a sling and wonders what he did to it.

"Good luck in there," Hank says as they meet in the parking lot. "The wife's on a bit of a tear."

Lynn detests Dale Patterson. If her restaurant weren't considered a public place she'd bar him from ever crossing its threshold. "Karla Norman needs a good slap" is what Lynn said to Hank about her engagement to Dale, or rather engagement*s*. Hank understands Lynn's point of view—if he were a woman he'd steer clear of Dale Patterson too—but there's been more than one time that Dale's had Hank busting a gut. True, the laugh is usually at the expense of someone else, like the banker, Norval Birch—Dale calls him Birchbark, which always cracks Hank up—but Hank figures if the butt of the joke isn't present, no harm done.

Dale takes his cell phone out of his back pocket and struggles to punch in a number with his good hand.

"What happened to you anyway?" Hank asks.

"Nothing happened to me, for about the twentieth time this morning," Dale says.

"I guess that sling's a decoration, then," Hank says.

Dale gives him a look to kill.

Hank decides to beat it, leave Dale and Lynn to each other and good luck to the both of them. The yellow flyers that were dumped from the bus are still blowing around in the hot breeze. Hank notices that several of them have plastered themselves against the wire fence that surrounds the parking lot, making it look like a fairground after the carnival has packed up and gone.

"I've got calves to gather," Hank says, starting toward his truck. "No sense asking you for help with that gimpy arm, whatever you did to it."

"Why is everybody so interested in my damned arm?" Dale says. "It's none of your business."

Hank shakes his head and gets in the truck and slams the door. The coffee that he'd spilled on the floor the night before is not smelling so good and he rolls down the window before he turns the key.

"Have a good day there, Dale," he calls through the open window, taking the opportunity to grab the last word as Dale puts his phone to his ear.

Hank remembers that he was planning to drop something off for Lee Torgeson, some of Lynn's baking. He knows Lynn would send muffins or a pie—maybe even one of the key lime pies—but he decides to leave that for another day. Best to wait, he thinks—after years of experience—for whatever has put her in such a temper to pass. As it always does.

The Manager

On Norval's desk at the bank, between two decorative horse-head bookends purchased by Lila, are a half-dozen historical texts on the area in which Juliet is situated. When Norval first moved to Juliet to assume the role of bank manager, he read these books in an effort to understand his new mercantile parish. He read, for example, that in the nineteenth century, before the area was opened up for settlement, it was declared to be unsuitable for crops by a geographical adviser to the British Parliament. The man's advice was not heeded, and sometimes when Norval looks out his office window and the air is the colour of sand, he thinks perhaps it should have been. On such days—and today is one of them—he wonders how he ended up here, and if what had been described as a promotion had actually been a punishment for some corporate mistake he was not aware he'd committed. With the oppressive heat building already, Norval is thankful for the air conditioner installed in the window behind him even though it's noisy.

He checks his calendar and sees that his only official appointment is the late-afternoon teacher interview at the school, and his morning is free and clear for dealing with the farm loan payments coming due. He turns on his computer and generates his client list, and at the top of that list is Blaine Dolson's name.

In spite of all the ads on TV that tell you a financial institution holds your ticket to a prosperous future, Norval cannot think of any way for his bank to help Blaine Dolson get back on his feet, let alone prosper. Blaine's just got in too deep. He's working on the highway crew to make ends meet, and still there's barely enough money coming in to pay the interest on his remaining loans. What will happen when the new highway's done? Blaine has half a dozen kids. Norval recently saw a documentary on American TV about families living in their cars. How can that be happening in one of the most affluent countries in the world? And how will Norval live with himself if it comes to that for the Dolsons, when the same institution that pulled the rug out from under Blaine is going to provide Norval with a comfortable, if not extravagant, retirement?

Then Norval feels a little flash of anger on his own behalf as he thinks about how *hard* this job is, and how he agonizes over clients like the Dolsons and is not just sitting in here playing solitaire. He spends a good portion of every day worrying about families who have fallen on hard times, and what will happen to them, and what will happen to the whole town if the farm economy plummets again, or tanks completely. He cares about these things. If it were up to him, he would bail Blaine Dolson out in a minute, open up the safe and hand over a bag full of money, but that's not the way it works. Well, there is one thing he can do. It's not much, but he decides to ignore Blaine's name and take it off his priority list, for a few days at least.

He turns his attention to the Pattersons. They are not in a dire state, but there's a quarterly payment due and he hasn't heard from them. The senior Patterson, Andy, is a reasonable man to deal with, but the son is an unpredictable hothead. Norval is not sure what will happen when Andy decides to retire and let Dale take over. Norval just hopes that Andy keeps himself in the

picture for a while. At least he's willing to listen when Norval
presents the bank's perspective on his options.

He clicks to open the file, and picks up the phone and punches
in Andy's phone number. No one answers, but after three rings
a man's voice—it sounds like Dale—asks the caller to leave a
message, and so Norval does. *Just wondering if Andy is available
to come in to the bank as soon as possible; hope things are well with
yourself and the wife, hope to hear from you soon.* A pleasant-
sounding goodbye, and Norval hangs up. Then he double-checks
the phone numbers and realizes that he's accidentally called
Dale's cell phone. He calls again, Andy's number this time, and
leaves the same message.

At this point, Marsha—Norval's jack-of-all-trades bank
employee—brings him a dozen letters to sign, and he gets himself a cup of instant coffee before settling back behind his desk
to check them over. He sets his mug down next to a framed photograph of Rachelle in her graduation cap and gown, which he'd
installed to remind himself that she'd at least completed her
grade twelve before she carelessly tossed away her future. In the
photograph she looks poised and mature, ready for a career as a
teacher or a journalist or an engineer, anything was possible just
a few months ago. He sighs audibly, then turns to the letters.

Before he's finished reading the first one, he hears a pounding
on the front door of the bank, which is not yet open to the public,
and when Marsha unlocks the door, Norval hears the younger
Patterson's angry voice. Norval listens, regretting now the mistake of the phone numbers.

"I want to see that Norval Birch," Dale says.

"The bank's not open for another ten minutes," Norval hears
Marsha say. "Do you have to see him right now?"

"Right this damn minute," Dale says, and then Norval hears
his boots stomping across the insubstantial floor, he can almost

feel the floor giving under Dale's weight, and there he is, in Norval's office doorway, with his left arm in a sling.

"Sorry, Norval," Marsha says from behind Dale.

"You might as well come in, Dale. I can see you've got something pressing on your mind."

"I'll just keep the door open, shall I," Marsha says, and leaves, although Norval is pretty sure she's going to stay close enough to hear what's going on. All of ninety-five pounds, and she doesn't seem to be the least rattled by the Dale Pattersons of the world. Maybe *she* should be the bank manager.

Dale enters the office and instead of taking the chair placed across the desk from Norval, he pushes it out of the way with his good arm and leans over Norval to better make his point. But before Dale can speak, he grimaces and straightens up, obviously in agony, and as he does so his good arm knocks a bookend and a couple of Norval's books to the floor. The remaining books teeter, and then they fall too, leaving only one flat-sided plaster horsehead behind. Dale ignores the books, takes a moment to recover from the pain and then picks up the photograph of Rachelle. Norval can see beads of sweat on Dale's forehead.

"Maybe you should sit down," Norval says.

"I wonder," says Dale, ignoring the invitation to sit, still staring at the picture, "if you called to give me a personal invitation to your daughter's wedding." Then he looks at Norval, waiting for a response, and Norval actually thinks he might be serious.

"I'd have to check with the wife on that," he says. "She's got a list as long as your arm." He wishes he hadn't said the word *arm*. He tries to look Dale in the eye and stay calm and say what he has to say. He wishes Dale had brought Andy with him.

"I meant to call your father's number, Dale," Norval says. "It's your father I'd like to talk to, about the loan. I'd feel more comfortable if he were here."

"I could give a rat's ass about your comfort," says Dale.

Norval takes a deep breath. "Fair enough," he says.

Dale begins to tap Norval's desk with Rachelle's photograph. "So, Birchbark," he asks, "when is this fancy wedding anyway?"

Birchbark. The disrespect is unbelievable.

"I'd prefer Norval," he says. "October, after harvest." He pauses, then says, "Dale, tell your father that I'd like to talk to him. There's a payment coming due at the end of—" but Dale raises his good arm, still holding the photograph and aiming it for emphasis in Norval's direction, and says, "Stop."

"There's not necessarily a problem, I just need to know—" but again Dale says, "Stop."

Norval stops. The two of them stare at each other, Dale aiming at Norval with the photograph of Rachelle. When it's clear that Norval is not going to try to use bankers' words or talk loan payments, Dale lowers his arm and sets the photograph down.

"You think you've got it made, don't you, Birchbark."

"Not really," Norval says.

"I know who that daughter of yours is marrying. We'll see how she does, eh, see how her finances look in a couple of years."

That almost makes Norval laugh. The idea that he, a banker, would not have thought that one through. Norval clears his throat and says, "The loan is in your father's name, so he's the one I need to speak with."

A smirk crosses Dale's face. He says, "Not for long, Birchbark. The old man's retiring. Haven't you heard? It's me you'll be dealing with from now on."

And at that moment Norval understands why Dale came to the bank and pounded on the door, unable to wait for an appointment or even the regular hours of operation. He'd been bursting to deliver this news and let Norval know there'll be no more Mr. Nice Guy when it comes to dealing with the Pattersons.

Dale tips his cap and then kicks at the books on his way out of Norval's office. In the doorway he stops and says, "You'll be hearing from the lawyer about the transfer, but you talk to me from now on. *Mister Birch*. There. Does that suit you better?"

"Yes," Norval says. "Mr. Birch is definitely an improvement."

As soon as Dale is gone from his office, Norval realizes that his heart is pounding. He doesn't know why, he's not afraid of Dale and he's experienced at dealing with this sort of behaviour. He looks at his hands—shaking like a palsied old man's. He's disgusted with himself. Maybe he just doesn't have what it takes to be a bank manager any more. If he were a boxer or a race-car driver, he'd have to say he's lost his nerve. What if there were a real threat? What if someone—one of his several frustrated and unhappy clients—decided to walk through the front door with a shotgun and wave it in his face? It could happen, there's no shortage of guns out there.

He gives himself a talking-to. Most of his clients are dignified and ever-optimistic people who keep their frustration in check even when they have good reason to boil over. Their ancestors survived the thirties when blowing dust drifted against the doors of their houses, creating a people who believe you can survive anything if you just hang in there long enough, who believe bad times are cyclical. *Next year we'll get rain. We're due for it.* How many times has he heard that? No, if he's going to worry about danger in the bank he should worry about robbery, which is always a possibility.

In fact, there *had* been a robbery five years ago, a real one with guns. The RCMP had caught the bank robbers in no time by following them with a helicopter through the sand hills northwest to the ferry crossing, and they'd had the operator hold the ferry on the other side of the river and there was no place for the robbers to go, nowhere to hide in such wide-open country.

Norval remembers the two men with balaclavas ordering him and Marsha—the only two people in the bank at the time—to lie face down on the floor with their arms and legs spread. He doesn't remember his hands shaking then, the way they are now. If it weren't so early in the day, he'd have a drink. Noon, even, but ten o'clock—sadly, far too early.

Norval walks around to the front of his desk and picks up the fallen bookend. One of the horse's ears is chipped off. This makes the horse look sad, defeated. Like some of his clients, he thinks. And then a picture of the Dolson family pops into his head. A man, his wife, a bunch of kids, all lined up, sad, defeated and humiliated. Norval blinks, trying to rid himself of the sorry image. What is wrong with him? Not all of his clients are in the red, for Christ sake. Look at young Lee Torgeson. Norval had worried about what might happen with the old pair gone, but Lee appears to be doing fine. Why can't he think more about the Lee Torgesons in the community, and less about clients like the Dolsons? And Juliet certainly has its share of prosperous business people. It's not like the whole town is on a fast track to destitution.

He calls to Marsha, rather more abruptly than he ever speaks to his staff, and when she comes to the door, he says, "Clean up this mess. I'm going to the café for coffee." Then he adds the word *please*, ashamed of himself.

He steps outside and walks toward the entrance of the Maple Leaf Café, which used to be the Double Happiness before the Chinese family that owned it moved on. As he passes the street-level window he looks inside and sees a cap that might be Dale's. And even if it isn't Dale's, he thinks, it's likely the cap of some-one else whose finances he knows intimately. He passes the restaurant by. Even though he would love a cup of fresh coffee, he doesn't want to see any of his clients, no matter what their financial situation.

He decides to walk around the block before returning to the bank, grab some air, even though it's already hot. As he passes the garbage stand behind the hotel, a stray dog trying to break into a trash can lifts his head and stares at him. He doesn't recognize the dog, wonders where it came from.

By the time he gets back, the bank is open and Belinda, the part-time teller—or more officially, customer care representative—is in place behind the counter. From the look she gives Norval he knows that Marsha has filled her in on the morning so far. He apologizes to Marsha for being less than polite when he asked her to pick up the books.

"Oh, you never mind, Norval," Marsha says. "Dale Patterson can do that to a person. You're entitled. What happened to him anyway? He looked like the lion with a thorn in his paw, that one from the Bible. Was it Daniel who took the thorn out?"

"Saint Jerome," says Norval. "Daniel got thrown to the lions. None of them had thorns that I know of."

"Don't you just know your Bible inside out," says Marsha.

"Not really," says Norval. "Just the lion parts."

"So what did he do to his arm?" Marsha asks.

"I have no idea. He doesn't tell me his secrets. I'm only his banker."

At that moment, a woman he doesn't recognize and her young son come into the bank. Norval tries to switch on his most affable bank manager persona.

"Good morning," he says. "Welcome. Nice summer day, isn't it."

The woman looks at Norval, suspicious of his friendly manner. He directs her to Belinda and returns to his office and sits at his desk, on which the books are once again neatly ordered. He sees that Marsha has even glued the horse's ear back on. He wipes Rachelle's photograph with a tissue and then puts it in its proper spot.

Through his open door Norval can hear the woman telling

Belinda at the teller's window that her son has seven dollars in pennies and he'd like to open a bank account.

"Seven hundred pennies," Belinda says to the boy. "What a lot of money. I wonder if you'd like to take your pennies home and wrap them for me in these paper wrappers. That would be fun, wouldn't it?"

"If it's all the same to you," the mother says, "we'd rather not."

"But I really can't take all those pennies if they're not wrapped," Belinda says. "I'm sorry, but that's our policy."

"Well, then," the woman says, "I'd like to speak to the manager about that policy."

The manager. That's him, Norval Birch. Norval sighs so loudly he worries that Marsha and Belinda and the woman and her son can hear him. What is wrong with him, he wonders, this feeling that he's not *handling things*? He'd blame it on Dale Patterson, or Kyle passed out in the backyard, or Lila and her list, except that this feeling has been here from the moment he woke up in the dark with thoughts of a tree falling on the house.

Or maybe it began five years ago when he and Marsha were spread-eagled on the bank floor, the smell of floor wax in his nostrils, his eye fixed on a toothpick that someone had dropped, and he'd marvelled at the workmanship, the smooth surface and the perfect points on each end, all that work for something you get free from the counter of any coffee shop. What a crazy thing to think about while you're being robbed.

Or maybe the feeling set in before that—long before—when he stood with Lila in a parking lot in the city, his chest swelling with the thought of himself as her saviour. He'd brazenly led her to believe that he was capable, that he had a road map to their future, and that he knew how to read it. Twenty-five years ago that was. Such foolish confidence. Now long gone—and what has replaced it? Nothing. A gaping hole for the wind and sand to blow through.

She's in his doorway now, the woman with the penny complaint. She doesn't wait for an invitation to speak.

"We have a problem, Mr. Birch," she says.

Crush

Through the waves of heat rising from the surface of the packed roadbed, Blaine Dolson studies Justine, the flag girl. He sees her scan down the road for traffic, and when none appears to be coming, she heads for the portable johnny-on-the-spot. She's supposed to wait for the scheduled breaks, but the foreman appears to be dozing in the cab of his truck. Blaine watches as she leans her flag against the blue plastic biffy and steps inside and closes the door.

It's ridiculous, this obsession he has with Justine, but he tells himself it's a fatherly kind of concern. She's the only female on the crew. The other flagman is a boy so shy you can hardly get a word out of him. Blaine doesn't know which of the two gets it worse: Justine because she's a girl, or the other kid because he's so timid. He doesn't care about the boy's whereabouts though, just Justine's. He watches her *all the time*. When the packer is facing east, she's there in front of him, and when he has to go the other direction, he anticipates the end of the stretch so he can turn his rig around and get her in his line of sight again, her white T-shirt catching the sun. It's as though he's thirteen years old with a crush, only she's not much older than Shiloh and he's definitely old enough to know better.

Where Justine is concerned, Blaine doesn't trust the intentions of a single man on this crew (with the exception of the shy kid, and maybe not even him). Every one of them leers openly at her. Blaine thinks of his wife, and of his daughters when they get to be Justine's age. If these men acted the way they talked, they'd all be in jail. And because they've noticed that Justine is friendly toward Blaine, they've taken to making vulgar suggestions in his presence about what she *really wants*. He ignores them as best he can. He doesn't like any of these men, but he knows enough not to let that show. Justine needs a guardian out here—at least that's what he tells himself.

The foreman is no help. A committed alcoholic, he spends most of the time in the cab of his truck either not so secretly drinking or trying to recover from the night before. Every once in a while he crawls out and gets ugly with someone who looks at him the wrong way through the cab window. He's downright cruel to the timid kid, and he tore a strip off Justine a few days ago for being late. She'd had car trouble and the foreman himself had got stuck holding the yellow SLOW sign for half an hour. When Justine pulled up, the rest of the crew—at least those close enough—watched to see what would happen, getting some kind of sadistic pleasure out of watching the foreman's angry posture, imagining amid the roar of machinery the words he was shouting at Justine, anticipating her humiliation and the tears that were bound to come. But Blaine, who was nearby on the packer, saw Justine's chin go up and her back straighten, and he saw that she was actually taller than the foreman. She didn't seem fazed by whatever it was he said to her, and later at lunch she told Blaine—looking right at the foreman holed up in his truck alone—that she felt sorry for him because he was so short and a pathetic alcoholic to boot. The foreman would have fired her on the spot if he'd overheard that.

Blaine admires Justine's spunk. She's completely different from Vicki, who was so innocent and naive at Justine's age. Vicki even liked to be tickled—still does—and reminded Blaine of a little girl. He remembers the day they were married in the United church in Juliet, how an overwhelming feeling of protectiveness for Vicki sprang out of nowhere as he watched her walk toward him up the aisle in her long white dress. She was not especially delicate, but she was small and she had blue eyes and a mass of curly blonde hair. In those days, the way she deferred to him on everything made him feel like marriage was the best medicine going for a man's ego, and that he was doing his job as her husband. He remembers the time shortly after the wedding that she had a flat tire three miles from home and she sat by the side of the road in her car and waited for him to come looking for her, even though she could have walked home in less time than it took for him to realize she was missing. He'd thought it was funny, and told the story often. It was an example of how Vicki *liked* to need him, and he liked to look after her. But as the children came, Shiloh and then the others, he felt the same feeling of protectiveness for them, and as more children arrived there was less and less of it to go around, and he began to grow irritated with Vicki. Sometimes she actually seemed incompetent as the house gathered dust and dinner was late and the dishes piled up in the sink until she felt like doing them. Her innocence began to look like an act, a pretense that he thought she should give up.

So why, Blaine wonders, with the sounds of heavy machinery droning through his protective headphones, if he wants Vicki to be more independent, does he not want her to get a job in town? He has nothing against women working. He admires Justine's ability to stand out in the sun all day and deal with this crew of men who don't really believe in her right to be here. Would he want Vicki working as a flag girl on a road crew? Definitely not.

But why not as a clerk in the grocery store, or a receptionist in the insurance office? These are both possibilities that she's raised with him. He uses the kids as his excuse for not being in favour of her working, and it's a legitimate excuse when you consider the cost of babysitting. But the kids aren't the real reason he's so opposed. It all goes back to the responsibility he accepted when they were married, his promise to look after Vicki and whatever family they might have, and his inability to admit that he's failed, that he can't look after them any more, and that he needs his wife to help put the food on the table.

What would his father think if he were still alive? Blaine knew his father was in the dark ages long after a lot of men had crawled out, but he'd always told Blaine that a woman working was a sure sign of a weak husband. Blaine can well imagine what his father would say about the situation he's in today. He doesn't know himself how he got here, except that he'd let the debt accumulate in good years and was stuck with it when the times turned. Even when Blaine first took over the farm, his father had been there every day telling him he was doing things wrong if Blaine attempted to change anything at all. If he were alive, he'd have his proof. Blaine knows it's not that simple, you can't keep doing things the same way forever, but even if his father was wrong in the nature of his criticisms, Blaine obviously had done *something* wrong to get so far under. It kills him that there's nothing left for his sons, especially Shiloh. He knows he acts sometimes like Vicki is to blame, like this morning when he was so impatient with her, but he also knows she's not responsible. The real blame goes to culprits so abstract he can't put a face to them—trade agreements and government subsidies and corporate monopolies. He's no economist, and that's what you have to be these days to understand what's going on.

There is one real face to all this, though. It was Norval Birch who froze Blaine's line of credit, and it was Norval who turned down Blaine's refinancing plan, even as he had earlier approved—encouraged—Blaine's accumulation of debt as a modern-day farming practice. Now the banks are making huge profits as Blaine goes broke, and who represents the bank in Juliet if not Norval? Blaine can just see him sitting behind his desk, his salary assured no matter what is happening with his loan clients. When Blaine wakes in the night and Vicki is trying to snuggle up in her flannelette nightie, reminding him of his failed promise to look after her and the kids, he seethes with anger, and he thinks of Norval. He thinks of him in a night-vision of angry colours, blood red and midnight blue. He's always angry these days as the sun burns his neck and he smells the heat and tar and hears the rumble and whine of heavy machinery, and he thinks he's working in the flames of hell, paying for sins he doesn't remember committing. He's angry with people he knows he shouldn't be angry with, confused about men and women and what makes a good husband. Vicki tells him he *is* a good husband in spite of all that's happened, but she's fooling herself.

From his perch on the packer, Blaine can see a car approaching, going fast. Justine's flag is still leaning against the blue biffy. The car doesn't appear to be slowing, and it passes the crew at a dangerous speed. The foreman jumps out of his truck, first shaking a fist after the car, and then apparently looking for Justine and shouting where the hell is she, impossible for anyone to hear amid the construction noise. The biffy door opens and Justine steps out and notices the ranting foreman coming toward her. She picks up her flag and shouts something back, Blaine can't hear what. The foreman is still yelling, stepping toward Justine, just a few feet from her now, with his arms waving and his dwarfish body bouncing with anger. There is no other crew around, Blaine is the closest, and he wonders if he should get down and intervene.

But then he sees Justine's hands rise emphatically and she moves forward so aggressively that the little foreman has to step back. She actually shakes a finger in his face. It's the funniest thing. The foreman tries to get in another lick, but once again Justine steps forward and he steps back. Blaine doesn't know who gets the last word in, but he sees the foreman turn around and climb back into his truck cab. He watches Justine return to her position, and when he catches her eye he gives her the thumbs-up. She laughs. He wants to laugh with her. He imagines the two of them laughing, she the beer-ad girl in a white T-shirt, her brown arms testifying to health and happiness, and he the picture of strength and vitality, the independent man of the West, red-necked from outdoor work and proud of it.

He turns his rig around even though he's not at the end of his pass. He suddenly doesn't want to look at her, she's too young, and she's just inviting trouble by being here. He even feels a moment's anger at her, for being so careless, for taking this job in the first place among all these men who have no respect for women and resent the fact that she's collecting another man's salary. And then he realizes that his anger at Justine is the same as his anger at Vicki, and he's tired of it, tired of being angry. When he gets to the end of the stretch he turns his rig around again and drives back toward Justine. White T-shirt. Smiling. Waving at a car that slows down in response to her sign. Spinning her sign in the gravel once the car has passed.

She looks bored. She takes off her hard hat and adjusts the ball cap she wears underneath to provide a better peak against the sun. She puts the hard hat back on and spins the sign once more. As Blaine draws closer, he can see that her lips are moving and at first he can't figure out what she's doing—talking to herself?—but then she begins to bob her head and she even does a little dance step, and he realizes that she's singing.

Singing. Right out loud. Out here in the middle of nowhere. Like Daisy, in her own world, putting on a show for an invisible audience. He tries to look away so Justine won't be embarrassed at being caught. Only she isn't embarrassed. Not at all. She sees him watching her and she grins and does her little dance step again, for him this time.

He nods his acknowledgment, and now he's the one who is embarrassed: that he's been so obvious in the way he watches her.

His face is so red from the sun no one could possibly know he's blushing.

So Gay

Shiloh walks down Main Street, not really sure where he's going, but he knows he doesn't want to traipse around to all the stores in town with his mother. Maybe he can find someone to hang out with. Then he hears her car coming up behind him, its familiar engine knock, and Daisy calls out the window, "Hey Shiloh, where're you going?" and Vicki pulls alongside him and says, "Hey, where are you off to, stranger?"

"Nowhere," he says without stopping.

"Hop in, then," Vicki says.

He ignores her.

"Oh, for God's sake, Shiloh," Vicki says. "Since when did I become the enemy?"

"I don't want to be dragged all over town on some dumb shopping trip."

"All right. Fair enough," Vicki says. "Why don't you meet us at the swimming pool. In what . . . an hour?"

She waits for him to answer, so he doesn't. He just keeps on walking, but she won't go away, she follows alongside.

"Okay, okay," he finally says, just to get rid of them.

"I want to go with Shiloh," Martin says.

"Well, you can't," Shiloh says. "So get that out of your damn head right now." He knows he sounds just like Blaine.

"Shiloh's growing up and he wants to be left alone," Vicki says to Martin. Then she says to Shiloh, "Watch your language when you're talking to the little ones, mister. There's no excuse for being rude."

He hates almost every single thing she says these days, and then he feels bad.

"One hour," she says. "Don't keep us waiting."

"Two hours," he argues. He knows she won't be ready in an hour anyway.

"No, Shiloh," Vicki says. "We have to get home."

"An hour and a half, then."

Vicki looks at her watch. "Okay," she says. "An hour and a half, but don't be late."

After she's gone, Shiloh sits on the curb and gloats. It's so easy to get his own way with his mother. Then he realizes he has to find something to do for the next hour and a half. There are a few town kids he doesn't mind—Mark Matheson and Brad Weibe are okay—but Mark's family has a cottage and they go there for pretty much the whole summer, and he thinks Brad's away at a hockey camp. He doesn't usually see much of the other kids during the summer, and so he feels funny just dropping by some-one's house. He decides to wander around town, hoping a plan will reveal itself.

He walks up Main Street, but the only familiar person he sees is Brittney Vass, who is coming toward him with her mother. He just about dies, and would cross the street to get away but it's too late. Brittney's father has the insurance business in town and they have money. He knows the other girls think she has the best clothes, and she's good at sports and won the girls' athletic award at the end of the school year, even though she was only in grade seven. Once, when Shiloh missed the bus after school, he watched the girls' basketball team play—or more correctly, he watched Brittney play—while he waited for his mother to come and pick him up. There were several boys from his class watching, but they were boys who played on sports teams too, which meant they were all town kids. Shiloh stood by the gym door and when Brad Weibe waved him over to the bleachers, Shiloh pretended he didn't see him. Still, he couldn't help but see the other boys look his way and laugh. When he got to school the next day, someone had written in chalk on the wall of the school SHILOH DOLSON IS SO GAY. Again, he pretended he didn't notice and by recess it was gone, or at least rubbed out so you couldn't read it.

Shiloh notices how much taller Brittney is than him, and as she and her mother come closer on the sidewalk he tries to pull himself up and at least give the impression of tall. He sees that Brittney is wearing lipstick. When they pass, she doesn't even give him a glance. You'd think she'd never seen him before in her life. He hears her mother ask, *Wasn't that the Dolson boy?* but he can't hear Brittney's answer. There might not have been one.

Anyway, he hates her. He hates all the girls in his class, but at the same time he wants to watch Brittney walk down the sidewalk. He tries to think up some excuse to turn around and go the other way after her, toward the hardware store maybe, or the post office. But it would be so obvious. She'd know and she'd call up her friends, the other cool girls, and tell them he was following her around, stalking her even, that's how girls are. She'd get on the phone as soon as she got home and they'd rip him apart, talk about how short he is, or how funny his voice sounds. So instead of following Brittney, he goes to the schoolyard. He searches the ground for a soft rock, the kind that you can write with, and he scrawls BRITTNEY IS SO GAY on the brick wall and, as an afterthought, GIRLS ARE SO FUCKING GAY. Then he goes to the little kids' playground, drops his backpack in the grass, and sits on a swing and scratches the letters in Brittney's name with his foot in the dirt, and rubs them out, and writes them again.

A car coming slowly up the street catches his attention. It gets to the end of the block and then the driver does a U-turn and comes back. The car stops by the curb bordering the playground and a woman steps out, no one Shiloh recognizes. She's wearing high heels and a light blue suit and big black sunglasses. Shiloh watches as she leans against the car and stares at the school. She lights a cigarette and then notices him on the swings. He looks away but he can still see that she is coming toward him, tottering through the sparse and dusty playground grass on her high heels.

"Do you go to school here?" she asks when she reaches the swings.

Shiloh says, "If you want to smoke you have to be at least a block away from the school. That's the rule. I thought everyone knew that."

"Oh," she says. "Well, I'm not from around here."

"That's the rule everywhere," Shiloh says. He knows he's being rude, but it feels good. She's a stranger. Who cares what she thinks?

"I don't imagine anyone's going to enforce the rule during the summer," the woman says. She takes a drag on the smoke and then butts it out in the dirt, grinding it beneath her shoe. *Her fancy city shoe*, Shiloh thinks. No women here wear shoes like that, at least not where he sees them. She picks up the butt and holds it in her open palm.

"So is this a pretty good school, then?" she asks Shiloh.

"It sucks," Shiloh says.

"You like the teachers? The principal?"

"They suck too. This whole town sucks."

"That's kind of what I thought," the woman says. "Call it a first impression." She looks like she might be about to ask him something else, but then she turns around and walks back to her car. She stops to read what Shiloh wrote on the wall of the school before getting in her car and driving away, this time not slowly. She even spins her tires.

Shiloh is wondering what he should do next when a kid comes into the schoolyard with his white dog, some kind of little terrier. Shiloh recognizes the kid from the reading buddy program. He wasn't his own reading buddy, but he was in the same class of grade ones and twos—the one that Daisy is in. When the reading buddy program started up, Daisy wanted Shiloh for her partner but the teacher said no.

The kid recognizes Shiloh, and comes to the swings and asks him if he wants to play Frisbee with the dog. The kid has a lisp. Shiloh says sure, and they take turns throwing the Frisbee, which the dog is pretty good at catching. Shiloh tries throwing it harder and the dog runs like crazy and picks the Frisbee out of the air. Shiloh keeps trying to throw it farther and farther, but the dog always manages to get there and catch it. The kid gets more excited about how far Shiloh can throw the Frisbee than he is about the dog's ability to catch it. He keeps saying, "Farther, Shiloh, farther." The kid's own attempts to throw the Frisbee are pretty bad, so Shiloh gives him a lesson. The kid thinks it would be a good idea to invent a Frisbee that would come back, like a boomerang. Shiloh hangs out with the kid and his dog until the kid decides he should go home. As the kid is leaving he sees the writing on the school wall and he wants to know what it means.

"Nothing," Shiloh says. "Just some dumb crap."

"Someone's going to get heck," the kid says. He pronounces it *thumb one.*

"It's summer," Shiloh says. "You can write whatever you want on the school in summer."

After the kid leaves, Shiloh heads across the lawn in front of the school. There are a couple of high school girls—grade ten or eleven—on inline skates in the parking lot. They're wearing shorts and tank tops, and they're all geared up with helmets and knee pads and wrist guards. Shiloh hardly dares to look at them. In fact, he decides to skirt the parking lot altogether.

But then one of them yells to him, "Hey, Shiloh, want to see a cool trick?"

How would they know his name? He must have heard wrong.

"That's your name, isn't it? Shiloh Dolson?"

He keeps on going with his head down.

"What's the matter? Cat got your tongue?" And then the other girl says, "We think you're cute, Shiloh. Come and see us in a couple of years." This is immediately followed by the sound of girls laughing, completely pleased with themselves.

He hates girls. He crosses the street and heads down the alley that runs behind Brad's house. He doesn't expect him to be home, but he looks over the back fence anyway, and sees that the house looks quiet and locked up. There's usually a camper trailer parked on a pad behind the house and it's not there. Shiloh takes this to mean the whole family has gone to the hockey camp. That makes sense. Brad's parents are the town's biggest hockey fans, along with Greg Bellmore's mother. Greg Bellmore, who played eight seasons in the NHL and never lived in Juliet, but his mother married a Juliet teacher, who died a year later. Mrs. Bellmore (she kept the name Bellmore because of her famous son) had stayed, and now the town talks about Greg as though he was born here. In the winter Mrs. Bellmore hangs out at the rink every day along with Brad's dad, who doesn't work because of an accident he had several years ago and now is just a hockey fan. The two of them had headed a committee to raise the money for a new rink and they'd been so successful that the rink is practically theirs. The rink has NO SMOKING signs everywhere, but Brad's dad and Mrs. Bellmore are allowed to smoke during practices. They have to butt out during games, though, when the bleachers are full of other smokers who are expected to follow the rules. One Saturday when Shiloh was killing time in town he had gone over to the rink to watch Brad practise and he'd sat in the stands behind Brad's dad and Mrs. Bellmore. They talked on and on about Greg and Brad as though they weren't even real people. Mr. Weibe talked about Brad as though he were already in the NHL.

Shiloh continues on down the alley, pretending that he doesn't know Brittney Vass lives just a block away from Brad. When he comes to her house he looks over the fence and there she is, suntanning in a lounge chair beside an inflatable kiddy pool. She's wearing a bright blue bikini and music is blasting from a portable CD player that is attached to an outlet by a long red extension cord. Her eyes are closed and she dangles one foot in the pool. The lounge chair and the pool are on a low wooden deck, and there are pots with flowers in them everywhere. Shiloh can't help it; he stops and stares over the fence. The yard is like a park and Brittney looks so grown up. He doesn't even recognize the music she's listening to. He tries to commit it to memory so that if he hears it on the radio he'll be able to find out who it is. He leans against the fence and closes his eyes, taking in the music, and when he opens his eyes again Brittney is sitting up in her lounge chair and looking right at him.

He jumps back from the fence and walks quickly away down the alley. How could he be so stupid, like a kid drooling for candy, and how could he be even stupider and look back just in time to see her grab her CD player and run into the house, dragging the red extension cord after her, as though she were being chased by some kind of creepy pervert? The cord catches and she yanks it free, and then the screen door to the Vass house slams shut and Shiloh feels like the whole town is slammed shut. It's not his town. He's just a farm kid. His parents don't raise money for hockey rinks, and they don't have a cabin for summer holidays, and he doesn't have a backyard with a deck and flowerpots.

He breaks into a run and when he gets to the end of the alley he turns up the street toward the swimming pool, still running. When he gets to the swimming pool he'll tell Vicki they have to go home *right now* and do the beans like Blaine said. He runs along the sidewalk with the memory of Brittney Vass and her red extension cord chasing him, and when he gets to the pool he has to stand under a tree and catch his breath. He can see his brothers and sisters—four of them anyway—in the blue water, and now he's so hot and sweaty that the water looks inviting and he thinks maybe he should go for a swim, just a quick one to cool off, and he realizes that he's left his backpack somewhere. The schoolyard. He'll have to go back for it.

His life has turned out to be so crappy, he thinks. It damn well better improve before school starts again. If it doesn't, he'll quit school and move. He hates this dump. Anywhere else would be better.

Solo

Dan

Lee is amazed that the horse goes forward so willingly in the late-morning heat across a seemingly endless tract of low dunes and sand flats. Creeping juniper stands out here as an oddity, a sprawling evergreen shrub where tall cactus would be more expected. The breeze—not strong enough to provide any relief—sends wisps of sand snaking their way across the surface. Little snakes of sand. Lee wonders if that's how the hills got their name. He watches the surface shift before his eyes, fine wavy patterns appearing and then vanishing again. *You could stand out here and watch your own footprints disappear,* he thinks.

Out of curiosity, he asks the horse to stop, and he watches the sand blow into the hoofprints, feathering the edges and slipping into the holes. As Lee looks back the way he came, he sees his trail becoming less distinct and then disappearing not far from where he's standing, so that it looks as though the horse emerged out of nowhere. He asks the horse to move forward again and they create new prints, sharp-edged for only seconds.

Besides feeling the effects of the sun, Lee is now feeling the effects of over thirty-five steady miles horseback. He's thirsty and saddle sore, and he wishes he'd thought to put a cap on his head when he started out. He reaches behind the cantle where he tied his jacket and loosens the saddle strings, planning to use the jacket as a makeshift head covering, but it slips out of his hands and slides to the ground. He doesn't bother stopping to pick it up. It's an old jacket, ripped around the pockets and not much good any more without Astrid to patch it. He looks back and watches it settle in the sand, and wonders how long it will be before it's completely covered. He thinks again of Willard's camel, wonders if her remains are buried out here somewhere. He pictures a dead camel with clouds of sand blowing over its body, creating a mound, the beginnings of a new dune. Is this how the ancient Egyptians came up with the idea of the pyramids, after watching the wind build massive sand monuments over the dead bodies of camels and horses?

As the sand soaks up the sun's heat and discharges it back at him like a giant furnace, he stands in the stirrups to try to take some pressure off the tender places, tries to readjust what Lester referred to as his "equipment." He remembers when Lester first said to him, *Don't get your equipment in a knot,* and Lee understood then that Lester thought he was old enough to talk a certain way when they were out of the presence of women. There's no adjusting that relieves all the sore spots—taking the pressure off one puts more on another—and he feels an inkling of regret that he made the impulsive decision to cross this desolate strip in the heat of the day. But it's too late now. He must be more than halfway to the Catholic church, and it would be crazy to turn back. There's a good well in the churchyard, or at least there used to be. He closes his eyes for a few seconds and thinks of water, cool water, like in the old cowboy song that Lester had on a vinyl record. Lee sings for a while, only half remembering the words, something about a cowboy lost in the desert with a horse or a mule named Dan, their throats parched and their souls crying out, but then Lee decides singing takes too much energy and, anyway, the song is depressing and it's just making him more thirsty.

"Dan," he says out loud. "That's a good name for you." The horse turns his ears in Lee's direction.

The beating sun adds a silvery sheen to the grey-gold colour that stretches as far as Lee can see. The horse steps without hesitation into the shimmering hot sand, his head high, moving forward, keeping up the same steady pace. He's an efficient machine, Lee thinks jealously, built for distance, while the man on his back is miserable and about to die from thirst, or at least that's how he feels.

Until finally Lee sees a road to the northwest, and then the old war memorial comes into view, which means the church is not far ahead and, more important, the well. He turns toward the road and travels westward in the shallow ditch. Sweet clover tempts the horse and he tries to snatch at it, but Lee keeps him moving past the stone memorial and toward the church. Another half-mile and he can see it, a small fieldstone building with white trim, the wooden steeple and cross reaching into the sky. Across the road from the church is George and Anna Varga's home place. The sun reflects brilliant green off the distant poplars and caragana hedges of the Varga yard. Lee knows, without a doubt, the relief that real desert travellers feel when their instincts or their animals successfully lead them to an oasis.

When he reaches the churchyard with its mowed grass and neat picket fence, Lee slides to the ground and carefully lets his body absorb its own weight. Without having to look, he knows the insides of his calves are chafed. He hobbles into the churchyard leading the horse, and latches the gate behind him. The roof of the church has an overhang and Lee makes for the shade it creates and removes the saddle and bridle. The saddle pad is soaked with sweat. As soon as the horse is free, he's into the dry grass edging the church's foundation.

Lee heads for the well and takes a long drink directly from the pump, and then splashes water on his head and back, soaking his shirt. There's a bucket hanging on the pump, which he fills for the horse. He lets him drink a bit, and then he splashes water on the horse's neck and chest to rinse off the sweat and cool him down. The horse shivers as the cold water hits him, and moves away from it. Lee fills the bucket again and this time he lets the horse drink what he wants, and then he drinks some more himself before stretching out in the shade. He thinks of food and is tempted to go rummaging in the church for something to eat, but he closes his eyes instead. As he nods off, ripples of sand pass endlessly in his head and then turn into waves of water lapping gently against the shore of a sandy beach.

He wakes from a sound sleep to find old George Varga staring down at him.

"So, young Torgeson," George says, holding out his hand to help Lee to his feet.

As he gets up, Lee tries to hide the fact that his body is sadly hurting. He's glad that George recognizes him, so he doesn't have to explain who he is.

The horse is nowhere in sight.

George sees Lee looking and points around the side of the church. "Damn bugger's eating my grass," he says. Then he waves his hand in dismissal and adds, "Saves me mowing."

Lee senses George waiting for an explanation, so he offers, "I came across the sand." As he says it, he realizes it's not much of an explanation.

"From your place?" George asks.

Lee nods, expecting disbelief, but George says, "Well, better come on over to the house, have some lunch. Fill the belly before you go. Long way back home, long ride ahead of you." The words *long ride* resonate but are quickly replaced by thoughts of food.

Lee follows George through the churchyard gate and across the road to the original Varga homestead, where he knows George lives with his sister Anna. As they pass through the trees, he sees a mobile home with a framed porch built onto the side and a carefully tended flower bed in front. The old farmhouse is still standing, but it's badly weathered and not in use any more. It's rumoured that George is filthy rich, but you'd never know it from the twenty-year-old pickup truck parked in the yard. Lee takes note of the tow hitch and looks around for a stock trailer, thinking about a ride home, but he doesn't see one.

George takes him into the porch, which turns out to be a summer kitchen, calling out to Anna that they have a visitor from down south, young Lee Torgeson—remember him, Lester's boy? "Get the boy something to eat, Anna," George says. "He's come all this way on a horse, just like the old days."

Then Anna speaks to George in Hungarian. It's intimidating, having her speak without Lee knowing what she's saying. She could be telling George to get him the hell out, for all he knows. But no, she's sending him into the trailer and down the hall to the washroom, and when he gets back she's already got food on the table: bread and cheese and cold meat, pickles and sliced tomatoes. A plate filled with cookies and cake squares.

"Sit, sit," Anna says in English. "All that way on a horse. You must be hungry."

"Like the Perry cowboys, eh," George says to Anna.

Lee isn't sure what George means, something to do with the legendary ranch, he supposes, how everything was done horseback in those days. Much of the pastureland in the district had been part of the original Perry lease, and there are old black-and-white photographs in the town hall. He shifts his weight on a wooden chair, trying to relieve the pressure on his bruises and saddle burns. His mouth is watering, but he waits until Anna offers him the plate of cheese and cold cuts. When she does, he digs in.

"We ate already," George says, although he takes a piece of cake in his big farmer's hand. Lee notices that he's missing a finger.

"So," George says, his mouth full of cake, "you're doing the hundred-mile ride, just like Ivan Dodge. Hundred miles on the same horse. Have to be. No fresh horse for you here."

Lee is hardly listening. He's busy making himself the best-looking sandwich he's ever seen, the kind Astrid used to call a Dagwood.

"You know the story, I suppose," George says.

Lee looks at him then, and George can tell he doesn't know what he's talking about.

"Lester never told you about that race?" George asks. "Before I was born. The riders changed horses—one of them anyway—right out there where the church is."

Lee tries to remember, but he doesn't think he's heard anything about such a race. He would have remembered a story with horses in it.

So George tells him. Anna knows the story too, and nods throughout the telling. How a cowboy named Ivan Dodge and another hand from the ranch came through the dunes and Ivan Dodge was well ahead of his competitor, and they were supposed to switch to fresh horses but Ivan shook his head when one of his crew led his change horse up and then he loped off on his Arab horse and rode his way to victory. How the other cowboy's horse tied up and he couldn't finish the race.

"There was betting that day," George says. "Not many won money. Only those with horse sense. They say that's inherited, horse sense. My old man travelled all the way to watch the finish out by your place, by that old buffalo stone. He didn't like to admit he bet on the wrong horse, but that's what he did. He had no horse sense."

"Get the book, George," Anna says. "Show him the picture."

Anna takes away Lee's empty plate and gets him a teacup. "Tea is good on a hot day," she says. "You wouldn't think so, but it is."

For some reason Lee tells her about the Bedouins and their tea ceremony. "They drink it sweet," Lee says, "and if they're outside they pour a few drops in the sand. It's a gift to the desert." Once he's said it he feels embarrassed, but Anna looks interested.

"Is that so?" she says. "They sweeten with honey, I suppose."

George returns with an old album filled to bursting with newspaper clippings, scraps of paper and photographs. He lays it on the table and flips through the pages, some of them falling free of the binding, and searches for something. He holds a magnifying glass over the pages as he looks. He shows Lee pictures of dead people in their burial attire, taken, George says, so their families could remember them. "Most dressed up they'd ever been," he says, "so good time for a picture."

"History," Anna says, indicating the book. "Varga history."

George points out a photograph of the stone foundation of a building. "The church," he says. "Soon as my old man got the house done, he started on the church. The house will be gone soon, next big wind, I suppose, but the church is still there. Better building. Or maybe God looks after it, eh."

As George flips through the scrapbook, Lee imagines the rash of activity that must have gone into building a community from scratch.

George finds what he's looking for, a newspaper article. He slides the book toward Lee, indicating that he should take the magnifying glass as well.

"His eyes are young, he doesn't need that," Anna says, but Lee takes it anyway because the article is faded.

It relates the details of the race: the two cowboys, the hundred-mile horse, said to be an Arab. *It is rumoured,* the article says, *that money exchanged hands, although no man is owning up to either winning or losing, perhaps because of the local women's well-known disapproval of gambling.* The way the article is written reminds Lee of Lester's old books. He studies the grainy picture of Ivan Dodge, who resembles a movie cowboy with his young good looks, his hat and his fringed chaps. Lee examines the faces of the people standing around him, men in old-fashioned clothing, looking as though they're dressed for church. He wonders if one of them might be Lester's father, but none looks familiar. He scans the article until he finds the name of the other cowboy, the one who lost, Henry Merchant. He doesn't recognize either name, Dodge or Merchant. They'd had their moment of fame, he supposes, and then left the district like so many others.

Anna takes Lee's empty cup from the table and carries it to the sink.

"George," she says, "when are you going to get me that dishwasher?"

"Waiting for a sale," he says. He leans toward Lee conspiratorially and says, "I already got a good dishwasher."

"What's he saying there?" Anna asks.

Lee laughs and decides it's time to go. "Thanks for the lunch," he says, and pushes himself away from the table. George rises too and Anna comes to see him out the door. He's thinking that George must have some kind of trailer for hauling animals and is about to ask—not because of the long ride, he'll say, but because he has work to do—when Anna warns, "You be careful on that horse. Look in the graveyard across the road. Pete Varga. Died when he got bucked off and hit his head on a rock." Anna shakes her head. "Such a tragedy."

"Don't worry," George says, "he's not going to get bucked off. Not a horseman like this one."

Lee says, "I don't know, fifty miles might be far enough." He waits for a response, hoping, but hope evaporates when George says, "You ride out, you have to ride back. How else do you get home? Now that you got food in the belly, good to go again. Let that Araby horse set his own pace and you'll be fine."

Lee thanks Anna for the lunch and finds himself walking with George back to the churchyard, knowing that there's no other way, he'll have to saddle up and ride the remaining fifty miles like Ivan Dodge did, no matter how sore he is, no matter how much it hurts to climb back in the saddle. He can already feel the pain of the horse moving under him once again, the seams of his jeans rubbing once more against raw skin. He badly regrets his decision to ride any farther than Hank's pasture.

"You didn't bring no hat?" George asks.

"It was dark when I started," Lee says.

George is wearing an old felt cowboy hat, battered and darkened around the band with years of sweat and grease. He takes it off, exposing a white forehead and thick grey hair, and hands it to Lee. "You better take this," he says. "You've got enough sunburn on that face for one day."

Lee doesn't really want to put George's dirty old hat on his head, but he takes it anyway because he knows George is right. He tries it on and it fits well enough to stay in place.

"I'll get it back to you," Lee says.

"Never mind," says George. "Time for a new one. You throw that one away when you get home."

The horse lifts his head and whinnies when George and Lee enter the churchyard. Lee offers the horse another drink and then tacks him up, and when there's nothing else to do, he mounts once again. The saddle doesn't feel as bad as he thought it would.

"So where'd you get this horse, anyway?" George asks. "Lester never had no horse like this. Just those heavy horses, eh, good for work."

Lee tells him. How the horse just wandered into his yard.

"Huh," George says. "Well, no one claims him, I guess he'll be yours."

"I don't think so," Lee says. "Someone will come looking for him."

"Tell you what," George says. "You ride the whole hundred miles and I'll give you fifty bucks."

George holds up his hand and Lee doesn't know what to do other than shake it.

"All right, then," George says. "Straight south. That's the way the Perry cowboys went. Good flatland. Won't be as hard going as what you've come through. Maybe someone will put your picture in the paper, eh."

"I hope not," Lee says. He tips his hat to George, and once they've crossed the road he lets the horse move into a trot. He doesn't give the fifty dollars another thought, and he tries not to think of the distance between here and home.

It feels better than he predicted it would to be moving again.

Ed's Window

Willard is certain that Marian is watching him through the living room window of the house—the window that Willard will always think of as "Ed's window." When they were building the house, Ed had gone to the drugstore and bought a magazine that featured an article on the latest in home design. This was completely out of character, but Willard later learned that Ed had marriage in mind and he wanted to build a house that would attract a woman. Although the house was essentially a prefab from the lumberyard in Swift Current, Ed had insisted they replace the standard living room window that came in the package with a larger window that he'd seen in the magazine.

There'd been no end of trouble with Ed's window. The lumberyard had to special-order and Ed went to the lumberyard every day to see if it was in. He happened to be there when it arrived, broken. Because Ed had helped to unpack the crate, the insurance company tried to use that to renege on its responsibility. The disagreement escalated to include the shipper and its insurance company, and the manufacturer. Ed's position was that he wasn't paying a cent for a broken window, no matter whose fault it was. Eventually, there was a settlement, but when the second window arrived, this time intact, the carpenters broke it when they were installing it, and a third window had to be ordered. Again, Ed held to his position, not one red cent, and the lumberyard was forced to order and pay for a third window. This one was installed without incident, but over the entire first year that Ed and Willard lived in the new house, Ed fought with the lumberyard because the window iced up on the inside in the winter, and when the ice melted in the spring, water leaked into the wall and the Gyproc got wet and disintegrated. Ed could probably have fixed the window and re-plastered the wall himself, but it was a matter of principle. And there was some urgency for Ed, because he had plans. The window had to be right before he went looking for his bride, who eventually turned out to be Marian.

To this day, Willard does not know how they met. He only knows that Ed went out all dressed up one day in January—a good month for a new start—and was gone for the better part of a week. Willard was left alone, not really worried because Ed had always done things without telling anyone. Ed said nothing when he got home about where he'd been, but Willard knew that Ed was just dying for him to ask, which was reason enough for Willard not to. Ed made several other forays out into the world that winter and spring, in between rounds of lodging complaints about the window, and in July—once the window was resealed and the wall plaster was sanded and painted—he showed up with Marian and introduced her as his wife. Willard said, *Pleased to meet you,* and he remembers that Marian said the same, only she sounded genuinely pleased, which was somehow surprising.

Willard looks up from his fence repairs to check for Marian in the window. He can't really see her. The house is too far away and too dark inside, but just the same, he suspects she's there. Willard has a makeshift workbench set up on the tailgate of his truck. As he rips the blackened, damaged boards off the fence and measures up for new ones, he wonders where Ed got the idea that a window would tip the scale for a woman considering marriage to him. He tries to remember, when Ed first brought Marian home, whether she was as impressed by the window as Ed thought a woman should be. It's not as though the window looks out over a green meadow or a pretty little creek. Ed had insisted the window face out over the drive-in lot.

The next time Willard looks up, he sees Marian crossing the yard with a thermos. She's wearing sturdy shoes and a housedress, and she's pulled a John Deere cap on over her hair, which she has tied in a ponytail. Willard thinks she looks a little like the young girls in town with their caps and ponytails, only Marian's hair is mostly grey, and not some wild shade of red, or even blue. He overheard a couple of girls in the grocery store one day, and they were buying Kool-Aid to put in their hair.

He stops work and lays his hammer on the truck's tailgate.

"You looked hard at it," Marian says. "I thought you might want some iced tea."

"I never turn down moisture," he says.

"There are sandwiches in the fridge," Marian says. "I imagine you'll want to have lunch inside, what with the heat. You can come in whenever you're ready."

"Another half-hour here ought to do it," he says.

Marian sets the thermos down on the tailgate, next to the hammer.

"I just heard on the radio that we might get rain later in the week."

"Too late now," Willard says. "Anyway, I'll believe that when it happens." He looks to the west and there's not a cloud to be seen. He takes off his work gloves and unscrews the top on the thermos.

Marian turns to walk back to the house.

"Wait," Willard says.

She stops and looks at him. The anticipation on her face tells him she thinks he might ask her something important.

"I was just wondering," he says, "what you thought of Ed's window there, when he brought you to the house that first time."

"Ed's window?"

"The picture window," Willard says, nodding toward it. "Did you think, *Now there's a window right out of a magazine?*"

"I'm not sure what you're getting at," Marian says.

"He didn't ever make mention of the window?"

"Not that I can recall."

Marian looks puzzled. Willard doesn't know what else to say. He's sorry he mentioned the window, and Ed. He hasn't talked to Marian about Ed since they buried him, and even in that difficult time they didn't say much. Marian had asked him what hymn they should sing at the funeral and Willard had said probably no hymn as Ed was an atheist, but maybe "Amazing Grace" would do. Ed would agree that people were wretched, and if you stretched it, "I was blind but now I see" might refer to Ed's political enlightenment.

Marian finally says, "Well, it was night, as I recall. And there were no curtains. I looked out and thought, *If I'm going to live here, the first thing I will do is make curtains for that window.*"

"Hah," Willard says. "Did you tell Ed that?"

"I don't remember, but I did go out and buy material and of course he thought that was a waste of money. When I brought the fabric home he said, 'You're not going to cover up that window?' 'Oh yes I am,' I said. No woman wants to stand in a window that big, for all the world to see, unless she's a you-know-what kind of woman."

Willard feels himself flushing at this reference to a prostitute. He and Marian absolutely don't talk about things like that.

"But I had a different thought the first time I saw the window in daylight," Marian says. "I looked out and saw the movie screen and the speakers lined up in the sand, and I thought, *If I had one of those speakers in the house I could sit in the window and watch movies every night.* Well now I can do that, can't I, since we updated the sound system."

That's true. There's a radio in the living room and sometimes, when Marian isn't helping Willard in the concession stand, she tunes it to the movie frequency and pulls a chair up to the window. When Willard sees the lights go out right after the movie starts, he knows Marian is settling in to watch. He's been curious over the years about which movies she selects. She doesn't like violence or the horror movies that the kids are so fond of, but she doesn't seem to like the romances either. She likes musicals, and movies set in other countries, and once she starts watching a movie she commits herself to it. When the movie's over, she draws the curtains and turns the lights back on.

"Why all this interest in the window?" Marian asks.

Willard says, "Ed put that window in as a special drawing card, when he was looking for a wife."

Marian starts to laugh, right out loud, in a way that Willard has rarely seen. The only other time that comes to mind was when he put her up on Antoinette and took her for a camel ride around the drive-in lot. She'd laughed like a girl, so hard that Willard thought she might fall off. He figures she enjoyed the camel ride as much as anyone ever had, even young Lee Torgeson.

Marian walks back to the house laughing, and when she gets to the door she turns and waves at Willard. It's the oddest thing and throws him completely, so he waves back without knowing why they're waving at each other when neither of them is going anywhere.

He turns to the thermos and unscrews the top, and as he does, he hears ice cubes clinking against the glass liner and just the sound of ice cools him off a degree or two. He takes a swallow, and feels the tart lemon taste, and thinks how lucky he is to have Marian looking after him, and then he puts the thermos down and quickly goes back to work.

It's the best thing about work, he thinks, how it keeps worry at bay.

Blue Pool

Norval has pretty much spent the morning staring at the walls of his office and when lunch hour arrives he decides to go home and eat with Lila. On his way, he passes the swimming pool. There's Rachelle in her bikini, perched up on the high chair, protected from the sun by an orange umbrella. An orange cap is the only thing identifying her as a lifeguard, that and the fact that she's sitting in the chair.

For a hot day, the pool is quiet. Just a few young children in the shallow end and a half-dozen rowdy ten-year-olds lining up to do cannonballs off the diving board. There are two adults swimming laps, one of them a woman with a giant plastic flower on the top of her bathing cap. Both swimmers are wearing goggles, so he can't tell who they are. The absence of teenagers sprawled on the pool deck likely means they're all still asleep, as Rachelle would be if she didn't have this job. Norval would like to march over to the fence and give her a good talking-to about her disappearing act of the night before, but of course he can't, she's at work after all. At least she showed up for work.

She hasn't seen him yet. He stands behind one of the elm trees that line the sidewalk and watches her. She could still see him if she looked his way, but she's keeping her eye on the boys. Norval notices Vicki Dolson standing in the shade of the change building reading a book. So some of the children in the pool must be hers. He always feels terrible when he sees Vicki. He can well imagine the conversations she and Blaine have in bed at night about options and blame and where to turn next.

A small girl in a bikini gets out of the shallow end of the pool and runs back to Vicki, who unfolds a towel and lays it out for her. The child lies down on her back, as though she's suntanning, even though Vicki has placed the towel in the shade. They look so ordinary, Vicki and the little girl, that Norval dares to hope maybe the Dolsons will be all right if Blaine can keep working construction.

The blue water looks inviting. Norval wonders if he should perhaps take up swimming for exercise in the summer. He's been told by his doctor to get on a regular exercise program, and Lila has certainly been after him about fitness. Once in a while he'll agree to walk with her around the town perimeter in the evening. Lila dresses in an exercise outfit and pumps her arms as she walks, and tries to get Norval to do the same. Normally an intense socializer, Lila is curt when they run into people they know, other couples in exercise wear. They exchange hellos without stopping, in recognition of the fact that they're all out for *earnest* walks, and doing something too important to be interrupted.

"This is not relaxing," Norval has said to Lila about the pace she sets. "It's causing my blood pressure to rise."

Lila explains to him about resting and working heart rates. She sounds like the coach of a track team. He wonders how she got to be such an expert on these matters.

But swimming. He used to swim, it's something he knows how to do.

As he watches from behind the tree, Rachelle gets down from the chair and calls to one of the boys. Norval can tell it's a Dolson by the way Vicki looks up from her book. Norval thinks Rachelle is about to reprimand the boy for fooling around, but then he sees her demonstrate a swimming stroke with her arms, perhaps the breast stroke (Norval never did master that one), and the boy strikes out across the pool. Rachelle nods approval. Then the boy gets out of the pool and climbs back up to the diving board, the highest one. Four other boys see him and they gather like sharks below the board. The Dolson boy walks to the end of the board, bounces a few times and then jumps, pulling his knees to his chest and hitting the water with a splash. As he comes to the surface, the other boys swim toward him and push him back under. When he comes to the surface again, they push him under once more. Norval is alarmed, but Rachelle is there right away. She blows her whistle and shouts so loud that Norval can hear her from his hiding place.

"You boys," Rachelle says. "Out of the pool!"

They look at her, and then one by one they swim to the edge and scramble out. Rachelle points to the chain-link fence and they line up. The Dolson boy starts to get out too, but Rachelle says, "Not you. You can stay in."

Vicki looks up from her book, but then goes back to reading when she sees it's not her own kids who are in trouble with the lifeguard. Rachelle gives the boys a lecture on dunking, all the while keeping her eye on the children who are still in the pool. The boys by the fence stare at Rachelle, completely infatuated by an older woman in a bikini. They sit down on the cement as she imposes a five-minute time-out.

Nothing has changed since his own childhood, Norval thinks. He decides to make his presence known and he steps out from behind the tree and waves to Rachelle. She waves back, and Norval heads down the sidewalk toward home.

When he gets there, he discovers the house is empty. Lila comes in shortly after, sporting a sleek hairdo.

"Oh, you're home," she says, checking herself in the hall mirror. "Thank goodness for Karla Norman. She knows how to do hair, that's for sure, even if her family is as trashy as they come." Then she tells Norval there's a niçoise salad in the fridge.

He announces that he's going for a swim at the pool, and would Lila mind packing up his lunch, he'll eat it at work?

She can't believe it. "You're going swimming? Today, just like that?"

"The pool is practically empty."

"Do you even own a swimsuit?" Lila asks.

"I believe I do," he says.

Norval goes up to the bedroom and rummages in his bureau drawers. He finds a swimsuit, an old-fashioned, eighties-style suit with long legs and bright yellow and pink splotches, reminiscent of the *Miami Vice* days.

When he carries it downstairs she takes one look and says, "Oh my God, you're not going to wear that. You'll humiliate Rachelle from here to next week."

"I don't think the style of my suit matters."

A look crosses Lila's face. "You're not doing this on purpose, are you, to punish Rachelle over last night? Because there's no need. She spent the night at Kristen's. Everything is fine."

"I'm not going to punish Rachelle by going swimming," he says.

"Because that would be childish, Norval, even for you."

"Even for me? What in the world is that supposed to mean? I just feel like going for a swim. You're the one who's always telling me I need exercise."

Lila hands him an insulated nylon lunch bag and says, "Well, that's a switch."

"And I hardly think that I, the hard-working breadwinner of this family, deserve to be called childish. You have no idea what I have to put up with every day, Lila."

"Okay," she says. "I'm sorry. Good for you. I commend you, Norval. Just don't embarrass Rachelle. What are you taking for a towel?"

"What should I take?" Norval asks.

Lila shakes her head and goes to find him a towel. She returns with a proper beach towel. "It doesn't match your suit," she says as she hands it to him.

"Is that required?" he asks. "Will it work better if it matches?"

"We don't own a towel the same colour as that suit," Lila says. "Thank God."

Before Norval leaves, she says, "I made arrangements for the wedding party hairstyles this morning. You have to make these arrangements well ahead of time."

He waits for what he knows is coming.

"I'm counting on you, Norval, to take care of the church business," Lila says.

"Not to worry," Norval says. "I will be so invigorated after my swim that I will march over to the church and put God's House in order."

By the time he gets back to the pool the Dolsons and the adult swimmers have gone, and he's amazed to find the pool is empty. He can see Rachelle standing in the shade, leafing through a magazine. She's pulled a sleeveless orange T-shirt on over her bikini, LIFEGUARD written on the front. Norval goes to the pool entrance and gets out his wallet to pay the girl at the ticket window.

"Slow day, eh," Norval says to the girl as he hands her a five-dollar bill.

"No kids allowed in the pool at noon," she says by way of explanation. "And also, you have to get out of the pool if we get a storm. It's a rule. No one in the water if there's lightning. You won't get your money back, just so's you know."

The sky is blue, like every other day this summer, and there's not a cloud in sight.

"I'll take my chances," Norval says. "But thanks for the warning."

When Norval comes out of the change room onto the pool deck, Rachelle looks up from her magazine.

"Holy crap," she says, staring at his suit. "What are you doing here?"

"What do you think?" Norval asks, dropping his towel on the cement.

"Can you even swim?" Rachelle asks. "Because if you can't, you have to go in the shallow end. You have to be able to swim two widths to go in the deep end."

"Believe me," Norval says. "I can swim."

He goes to the edge of the pool and wonders if he still can. He thinks about diving in but then changes his mind and lowers himself carefully into the blue water. He doesn't want his daughter to have to rescue him. She comes to the edge of the pool and watches him. The water is surprisingly cold.

"Don't watch too closely," Norval says, treading water and trying to catch his breath. "I'm not an Olympic swimmer or anything like that."

"That bathing suit is almost ugly enough to be cool," Rachelle says.

"Tell your mother that."

"I can't believe she let you out of the house with it."

Norval strikes out across the width of the pool with a stroke he used to call the Australian crawl. He wonders if they still call it that. He makes it across, but then he has to stop for a rest. He hangs on to the cement lip, breathing hard.

"Can you make it back?" Rachelle shouts. "Maybe move to the shallow end."

Norval strikes out again and struggles back to where Rachelle is still standing.

"That wasn't very impressive, was it," she says. "We offer a stroke improvement class for seniors. Maybe you should take that."

"Can I stay in the deep end or not?" Norval asks between gasps.

"I guess so."

"Go back to your magazine, then."

"Oh sure," Rachelle says. "And you'll drown and it will be my fault." She climbs up into the chair under the umbrella.

Norval rolls over onto his back and floats. He hears the girl from the ticket window call to Rachelle, but he can't hear what she's saying.

Rachelle says, "Wait 'til this guy's finished. He won't last long."

Norval swims a few more laps. He closes his eyes and feels the water on his body, remembers the feeling of buoyancy. He realizes that Lila is probably right, he should do something more to keep himself in shape. He swims back and forth, trying to remember how to breathe properly, and thinks about the strange reality that his irresponsible daughter is at this moment guarding his life. He remembers the time he once saved hers, when he found her hanging from the swing set in the backyard, the string ties on her sweatshirt caught somehow in the chains. He'd got there just in time. She was already turning blue. He'd sawn the swing set into pieces with a hacksaw after that, and taken it to the dump. He can still feel sick at the thought of how close they came to losing her. He felt no satisfaction in the knowledge that he'd saved her life, only terror that he might not have.

The pleasurable in life, he thinks, is never without a flip side. Sadly.

This water, that feels so good.

Vengeance

Lynn's been angry all morning and anyone with sense is staying out of her way. Angry, as in, *If I get my hands on this flirty little bitch Joni, she'll soon see who she's up against.* All through the lunch-hour rush she's sharp with Haley and she even has to apologize to the poor girl for making her cry over a broken cup. Lynn herself breaks a plate in the kitchen by slapping it down on the counter so hard it slides right off the other side and onto the ceramic tile floor.

When the restaurant clears and Lynn finally has time to sit by herself at a table and have a bite to eat, she thinks about how, lately, she's been *letting herself go.* She was conscientious for years about doing her yoga every night, no matter how tired she was, but for . . . what? six months now? a year? . . . she's given up on keeping in shape. And the funny thing is, she feels more self-absorbed now that she's given up than she did when she was trying. When she gets up in the morning and looks in the bathroom mirror she sees lines and wrinkles. When she walks past the full-length mirror in the bedroom she sees a thick body without a waist. When she looks in the mirror in the washroom at the Oasis, she sees hair that is streaked with grey and badly in need of styling. And as she works away at whatever she's doing, she puts all these glimpses of herself together into a picture of a thoroughly unattractive middle-aged woman who will never again get a compliment on her appearance, unless it's from another middle-aged woman who understands the meaning of *relative*. Even her daughters have noticed her declining appearance. The last time Leanne was home, she urged Lynn to join her on a spa weekend. "You look like you need one," Leanne said. As if someone who owns a restaurant can leave for the weekend, just like that.

Lynn wishes she'd appreciated her looks more when she still had them. She keeps coming back to that little slip of paper in her pocket, and to the thought that Hank hadn't appreciated her looks when she was young either, because if he had, what had he been doing sleeping with someone else? Is it possible that she's wasted herself on Hank? If she'd held out that time she left him, might she have done better? Might she have met a man who was positively bowled over by her, who thought she was Helen of Troy? Well, it's too late for that now.

By the time Lynn finishes her lunch she doesn't know if she's depressed or angry, and if she is angry, whether she's mad at Hank or herself, and if she's depressed, what she's depressed about. Not just the slip of paper from Hank's pocket, because the concern with her loss of looks predates its discovery. Even so, all morning long, every fifteen minutes if she could manage it, she'd gone to the phone and dialled the number on the piece of paper and then hung up. She knows her behaviour is crazy. Maybe she just wants to torment this Joni person for daring to give her husband a phone number, and for daring to be young (she has to be young: the handwriting, the loopy little circle above the *i*). She can just see her: Joni with her little waist and perky breasts. She hopes she has unattractive calves. Lynn used to have good, well-shaped legs.

She can't stop herself, she keeps thinking about those years when she was at her most attractive, and they were the same years that Hank was still travelling the amateur rodeo circuit with his buddies. He was no longer a regular weekend warrior and, yes, he stayed home when there was crop to put in, hay to take off, calves to ship, an event to attend with Lynn and the girls. But she knew where his heart was, where he'd rather be if he hadn't accepted the role of family man. Heaven to Hank was a weekend of rodeo and coming home late on Sunday night to all the benefits of marriage: Lynn's good cooking, the adoration of his children, clean laundry and, of course, sex. The truth is, she hated those years. She was always tired from being both homemaker and Hank's hired hand. She worried that he'd get hurt, and then where would they be? Or that he'd cave to the temptation of the rodeo groupies, of which there was no shortage, and she knew what cowboy church was for on Sunday morning. Even after Hank swore off booze and promised that rodeo for him was a good ride and a lot of hanging around the chutes with the other cowboys, the marriage was clouded by suspicion and resentment.

Until that August when Dana was eight years old and got sick with meningitis and almost died. Hank pretty much sat by her bedside until she got better, and after she was well again, Lynn had taken both girls and left for a while, went to her parents' place. She couldn't even tell Hank why, what was wrong, what he could do to fix things. When Lynn did go back, not too long before Christmas, she still couldn't explain what had caused her to leave, but Hank seemed to understand. And Lynn herself had been truly regretful when she walked back into their house and saw the look of relief on his face. Instead of thinking about Hank's weekend absences and the dalliance that had hung over their marriage for so long, she'd thought what her unhappiness had done to him. For the first time, she recognized that her own dissatisfaction with married life was not entirely Hank's fault.

And then that same year, both of Hank's travelling partners got married, one at Christmas and the other in the spring, and although no announcement was made, they all gave up rodeo for good and settled down to being plain old-fashioned mixed farmers with wives and children. Hank bought another quarter-section of cultivated land, and leased another of pasture so he could expand his operation. He loved his girls. Lynn believed that he loved her—that he had never stopped loving her. The night with the rodeo girl faded into a memory in the same league as high school. The threat of another woman never again reared its head.

Until today.

Lynn gathers her lunch plate and coffee cup and takes them to the kitchen, where Haley is pretty much hiding from her.

"Don't worry," Lynn says to her. "I'm over it. You can sweep under the tables now. Please."

Haley grabs the broom and dustpan and hurries for the door, not believing that Lynn is over whatever was bothering her. And as Haley leaves the kitchen, Lynn stares after her, at her tiny waist and her skin-tight jeans, and thinks about how her own daughters are grown up and don't need her any more, and once again how she's let herself go. She can just hear the snobby town women like Lila Birch: *Lynn Trass has sure let herself go, hasn't she, too bad, she used to be quite attractive.* Women like Lila go to

fitness classes in fancy outfits and have treadmills in their base-
ments. Well, who but the banker's wife and the doctor's wife
have got time and money for that?

Obviously, she's not over it. She goes once again to the pay
phone and dials Joni's number, lets it ring until a girlish voice
says hello, and then she hangs up.

It doesn't make her feel good to do this. It just makes her feel
older, and more depressed about being older. And then this makes
her want to dial the number again, and this time the voice says,
"Who is this? I can trace the call, you know. If you call again,
that's what I'm going to do."

Lynn slams the phone down. They can't trace calls from a pay
phone, can they? She thinks about how embarrassing it would be
to get caught. But she's not giving up, she's not done with young
Joni yet. She's got a cell phone out in the car for emergencies and
she's pretty sure you can't trace cell phone calls.

She goes to the door of the restaurant and yells to Haley, "I'll
be right back. Everything okay in there?"

"No problem," says Haley, who thinks Lynn is acting pretty
strange today, all these trips to the foyer. She followed her once
and peeked through the glass door to see where she was going,
and saw that she was dropping a quarter in the pay phone. Now
she watches as Lynn goes to her car. She almost expects her to
get in and drive away, go on some mysterious errand, but Lynn
doesn't, she gets something from the car and then walks back
toward the restaurant, so Haley ducks behind the counter and
makes like she's interested in what's under the glass. Not gum
and candy bars like you might expect, but Hank's barbed-wire
collection. IMPROVED 2-POINT TWISTED, Haley reads on a card
next to one of the samples of wire. *Twisted is right,* she thinks,
and then, *I come from a town where people collect barbed wire.*

As Lynn comes through the restaurant door, Haley notices that she's tracking a piece of yellow paper under her shoe, a flyer of some kind, and it drops right next to where Haley is standing, so she bends over and picks it up.

"'The end is near,'" Haley reads out loud.

"What's that?" Lynn asks.

"'The end is near,'" Haley says, holding out the flyer. "That's what it says."

"Oh for heaven's sake," Lynn says. "Throw it out."

Haley does. Then she goes to the washroom, and when she comes back she says to Lynn, "Do you think I have too much body fat?"

Lynn just about chokes. "You can't be serious," she says.

"I don't know," Haley says. "That's why I'm asking. Those athlete girls—the really competitive ones—have no body fat. They don't even have periods, I read, because they don't have any body fat."

"You're not fat," Lynn says in exasperation. She'd like to shoot the girl. Wait thirty years, she thinks, and then you'll know for sure what body fat is. No periods and a whole lot of body fat. Just you wait.

"Anyway, I guess I'll go now," Haley says. "Seth is picking me up. See you tomorrow."

Lynn watches as Haley goes outside and stands in front of the restaurant, waiting for her ride.

Haley's replacement is late. Lynn schedules the girls so they overlap by fifteen minutes just to make sure she's not stuck on her own, especially for the supper hour. She'd better call now and make sure her next girl is coming—she thinks Rosemary is scheduled until closing, an extra-long shift. On second thought, there's another call she should make first, while she's alone. She gets out the cell phone and dials Joni's number, but this time a voice tells her that the number is unavailable. So Joni has her phone turned off. Well, Lynn thinks, that won't last long since phones are like oxygen to girls these days. She calls Rosemary's home number and is told by her mother that her boyfriend picked her up half an hour ago. Rosemary's mother wonders if something has happened.

Lynn assures her that nothing has happened. Kids, she says, they have no sense of time.

Ten minutes later Rosemary walks in the door. "Here I am," she announces cheerily.

As though the whole world has been waiting for her.

"Call your mother, Rosemary," Lynn says. "Let her know you're here."

Lynn sticks the cell phone in her apron pocket, wondering if she's going crazy.

Somewhere Else

Shiloh Dolson is standing on the highway with his thumb out. This is a change in plan, but after he'd gone back to the school-yard for his backpack and then returned to the swimming pool, his mother was gone. He'd checked the parking lot for her car and it wasn't there. He thought about walking up Main Street again looking for her, but instead he walked to the western edge of Juliet with some vague notion of going to the highway construction site where his father is working.

But cars keep passing him by. He's about to give up when, finally, a couple in a half-ton stop and a woman opens the passenger door for Shiloh to hop in. He likes the fact that she slides over on the bench seat to make room, and doesn't expect him to get in the middle, like a kid. He puts his backpack on his knee, noticing that the seat behind them is stuffed with suitcases and boxes. The radio dial is set on the local station, a program called *The Trading Post* that Shiloh's mother sometimes listens to. A man named Ernie is trying to sell an old black-and-white television. The picture doesn't work, he's saying, but the sound comes in clear as a bell.

"Now who would buy a wrecked black-and-white TV?" the woman asks, looking at Shiloh as if he should know the answer.

He notices that her eye makeup is smeared, as though she might have been crying. She has feathery yellow hair cut all different lengths and Shiloh thinks she looks like a canary.

She says to Shiloh, "What possible use could an old broken-down TV be?"

Shiloh says, "You could put it somewhere you don't need to watch it, and listen to the sound," just as Ernie is saying pretty much the same thing. The shop, Ernie suggests, or maybe the garage. "That way," Ernie says, "a guy can keep up with his programs and still get his work done." The announcer asks Ernie how much he wants for the TV and Ernie says three dollars or best offer.

"Why doesn't he just give it away?" the bird woman asks.

"He's having fun, Janice," the driver says. "You remember what fun is."

Shiloh looks at him. He has tattoos on his forearms, like he just got out of the army, or maybe jail.

"Who knows how many calls he'll get because of that TV," says the driver, whose name turns out to be Terry. "Keep Ernie busy most of the day."

"Well, that's sad," Janice says. "To think someone could be so lonely."

"He's not lonely," Terry says. "He's inventive."

"I hope I'm not going to cry again," Janice says. "I'm getting tired of doing my eyes." Then she says to Shiloh, "You're just a kid. Close your eyes if you don't want to see crying."

There it is again. *Just a kid.*

"I'm not a kid," Shiloh says, trying to sit taller.

Terry snorts, but he doesn't say anything.

Shiloh puts his arm across the seat-back behind Janice, the way he's seen his father do when he's riding with someone else. He's careful not to touch her.

"You shouldn't take a ride with strangers, you know," Janice says. "Where are you going anyway?"

"There's a construction site up ahead," Shiloh says. "I've got a job there."

"I'm not buying that," Terry says. "You're too young to work construction."

Up ahead, the flag girl and her SLOW sign come into view. Terry whistles at her as they approach and Janice gives him a playful smack on the arm. Shiloh can see his father's truck parked in the ditch, his father on the packer with his back to them.

"So you want out here, then?" Terry asks.

"No," Shiloh says. "There's another site up ahead." He turns his head away from the packer as they pass slowly, and then he makes a decision that surprises him. He asks, "How far are you two going anyway?" Once he's asked, it seems as though this had been his plan all along.

"I don't know if we should tell him," Janice says to Terry.

"Why not?" Terry asks.

"Well, duh," Janice says. "We're on the run in case you didn't know."

"We're not on the fucking run," Terry says.

"It doesn't matter to me if you are," Shiloh says. Then he asks, "How far west?"

"A lot farther west than your construction site," Terry says.

"Are you going as far as Calgary?" Shiloh persists.

"Is that where the construction is?" Terry asks. "Calgary?"

"I lied," Shiloh says. "Bible school. I go to summer bible school in Calgary. I was supposed to catch the Greyhound, but I missed it." He congratulates himself for coming up with this.

"Well, you're just lucky we came along, then," Janice says.

"I guess," Shiloh says, thinking that Janice is about as smart as the canary she resembles. "Anyway, I'll get a lift to Calgary, if you don't mind."

"I don't think so," Terry says.

"Terry," Janice says. "The kid's on his way to bible school." She turns to Shiloh. "Just ignore him," she says. She pauses for a minute, then asks, "So, how many brothers and sisters do you have? What's your mom like? Do you have any pets?"

Shiloh doesn't answer her. Instead he says, "This radio station is so lame."

A woman is trying to sell living room furniture. "I have a sofa," she is saying, "harvest gold, a little old-fashioned but in good condition. And a recliner, slightly worn. And two wingbacks, and a set of drapes, harvest gold also."

"What are wingbacks?" the announcer asks. "Sounds like ducks. Wingback ducks."

"Chairs," the woman says. "They match the sofa set."

"How come you're selling all your furniture?" the announcer asks.

"I've had the good fortune of winning a little money on the lottery," the woman says. "My daughter thinks I should give it away to charity. She's born-again, and she doesn't believe in gambling and says the only way it's okay is if I give away the money, but I've ordered new furniture. I think I deserve that, even if my daughter doesn't think so."

"Maybe that daughter will be at your summer bible school,"

Terry says. Then he says to Janice, "The kid's right. Change the station."

"Just let me hear how much she's asking," Janice says.

"I'd like eight hundred dollars for the works," the woman says. "It all matches."

"Way too much," Janice says. "She'll never get that for used furniture, especially not if it's harvest gold."

She fiddles with the dial but doesn't find anything to her liking and finally shuts the radio off. "I think it's great that you're going to bible school," she says. "What do you do at bible school anyway?"

"Bible things," Shiloh says. Then he adds, "We sing. Hymns and junk like that."

"He's not going to bible school, Janice," Terry says.

"Is that true?" she asks Shiloh.

He doesn't answer.

"Oh," says Janice. "Well, I guess that doesn't surprise me. Probably a good thing. Those bible girls are all so dowdy. They don't wear makeup, you know. God, I just hate to think. You should see me with no makeup."

Shiloh listens to Janice and thinks she's like a hard rubber ball bouncing around on a piece of concrete, veering off in whatever direction the surface sends her. He wonders what they're running away from. The only thing he can think of is the police.

As though she can read his mind, she says, "We're really in love, you know, me and Terry. His wife and the whole town hate us, but they don't understand."

"Janice," Terry says. "He's a kid. Stop telling him stuff, for Christ sake."

There's a box of Kleenex on the floor at Shiloh's feet and Janice reaches down for it, and then sits with it on her lap.

"I'm not a kid," Shiloh says.

"Yes, you are," Terry says, "and this is as far as your ride goes." Terry pulls over onto the shoulder and reaches across Janice to open the passenger-side door. "Out you go," he says. "Running away is serious business. Believe me, you're not nearly old enough. Wait until you're our age and then maybe give it a try."

"You go back home," Janice says, beginning to sniffle again. "And watch who you get in a car with. If you smell booze, don't get in."

"Thanks for nothing," Shiloh says as he slams the door. "And I hope you get caught."

Janice and Terry pull back onto the highway and he watches after them until their truck disappears. He doesn't bother sticking his thumb out again. He doesn't want to go to Calgary any more, but instead of crossing the highway to go back to Juliet he steps down into the ditch. The hay has been cut, but the round bales are a long way apart because it's such a dry year. Shiloh walks toward the closest one, and when he gets there he settles down on the north side where he's hidden from the traffic. He can hear the vehicles passing, cars and farm trucks and semi-trailers, and even a police car with its siren going. He opens his backpack and takes out the bag of cookies. He closes his eyes and eats an Oreo and smells the cut grass and the sage growing along the fence line. A meadowlark sings from a fence post close by. The east and west traffic sounds compete with each other like duelling banjos, and as Shiloh listens, his bad day vanishes. The ditch doesn't feel like any particular place, and it could be any hour. In the shade of the hay bale, the temperature is neither too hot nor too cold. It's perfect. As Shiloh nods off, he thinks, *I got to somewhere else after all.*

A Good Map

The Watch

The words *mortal wounds* keep popping into Lee's head. Astrid used to tease him when he was little by saying, "I think it's a mortal wound," whenever he would acquire a cut or a scratch needing her attention and a Band-aid. He feels now as though his saddle-sore body needs attention, and he rides with the phrase repeating over and over, and after a while it switches to *mortal remains,* which he doesn't like the sound of. And then for some reason *earthly possessions,* which is better because it leads him to think about things other than pain and discomfort. Astrid's tea service, for example. How it needs polishing. Where the polish is kept. And what *Use the silver tea service* might mean, and in what context it could be taken as practical advice. In the light of day it seems simple: be hospitable. Astrid was always hospitable, and she admired people who used her well. Lee always thought that was a funny way to put it: *She used me very well.*

The going is a little easier on this leg, as George said it would be. The ground is still sandy but the surface has been contained by the roots of grass and pasture sage. There are no more dunes, just sporadic patches like children's sandboxes that have been allowed to spill over onto backyard lawns. Lee is grateful for George's old hat, which is keeping his face shaded from the sun. He's no longer thinking about who might haul him the rest of the way; he knows no one along this stretch. He tries to focus on the ground that he's covering, where he is in proximity to home. A map begins to develop in his head. He almost wishes he had a piece of paper and a pencil with him so he could record his route. There are photographs of ancient maps in one of Lester's atlases and Lee remembers the curious drawings included by the early mapmakers: exotic birds and animals, unusual landmarks, depictions of significant events along the way. Cartography was an art, Lester told him, before it was a science. Lee tries to remember the landmarks he's encountered so far, mapping them in his head and adding little anthropological details much like the quotations he once kept about the Bedouins in his scrapbook: *The dunes provide a handy place for local teenagers to drink their ritual beer away from the watchful eyes of adults.* Or, *George and Anna Varga are an interesting study of lifelong familial companionship, and Anna's kitchen is welcome relief for the hot and hungry traveller.* He has no idea where the word *familial* came from.

He crosses a Texas gate into what he assumes is community pasture, and he sees signs of cattle: droppings baked dry in the sun, narrow trails that wind their way toward water. He follows one of these cattle trails, and when it reaches the lip of a coulee, Lee decides to get out of the sun for a while. The horse edges down the south-facing drop, picking his way through clumps of cactus. As they descend farther, they encounter low shrubs and scruffy stands of willow and black poplar, the welcome relief of shade.

There's a creek running through the coulee, not much of one, but when they get to the bottom the horse immediately steps into the shallow water and drinks. Lee closes his eyes and listens to the quiet sound of birds and leaves rustling. When he feels the horse shifting beneath him, he opens his eyes and realizes just in time that the horse is about to drop and roll in the water. Lee lifts the reins and gives the horse the heel of his boot, and the horse does a little start as though he's just realized that a rider is still up there.

Lee decides to give the horse a break by leading him through the coulee for a ways. He slides to the ground and splashes himself with water, and then sets off on foot. He discovers it feels good to walk. The horse follows him willingly, tugging just once in a while as he snatches at a mouthful of grass.

Lee has to keep his eyes on the ground to avoid tripping on roots and deadfall. Even so, he steps on the rotten branch of a black poplar, and it snaps, and one end flips up and Lee sees a glint of metal, hardly noticeable except that the sun is shining through the trees right on it. He stops and brushes the dry grass away, and sees that it's a tarnished and rusted pocket watch. He uses his shirt to wipe the dirt from the watch and tries to open the face but it's too rusted. For the second time today he thinks about Lester's pocket watch, the one he'd broken and thrown away in the sand in order to conceal his crime. As he walks through the deadfall, putting off the return up into the hot sun, he remembers how he'd surprised himself with his ability to lie, straight-faced, when Lester found the watch was missing.

Lee knows the empty velvet box is in Astrid and Lester's bedroom closet because he'd put it there himself, with the blankets and photo albums and other possessions, after one of the neighbour women found it when she was helping him with Astrid's clothes. He'd hardly been able to bring himself to touch the box, he'd felt so guilty at seeing it once again. It brought back shame, for the old crime, and for every ungrateful thing he'd ever said or done.

Now, with a different watch in his hand, he thinks again of how it all started with temptation, with his knowing the watch was in Lester's drawer because Astrid had shown it to him one Saturday when he was eight years old and feeling dejected because Lester had lost patience with him. Lester had been trying to repair a combine and he needed Lee's small body to reach into a tight space he himself couldn't get to, which Lee did but he couldn't figure out what he was supposed to do after that, couldn't follow Lester's instructions, and Lester finally said, "You might as well go to the house." *Go to the house* was the ultimate dismissal. It was what Lester said to the dog when he was getting in the way. All the dogs they ever had were trained to go to the house and lie on the step, banished, at Lester's command.

Astrid, feeling sorry for him, took him up to the bedroom and opened the top drawer of the oak dresser, and withdrew the velvet box. Inside was a man's silver pocket watch on a chain—a fob watch it was called—and Astrid said it came from Norway and had belonged to Lester's grandfather. "That would be your great-great-uncle," she explained. An impossible number of years for Lee to comprehend. Astrid told him the watch was an heirloom, and that Lester used to worry about who would get the watch, "but now he doesn't worry about that any more," she told Lee, "because he has you, and someday the watch will be yours."

Astrid let Lee touch the watch. He asked her if it worked. She said it did, but it was delicate because it was very old, so she didn't want to risk winding it up. Lester, she said, would be upset if he even knew she was showing Lee the watch. After Lee had a good look at it, Astrid put the watch away and they went back downstairs. "Remember," Astrid said, "that Lester may seem impatient sometimes, but you're like a son to him."

A month or so later, when Astrid was in town and Lester was in the field, Lee took the watch out of Lester's drawer again. He'd only meant to look at it, but the temptation to see if it worked was too great, and besides, he already thought of the watch as his. He wound it and listened to it tick. Then he wound it some more and it stopped ticking. He tried to unwind it and the winding mechanism came off. Through the bedroom window Lee could see Lester coming into the yard on the tractor and he panicked. He put the blue velvet box back in the drawer and the watch in his pocket and ran downstairs and outside to get his bike.

He rode along the dirt trail into Hank Trass's sandy lease northwest of the farm, climbed through the wire fence and up the first sand hill he came to, and pitched the watch as far out into the sand as he could throw it. Then he ran back down the hill, his shoes filling with sand, and he found a stand of poplar trees that had been covered right up to their leafy branches, so they looked like trees that had been chopped off and stuck back in the sand, and he stayed there all afternoon. When he got home Astrid sent him to his room without supper because he'd been gone so long.

The watch wasn't missed for a year. Then one day Lester took Lee upstairs to show him something and Lee knew it was going to be the watch. When the watch wasn't in the box, Lester called Astrid and Lee was terrified, sure that Astrid would know. But Astrid looked at Lee, and then she told Lester that she'd sent the watch away to be cleaned and it had gotten lost in the mail. She sent Lee to his own room and then she and Lester had a hushed discussion behind their closed bedroom door. Afterwards, Astrid had come to Lee's room and asked him straight out if he had taken the watch. Lee had shaken his head and the watch was never mentioned again.

All through his school years, whenever Lee went up the road and west onto Hank's lease, he couldn't help looking for the watch. He knew the chances of finding it were slim, and he didn't know what he'd do if he did happen to find it, but he believed it was possible that one day he would be walking and there it would be. The sand was constantly changing, after all, covering and uncovering roots and bones and objects discarded by their owners. But he never found it.

Lee slips the rusty old watch in his pocket, throws the reins over the horse's neck, and lifts himself into the saddle. He groans out loud—like an old man, he thinks, but who's to hear—and once again settles into a position that can't in any way be called comfortable. Luckily, the expectation for comfort is long gone.

Although the shade of the coulee is preferable to the heat of high ground, Lee knows the creek will wind and cut back endlessly, adding miles to the journey, so he urges the horse toward the north-facing slope. At the top, he sees a pair of antelope stock-still and staring at him. Up ahead, a fence and a waving field of yellow wheat. The crop confuses him for a minute, and then he realizes that he's ridden far enough south that he's back into cultivated land. To the west he can see a farmyard. He tries to remember who lives there: it's the old Stanish place, he thinks, recently bought by a couple from Ireland. There was a story about them in the local paper, how they couldn't afford to buy land in Ireland so they looked at Canada. They were planning to raise sheep and found the people of Juliet friendly and helpful. Lee looks for signs of sheep but he doesn't see any. In fact, the place looks deserted and run-down.

He watches as the antelope bound away from him and scramble through the fence, down on their knees and up again so fast it's as though they've run right through it. He adds the fence and the farmyard to the map in his head and composes a notation: *The land to the south is marked by fences, a sure sign that the settlers of the area intended permanence rather than a nomadic lifestyle.* Then he gets carried away: *A deserted farmyard is a sad reminder of the failed homesteader, who gave it his best effort and then left again with all his earthly possessions, mortally wounded by the loneliness of geographic isolation.*

He sees a gate in the wire fence and turns the horse toward it.

Daisy Breaks Something

"When are we going to drop this cake off?" Martin asks. He's still got it on his lap while Vicki drives her old Cutlass up and down the streets and alleys of town looking for Shiloh, and then she gives up in annoyance.

"That boy," she says. "He has a thing or two to learn."

"What?" Daisy asks. "What does he have to learn?"

"Many things, Daisy," Vicki says. "Too numerous to mention. And you'll have to learn them too, unfortunately."

"Will I be bad like Shiloh?" Daisy asks.

"Shiloh isn't bad," Vicki says. "All teenagers have things to figure out and it makes them moody. And don't ask me what *moody* means. Ask your father."

Daisy turns her attention to another topic: they could stop at the Saan Store, she suggests, and look at toys and maybe Shiloh will see the car parked out front. Vicki agrees to this plan before she takes time to think about it, and once the kids have their hearts set on it, she can't back out even though she knows the afternoon is passing. She angle parks on Main Street in front of the Saan, and the kids throw open the car doors before she's barely stopped, and they're into the store and heading straight for the toy section before Vicki can give them the usual warning about don't break anything because she can't afford to pay for it right now. To give some purpose to this stop, Vicki checks the hardware section for blanchers. The clerk—obviously displeased because the kids appear to be treating the toy section like a day-care centre—suggests that Vicki try Robinson's. So Vicki gets the kids to put all the toys back and they cross the street. At Robinson's, the kids do the same thing they did at the Saan. Daisy even asks the clerk for a piece of paper and a pencil so she can write down all the choices for Christmas. The clerk—a teenage girl Vicki doesn't know—tells Daisy it's too early for a Christmas list, Santa hibernates in the summer, doesn't she know that—but she ends up giving Daisy a pencil and a discarded till receipt.

The bell on the glass door of the shop rings and Vicki sees Marian Shoenfeld from the drive-in enter the store. She watches as Marian walks with purpose toward the clothing section and stops in Women's Wear. Now Marian is a woman who would have her beans in the freezer the day they were picked, thinks Vicki. She probably has her whole house in order, top to bottom—or more correctly, Willard's house, she supposes. She sees Marian take a mint green outfit off the rack and hold it up to herself in front of a mirror. It looks like a pantsuit of some kind, slacks and a vest. Curious that Marian is buying a new pantsuit. Maybe she's going to a special event, a wedding or a graduation. She doesn't think Marian is the kind of person who would buy a new outfit without a reason.

Marian takes the green outfit into a change room and Vicki goes back to looking for a blancher. Her eye travels along the row of cake pans and muffin tins, fridge-to-microwave containers, no-stick frying pans, stovetop kettles and cookware sets, colanders and sieves and, finally, canning supplies, and she concludes that Robinson's does not have blanchers. She won't bother asking the clerk; she can tell by looking at the girl that she wouldn't know a blancher if it jumped up and bit her.

She heads back to the toy section, where another young clerk is in the aisle with the kids, giving them instructions as though she's their teacher and they're on a field trip.

"Put one toy back before you look at another," she instructs. "You wouldn't leave things lying all over at home, so you don't do that here either. And I hope at least one of you is planning to buy something."

Normally this would make Vicki mad but right now she doesn't have time to be snippy with the girl. She tells the kids to put the toys back where they found them, which they do without arguing.

"Okay," she says. "One more place to look and then we have to head home." She herds them out the door and then down the block for one last stop at Jackson's Hardware. She decides that if Shiloh hasn't found them by the time they're done there she'll drive home without him and let Blaine deal with him later. It wouldn't hurt Shiloh to stew for a while anyway, although she doesn't imagine being left behind will teach him much. It will just give him another reason to be irritated with her. Well, at least she can use his disappearance as an excuse for her extended stay in town.

As they enter the hardware store, old George Varga from up north is just leaving, positioning what looks like a new hat on his head. He holds the door for Vicki and the kids, and as soon as they're inside the kids head for the back. There aren't any small toys here, but there are plenty of tricycles, bicycles and other riding toys, and a bright red plastic wagon that the twins have their eyes on. The store is air-conditioned, and Vicki feels the relief from the heat outside. Mrs. Jackson, a middle-aged woman (who dresses very well for a day of standing behind the till in a hardware store, Vicki thinks) is admiring her newly manicured fingernails. Vicki guesses that she's had them done at the new place in Swift Current, called Pretty Pinkies. The young girls get wild patterns and rhinestones, but Mrs. Jackson's nails are just plain red.

She asks Mrs. Jackson if she has blanchers in stock.

Vicki sees Mrs. Jackson's eyes leave her new nails and dart around the store trying to fix on the kids. Why does this happen everywhere they go? Vicki wonders. Her kids are not bad. They don't steal. There are a lot of them, but what's wrong with that? She and Blaine are keeping the numbers up in the Juliet school. The twins will be a bonus in the fall, a double addition to the kindergarten class. She and Blaine should be thanked for having so many kids.

"I'm sorry, Vicki," she says, "they're all gone. I didn't bring many in from the warehouse this year because of nobody having any garden. My own garden went to the grasshoppers. They just devoured it. I'm especially sorry not to have any green beans."

Vicki considers telling her she knows where she can get some, but says instead, "I just happened to be in town today, you know, and thought I would pick up a blancher."

Mrs. Jackson says she can have one in for her by tomorrow afternoon, and Vicki is about to say that will be too late—even now she's going to need ten stoves and forty blanchers to get the beans done before Blaine gets home—when a loud crash comes from the back of the store, and a child starts to howl at full volume.

"Mom," Martin shouts, "Daisy's broken something."

Vicki assumes that means a limb. Mrs. Jackson assumes it means a piece of merchandise. They're both right. Daisy had been climbing up and down the cans in a pyramid-shaped display of barn paint. She fell from the fourth row and landed on her wrist. The cans luckily fell the other way, but one of the lids came off and paint is now spilling out in a widening pool of deep red. The paint has already run under a refrigerator and an apartment-sized clothes dryer by the time the two women get to the back of the store. Vicki's first thought is that the paint is the same colour as Mrs. Jackson's new fingernails, even as Daisy is screaming loudly enough for the whole town to hear. Vicki tries to examine Daisy's arm, but Daisy won't let her touch it. Mrs. Jackson grabs a package of paper towels off the shelf and tries, unsuccessfully, to stop the paint spill from spreading. The other four kids stand in a row and watch, their eyes wide.

"You're in trouble now, Daisy," says Martin. "The lady has paint on her trousers."

Vicki wonders where Martin got the word *trousers,* what a funny word for a child to use. She glances at Mrs. Jackson and, yes, she has paint on the hem of her beige pants, and on her shoes as well. It's a disaster. She feels so bad but she doesn't know what to do, and she doesn't know whether Daisy is really hurt or just crying because she's afraid she'll catch heck for spilling the paint. There are no bones sticking out, but still, something could be broken in there. She decides she'd better get Daisy to the Health Centre and have her arm checked by the doctor. Mrs. Jackson thinks so too. Vicki doesn't have a clue what to do about the paint.

"What a mess" is all she can think of to say.

Mrs. Jackson is thinking the same thing, but she hustles the family to the front of the store, saying, "Never mind that. Just get her to the Centre. Poor little thing, I hope the doctor is in." There's only one doctor, and he covers the health centres in three communities. Vicki says that she'll come back to clean up the paint, and Mrs. Jackson thinks, what a circus that would be, Vicki and her kids cleaning up all that enamel paint.

"Don't give it another thought," Mrs. Jackson says. She's hoping the appliances aren't damaged. If they are, she certainly can't ask Vicki and Blaine to contribute to their repair; from what she's heard, it's a wonder Vicki can afford to buy a blancher. Anyway, how can she be angry when the little girl is crying so hard she can't catch her breath? How can one little girl make so much noise? It's causing her ears to ring. If all the Dolson kids screamed at once, the whole town would go deaf.

"Drive carefully," Mrs. Jackson says as Vicki hurries the kids to the car.

"If you happen to see Shiloh," Vicki calls to her, "tell him to wait here on Main Street. I'll come back for him."

Mrs. Jackson has no idea who Shiloh is. Another of the many children, she supposes. She can still hear Daisy screaming as Vicki turns off Main Street at the corner. Mrs. Jackson thanks her lucky stars that she and Mr. Jackson weren't blessed with children. She just could not have stood it.

"Daisy," Vicki says as they turn the corner and head toward the Health Centre. "I know you're hurt but you're going to cause me to get in an accident."

"I'm the one who was in an accident," Daisy manages to say between wails. "It was an accident, I promise." Then crying again.

"I know it was an accident," Vicki says. And before she can stop herself, "Everything that happens to us is a bloody accident."

"You said *bloody*," says one of the twins. He has to shout to be heard over Daisy's crying. "I'm telling Dad."

"Nobody tell Dad anything," Vicki says. "Leave that to me, if you don't mind." She doesn't know what she'll tell him about today. One thing for sure, he'll be furious.

"What's bloody?" Lucille asks, her tiny voice a squeal as she tries to raise it above the racket. "Is Daisy's arm bloody?"

"All of you," Vicki says, raising her own voice. "Shut up. Shut the bloody hell up right now."

The silence in the car is instant. Even Daisy stops. Vicki never yells. The children look at her in shock.

There are at least ten seconds of blissful quiet before Daisy starts up again. With renewed vigour.

Temptation

When Blaine's crew shuts down for the day, Blaine sits in his truck, parked in the ditch, and watches the rest of the men get into their vehicles and leave the construction site. He can see that Justine is doing the same thing he is, sitting in her car, waiting. When they're the only two left, he watches as she tries to start her car, to no avail. He navigates his truck up out of the ditch and pulls alongside Justine, the vehicles facing and the open driver windows side by side.

"Problem with the car?" Blaine asks.

"It always does this," she says.

"Want me to have a look?"

"That's okay. It'll start eventually. You have to ask just right."

"Must be a woman, then," Blaine says.

"Ha ha," Justine says.

There's an awkward silence, and then Blaine says, "Hop in if you don't feel like waiting around. I'll give you a lift into town. If you're sure you don't want me to have a look."

Justine rolls up the windows in her car before getting out and into Blaine's truck.

"It'll still be here tomorrow," she says. "You can look then. Or maybe someone will steal it, which would actually be great."

Blaine backs off the approach, puts the truck in gear and guns it. They fishtail along the unfinished stretch of highway.

"Yahoo, cowboy," says Justine, laughing.

Blaine tries to think what he can talk to her about, now that they're alone together. He wonders if there's any chance she engineered this ride to town with him, and the possibility makes him nervous, and eager at the same time. Maybe too eager. He stands a chance of making a fool of himself.

"So, how's the job?" he asks.

"Kind of boring," she says. "But a job's a job."

"The guys treat you all right? Some of them are a little rough."

"They're all talk," she says. "Anyway, I'm just the flag girl. Not much of a threat. Might be different if I was the foreman. That might not go over."

Blaine laughs. "You're right about that," he says. "I'd have a little trouble with you as the foreman myself."

"Well, I'd do a better job than the alcoholic hobbit," she says. "He's so pathetic." Her tone is completely dismissive. "Anyway, someday I *could* be the foreman of a crew like this. Then they'd have to watch their own asses instead of mine."

Such confidence, Blaine thinks. Only the young. They reach the end of the construction and Blaine angles the truck around the barricade and onto the pavement.

"Do you want to grab a cold beer somewhere?" Justine asks, as though they were old friends.

Well, they are, sort of, he supposes. Still, he doesn't know what the suggestion means. She might be playing with him. He decides to ignore the question.

"So you're a university student," he says. "How'd you end up in Juliet?"

"I applied on that government Web site for summer jobs and this is what I got. I don't mind. I'm staying with a pretty nice family. Room and board."

Blaine asks her what she's studying and she tells him engineering.

"No kidding," he says.

"There are girls in engineering these days, you know," she says. "I heard they have a quota, but I'm not sure if that's true."

"Hey," Blaine says. "You're in Juliet. It's going to take us a while to catch up, guys like me anyway." He adds, "Old guys like me," with emphasis on the word *old.*

He half waits for her to tell him he's not old, but then is glad when she doesn't.

She says something else, though, that makes him doubt his own hearing. She says, "We should just keep on driving. Or maybe head south. We could go across the border into Montana for a beer."

"Why would we want to do that?" Blaine asks. Carefully. Something is coming back to him here, some knowledge of a game he hasn't played since he started dating Vicki. There's a skill to checking out a situation like this without committing yourself.

"No reason," says Justine. "Just for something to do. Something crazy."

Blaine looks at Justine and thinks how young and pretty she is. She's wearing lightweight coveralls with her white T-shirt underneath, stretched tight across her small breasts. The T-shirt is so white it's practically luminescent even though it's dusty from her day on the highway. Is she young enough to be his daughter? He calculates. Yes, she's that young. Or he's that old, depending which way you look at it. If she's genuinely asking him to take off down the road with her—and she appears to be—he's in the middle of a serious wet dream. Either that or a beer commercial.

"I'm a married man, Justine," he says.

"I know that," she says. "I asked around. Kids too. Anyway, I've seen your wife and kids in town. You're lucky."

Blaine snorts, he can't help it. "If you think I'm lucky, you've got a shingle flapping on the roof. If I were lucky I'd have a million dollars instead of a pile of debt."

"Oh," Justine says. "I see. Well, I'm pretty lucky. You can hang around with me for a while and see if it rubs off."

When they get to Juliet, Blaine turns onto the access road into town.

"Where do you want dropped off?" he asks.

"So we're not going to Montana, I guess," Justine says. "Too bad. You can drop me at the post office, then. I'll pop in and get my mail. That will have to be fun enough for today. Maybe I'll have a letter from my boyfriend."

"You have a boyfriend?"

"Wouldn't you like to know," she says, and then, "No, of course not."

Blaine doesn't know what *of course not* means, why she said that. He angle parks in front of the post office and turns off the ignition. Justine makes no move to get out. It's like they're teenagers parked out in the country on a side road, only they're in the middle of downtown Juliet. Blaine gets self-conscious, sitting on Main Street in full view of the world with Justine sitting next to him. If she stays in the truck, it's more than just a ride. To anyone walking by, there's something going on.

Justine says, "It's just that you're the only one out there who seems to have a soul. The others are all about, well, you know, watching my ass."

All Blaine can think of to say is "You'd better get out. People talk." He doesn't mean to sound rude but it does sound that way, at least to him.

Justine opens the door to get out and she's half in and half out of his truck, looking at him with her big dark eyes, and she says, "You were serious, I guess, about being married." There's a moment, then, when he knows that he is capable of making a bad decision, comes so close. He wants to slide across the bench seat and grab her, pull her to him and take a break from his life of attachment and worry and, yes, if he could forget all that he might feel good again. Never mind that he's too old for her. Never mind that her interest in him makes no sense. What she's offering, from his perspective anyway, is escape—if only momentary—and he would so badly like to accept.

But he doesn't. He's lost almost everything, but he still has a family and he knows for certain that Vicki would never, ever betray him with another man. "Forget about married men, girl. You can do way better than the likes of me."

"That's honourable," she says. "But I'm not sure about that. Anyway, see you tomorrow. Same as always."

Blaine watches as she goes into the post office and then comes out again flipping through several envelopes. He wonders who they could be from. Not her girlfriends, in this age of e-mail and text messaging. She crosses the street and takes the first right onto a block of new houses, split-levels with double garages and landscaping. He doesn't want to know where she lives, but he can still see her and so he watches as she turns up the walk of the second house from the corner.

She was just playing with me, he thinks. Now that she's gone, it's as clear as day.

Blaine steps out of the truck and goes into the post office to pick up his own mail. He gets out his key, opens the stainless steel mailbox, and finds it empty. Just then Mrs. Bulin walks by and sees the open box.

"Hi there, Blaine," her voice says from behind the wall of boxes. "Vicki was already in for your mail. Do you think we'll get rain anytime soon?"

"Jesus H. Christ," Blaine says under his breath. "When was Vicki in?" he asks Mrs. Bulin.

"Quite a while ago," Mrs. Bulin says. "Before noon, I think. Did you hear they had rain north of the river? Andy Patterson was to a sale at Elrose on Wednesday and he said they had three-tenths up there. He said it's too late for the crops but a good rain might help the pastures. I didn't think Andy looked too well. He probably shouldn't be running around the country to sales."

Jesus Murphy, that woman never shuts up, he thinks. He slams the mailbox shut and goes back to his truck, fuming. Not about Mrs. Bulin's chatter, but about her eyewitness report that Vicki was on the move. As usual.

Penance

In the late-afternoon heat of the Juliet school staff room, Norval waits—along with the principal and the director of education, who are both dressed in golf attire—for their job applicant to show up for her interview. "She probably got lost," Norval offers by way of explanation. He once again peruses her letter of application, thankful that her qualifications trump Mrs. Baxter's. He can't understand why the other two on the hiring committee are so unconcerned about Mrs. Baxter's campaign to weasel her way into this job, despite the fact that she has never been to anything remotely like a teachers college and would surely force the girls of Juliet into a time warp marked by crocheted toilet-roll covers and family-values rhetoric as outdated as Elvis Presley.

He checks his watch. Their candidate is now twenty minutes late. Half an hour passes, the director and the principal obviously impatient for their golf game, forty minutes, and finally they are forced to give up. There is no discussion about Mrs. Baxter. They all know the consequence of this no-show. The director gets his car keys out of his pocket and says to the principal, "Tee time, then," and to Norval, "One of these days you're going to join us and discover the pleasures of golf."

Once they're gone, he tosses the candidate's resumé in the bin for shredding and considers resigning from the school board.

The staff room phone rings. Norval hopes against hope that it's the late job applicant calling with a good excuse, but it's Lila.

"Good," she says, "I'm glad I caught you. Your cell phone is turned off, you know."

Norval feigns surprise at that.

Lila wants to know if he's done what he said he would do, which is go to the church and talk to the caretaker about the renovations. "You promised," she adds.

Norval doesn't remember promising exactly. What he would really *like* to do is go to the hardware store and buy a lawn mower and forget about Lila's plans. He says, "You're talking as though these renovations of yours are a done deal."

"They're not a done deal, Norval. That's why I want you to speak with Joe. Everybody knows he runs the maintenance committee. That church is a disgrace. We can't have the wedding there with things the way they are. Surely you agree with me."

Norval stops himself from saying that weddings take place in the church pretty regularly with things the way they are.

"I'll see what I can do," he says.

"I know you," Lila says. "You won't want to be too pushy, but you can't expect a caretaker to have any sense when it comes to decorating."

To get Lila off the phone, he *promises* to give Joe all of her suggestions.

"Don't call them suggestions," Lila says. "Insist. Speak with authority." Then she runs through her list of what needs renovating before the church is good enough for the wedding that she has in mind, even though she'd already written it all down for him: new carpet in the foyer (or ceramic tile might be nice);

new light fixtures in the basement reception hall; the pews need refinishing; and of course everything needs paint. Be specific about the colours, she tells Norval. Those are the main things. The kitchen could certainly use new china, she says, but they can rent something decent for the reception if that's not possible. Norval knows that the maintenance committee is concerned with the mouldings on the four stained-glass windows in the church, which have been leaking in a heavy rain. Perhaps, he says, their priorities are already set, what with the state of the windows. He doesn't say that the chance of any renovation happening before October is next to none.

"Well, that's fine," Lila says, "but cosmetic upgrades are what will bring people into the church. It makes sense from a business perspective. Use that argument."

Once Lila is finally through (though not before reminding him to turn his cell phone on, what good is it otherwise), Norval calls the caretaker to see if he will be around. He doesn't want to do this, doesn't want to embarrass himself, but he suspects he will be more embarrassed if he doesn't talk to the caretaker and Lila does.

No one answers. Joe's awkward voice message tells him that he is in the church somewhere, or perhaps in the yard, or perhaps out on an errand, but he is in and please leave a message. Norval waits for the beep and then tells Joe he will be by at five to talk about the wedding plans, knowing that Joe's hours at the church commonly run into early evening. He doesn't mention Lila's renovations.

Norval decides to turn Joe's temporary absence into his opportunity to stop and buy his new lawn mower. The heat of the day isn't waning at all, and as he walks the few blocks to the hardware store, he recalls how good the pool water felt earlier, which causes him to recall that he left his wet bathing suit sitting in his office. He decides to leave it there rather than go back to the bank for it.

As he opens the door to the hardware store, Vicki Dolson and her pile of kids come screaming out, almost knocking him over. One of the kids is literally screaming, and Vicki is trying to comfort her as she ushers the kids to the car. It's the second time today he's seen Vicki Dolson, and he feels the worry and responsibility once again. He watches as she gets the kids into the car and the doors closed, the little girl screeching as though she's being murdered, Vicki's life the very picture of chaos. She backs the car out too quickly and almost slams into the side of a half-ton coming down the street.

Norval notices Mrs. Jackson watching through the hardware store window. He steps inside and Mrs. Jackson says, "Oh dear," and he soon sees that *oh dear* is in reference to the barn paint that has spread like a spill from a wound all over the floor at the back of the store. Right in the spot where his new electric lawn mower is located. Its wheels, along with the wheels of a gas mower and an old-fashioned manual push mower, are now sitting in paint. Mrs. Jackson looks as if she has no idea what to do.

"I just don't know where to start," she says.

Norval doesn't want to help Mrs. Jackson clean up the paint, doesn't want to at all, but he offers just the same. She thanks him, but says Mr. Jackson will be by soon, he'll know what to do.

"Still," Norval says, "I think we'd better wipe up the worst of it before it starts to dry. Then you'll have a real mess on your hands."

Mrs. Jackson stands staring at the spill. Norval can see that she already has paint on her shoes and her pant legs.

"You might want to get your clothes cleaned up," he says. "Before it's too late."

"I imagine it's already too late," Mrs. Jackson says. She hands Norval an opened package of paper towels, and retrieves a pack of heavy-duty garbage bags from the store shelves. He gives the pool a swipe with a wad of paper towels, trying not to step in it. The paper towels push the paint around without actually absorbing much. When Norval lifts the wad of paper towel off the floor, red paint drips onto the toe of his loafer and he has to get a clean sheet to wipe it off. Again Mrs. Jackson suggests leaving the clean-up for her husband, but Norval insists, perhaps beyond reason. Mrs. Jackson wonders aloud if it would help to sprinkle wood shavings over the paint and Norval agrees that this might be worth a try.

While she moves out of the way whatever merchandise she can manage—the lawn mowers, some garden tools, the other cans of paint that fell, thankfully, without the lids popping off—Norval walks down the block to the lumberyard and buys a bag of shavings, which he carries back to the store on his shoulder, sweating profusely into his shirt and jacket. Mrs. Jackson finds him a pair of rubber boots—again, new merchandise off the shelf—because it is apparent that it will be impossible to do this job without stepping in paint. Norval takes off his sports jacket, puts on the boots and stuffs his pant legs inside, and then he wades right into the mess and struggles to drag the refrigerator and spin dryer aside. Of course they drag paint with them, but at least the extent of what they're dealing with is now revealed. Between the two of them, they get shavings sprinkled all over the spill and they do, indeed, absorb at least some of the paint. Norval shovels up the now-red shavings and dumps them in garbage bags, and then he attacks the floor with paper towels. When they have the worst of the disaster taken care of, Norval steps out of the boots and back into his leather shoes, and carries the bags out back and leaves them against the brick wall of the building. The same stray dog that he'd seen earlier is now sniffing at trash cans in this alley, and he stares at Norval just as he did before.

Mrs. Jackson keeps saying she can't thank Norval enough and insists that she and Mr. Jackson can take it from here, and so Norval finally does what he came to do, which is manoeuvre his shiny new lawn mower up the aisle toward the front of the store. He notices that it's leaving red tire tracks, so he flips it upside down and gives the tires a rub with more paper towel. Mrs. Jackson, who follows Norval up the aisle wiping paint marks from the floor, tries to convince him to leave the lawn mower until she can get it properly cleaned, but Norval doesn't want to wait. He tells Mrs. Jackson that the paint on the tires won't make a bit of difference to how the mower cuts the grass, so she gives him a whopping discount, and thanks him again for helping with the paint.

"That Vicki Dolson is a nice enough girl," Mrs. Jackson says, "and she's got her hands full, that's for sure. She offered to help clean up, but she won't be back. How she can afford to buy anything . . . well, I'm sure you know all about that."

Once again Norval feels the weight of *what he knows,* and Mrs. Jackson must recognize the look on his face because she says, touching his arm, "Such a difficult job you have, Norval." He simply nods and leaves the store, wheeling the lawn mower in front of him, with his jacket draped over the handles. He has red paint on his hands, and when he looks down he sees a spot on his pant leg, another on the sleeve of his shirt. Red for guilt, he thinks, how damned obvious. He wonders if, now that his clothes are probably ruined anyway, he should go back to the store and have Mrs. Jackson daub sample spots of all Lila's preferred colours for the renovations on him. Come to think of it, the red colour he's already wearing would probably fit with Lila's idea of a more modern look for the church. He recalls seeing cranberry on the list, along with taupe and olive green.

Norval pushes the lawn mower along the sidewalk, over cracks and gouges and through unmarked intersections, until he comes to the neat-looking United church, with its beige lap siding and its caragana hedge on three sides. An arch-shaped sign on the lawn names the church as St. Andrews, and informs of Sunday service at eleven o'clock with the reverend Mary Marshall at the pulpit. Juliet shares the reverend with three other communities and gets her only once a month. The other Sundays, a lay minister takes the service. Sometimes, the lay minister is Norval.

He looks up at the roof of the church and sees that the shingles on the south side are curling up. The paint is peeling on the south side too, and Norval has the reluctant thought that perhaps Lila is right, the church is in need of a touch-up, although not because of Rachelle's wedding. He wheels the lawn mower around to the side of the building and parks it by the door that leads to the basement reception hall and Joe's office. Norval tries the door and it's open. Joe must be here, then. Norval wonders briefly about the wisdom of leaving the new lawn mower outside unattended, but it's hidden from the street by the caragana hedge.

From the side door landing, he has the choice of going downstairs into the hall, or up four steps to the chapel door. This is the minister's entrance, and leads to the pulpit and the choir loft, if you can call the ten or so banquet chairs lined up behind the pulpit a choir loft. Because the basement is dark, Norval chooses to go up the steps, but when he enters the chapel, Joe isn't there either. He decides to wait. He sits in the front row of pews and sees that the list of hymns from last Sunday is still on the board, among them one of his favourites, "Blessed Be the Tie That Binds." He tries to imagine himself sitting here, in this very spot, having just watched his daughter tie herself to matrimony with Kyle Hoffert. Will he be able to act happy and blessed, for Rachelle's and Lila's sakes?

He looks at the stained-glass windows, two on either side of the church. Although the windows are not at all fancy and are patterned with simple geometric shapes, mostly green and yellow, they are pretty, especially on the west side with the late-afternoon sun shining through them. He thinks that maybe this is the first time he's ever sat in the chapel by himself. He's practised his sermon here a few times, but with Lila watching and writing her comments on a pad of paper. Notes, she called them, which she'd learned how to give in her year at theatre school.

Norval checks his watch again. He really should call Lila and let her know he's waiting for Joe. She'll have dinner ready. He takes his phone out of his pocket, turns it on and dials his home number. When Lila says hello, he surprises himself by not saying anything. "Hello?" Lila says again, and again he doesn't answer. He's not sure why. Perhaps he doesn't want to hear the sound of his voice echoing banalities in the empty little church. He does know that he feels quite a sense of satisfaction as he pushes the Power button off and puts his phone back in his pocket. And for the next while he loses track of time and sits by himself in the quiet with the sun coming through the west windows, spraying oddly coloured light around the room.

Change of Heart

An Empty House

When Blaine pulls into the yard at home, he doesn't see Vicki's car. He calls out as he walks into the house, but there's no answer. Not even Shiloh is home. He checks the voice mail to see if Vicki has phoned, but there's only a message from Hank Trass, wanting to know if by any slim chance Blaine is home, and if so, whether he'd mind giving a hand gathering calves from along the railway tracks. There's no time on the message indicating when Hank called. It's probably too late, Blaine thinks, but he gives Hank a call back to check, and there's no answer.

As Blaine stands by the phone, he sees the tubs of beans on the kitchen floor, and the two blanchers on the counter. There's a white tea towel on the counter and the way it's been tossed there instead of hung on the towel bar annoys him so much he feels as though he could strangle someone with it. He picks it up and hangs it where it should be, and as he does so it reminds him of Justine's white T-shirt, and in that moment the towel and the beans and the blanchers and the garden and Vicki and the kids become such a weight, such a terrible crushing weight. He would think he were having a heart attack, except the weight is everywhere: on his chest and his head and his thighs, his whole body. He looks at the tubs of beans and he thinks, *Vicki is right,*

a crop of beans from a vegetable garden, what's the point? What's
the point of beans when you can't grow anything else? It's all
just too fucking pathetic. He's pathetic, worse than the alcoholic
foreman, and the thought of how close he came to making a
complete ass of himself is humiliating. Justine is probably on
her phone right now telling some other girl-engineering-student
about the fun she had with him on the way into town, fun with
an old hick out here in Hicksville. The beans stare up at him
from the kitchen floor and he decides to do his wife a favour. He
carries them outside, one tub at a time, and he throws them all
in a pile in the yard. Then he soaks the beans thoroughly with
kerosene and throws a match on the pile. He watches as thick,
choking black smoke rises into the air, and when he's sure the
beans are going to burn he goes back into the house. On the way
in he looks at the rain gauge that's attached to the railing on the
step. He does this out of habit. There's nothing in the gauge but
dust and bits of chaff. Anyway, what does it matter? Even if it
was the right time of year for rain, it wouldn't fix his problems.

Blaine goes inside and lies on the floor in the living room,
stretches out and stares at the stippled ceiling. When he was a
kid he used to lie on the floor and pretend the sparkles were stars.
He looks over at the painting of his parents above the couch, with
his father's brand burned into the old-fashioned wooden frame.
The painting, a copy of a photograph, had been Vicki's idea for
Blaine's parents' anniversary one year. The artist had suggested to
Vicki that he do the painting in sepia to give it a western look and
Vicki had liked that idea. When Blaine's mother moved into her
condo, she'd returned the painting to Blaine and Vicki. Now his
parents—dressed in their Sunday clothes, Blaine's mother with
her hair newly curled—stare down at him and remind him of
the abysmal job he's done of looking after the place, how he's lost
most of it, and might as well give up the remaining quarter for all

the good it's doing to hang on to it. He wonders if the same thing will happen to the Torgeson kid. If it does, he hopes it happens quickly, before he's got a wife and a bunch of kids to support. He remembers Vicki telling him that Lee won some kind of scholarship to go to university, and he turned it down to stay home and farm. That's a decision the kid might live to regret.

Blaine closes his eyes and tries to imagine a life somewhere else. In Swift Current maybe, working at the stockyards or the auction, living with Vicki and six kids in a rented house. But could he afford to keep his family in the city? And could they be happy there? The weight on Blaine's body gets heavier and heavier and he doesn't know if it's sleep that's coming on or death, and he doesn't much care. With his luck, he thinks, it'll be sleep, which it is, and he dozes off right there on the floor, stretched out on his back like a dead person, but still very much alive whether he likes it or not. He dreams of driving around in the sand dunes. In the dream, the truck skims lightly over the sand like a hydroplane over water. Vicki and the kids are in the truck box under a blanket, all but Shiloh, who is on the seat beside him. They have no possessions but a picnic basket, and they're looking for water. In the dream, Blaine feels in his bones that they're headed in the right direction. Shiloh sits attentively beside him, absorbing whatever it is that Blaine has to teach him about survival.

When Blaine wakes up, he looks around, half expecting Shiloh to be sitting on the couch staring at him. But the house is quiet, still no sign of Vicki and the kids. Blaine hauls himself up off the floor and calls Hank Trass's number again. No answer. He decides to trailer his horse over to Hank's just in case he's needed.

When he's halfway across the yard he can see that there's a problem. The horse is lying down—not in itself unusual—but he's stretched out all wrong, and when Blaine calls, he doesn't lift his head to look. Blaine quickens his steps and as he enters the pen he can see that the horse is too exhausted to greet him.

"Hey, Buck. Hey, buddy," Blaine says, an urgency in his voice. "Up now, buddy, on your feet." The horse is wearing a halter and Blaine takes it and tugs, encourages with the toe of his boot. "Up now," he says over and over, and the horse, willing to please, looks at Blaine and somehow manages to struggle to his feet. The evidence of his frantic kicking and thrashing shows in the patches of skin rubbed raw on his head and belly, and in the sweat marks on his neck and chest. Blaine suspects colic. It's obvious that the horse has been in distress for some time. He places his ear against the horse's belly, listening for gut sounds, and he hears nothing.

There is no home remedy for this. There is no money for a vet bill. The horse must be in incredible pain and it breaks Blaine's heart that he's been suffering, probably all day. Blaine knows what he has to do. It's not that he's never had to put a horse down before, but this horse—the last one—now represents every ambition that he's ever had and his last bit of hope, however unreasonable, that things might turn around. His dark heart, already close to bottom, sinks further, even as the anger rises. Anger at Vicki. If she'd been home, she would have noticed that something was wrong, or even if she hadn't noticed, one of the kids would have.

Blaine goes to the house for a rifle, kept with several other rifles in a locked cabinet, and then to the bedroom where he keeps the shells hidden in a locked box on the top shelf of the closet. He slips the shells into his pocket and goes back to the pen, where the horse is once again down. Blaine gets him up on his feet and this time he leads him out of the pen. The exhausted horse rallies to follow Blaine on unsteady legs, toward the place on the quarter where the land dips and where, for a hundred years, the bones of the Dolsons' animals have been bleached by the sun.

But Blaine can't do it. Just as he is about to lead the horse through the wire gate, he decides he can't, not yet, not without trying, who cares about the money; they're already so far in debt it won't make any difference. Maybe the vet can work a miracle and save the horse, save Blaine's hope, his very life. He leads the horse away from the gate and toward the trailer, which is parked in the shade of the barn, leaves the horse standing, barely able to keep himself upright, while he backs the truck up to the coupling, and then he swings the trailer door open wide and asks the horse to get in. The quivering horse tries, gets one front leg up, and then the other, but he just doesn't have the strength to lift his back legs. So Blaine lifts for him, lifts one back foot into the trailer and leans all his weight on the horse's hip trying to get him to lift the other and step into the trailer—just one step so Blaine can close the trailer door. The horse leans against him and for a minute Blaine is sure that the horse is going to fall back on him and he shouts, "Get up there, get ahead," and finally the horse takes the step up, one is enough, and Blaine quickly swings the door closed and latches it. He sees the gun where he left it leaning against the barn and decides to take it with him, in case there's nothing the vet can do.

And of course there is nothing the vet can do. Just as Blaine is turning onto the service road in Swift Current, he hears a crash in the trailer and feels a sway. When he pulls into the clinic, the vet is outside in the yard and comes over to see what Blaine has for him.

"Not going to be good," Blaine says as he's unlatching the trailer door.

When Blaine has swung the door wide, the two of them stand looking at the dead horse. The vet shakes his head in a gesture of understanding.

"Sorry, Blaine," he says.

"Colic," Blaine says. "Had a hell of a time getting him in the trailer."

"Probably couldn't have saved him, that far gone," the vet says. "Anyway, the surgery doesn't always work. Lot of money for a gamble."

He knows, Blaine thinks, *everyone knows my financial situation.*

"I would have spent the money," Blaine says, "if there'd been a chance."

The vet says, "I guess we'd better get him out before he's wedged in. You don't want that."

And so Blaine's last remaining horse doesn't get to lie with others on his last remaining quarter, and is instead dragged with chains around its hind legs to wait with a dead cow, flies already buzzing around its eyes, for sanitary disposal. The two large animals lie in a grassy area behind the clinic, well out of sight of the town families bringing their cats and dogs for rabies shots and neutering and euthanasia.

"No charge," the vet says to Blaine. "The truck's coming anyway for the cow," and Blaine doesn't argue.

He doesn't go straight home. He decides to have another look around town for Vicki's car. He drives up Main Street past the post office, turns and drives by the house where Justine lives, past the swimming pool just as Norval Birch's daughter comes out and gets in her boyfriend's truck—that god damned Norval Birch, the source of all his problems—a U-turn at the corner and back up Main Street and past the hotel, no sign of Vicki's car in the parking lot. The schoolyard, Blaine thinks, the playground maybe, and on his way there he passes the United church and who is standing on the sidewalk looking up and down the street, stunned as a rabbit in the headlights, but Norval Birch himself. He's just standing there in a daze, and Blaine takes his foot off the gas and slows to watch as Norval turns and goes around the side of the church.

Blaine has no idea why he stops the truck. What can he say to Norval that he hasn't said twenty times already in Norval's office in the bank? But he does, he parks and opens his door to get out, and when he sees the gun leaning against the seat on the passenger's side, he picks it up. He can't say why. He's hardly aware of it in his hand when he follows the sidewalk to the side door of the church. And when Norval hears footsteps coming down the stairs to the basement, he thinks it's Joe the caretaker and goes to the foot of the stairs to meet him, and who does he see halfway down the narrow staircase but Blaine Dolson, with a rifle in his hand.

"Blaine," says Norval, trying to sound nonchalant, trying not to look at the rifle; trying, in fact, to pretend that he's just run into Blaine coming out of the Co-op, and it's not a gun in his hand but rather a quart of milk or a loaf of bread. "Pretty hot day, wasn't it," he says. "I don't know about you, but I'm ready to go home and put my feet up."

Blaine just stares at him, not moving up or down the stairs. Norval has never before been afraid of Blaine. He's seen him angry, yes, but he's never once feared that Blaine would cross the line and become a threat to his safety. Not Blaine Dolson.

"So what are you doing here?" Norval asks. "Myself, I'm waiting for Joe. He should be here. Not sure where he's got to. The wife has it in her head that the church needs some upgrading— paint, flooring, that kind of thing. I don't know. There are other more important needs, if you ask me. Take the windows upstairs. A strong wind could do some damage there." He's babbling, he knows it, but he's unnerved by the gun. He, Norval, doesn't own a gun. Never has. He wouldn't know what to do with one. He'd barely known what to do with a water gun when he was a kid.

"Is that gun loaded?" he asks. He doesn't like the sound of his own voice. He sounds weak and scared.

"No," says Blaine.

"Can I help you with anything?" Norval asks.

"Coming from you, that's a very funny question."

Norval feels panic rising. He tries not to be afraid—it's Blaine Dolson, he tells himself—but Blaine is still standing in the stairwell, hardly stirring, just staring down at Norval, and *he has a gun and it might be for me.* The seconds tick by. The stairwell is not especially well lit (another of Lila's complaints) and Blaine's face is in shadows, so it's not hard for Norval to imagine menace in his eyes. Norval prays the gun is truly not loaded. He prays that Joe will show up.

He musters the courage to speak again. "What can I do for you, Blaine?" he asks. It's a question he's asked so many times in the comfort of his office chair, trying to sound upbeat and optimistic, trying to sound like an expert on finances and agro-business, but when he asks it here, in the musty church basement, away from his desk and whatever clout his promotion to bank manager has given him, he is shocked by how false it sounds. Just as false as Lila's performance in her long-ago Shakespearean debut. He remembers the pain of sitting in the audience and hearing Lila's struggle to infuse her lines with truth, and that's just what he's doing now, struggling to sound credible, as though there's actually something he can do when he asks Blaine, *What can I do for you?* A man who has lost everything through no real fault of his own, he did everything that Norval advised. He remembers Blaine's little girl howling in the hardware store, and he thinks, *This man has mouths to feed,* and he hears himself saying, "I'm sorry, Blaine. I'm sorry I asked that. There's nothing I can do. Not a thing. It's all bullshit." And he feels himself sitting down on the bottom step of the narrow staircase, and he's afraid— terrified—when he sees Blaine take a bullet out of his pocket and slip it into the gun's chamber. Norval sits at the foot of the stairs in the bad light of the church basement with Blaine and his gun just a few steps away and thinks, *Give it to me. Give me whatever I deserve.*

Only Norval hasn't seen Blaine reach for a bullet, he's only imagined it, and Blaine doesn't give him anything. He stares at Norval, and then he turns and leaves without saying another word, thereby dismissing him, and Norval thinks, *Of course, of course. That's what I deserve. Nothing. Exactly nothing.*

The realization that he deserves nothing is such a relief.

That, and the fact that Blaine Dolson was able to see right through him, as if he were made of window glass.

Only a Breath

The Health Centre is located in a wing of the nursing home. Dr. van Riebeeck points the rest of the kids to the row of waiting room chairs, and then leads Vicki and Daisy into the treatment room. It's after hours because the Centre closes at four o'clock, and Vicki is lucky she caught him. As she pulled into the parking lot, Daisy still screaming, she'd seen the doctor walking to his car and had driven right for him, honking the horn. The doctor froze and a look of fear crossed his face as though he thought Vicki might be about to run him down. When she saw this, she slammed on the brakes and Daisy was thrown forward into the dash, which made her scream even louder. Lucille started to cry too, because her ears hurt, she said, couldn't Daisy be quiet now that they were here?

Vicki jumped out of the car, apologizing to the doctor but quite certain that something was really wrong with Daisy's arm— even Daisy should have given up howling by this time. They all trooped into the Health Centre after the doctor unlocked the door and switched the lights back on.

"Now you lot behave yourselves," Vicki had said to the rest of the kids when they got inside. "We don't need any more excitement."

From the open doorway to the treatment room, Vicki keeps her eye on her brood and on Daisy at the same time. She watches as Martin seats himself in a wheelchair waiting by the receptionist's desk, and then all of a sudden the chair is rolling across the vinyl flooring, and then all the kids get into the picture and they and the chair disappear from view. Luckily, the doctor's back is to the door.

"I think you're going to have to take this girl into Swift Current," the doctor says in his South African accent while Daisy cries and holds her arm away so that he can't get a good look at it. "Here, little girl," he says, reaching out his hand as though he were offering it to a dog to sniff.

"Daisy," Vicki says, tired of the racket and the whole complicated day. "For heaven's sake, let the nice doctor look so we can get you fixed up and go home." To the doctor she says, "Please do what you can here. I can't take all these kids into Swift Current now. I just can't." She knows she sounds like she's begging, but she doesn't care.

Daisy stops crying for a few seconds and retreats to a far corner of the room. The doctor turns to Vicki. "Why don't you wait with the other children," he says. "Perhaps she'll be better if you aren't in the room. That sometimes helps with the difficult ones."

Vicki wants to tell him that Daisy is *not* a difficult child, but then she looks at her daughter cowering in the corner like a wolf pup. She leaves the room, closing the door after her, and listens for the crying to start up again, but it doesn't.

The waiting area is deserted. Vicki can't see the other kids anywhere. She steps out into the parking lot, thinking they may have taken the wheelchair outside, but they aren't there either. They must be in the nursing home, then, visiting Mr. Cruikshank, a Second World War veteran who has a major league baseball he likes to show the kids. She knows Martin and some other boys from school sometimes visit him during the noon hour. After Mr. Cruikshank has had his lunch, Martin tells her, he takes them back to his room and asks one of them to go to the drawer and get his baseball, which is in a red satin bag made especially for the ball by his daughter. Apparently he caught it at a game in Ebbets Field in Brooklyn in 1947, after the war and before he returned home to Saskatchewan. He can't remember the name of the player who hit the ball, someone who got sent back to the minors and disappeared from baseball history.

Vicki walks around the corner to the nursing home entrance, passes through the lounge with its big-screen TV, and goes down the short hallway that she knows leads to Mr. Cruikshank's room. She's familiar with the building, having visited elderly neighbours here many times. The hallways and public spaces in the home are decorated cheerily with wicker baskets and dried flowers and little brass pots that look as if they belong in an English country garden. The bedrooms are jam-packed with odd, mismatched furniture from the last places the residents called home, the places they left in a flurry of dispersal, saving only the few favourite items that would fit in one small room: an armchair, a dresser, a small television set. There are crocheted afghans and home-made quilts with matching pillow slips, and almost all of the residents have brought with them a picture to hang on the wall above the bed or the armchair: a generic oil painting of maple trees in the fall; a calendar print of a lone cowboy; or perhaps a paint-by-number completed years ago by a member of the family. And photographs. Every surface in every bedroom is covered with framed photographs of ancestors and descendants, babies and children, teenagers in graduation caps and gowns, family portraits. Reminders of the past, and reminders that the world is still happening out there.

As Vicki approaches Mr. Cruikshank's open doorway, she can hear him telling the story of how he caught the ball in his army cap, and how he wishes he'd stood in line to get some of the players to sign it but he didn't, there you go, too late now. She peeks around the corner and her children are all listening to Mr. Cruikshank's story, calm as can be. Lucille is sucking her thumb, leaning up against her big brother Martin on the floor. The twins are both seated on the edge of the bed. She can't see the wheelchair; they must have ditched it somewhere.

Vicki hears Martin ask, "What should I be surprised about? You said I would be surprised."

"I said that?" Mr. Cruikshank asks. "Well, I suppose I was referring to the player who hit the ball and how he went back to the minors and then who knows where, and I imagine he was surprised by how his life turned out because he thought he was going to be a big-leaguer and get into the Hall of Fame, but other things happened to him instead. Important things, I imagine. You'll be surprised too. That's what I meant."

Martin says that doesn't really make sense, and then little Lucille sits up and looks at him and puts her finger to her lips. "Shhhhh," she says to him, "be polite."

This makes Vicki smile, especially since Lucille's hair still looks so funny.

Just then a nurse's aide arrives to take Mr. Cruikshank for his bath. Mr. Cruikshank asks Martin to put the ball back where it belongs. "Be careful of the bag," he says. "It's special, my daughter made it for me."

On the way back to the Health Centre, Vicki pats Martin on the head. "You're a sweet boy," she says.

Martin doesn't like to be called a sweet boy. He runs ahead.

The door to the treatment room is still closed. Vicki puts her ear to the door and is relieved to hear silence instead of Daisy screaming. There's a stack of children's books on a table, so she seats the kids and reads aloud to them from Dr. Seuss.

When the door finally opens and Daisy emerges, she has a plaster cast on her arm.

"I'm assuming it's a hairline fracture," the doctor says. "The cast will stabilize it but I want you to take her into Swift Current tomorrow, just to be sure." He hands Vicki a referral.

Daisy is admiring her cast. She's tapping it with a pen the doctor gave her for getting people to sign it. She can't believe the cast has turned so hard. It's magic.

"Thank you so much," Vicki says to the doctor. He looks exhausted. There's a rumour about town that he'd like to go back to South Africa, and if he does, it will be almost impossible to replace him. "We're so lucky to have you here," Vicki says.

The doctor nods, as though he agrees with her.

"You be careful with that arm," Vicki says to Daisy a few minutes later as the kids pile into the car. "The doctor's gone home for supper and he doesn't want to see us again for a while, I can tell you that." The other kids agree that Daisy should get to sit in the front. The chocolate cake is on the seat and Vicki picks it up and hands it to Martin in the back. No one asks why they aren't dropping it off at Karla's.

It's now almost six. Vicki drives around town to have one last look for Shiloh. The streets are deserted. She's starting to get worried, but she supposes there'll be a message when she gets home; he'll be going to the drive-in with someone else's family, a friend from school, that boy who plays hockey. Right now she's too tired to decide whether punishment is in order, grounding perhaps. She turns toward home, trying not to worry about Shiloh or the beans or Daisy or Blaine's lunch for tomorrow. She can't believe that in all that time in town she didn't buy anything for Blaine's lunch. All she did was lose Shiloh and break Daisy's arm. She'll have to mislead Blaine a little about the details of Daisy's accident, she thinks. Perhaps she can tell the story without giving the exact time. They went into town for a blancher and a few groceries, then Shiloh disappeared and Daisy had a wreck and it took forever to get a doctor to look at her, and then back to trying to track down Shiloh, and by then the stores were closed and where in the world does the time go?

They pass the Petro-Can and Vicki decides she'd better stop at the convenience store to pick up frozen Pizza Pops for supper. She doesn't dare try the debit card again, but she can write a cheque. Blaine hates Pizza Pops—he says he can't stand the smell—but at least they're fast. Vicki buys a dozen. There's a canned ham on the shelf and she buys that too. And coffee. So the day wasn't a complete waste. At least Blaine will get a decent lunch tomorrow. Maybe the smell of Pizza Pops will make him so mad that he'll forget about the beans. Daisy's arm will help too. And Shiloh will be a distraction, how he's getting home and whether someone will have to drive back to town for him.

So everything will be all right after all, and anyway, what's another day? What does it matter whether the beans get done today or tomorrow? There's just a few hours of darkness—one sleep, as the kids say—between this day and the next, just like there's only a breath between being alive and being dead. She heard someone say that on the radio once—some famous person who was dying, one of those people who *thinks* about things— and it made a lot of sense. The image of a dying person's last breath had come back to her many times since then, and it was a comfort. It made dying seem like something you could actually do without being terrified out of your mind.

By the time Vicki pulls into the yard and turns the car off, she's decided not to worry about whether Blaine will be mad that the beans are still sitting in plastic tubs, although she can't quite convince herself not to worry about Shiloh. She runs her fingers through her hair and has a quick look at herself in the rear-view mirror.

Lucille notices and says, "You look pretty, Mom."

Vicki accepts the compliment, but really she thinks she just looks worn out.

Cocktails

This has never, ever happened in all the years of Marian's living in this house. Not while Ed was alive. Not since his death. Come to think of it, Willard has never entered any house at what they call "happy hour" and had a fancy alcoholic beverage waiting for him on the coffee table. He walks in the door after a day of odd jobs around the yard, and there's Marian, sitting on the couch in an outfit he's never seen before, with her hair piled up on top of her head, and two glasses of green something-or-other on a tray, along with some kind of tarts or pastries on a plate. It's so unusual that he decides the drink is not for him after all, she must be expecting someone else, another lady from town.

"I'll just get out of your way, then," he says, and starts down the hall to his room. He's not sure what he'll do in there while Marian entertains, but it's what comes to mind in a moment of awkwardness. Outside would be better, at least he knows what to do outside.

"Willard," Marian says to his back, "I thought we could have a drink before supper."

He can smell a roast in the oven. That's unusual too, for such a hot day.

Willard stops, not quite sure what to do now. "You mean me? You and me?"

"That's right," Marian says. "I found a recipe. 'Perfect for a summer day,' the magazine said. I thought I'd try it out. You're the guinea pig."

"I'll just wash up, then," Willard says, and continues down the hall.

This is very strange, he thinks in the privacy of the bathroom. He washes the day's dirt off his hands and face, and looks at himself in the mirror. He has grey stubble all over his chin. He wonders how many days it's been since he shaved. Shaving is not a thing he does very conscientiously, and sometimes he leaves it long enough that he tells people he's growing a beard, even though he never really is. He thinks about Marian in a new outfit with her hair done, and decides he has to shave. There's hardly ever a time when Willard shaves for a reason other than his face gets itchy or he gets tired of looking at stubble in the mirror, but shaving will buy some time while he tries to figure this out.

He gets his electric shaver out of the drawer in the cabinet and goes to work on his beard. Is it the change of life? he wonders. He has no idea how old Marian is. Younger than Ed by a good bit, that's all he knows. Or maybe today is her birthday and that's what the drinks are in aid of. She knows when *his* birthday is—every year she bakes him his favourite carrot cake and gives him a card that he's never sure what to do with because he knows she doesn't like paper left lying around, so he reads it and says thank you and puts it in the recycling, hoping that's the right choice—but he has no idea when her birthday is, and as far as he knows, no one else does either. He can't remember a time when a birthday card came in the mail. He should ask her when her birthday is and take care to buy her a card. Although if it's today, it's too late.

Once he gets his face cleaned up, his work shirt looks comparatively dirty and ragged around the collar. He decides to slip into his bedroom and change into a clean one. While he's doing this, he has the thought, once again, that Marian is about to tell him she's leaving, and this is her way of delivering the news. Maybe she needs a shot of alcohol to get the conversation started, or maybe she thinks Willard will need a shot of alcohol to receive the news that he's going to have to look after himself from now on, and run the drive-in alone, and listen to his own voice as he sits at the supper table eating fried eggs and canned pork and beans while the recycling piles up around him, the *Western Producer* and all the flyers that appear in his mailbox, and the dishes pile up in the sink until he's forced to wash them, or maybe he could get into the habit of using just one plate and one knife and fork, and that way he could manage to get them washed up after each meal. He hopes he won't turn into one of those old bachelors who sleeps in the same sheets until they wear out, and then doesn't bother with sheets at all, and eventually doesn't bother washing the one dirty plate, just gives it to the dog to lick and calls it good enough. He's heard the stories, he knows there are a few of those old men around the countryside. Elton Sutter, for example, who had a famous fit when some of the ladies in town decided to surprise him with a clean house. Story was, he came in from the field one night and saw his house all spiffed up. The ladies didn't get a bit of thanks for their trouble, even though they'd left a big pot of beef stew on the stove and a bag of homemade buns on the table. Elton had taken the pot of stew and thrown it to the dogs. Or at least that's what he told people. Willard suspected that he'd eaten it but just didn't want to admit it. What man who cooked for himself could turn down a good homemade stew, no matter what the circumstances?

Once Willard has changed into a clean plaid shirt, he's embarrassed to go out to the living room and join Marian. What will she think when she sees him all cleaned up? She might assume something—the wrong something. Well, maybe not wrong; he wants her to stay, but he knows he has no right to expect that. He gets so self-conscious about having cleaned himself up that he sits on the bed for a while like a kid with a crush, when the object of his crush has given some sign that she just might be interested. Willard remembers this from a long time ago. Maybe that's why he never married. He just couldn't stand it—the idea that some pretty little girl might actually like him, and that he'd never be able to live up to whatever idea she had in her head about who he was, but it had to be a wrong idea, because if it was right she'd like someone else and not him. Ed, probably. There was that time when one of the pretty little girls had invited him to dance with her and he'd actually done it and thought of nothing else for days afterwards, had dared to dream of marrying this girl, and then found out that she had her sights on Ed and not him, and that he'd been her sly introduction. When she found out that Ed wasn't interested, she turned cold as ice, wouldn't even say hello to Willard on the street. For fear of encouraging him, Willard supposed.

Well, he can't sit here on the bed all day when Marian is sitting out there on the couch waiting for him. She's waited long enough already. What Willard decides to do is put his old work shirt back on, that way the change won't be too drastic, but when he does he can smell the dust and oil on himself and he thinks he can't go out and sit with Marian like that, it wouldn't be right when she's gone to the trouble she has, so he changes once again into the clean shirt. Then he clears his throat and runs his hands through his hair and goes to face the music, whatever that music might be.

When Marian sees him she says, "Don't you look nice," which throws him completely for a loop and makes him think he should have left the old shirt on after all.

"Sit down, Willard, and give this a try."

He sits, not beside her on the couch, of course, but in the armchair opposite where she is sitting. Ed's chair. She hands him one of the glasses. "It's supposed to have crushed ice in it," she says, "but the ice melted. I hope I didn't add too much gin."

"Sorry," Willard says, taking the drink. "I guess I took too long."

"Doesn't matter," says Marian. "It's worth it, to see you clean-shaven. I thought you were growing a beard again."

Willard takes a sip of the drink. It tastes like mint.

"Good," he says. To tell the truth, it tastes more like peppermint soda than an alcoholic beverage, but he isn't going to say that. He's not sure what to say because he doesn't know what would be the *right thing*.

Marian picks up the plate of pastries and holds it out for Willard.

"Try these," she says. "They're supposed to be perfect for a summer day too."

Willard thinks it's a little strange to be eating dessert before dinner, but when he bites into one of the pastries he realizes that it's filled with egg. Cold egg and cheese.

"Umm," he says, not committing himself, not used to the idea of cold egg in a tart, although it's pretty darned good. He remembers Lynn Trass's green pie and thinks it's his lucky day, as far as sampling home cooking goes.

"Hors d'oeuvres," says Marian.

"Good," says Willard. He takes another. Marian looks pleased.

"There's a new movie tonight," Willard says.

"Yes," Marian says. "I saw the poster. A love story, I think. I enjoy the love stories."

"Is that so?" he asks. He didn't think she did.

"I do, although they aren't what they used to be, are they."

Willard wonders if this is the last movie she'll watch through Ed's picture window. He looks at her hair and wonders what's holding it up there.

"Sometimes I find love stories to be disappointing in the end," Marian says. "There's something missing. Real life, I suppose that's what's missing. Even when the lovers die in the end. You'd think death would be about as real life as it gets, but death at the end of a movie seems artificial. Don't you think?"

Willard doesn't know what to think. He's still back on the word *lovers,* the way it so easily left Marian's lips and blended in with the rest of her words, as though it's a word you use every day like *rain* or *mail* or *gasoline.* But it's not one of those words. *Lovers* is a word you might not say once in your entire life. He's pretty sure he's never said the word *lovers.*

Then she asks him a strange question.

"Willard," she says, "do you think Ed had any idea he was a dying man?"

"What do you mean?" Willard asks.

"You don't just up and have a heart attack without there being something wrong with your heart. Do you think he knew?"

Willard has never thought about this before. "Ed never went to a doctor," he says. "So I guess not. It just hit him like lightning. That would be my guess."

Marian pauses and then says, "You know, it might not be a bad idea for you to have a checkup. Just to be sure."

Willard doesn't like doctors any better than Ed did. "I don't think there's anything wrong with me," he says.

"Will you promise me you'll go to the Centre if you ever do think something is wrong? If you have chest pain, say, or dizzy spells?"

This is just so strange. Marian is saying things that are getting right under his skin, or maybe even deeper than that. Her words—words like *promise* and *pain*—are burrowing all the way to his heart, the one she seems to be worrying about.

"I promise," he says.

"Good," Marian says, "because men are not very careful about their bodies."

There she goes again. The word *bodies*. It bites at his skin like a tick. How is it that this has never happened before? In all the years they've lived just the two of them in this house, her words have never had this effect. That last one—bodies—*has* made him dizzy. He lifts Marian's special summer drink to his lips and drains it. From far away he hears her saying, "Would you like another?"

"Yes, please," he says, and he can hear her laughing as she takes his empty glass to the kitchen.

When she returns she places the fresh drink on the coffee table and sits down again.

"We'd best be careful," she says, still laughing, "or neither of us will be in good enough shape to run the movie."

Why, Willard wonders, is she so happy? That laugh, a girl's laugh. He allows himself to think, *please stay,* even though he would never be able to say that out loud. If he could, he would use Marian's words, the potent ones. "*Promise* me . . ." he would say. Or, "It gives me *pain* . . ." But if he could say these things out loud he would be a different person, and he would have asked her to marry him years ago, and she might even have said yes because he would not be Willard, but someone else more interesting. He can't bear the thought of sitting at the table with her for the last time, eating roast beef—not now, not tonight—and he says, "Perhaps I'd better not," and stands.

"Perhaps you'd better not what?" Marian asks, a look of alarm crossing her face.

"One drink is about all I can manage," he says. "It was good, though. Very good. Thank you. I've just remembered. . . ." and he leaves without finishing the sentence because he can't think of what he might have just remembered.

He goes back outside and gets in his truck and drives away from the yard. Toward town. The Oasis. He'll go to the Oasis for supper. They're used to him there. He can sit at a table and eat his meal and probably no one will talk to him, but if someone does, it will be about the weather, or grain prices, or football. And he won't have to hear the words, *I'm leaving, Willard. I thought you'd better know. . . .*

Just go, he thinks, *just go while I'm not home, and I'll pretend that you've gone to visit relatives somewhere. Eventually, I will get used to the idea that you're not coming back.*

Bandito

There's nothing Lee can think of that might mark the south-west corner of the square. How, he wonders, did the Perry cow-boys know where to turn east in what would have been unfenced, wide-open prairie? And then he remembers the railway tracks and how they would have been right where they are now, and he decides to go south until he sees the tracks running parallel to the Number One Highway, and then change direction for the last time. There's a picnic grounds in a shady spot just north of the highway. If he can find it, he'll stop there and rest the horse again before the last leg of the ride. That's how he's thinking of it now: the hundred-mile ride.

He's in community pasture again, and to the east he can see a herd of maybe four hundred cows and calves stretched out over the land, the way the buffalo would have grazed in the past. The horse doesn't seem bothered by the cattle, although he has his ears forward and is obviously curious. He's not the kind of horse that Lee would expect to have much experience with cattle.

The bulls are still in with the cows and he can see one lying off by himself in the sun, his sizable head and shoulders giving him away. Lee remembers a story Lester told him about the days of the old cattle ranches, and how thousands of cattle died one winter when the snow and ice came, storm after storm, and the ranch hands couldn't do a thing to help the herds. He imagines what the prairie looked and smelled like in the spring with dead cattle everywhere. Those storms had marked the end of an era.

Lee hears the whinny of a horse behind him. The Arab's ears rotate and his head goes up and he answers. Lee looks back and sees a small herd coming toward them, heads high, led by a big bay with a white blaze. As they get closer the bay breaks into a lope and the others follow. Eight of them, Lee counts, heading straight for him. The little herd is picking up speed, the bay tossing his head, and when they reach Lee they split and pass him on either side, the bay kicking out in their direction, and then they're all off in a gallop through the pasture, good-looking ranch horses, six sorrels and the bay and a blue roan. At first Lee tries to hold his horse back, but then he lets him go. The horse, with some memory of the wild in his genes, instinctively runs with the herd, not toward a particular place, but away, running from something without knowing what it is, wanting to take his cue from horses rather than the man on his back. And then Lee feels a surge and the grey horse surprises him by trying to get out in front of the bay. *He wants to be in front,* Lee thinks, *the little bugger wants to lead rather than follow,* and Lee feels his heart pounding with the excitement of it, holds on to his hat to keep it from blowing off, exhilarated by the feel of letting go and the power of the horse, ears flat back, at full gallop beneath him. And they run for a mile before the bay slows and the Arab does get out front, and the bay splits off to the east and his little band follows him.

Lee gets the Arab pulled into a circle and slowed up and then stopped, the two of them panting at the lip of a cactus-covered drop down into another coulee. Lee can see the railway tracks and the highway off in the distance, the trucks and summer RVs passing like Dinky Toys. He's now at the southern end of the square, he realizes, three-quarters of the way around; just one leg to go and he'll have done the whole hundred. The horse is lathered as they move forward again, and content now to walk. Both horse and man welcome the cooler air as they amble down into the shade of the picnic spot.

The picnic grounds are neat with the garbage cleaned up and wood carefully stacked for the two barbecue pits, although the tables that were once painted red are now the grey colour of weather-worn pine boards. Someone has taken a sweep with a mower through the open space along the bank of a shallow, slow-moving stream and several decent-sized poplars provide shade for the picnic area. There are no cars. No people. It's quiet. The coulee is far enough off the highway that you can barely hear the traffic once you're down in the trees. The horse heads for the water and splashes with his nose before drinking.

A rapping sound behind Lee makes him twist in the saddle to find the source. There's Blaine Dolson's oldest boy, sitting at one of the picnic tables, rapping his knuckles on the surface as though he's trying to get Lee's attention. Lee wonders why he didn't notice him when he rode into the picnic grounds. Perhaps he was lying in the grass.

"What're you doing here?" Lee asks the boy.

"Just out for a walk," says the boy.

"That's a long walk from home."

The boy doesn't answer.

"Which one are you anyway?" Lee asks. "I get you Dolson kids all mixed up."

"Shiloh," he says. "The oldest."

"I knew you were the oldest," Lee says. "I just couldn't remember your name. But Shiloh. Sure, I remember now."

"Your horse looks pretty hot," the kid says, getting up from the picnic table and wandering over. "You better cool him down before you let him drink."

"I figure he knows what's best for himself," Lee says.

The horse lifts his head from the water and turns to look at the stranger who's appeared out of nowhere. Lee dismounts, carefully putting his weight on first one leg and then the other, and uncinches the saddle and lifts it off. He turns it upside down on the ground and lays the sweaty pad out to dry. Then he leads the horse into the creek and lets him drop and roll in the shallow water. He stands again and shakes himself, and Lee gets soaked. The splash of water feels good, like being under a garden sprinkler on a hot day. The boy follows as Lee leads the horse to the grass near the picnic tables. Lee is limping, walking like an old man, even though he tries to cover it up. His hip joints don't seem to engage properly.

"What's wrong with you anyway?" Shiloh asks.

"Nothing's wrong," Lee says. "It's been a long day, that's all." He notices the boy's backpack on one of the tables. "Don't suppose you have any food in that backpack?"

"Cookies," Shiloh says.

"Haul them out of there, then," Lee says.

Shiloh gets out the bag of Oreos. "There might be a few crumbs left," he says, handing Lee the bag.

Lee fishes in the bottom for a couple of half-pieces of cookie and a handful of crumbs. He's starving, and realizes that the lunch he had at the Varga place is long used up. He finishes what's left and then tosses the bag into the nearest barbecue pit.

Shiloh says, "I didn't know you had a horse over at your place."

"This one's not likely going to stay," Lee says. "It's a long story, but he belongs to someone else. You could say he's on loan for a couple of days."

"Handy with cattle, do you think?"

"Not likely," Lee says. "But you never know."

"So how far'd you come on him?" Shiloh asks.

"Long enough that I'm going to wish I had my own personal masseuse by the time I get home. Or a hot tub, maybe."

Lee looks past Shiloh and sees a pair of outhouses in the trees across the trail from the picnic tables. He hands Shiloh the reins while he goes to relieve himself in comfort—well, not exactly comfort because the smell is powerful, the flies are thick and there are two wasps buzzing in and out of the quarter moon that is cut in the door marked HOMBRES. While he's got his pants unzipped he decides to lower them so that he can see the damage done to his calves. His jeans stick to the skin rubbed raw and he has to peel them away to see the abrasions. There's no skin left in weeping patches on the inside of each calf around the tops of his boots. Two more raw spots blossom under his seat bones. Astrid always said he didn't have enough meat on him. A little extra padding would have helped. He gingerly pulls his pants back up, thinking about a pleasurable soak in the big old clawfoot, but also the sting of water on a fresh wound.

When Lee steps back outside, he sees that Shiloh has taken the horse over to a patch of long grass near the entrance to the picnic grounds. He's let the bit drop down and behind the horse's chin so he can graze properly.

"You okay there?" Lee calls. "Because I wouldn't mind stretching out for a few minutes."

"We're good," Shiloh calls back.

Lee looks around for a water tap and sees one near the picnic tables. He has a long drink, and then lets the ice-cold water run over his head and neck. Once he's cooled off, he lies on his back on top of a table. He puts George's hat over his face to block out the light, but then he has to take it off again because of the smell. He can hear birds in the trees and the faint sound of traffic from the highway. He drops off, even though he doesn't mean to.

When he wakes up he can't see Shiloh and the horse. He notices that the saddle and pad are gone. The boy's backpack is gone too. It doesn't register at first, and then he realizes Shiloh has taken the horse.

"Well, Jesus Christ anyway," Lee says, and hurries up to the top of the coulee.

He's just in time to see the rodeo. Shiloh's trying to get on the horse, but the horse keeps stepping sideways and snaking around so that he's facing the boy. Shiloh tries again and this time he gets a foot in the stirrup and is about to hop into the saddle when the horse moves his hip away once more, and Shiloh is dragged around in a tight circle, hopping on one foot until he can get the other out of the stirrup and back on the ground. Lee can see from the horse's ears that he's none too happy about this new development. Lee is about to shout a warning when suddenly Shiloh gives up on the stirrup, grabs hold of the horn and vaults, gymnast-style, from the ground into the saddle. The horse stands for a second and then—before Shiloh can get himself organized—jerks the reins out of his hands, gets his head down and bucks like a Calgary bronc.

Lee can't believe that Shiloh survives the first buck, but he does, and then the kid gets his legs under himself and rides the horse, for a few seconds at least. The fourth buck launches him, and Lee holds his breath and waits for Shiloh to hit the dirt, hoping that he doesn't come down on the saddle horn or land on his head like Pete Varga in the graveyard—and thinking about the horse too, whether he'll be able to catch the animal if he runs off, and how pissed he'll be at this god damned kid if the horse does run off. And then thud, Shiloh is on the ground. Lee can almost hear the air leaving the kid's lungs. He's lying on the ground, not moving, his backpack underneath him, but hanging on to the reins with a death grip. Not that the horse is trying to go anywhere. As soon as he's rid of the upstart rider, he drops his head and rips at the dry grass.

Lee runs. He forgets about his burns and blisters and runs for the kid, who is now gasping, his eyes wide, trying to suck air into his lungs.

When Lee reaches him, he kneels down and pries the reins out of Shiloh's hand, saying, "Relax. Relax and breathe. You just got the wind knocked out of you."

The boy struggles to breathe, nothing, nothing, panic in his eyes, but finally he draws a breath and then another, and Lee sits down in the grass beside him. The boy's breathing is getting closer and closer to normal.

"Are you hurt?" Lee asks.

Shiloh lifts his arms, and then moves his legs. Everything seems to be working.

"Just my pride," he says, and then Lee starts to laugh.

"What's so funny?" Shiloh asks, sitting up now, anger quick to surface.

"Come on," Lee says. "You were trying to steal my horse and you got bucked off. It's right out of Roy Rogers. If anyone tried to steal Trigger, he sure as hell got himself bucked off. I wouldn't be laughing if you'd busted anything, but you'll live. Hey, you lasted a few seconds there. Didn't make the bell but you did all right. You'll make a cowboy."

Shiloh doesn't say anything then, just drops his head and stares at the ground.

"So what are you doing out here?" Lee asks. "And don't tell me you went for a walk."

"I hitchhiked," Shiloh says. "Got picked up by a couple of freaks who were supposed to take me to Calgary but they went and dropped me in the ditch. Anyway, they did me a favour. I don't know anyone in Calgary."

"So how are you getting home?"

"Walk, I guess."

Lee stands up and brushes the dust off the pockets of his jeans. "Let's get going, then," he says.

He throws the reins over the horse's neck and steps up into the saddle, then holds out his hand to Shiloh. "Here," he says. "Neither one of us has much weight for him to carry."

"No way," says Shiloh. "I'm not getting on that crazy animal."

"Come on," Lee says. "He's had his say. He'll be fine now."

Shiloh looks skeptical but he takes Lee's hand and Lee lifts him up behind the saddle. The horse steps sideways and tosses his head, but then he walks off as though this is just another part of the job he somehow inherited by wandering into Lee's yard.

"So have you ever heard of Ivan Dodge?" Lee asks. The hot sun is now behind them and it's a relief not to be heading into it.

"No," Shiloh says. "Should I have?"

Lee reaches into his pocket and pulls out the old watch. "This could be his pocket watch," he says. He knows it's probably not, but it belonged to some old-time cowboy. He tells Shiloh the story of the hundred-mile race and he makes up a part about Ivan losing his watch and how Lee found it, the very watch, in a coulee. When he's done telling it as best he can remember he puts the watch back in his pocket.

"Is that it?" asks Shiloh.

"Well, it's a pretty good story, don't you think?"

To the north, they see another small herd of cattle. About twenty cows and calves are spread along the flat, most of the calves stretched out in the late-afternoon sun. Lee and Shiloh notice a coyote that is sitting in the grass watching the cows. He turns his attention to horse and riders briefly, but decides they're far enough away that he doesn't have to worry about them. He settles on one cow that is grazing on the edge of the small herd, her calf asleep in the grass nearby. The coyote stands, shakes himself nonchalantly and then approaches the sleeping calf. When he gets too close for the cow's comfort, she takes a run at him. The coyote backs off, sits and gives himself a scratch behind one ear, and then approaches again. Once more the cow runs him off.

"Cheeky bugger," Lee says.

He stops the horse and they watch as the coyote approaches the sleeping calf several more times, and each time is chased off by the cow. Finally the coyote decides he's had enough and he moves off to the north and disappears.

"He knew all along he wasn't going to get close to that calf," Lee says. "He was just having fun."

He asks Shiloh if he's good for a jog.

"Whatever," Shiloh says. "I'm in no hurry."

"We might as well get home before tomorrow," Lee says.

He urges the horse up into a trot and the animal pricks his ears forward as they head eastward, and then breaks into an easy lope. Lee can feel Shiloh immediately find the horse's rhythm. The kid can ride, Lee thinks. If the horse hadn't caught him off guard, maybe he could have rode through the buck, and then what would have happened? Lee would be walking the last leg of the hundred miles, just like the old Perry cowboy, the one who lost the race.

They're silent for a long time and the horse slows up to give himself a rest and Shiloh says to Lee's back, "My dad says you're lucky."

Without stopping to think, Lee asks, "How's that?"

"How you got all that land, all paid for."

Lee isn't sure how to respond, how much Shiloh knows about Blaine and Vicki's situation. At the same time, Lee is on the defensive, wondering what Blaine has said about him, his private business.

"It was passed on to me, just like Blaine's land was."

"Yeah, but it's different," Shiloh says.

Lee lets it go. It *is* different, and compared to Blaine he is lucky. He wouldn't let anyone get away with calling Lester lucky. Everything Lester had was earned through hard work and frugality. As for himself . . . he agrees. So far, just lucky.

"My dad's going to buy another herd of cows, you know," Shiloh says. "That's why he's working construction. Maybe this fall."

"Good," says Lee. "I hope that works out for him." He feels bad for the kid. An idea comes to him. "You ever have a 4-H calf?" he asks.

"Course," says Shiloh.

"I could use a hand once in a while, there on my own," Lee says. "You want another calf, you could earn one by helping me out. Few hours on a Saturday here and there, maybe after school. When your dad doesn't need you at home, that is. Think about it."

"I'll think about it," Shiloh says. "But we're pretty busy at our place. I might not have time." Then he says, "You can drop me near town, I guess. When we get there."

"I could drive you home from my place," Lee offers.

"I'll walk from town," says Shiloh.

A dust devil blows across the prairie, carrying dirt and sand into their path. Lee automatically closes his eyes. When he opens them again he thinks he can see Juliet in the distance, but it's just a mirage.

Handyman

Norval is sitting on the bottom step in the church basement, and Joe is standing at the top of the stairs looking down at him, obviously perplexed. When Norval tries to stand he realizes that one foot has gone completely to sleep and it crumples—the oddest sensation, no feeling at all, as though his foot has been amputated—and he has to put a hand to the wall to keep from falling over.

"What are you doing down there, Norval?" Joe asks, and Norval mumbles something about resting his feet.

He takes his hand away from the wall and brushes off his khaki pants, and now he can feel the pins and needles as his foot comes back to life, and he realizes that even with the foot awake, he has the sensation that he is floating.

"Is that your new lawn mower out there?" Joe asks. His deep voice booms down the stairwell.

Norval nods and manages to say that he just picked it up at the hardware store.

"We could use a new one here at the church," Joe says.

Norval lifts his foot and rubs his ankle, floating on one leg now, and says that Joe can have his old one if he wants to fix it up, and if it's better than the old one he already has. They talk about lawn mowers—gas versus electric, whether a riding mower is really necessary for anyone with a small property—while Joe stands at the top of the stairs and Norval floats around at the bottom, like a man in a life raft.

Finally Joe says, "I guess there's no point me standing here, is there," and he descends, and then launches into an explanation of why he is so late. He did get Norval's message, he says, but then his sister phoned and she had a leaky water pipe and it was spraying all over the laundry room and she didn't know how to shut the water off, so Joe had to rush over and do an emergency repair, and then he had to help clean up the water before it ran all over the basement and ruined the carpet. Why his sister didn't just call a plumber, he doesn't know. "But I guess," Joe says, "if there's a handyman in the family, you're going to call him first." And then he says, "What the heck did you do to your pants?" He's looking at the paint spot.

"Painting accident," Norval says. Nothing more. He doesn't want to explain about the Dolsons and the mess. "What time is it?" he asks. He could look at his own watch but it seems like too much trouble.

Joe tells him it's after seven.

After seven. That means he's been sitting on the bottom step for over an hour.

"Is everything all right, Norval?" Joe asks. "You don't seem quite yourself."

Norval pauses and thinks about whether or not he is all right, whether a person who is all right hovers in a church basement, whether a person who is all right would think, in the presence of a man with a gun, *Give me whatever I deserve.* Surely he was wrong when he concluded he deserved nothing. He begins to write a manifesto in his head, to list what he deserves other than nothing: I, Norval Birch, deserve a chance to . . . But before he articulates even one opportunity, he feels his feet hit the floor. Thud, he can almost feel the jarring in his ankles, right on up to his knees, and with his feet on the ground it seems so obvious that even if he does deserve more than nothing, he certainly doesn't deserve more than what he already has. The shiny new lawn mower outside is evidence of the adequacy of his life.

He sees that Joe is waiting patiently with a somewhat worried expression on his face, and so he segues from his state of mind into the real reason he is here. "I'm fine," he says. "It's just a bit awkward," he says. "The wife . . ." And then he clears his throat and stands firmly on both feet and takes Lila's list out of his pocket and explains to Joe, calmly but firmly, that the church is in need of cosmetic repair.

Joe looks at him as he speaks, listening, nodding agreement. He concurs that the lighting is a problem, as is the waxy buildup on the pews. Norval is careful to say *not your fault, Joe* several times throughout his discourse, and Joe nods, *no offence taken,* and he even agrees that a more modern look would improve the reception hall. They talk about paint colours—cranberry and taupe and olive green—and Joe says that green would be very nice on the walls as long as they keep the ceiling white so it's not too dark, and white trim—smart, yes. They run through all the items on Lila's list, giving them the same serious consideration, and when they come to the end, Norval folds the list in half and says, "Well, then."

Joe, still nodding, says that there is a meeting of the maintenance committee next week and he'll put this to them and he's sure they'll welcome suggestions. "Although," he says, "the stained-glass windows upstairs are in pretty bad shape. Something needs to be done there before it's too late."

Norval says he realizes the windows have to be a priority; they don't want the windows falling into such disrepair that they can't be fixed. Still, he uses Lila's argument when he says, "These other things are important too, if we want to keep weddings in the community."

"You're right," Joe says, nodding until Norval wonders if his head might bob off. "No argument from me," Joe says, "that the place needs sprucing up."

No argument, so much accord, but Norval knows—as he did before he phoned Joe earlier—that not one of Lila's demands will be met in time for Rachelle's wedding.

"I'd best get home," he says. "I'll be in the doghouse if Lila's supper gets cold."

Joe apologizes again for being late and tells Norval he can blame the cold supper on him.

Norval ascends from the basement and steps out into the sunlight, not at all worried that Blaine Dolson will be waiting. He knows he won't be. He sees his sports jacket hanging on the lawn mower and sticks Lila's list in the pocket, then wheels his new mower up the sidewalk toward home. In the kitchen, he drapes his sports jacket over the back of a chair and then manages to get upstairs to change clothes before Lila notices the paint stains. He places his phone on his bedside table before tossing his pants and shirt in the back of his closet, thinking he might even throw them out rather than explain.

When he gets to the kitchen his supper is indeed cold, but he's saved from Lila's reproach when he says he was talking to Joe at the church.

"Well, you could have let me know," she says, carrying his plate to the microwave just as the phone rings.

Norval is going to ignore it, but Lila says, "It might be Rachelle," which he takes to mean that Rachelle is off again, who knows where. He picks up the receiver and it's Mrs. Baxter, who has already heard a rumour that her rival candidate didn't show up for her interview. This should make Norval crazy—the way news travels, that nothing in this town remains confidential—but it doesn't. He calmly tells Mrs. Baxter that, yes, she is now officially in the running for the job, while he silently gives thanks that Rachelle will *not* be in Mrs. Baxter's class next year. He apologizes that he has to cut the call short but his wife has supper on the table, and of course Mrs. Baxter understands the urgency of a hot meal.

Norval returns the phone to its cradle, then sits at the table to enjoy his warmed-up, heart-smart stir-fry. He picks up the chopsticks that Lila insists they use with Asian food and examines them for crusted bits of the last meal they were used for. This infuriates Lila because her kitchen is nothing if it isn't clean. She sits across from him, wanting to know what Norval said and what Joe said, and what exactly did Joe promise?

"He promised," Norval said, "to speak with the maintenance committee. He's the janitor, Lila. It's not up to him."

"Oh, for heaven's sake," Lila says. "You're just not assertive enough."

"You know, Lila," Norval says, "I was almost shot today." He aims for his mouth with the green beans and lean beef strips that are pinched precariously between his chopsticks, then lifts his plate to shorten the distance that he has to transport his food.

Lila stares at him. "You were almost shot today?" she says, alarm in her voice.

Norval concentrates on holding the chopsticks the way Lila showed him. If Lila weren't here, he'd give up and get proper cutlery out of the drawer.

"Eating with chopsticks requires my undivided attention, Lila," he says.

"A robbery?" Lila asks. "Did someone try to rob the bank?"

"Not a robbery," Norval says. "At least not one where I was the victim."

Lila prods him for information, but he says no more and eats until his plate is clean save for a few grains of rice that he can't manage to pick up. Then he pushes his chair away from the table. "That was good," he says. "Hit the spot."

Norval goes to the living room, where he turns on the television and sits on the couch. He tries to find a news channel, but when he does he can't make sense of all the information that it throws at him: sports scores down the side, headlines scrolling across the bottom, someone talking at him, elaborating on a topic that is not related to any of the headlines on the screen. He starts to feel again as though he's floating.

Lila appears in the arched doorway, silent now, seething. "Norval," she asks, "what in the world happened today? You can't just say, 'I was almost shot,' and then sit there watching the news. What kind of a man does that to his wife?"

"What kind of man," Norval says. "Very good question. A lucky man, I suppose, when he can use the word *almost*."

He switches to the Weather Channel and watches the forecast for the Caribbean. The weather is not especially good in the Caribbean. Cuba is experiencing unusually high winds and below-normal temperatures. There's a short video clip of a honeymoon couple from Canada confirming the poor state of the weather. "It's sure not beach weather," the young woman says.

At that moment Rachelle storms through the front door.

"The wedding is off," she says when she sees Lila, and Norval on the couch.

"What do you mean, the wedding is off?" Lila asks.

"Just what I said."

"The wedding can't be off."

"Why not?" Rachelle asks.

"Because you're still pregnant, for one thing," Lila says.

"I am sick to death of hearing about that," Rachelle says, and goes to her room.

Norval and Lila hear the door slam.

"And what do *you* have to say, Norval?" Lila asks. "That is, if you will lower yourself to say anything much at all."

"It's a relief," Norval says.

"A relief. That's it."

"Yes," says Norval. "Exactly."

"I don't deserve this," says Lila.

And then Norval finds out that he, in fact, *does* deserve something after all. He grabs at his chest—*of course, why didn't I think of this?*—while Lila cries, "Norval, Norval, what's happening?"

Hurry Sundown

Rendezvous

When Lee passes through a gate on the western edge of Hank's home pasture, he sees right away that he was wrong the night before when he assumed Hank had moved his calves. Just inside the fence line there's a slough with a puddle of water in the bottom and the calves standing in mud around it. Lee remembers the open gate and hopes the calves didn't get out and cause Hank a bunch of trouble. He should have closed it.

He rides the half-mile through the pasture, the horse in no hurry now, thinking about Shiloh and how he slid to the ground and headed up the road toward town, and then he turned around and shouted back to Lee, "I might take you up on that offer of work, as long as my dad doesn't need me." Funny kid.

Up ahead, Lee can see the buffalo rubbing stone. There appear to be two people at the stone, one of them sitting on it. He wonders if the high school kids are in the pasture again. He asks the horse to jog one last time, and as he approaches he sees that the person standing is George Varga, wearing a new straw cowboy hat. And sitting on the rock is Karla Norman, the hairdresser, Dale Patterson's fiancée or ex-fiancée, hard to know which, depends on the day of the week. Lee can see one of TNT's famous cars—the black Trans Am, catching the sun like a show car—parked on the approach next to George's truck. George has a thermos and appears to be drinking coffee from the metal top. Karla, more interestingly, has a six-pack of beer beside her on the rock. Once the six-pack registers, it's like a magnet.

Old George grins like mad as Lee rides up and stops.

"You look like you could use a cold one," Karla says. "Well, almost cold." She pulls a bottle out of the box and twists off the cap.

"You have no idea how good that looks," Lee says. The mosquitoes are swarming now that the heat of the day is over. Karla has a can of insect repellent on the rock, but it's only the beer Lee cares about.

Karla moves to the edge of the stone and reaches to hand him the bottle. "Cheers," she says.

Lee tips back the bottle and swallows, feels the moisture on his dry throat. Never has a beer tasted so good, even if it isn't cold.

He wonders what Karla and George are doing here together—an odd pair—and then he realizes they aren't together. George came to see if Lee would show up at the stone like Ivan Dodge did. Karla, apparently, is here to drink beer with the mosquitoes. Lee notices that the rock looks festive in the daylight, with the coloured handprints on it.

"So," Karla says to Lee, "what have you been up to?" The horse stretches his nose toward her and she runs her hand down his face. He doesn't object.

"Just out for a ride," Lee says.

He thinks, *I came across the road on this grey horse—what? Sixteen, seventeen hours ago?—and just kept on going.* He can't say that.

George slaps his thigh. "Just out for a ride, that's a good one. Some ride."

Karla looks puzzled but she doesn't ask any more questions.

Lee drains the beer and hands the empty bottle back to her. Then he takes off George's old hat and holds it out to him. "Thanks for the loan," he says. "Saved the day."

George waves it away. "You keep it," he says. "I've got this new one."

Lee puts the hat back on and thinks he can feel sand embedded in his brow. "Best get on home, then," he says.

"Not so fast," says George. He pulls something out of his shirt pocket and Lee sees that it's a disposable camera, still in the foil packaging. George gets it unwrapped and then steps around so that he's not looking into the sun, and snaps a couple of photos of Lee on the horse.

"You should get yourself one of those digital cameras, George," Karla says. "You know, like a little computer."

"Computers," he says dismissively. "Don't know nothing about them." Then he takes a crisp new fifty-dollar bill out of his wallet and hands it up to Lee.

"I can't take that," Lee says.

"Why not. You earned it. Should probably be a couple of thousand by now, with inflation, but I'm not that generous."

"No," says Lee. "I can't."

"Take it," says George, and Lee finally does, not having the energy to argue.

"Well, I'm curious, that's for sure," Karla says, popping the cap off another beer, "but none of my business."

"Come on," George says to Lee, putting the camera back in his pocket. "I'll get the gate." He tips his hat to Karla and says, "Happy birthday there, Karla. Don't you drink too much and fall off that rock."

"It's your birthday?" Lee asks Karla.

"Yeah, but it's not like anyone noticed. I've been stood up, apparently. I should probably be thanking my stars for that."

He sees now that she's too dressed up for sitting out in a

pasture. She's wearing a lacy white shirt and a red beaded necklace. He wonders if it's Dale she was expecting, or someone else. Now that he's actually looking at her, he realizes that she doesn't seem especially happy.

"Well, happy birthday anyway," he says. "Maybe someone decorated that rock just for you." As soon as the words are out, he regrets them. They sound so lame.

But Karla knows what he means and looks down at the graffiti prints. "Thanks for the thought," she says, "but no one I know would bother." Then she says, "Oh crap. Now I'm feeling sorry for myself. Time to go home when that happens. Leave the gate open, will you. I'm going right after I finish this one."

Lee guides the horse toward the gate and George walks along beside him. When they're out of Karla's hearing George shakes his head and says, "I don't understand these modern women. Out here by herself drinking beer. Should be home raising babies."

It makes Lee thinks of Lester. He would have said pretty much the same thing.

They reach the gate and George opens it and stretches it out on the ground. Before he gets in his truck he offers his hand for Lee to shake and says, "That's quite the horse, there. Not built for dragging calves, but built for distance, sure as heck. Wait until I tell Anna. I'll show her the picture, eh. Maybe put it in the book."

After George is gone, Lee slips to the ground so he can walk the last quarter-mile home and limber himself up. He can see the dust of a vehicle coming from the south, so he waits for it to pass, shaking out his legs and taking a few steps on the spot. As the truck approaches, he recognizes it as Dale Patterson's.

It doesn't pass. It slows and pulls onto the approach behind TNT's Trans Am, and Dale gets out. He's got his arm in a sling.

"Torgeson," Dale says, but he's got no time to talk as he steps over the wire gate on his way to the buffalo stone. "Can't keep the little woman waiting."

So it's on again, Lee thinks. The mystery man is Dale. Too bad for Karla.

Dale suddenly stops and turns back to Lee and says, "That horse."

"What about him?" Lee asks, thinking maybe Dale knows where the horse came from.

"If you wanted a horse," Dale says, "you should have called me. I could have sold you a real one. What the hell good is an Arab horse in this country?"

He doesn't wait for Lee to respond and strides away through the pasture, cradling his bad arm with his good.

In fact, Lee has no response, other than he's not going to complain about an animal that just carried him for a hundred miles. As he leads the horse home, he thinks about Karla in her lacy shirt waiting for Dale, and about her crazy family, the Normans, all the stories, old TNT, and Karla's cousin who stabbed his mother. He wonders what someone like Karla thinks about *him*, the boy who was found in a laundry basket. Maybe nothing. But on the other hand, maybe she looks at him and sums up his life, as he did hers, by what she knows from talk. Not much chance that anyone will forget how he came to have the last name Torgeson.

He stops and loops the reins over the saddle horn and then walks the rest of the way home, letting the tired horse follow on his own. *Everybody knows everything in Juliet*, Lee thinks.

The Stars of Heaven

When Norval is stricken with chest pains, Lila is hell-bent on calling for the ambulance in Swift Current, but the pain subsides and Norval says he will go to the hospital only if Lila drives him. In fact, he says, why don't they just try to get Dr. van Riebeeck on the phone, but Lila says he isn't even certified in Canada yet, and anyway he'll send Norval to Swift Current, so why waste precious time? Since it's the only way Norval will agree to go, she loads him into the car. So as not to worry Rachelle, who's in her room brooding over her breakup with Kyle, Lila calls upstairs and says she and Norval are going for a drive.

"Fine by me," Rachelle's voice snaps back. "I'm going out any-way. And don't expect me home. I'm staying at Kristen's."

Not brooding, then.

On the way into town, Norval reports that the pain is gone. He doesn't tell Lila about the tightness, the feeling that an elastic band is wrapped around his chest.

"Probably angina," Lila says. "They'll do an ECG. And a stress test."

He doesn't want a battery of tests. He suggests they turn around and go home. He'll make an appointment for a physical, he prom-ises, but Lila won't hear of returning home.

"There's no need for anyone to die of a heart attack these days, Norval," Lila says. "So we're going to get this checked and make sure. Otherwise, I won't sleep. The surgeries for valve repair and blocked arteries and the like are very sophisticated now."

Surgery? He certainly doesn't want to be told he's going under the knife. He wonders when Lila became such an expert on the treatment of heart disease and he's tempted to say something sarcastic, but he doesn't because he knows she's concerned. He notices that she is driving fast.

"There's nothing to worry about," he says. "You'd better slow down or you'll have us stopped by the RCMP, and that won't get us there any faster, will it." He rolls the window down and feels the breeze on his face. The sky, which had been the blue of early evening when they left Juliet, is now quite dark—dark enough that he can see the stars, millions of them.

"Look at that," he says to Lila. "Such a clear night sky. No moon. The Milky Way in full force."

"What are you talking about, Norval?" Lila asks. "It's only eight o'clock. Of course there's no moon. It's still light."

Eight o'clock. Lila must be wrong. Still, when Norval looks ahead he can clearly see the oncoming semi with its shiny red cab, the gold colour of ripe crops on either side of the highway, the turquoise farmhouse that Lila always says reflects someone's idea of unique when it's really just a very bad decorating choice. So odd—the earth still bright with the colours of the day, and the night sky above, sprinkled with stars.

"The very lights of heaven," he says. It's a joke, he doesn't believe in heaven, and he's just thinking that he should explain himself to Lila, lest she misunderstand, when the stars disappear and Swift Current lies spread out before them, a small city tucked into a creek valley, and Lila is off the highway and onto the service road, still driving over the speed limit and following the green H signs that indicate a hospital.

And they're almost there, just a short distance from the brand-new facility on the edge of town, when Lila hears Norval say, "Tell Blaine Dolson it's not his fault," and she looks at Norval and in the evening light she can see that the pain is upon him again, the most agonizing, wrenching pain this time, and she steps on the gas and drives as fast as she can without losing control of the car, up to the Emergency entrance, leaning on the horn and saying, "Norval, stay with me, we're almost there." There's no one at the door, no one coming, and Lila pounds on the car horn until finally a nurse comes running, and another, and then it's all out of Lila's hands. Things are happening in slow motion—Lila has time to notice that one of the young nurses has pink streaks in her hair—and warp speed at the same time. They get Norval on a gurney and whisk him inside and down a hall, through a door into Emergency, a pair of nurses calling out for a doctor and the tools of their trade, wheeling Norval away, just like they do on the Life Channel, too busy to pay any attention to Lila. Maybe she should follow, she thinks, but it's too frightening. She holds back and then when she thinks, *I should be with him*, it's too late. The door that they've wheeled him through is locked. She looks around and sees no one. *Why is this hospital so deserted?* she wonders. *Where are the nurses?* Busy. Busy with Norval. So she waits. There are several armchairs in the waiting area and she sits in one of them, and it feels too soft, too obviously chosen for a person needing comfort. She stares at the television on the wall, one program turning into another, a sitcom, a nature show, nothing at all making sense, until a young Hutterite couple in their black clothing come through doors leading from ICU and sit across from her. The woman is crying and Lila can't stand it, she can't sit here and watch a woman cry a few feet away from her. She has to leave, *do something*. Move her car, that's what she can do.

She goes outside and gets in the car, which is still nosed right up to the Emergency entrance and in the way of hospital traffic, forcing anyone who comes along to go around it. There's a blinding bright fluorescent light over the entrance doors even though it's not yet dark, and it shines down on Lila as she sits, paralyzed, until a big truck carrying more Hutterites comes along and she finally starts her car and moves it so they can get by. As she parks properly in the visitors' lot, she thinks, *This is ridiculous, they'll be looking for me, Norval will want me.* She gets out of the car, locks it and walks back to the Emergency door.

A nurse *is* there looking for her, and she takes her to the doctor, who explains what has happened. "Is there someone you can call?" the nurse, an older woman, asks as Lila sits, unbelieving, with Norval's body—*his body!*—in the treatment room where he'd died, hardly more than a cubicle. And Lila thinks about saying *my daughter* but she shakes her head, no, there's no one to call. The nurse wants information from her, the spelling of Norval's name, his health card number, date of birth, what *funeral home* she would like them to call. *How can she ask that?* Lila thinks. But she has to, of course she does. The nurse is kindly. She tells Lila to take all the time she needs with Norval, and she even brings her a cup of tea, which goes cold on the stand beside the bed while Lila wonders, *How will I tell Rachelle?*

Eventually, the nurse suggests that Lila go home and get some rest. She offers to drive her when she gets off in half an hour— "I live out your way," she says. "Juliet, isn't it?"—but Lila says no. She turns down an over-the-counter sleeping pill too.

She doesn't want to go home. It will be true once she gets home, everything will change as soon as she drives the car into the driveway and has to face the house and the fact of Norval's absence. When she does finally leave the hospital, she goes to the drugstore and buys some makeup and a bottle of bath salts. Her mind is numb as her hands select cosmetics off the store shelves. She almost buys a bridal magazine for Rachelle before she remembers that the wedding is off. After the drugstore, she stops at a gas station and buys a quick-pick lottery ticket and fills the car up, and watches the young attendant wash the dust off the windows.

Now she has to go home. There is no place else to go. There is no more avoiding the truth of what has happened—no avoiding Juliet and her house and Rachelle and the kitchen table with Norval's dinner plate still on it—and she gets back in the car and drives toward the service road and the highway going west. All the way home, she thinks of Norval's last words and what he said before the pain took his ability to talk: *Tell Blaine Dolson it's not his fault.* He hadn't said, *Tell Rachelle I love her.* He hadn't said, *You're everything in the world to me, Lila.* He'd had no dying words for his wife and daughter, just a few words for a feckless client with too many kids.

But Norval hadn't known he was dying, Lila reasons. He'd just thought of something, some little detail having to do with Blaine Dolson's accounts, and out it had popped. It had been an abbreviated sentence, the full intent being something like, *They'll probably keep me in the hospital overnight and you'll have to take a few calls for me. If Blaine Dolson calls, tell him it's not his fault. There was an incorrect payment date printed on one of his bank statements. Just assure him it's our error and not his, and we'll straighten it out next week.*

But Norval had also said something about the lights of heaven. Lila can't remember what, she hadn't paid attention because Norval was always saying things like that, things that were too smart for her, or at least that's how they made her feel, but the reference to heaven—did that not mean he was thinking about dying? And if he was thinking about dying, shouldn't he also have been thinking about her and Rachelle, and not Blaine Dolson? It was selfish of Norval to waste his dying thoughts on a bank client, she thinks, and just as she pulls into Juliet she remembers what else he'd said that evening, about almost getting shot, and how he'd refused to explain himself and sat watching the Weather Channel, as though *he knew.* Oh my God, Lila thinks, he'd been having these chest pains all day and he hadn't said anything, and that's what he meant by "almost shot." She's furious, absolutely furious with him for not getting medical attention straight away, look what he's done by being careless, just look at how he's left her alone, how could he, and the word *alone* repeats in her head until she gets the car stopped in the driveway, and she pounds on the steering wheel in anger, furious with Norval for being so irresponsible, furious with Rachelle for getting pregnant and causing Norval so much stress, furious with the bank for sending Norval to Juliet in the first place and making him work too hard. And finally sobbing because she's lost him, the other half of herself, lost him for good.

When Lila eventually gets out of the car, the first thing she notices is that the grass is too long. Why hadn't she noticed that before? It was unlike Norval to let the grass grow. He's very fussy about the length of his lawn. She's even seen him measure it, as though it were a green on a golf course. She walks around the side of the house to the back and the grass in the backyard is overgrown as well. Then she notices the new lawn mower, and remembers that the old one was not working, and that Norval had been going on and on about needing a new mower.

She enters the house through the back door and the kitchen, and falters when she sees Norval's plate and the pair of chopsticks on the table. She stands in the kitchen, not sure that she can face the rest of the house, not sure that she can get through this. Perhaps if Rachelle were here they could get through it together. She should try to reach her, try her cell, or Kristen's, ask her to come home without saying why. But Rachelle will argue, demand to know, and Lila will break down, and she can't tell Rachelle over the phone. *Your father died tonight.* Not over the phone.

In the living room she stares at the couch, not believing that just hours ago Norval was lying there watching the Weather Channel. She can still see the outline of his body in the nap of the Ultrasuede fabric. Norval's couch. She'd always thought of it as his because he'd driven all the way to Regina in a borrowed truck to pick it up, and then when he got it home, she discovered that the company had ordered the wrong couch, only she'd never told Norval because he seemed so happy with this one. It was the most interest he'd ever shown in a piece of furniture and he complimented her several times on her choice. Because she was pretty sure it was an even more expensive couch than the one she'd ordered, she kept the company's mistake to herself, even when she noticed that the fabric had a tendency to hold the outlines of people's buttocks—a definite flaw, she'd thought, considering how much money she'd spent. She puts her hand down on Norval's couch and imagines his warmth. She wants to lie down on the couch and let herself sink into the outline of Norval's body, feel the warmth that she will never—is it possible?—feel again. But the couch is a shrine that she can't yet disturb.

Instead, she goes looking. For clues. Clues that Norval knew something was wrong—*You know, Lila, I was almost shot today*—a note perhaps, like a suicide note, a message for her or for Rachelle, a goodbye, last words like the ones people on doomed aircraft write on the backs of blank cheques or the insides of cigarette boxes, and which are found floating amid the debris in the North Sea or the Indian Ocean.

She begins with his sports jacket, which is hanging over the back of a chair in the kitchen. She finds a miniature appointment book—no PalmPilot, even though she'd wanted to buy him one; a cell phone was enough portable technology, he'd said. In another pocket, his keys. And a list—her own list—of items that he was to discuss with Joe. How could it be that just hours ago Norval was at the church talking about something as ordinary as paint? She hangs the jacket back on the chair.

She moves from the kitchen to Norval's den, where he has a desk, an armchair and a set of bookshelves. The desk is so neat you'd swear he hadn't done any work at it in years, and perhaps he hadn't. When Lila thinks about it, she has no idea what Norval did in here. He has a small TV on one of the bookshelves. Maybe he just came in here and watched the Weather Channel while

Lila and Rachelle were watching reality shows in the living room. She scans the books on the shelves: several on history and geography, a couple of decades-old university commerce texts, the poetry and devotional books Norval used for his lay services, a set of reference books of famous quotations, and a National Geographic atlas that had been a Christmas present from her, at Norval's request.

She remembers that when they first got notice they were moving to Juliet, Norval had special-ordered a number of Prairie history books from a bookstore in the city because he wanted to understand the place they were moving to. She'd tried to read one of them herself and hadn't got past the introduction. But Norval had devoured them all, read passages aloud to her that he found particularly interesting. He told her that apparently they were moving to a desert—*a desert, Lila, and I'll bet you didn't even know there was a desert in Canada.* Well, it wasn't much of a desert, but the first year they'd lived here Norval had taken her and baby Rachelle out into the dunes with a photographer for their yearly Christmas card picture. She'd objected, had wanted to use a studio photo, but Norval's heart was set on the dunes picture, so she relented. She wishes she had a copy of that photograph to look at right now, but she's not sure one even exists any more.

She checks the desk drawers. Nothing. They're empty except for a phone book, a pad of paper and a handful of pens, some of them with the bank's name printed in gold letters on the shaft. She holds the pad of paper up to the light to see if anything Norval had written was indented on the top page, but the pad looks brand new. The wastebasket contains just two spent scratch lotto tickets and a cellophane candy wrapper. The den is a perfect reflection of Norval, a perfect reflection of a man who kept everything to himself. She leaves the room, closing the door quietly as though she doesn't want to disturb a man at work.

Lila checks every surface in the house that might hold a last note from Norval—the dining room table, the telephone stand, the vanity counter in the bathroom—but she finds nothing. Norval's bedside table holds only his cell phone, a news magazine, his reading glasses and the clock radio. She gives up. On her way back downstairs, she opens Rachelle's bedroom door and is shocked to see her there, sound asleep on top of the covers, still dressed.

Now is the time. She *must* wake her and tell her. She says Rachelle's name, but when she gets no response, she quietly closes the door. *I'm a coward*, she thinks. *Without Norval, I'm not equipped for life.*

In the living room, she collapses into an armchair and looks once again at Norval's shape in the Ultrasuede, and once again she cries, but this time not in anger. She sits with a Kleenex box on her lap and a wastebasket at her feet, dreading the conversation with her daughter, dreading all that she will have to do in the next few days, all *the arrangements*. Tomorrow, she thinks, she will become a widow in the eyes of the world.

And there will be a funeral to plan, instead of a wedding.

Astrid's Secret

As Lee finally walks into his own yard, he studies the car parked by the house. He doesn't recognize it. Cracker comes to greet him, his tail wagging, looking back toward the house as though he's saying, *Look, another stranger*—the first one being the horse, all those hours ago. Now, he doesn't pay the horse any mind at all.

"Who's here, Cracker?" Lee says, reaching down to give the dog a pat.

As they approach the house, he sees Mrs. Bulin from the post office sitting on the step. He remembers her phone message, the one he'd ignored: *Give me a call, Lee. There's something I need to discuss with you.* Mrs. Bulin stands and stretches, giving the impression that she's been waiting awhile. She's wearing purple knee-length shorts and her thin legs are blue-white, as though they haven't seen a minute of sun all summer.

She says, "That's a long time to sit for an old girl like me. I was about to leave but I could tell from the dog that it was you coming up the road. Did you get my message?"

Lee decides ignorance is the way to plead. "Sorry," he says, "I haven't checked messages all day." It's not exactly a lie. He wonders what could be so important that it brought her out here. Surely not just an overdue bill for his mailbox. That would be beyond the call of postal duty, even for Mrs. Bulin.

"I wanted to talk to you," she says. "In private, I mean. Not in the post office."

Lee is tired and sore, and he can't think of anyone he'd rather *not* talk to more than Mrs. Bulin right now. He'd like to put the horse in a pen, thank him for the day's long ride with a cool bath and a good brush, then sit alone in one of Astrid's webbed plastic lawn chairs and drink another beer or two—cold this time—and watch the sunset. He would like to be rude and send Mrs. Bulin packing, but he doesn't because you have to be careful what you say to someone who daily sees and talks to the whole town. Anyway, Astrid didn't approve of rudeness and sent no one packing without a good reason. He hears her voice: *Use people well.*

"You'd better come in, then," Lee says. "Just let me put this horse away. Wait in the house if you want. The door's open."

"I might do," Mrs. Bulin says. "That step was getting a little hard on the behind."

Not something he wants to think about, Mrs. Bulin's behind, and neither does he want to think about her in his house, collecting information, sniffing for mould in the fridge, running her finger over surfaces to check for dust. He'll have to hose the sweaty horse down later, he thinks, after Mrs. Bulin is gone, which won't be long if he can help it. He leads the horse into the pen, and the horse pulls toward the water bucket. Lee removes the saddle and bridle and turns him loose. The horse takes a long drink and then goes looking for a good spot to roll. He snorts and paws at the dust in a few different spots, then drops to the ground and stretches and rolls the full length of one side of his body, flips himself over and does the same on the other side. He stands and shakes, dirt now coated to his hide. Even his head is covered in black dirt. He looks like a chimney sweep, Lee thinks, tossing a substantial forkload of hay over the top rail. Then he takes the saddle and bridle and drops them just inside the barn door, saving the cleaning for later. The pad is wet with sweat and he hangs it over a stall divider to dry.

When Lee gets back to the house he finds Mrs. Bulin sitting on a kitchen chair. She's staring at the stack of mail on the sideboard, her stock-in-trade. She's distracted, uncomfortable. She fidgets in her chair. She doesn't look as though she's been snooping around, which surprises Lee. He thought for sure he'd find her with her nose in a cupboard. He takes old George's hat off and lays it on the counter.

"I'll make tea," Lee says. "Unless you'd like something else." Although he doesn't have much else. He's saving the beer in the fridge for himself.

"Tea would be fine," she says. "Lovely."

As Lee puts the kettle on, she says, "That's quite a sunburn you've got. You should use sunscreen. Robert Redford looks like an old leather boot now. He used to be so good-looking."

Lee can feel the sunburn on his face and the back of his neck, he doesn't need Mrs. Bulin to point it out. He gets a couple of clean mugs out of the cupboard and puts them on the table.

"That cowboy movie," Mrs. Bulin says. "I saw it at the drive-in, a long time ago. I guess he's still good-looking for his age, when you think about it."

Lee has no idea what movie she's talking about. She looks down at her hands and grows silent—Mrs. Bulin, silent—and Lee wonders with a touch of alarm, *What could it be, the reason she drove out here?*

Then she says, "It's about Astrid. You know I see things, don't you. At the post office."

Lee nods.

"I see people every day, I see what comes in the mail. I get blamed for spreading rumours, Lee, but I can keep secrets. I'm actually very good at keeping secrets." She stops.

Lee doesn't prompt. He's standing by the stove, waiting for the kettle to boil.

"This has been bothering me," she says, and takes a deep breath. "I believe Astrid thought of me as a friend. We shared a secret, just the two of us, although we never spoke about it, not once."

And then Lee knows. He knows that whatever Mrs. Bulin has to say, it will be about his mother. Not Astrid, but his *real mother.* He places one hand on the porcelain stovetop, but it's hot from the burner and so he removes it again. Sticks it casually in his back pocket.

"Go on," he says.

"Near the end, I visited Astrid in the hospital, and she kept talking about work she had to do. Baking. Ironing. Laundry piled on the clothes dryer. I kept saying to her, 'It's fine, Astrid. You don't need to worry about that. It's all taken care of.'" Mrs. Bulin looks at Lee. "Is it all right, me telling you this?"

Lee nods. He doesn't know if it's all right or not. His mind is all over the place with questions about what Mrs. Bulin might know. Mrs. Bulin, of all people.

"Even though Astrid was in a fog," Mrs. Bulin continues, "she knew she wasn't going home again, and so she asked me if I would come here, to the farm, and at first I thought she wanted me to come and do chores. By this time, with the drugs and such, I didn't think it mattered who she was talking to—me, a nurse, a neighbour—but then I realized she wasn't talking about chores, and she knew it was me by her bed. There was something she wanted done, and it had to be me." She looks at Lee, who is now watching her carefully, waiting, his heart skipping beats, or maybe it only seems to be. "She asked me to come out here and find a box in her closet. An old candy box."

A candy box. Lee thinks about the closet, the one in Astrid's bedroom, the same closet that holds the blue velvet watch box. He can see the candy box, knows exactly where it is.

"I was supposed to find it and burn it," Mrs. Bulin says, "and she was so insistent and upset that finally I told her I had already done as she asked. I said I'd found the box and burned it, and she relaxed then. Settled right down. Only I was lying, of course."

She looks at Lee. "So that's it. And now it's been bothering me, the same way it bothered her. That I didn't do it when I said I did. I thought about coming out here when you weren't home and finding it, but I couldn't do that. So then I decided to just tell you. And when I got here tonight and you weren't home I thought again about what she'd asked me to do and how I could still make good on my promise, but that just didn't seem right. I suppose I decided the candy box was something you should know about."

The kettle is boiling. Lee looks for the teapot but it's not on the counter where Astrid used to keep it. He doesn't usually make a pot of tea for himself, just puts a tea bag in a mug. His eye lands once again on the silver tea service and he hears Astrid's voice, *For company, use the silver tea service,* and so he does. He takes the pot out of the oak cabinet and rinses it out at the sink, and then drops a tea bag in. Even though the pot is tarnished. He carries it to the table and places it in the middle.

"Do you have any idea what's in this box?" Mrs. Bulin asks.

"No," Lee says. He imagines things: photographs, adoption papers, mailing addresses and telephone numbers. "Do you?"

"I believe I do," she says. "But I'll leave this with you now. I've done what I thought I should. I hope I did the right thing." She stands up from her chair. "Thanks for the offer of tea but I think you'll need time to yourself."

Lee doesn't know what to say. He feels neither gratitude nor animosity toward Mrs. Bulin, just that she has been a messenger, delivering an old package that he suspected was out there somewhere in the world but would never arrive in his hands.

She stands but seems not quite ready to go. She says, again, "It still bothers me that I told Astrid a lie, but I was trying to make things easy for her. 'Don't you fuss, Astrid,' I said. 'There's absolutely nothing to worry about. I baked bread and I did the ironing. I cooked Lee a big pot of stew and I put that box you're worried about in the burning barrel and lit a match to it. So everything's been taken care of.' That's what I said to her."

She's still looking at him, waiting. Lee thinks he's no better at this than Lester was. Talking. Alleviating guilt, his own or anyone else's. He says, "You can make me that stew anytime you want."

Mrs. Bulin says, "You don't know what you're asking. I can't make a good stew for love nor money." It's left hanging, whether or not that part of the lie will be annulled.

After Mrs. Bulin leaves, Lee pushes his chair from the table and climbs the stairs to Astrid and Lester's bedroom. As he stands in front of the closet door, he thinks of the candy box as a gift that you get to open at a designated time. He doesn't know if this is the time or not. He feels a strange sense of euphoria, like he did out in the sand, in the hot sun. Whatever is in the box, he decides, he has to know, and he opens the closet door.

And there it is, where he knew it would be, under a neat little pile of pillowcases, the special ones with the crocheted edges. The box is an ordinary old chocolate box, the kind Astrid used to save for storing odds and ends before she discovered snap-top plastic containers. It cries out with secrecy, the way it's placed underneath the linens. Why had he not realized before? Lee's heart begins to beat faster again as he lifts the pillowcases, sets them aside and then reaches for the box.

It contains a half-dozen or so postcards wrapped in an elastic band. Lee removes the postcards and then sets the box back on the shelf. The ancient elastic band crumbles and the cards, seven of them, fall open in his hands. He sees that they all have the same photo on the front—an old three-storey building with some kind of ivy clinging to the red bricks, a sign over the doorway reading KELSEY HOTEL. When he examines the printed caption on the back, he learns that the hotel is in Winnipeg. The postmarks are over twenty years old, dating from the time of his childhood. Lee knows without reading a word that the messages, neatly written and never signed, are from his mother.

He carries the cards to Astrid and Lester's bed, his heart beating wildly now, and sits down and tries to read the messages even though his vision is blurred. He tries to stay cool. None of this really matters now, he tells himself, he's simply curious. He can't focus, but he keeps trying, and gradually he's able to read and translate the writing into words. The first card contains eight lines of the children's verse "Pease Porridge Hot," which he knows by heart. He goes through the cards and sees they each contain a verse.

"Ladybird, Ladybird," he knows that one too. "The Lion and the Unicorn." "Ride a Cock Horse." "Old King Cole." "The Owl and the Pussycat." And, finally, "The North Wind Doth Blow." Six or eight lines of verse, no signature. He recognizes them all, every verse, from Astrid's bedtime recitations. He shuffles the cards and reads them again, savouring the familiar words.

Lee looks at his hands and can't believe how they're shaking. He becomes conscious of his breathing, too conscious, and it seems that he's getting it wrong as he tries to breathe properly, too shallow, too deep. How, he wonders, can you get breathing wrong, something that you've done without thinking all your life? He feels dizzy and lies back on the bed. The cards are on his chest, too heavy, much heavier than seven postcards should be, and he swipes them off, sends them flying to the floor. He tells himself to breathe, the same way he told Shiloh Dolson to breathe when he got bucked off the horse, he can hear his own voice, *breathe, breathe,* and he manages to get himself calmed down and the weight lifts off his chest and he's able to sit up and think again. He pieces together the journey that took the post-cards from his mother's hand to Astrid's closet, at the same time thinking, *For a few minutes there I was almost dead.* He wonders if that's what Shiloh thought once he got his breath back.

Lee picks up the cards and this time he sorts them according to the dates on the postmarks and reads them carefully once more, in the order they arrived. It's as though Astrid and his mother are in the room with him, Astrid's voice, his mother's hand. His mother had sent the cards hoping that Astrid would read them aloud and there would be some kind of connection among the three of them. And Astrid had complied. Although she hadn't read the cards aloud or showed them to Lee, she'd recited the verses, all seven, over and over again at countless bedtimes, until Lee outgrew them and lost interest.

No sooner has Lee pieced this together than the anger comes, unbelievable anger, at a woman who wanted to disappear but not completely, who would take the time to write a postcard but not to actually show up. Anger on Astrid's behalf, because these cards arriving in the mail must have frightened her, tormented her with the possibility that Lee's mother *would* show up and perhaps take Lee away. And then anger at Astrid for keeping the cards a secret, and anger at himself for being angry with a woman who had loved him like her own. Thoughts of the post office and Mrs. Bulin, the worry that she must have caused Astrid—who almost always got the mail, rarely Lester—because anyone will read the back of a postcard, and especially Mrs. Bulin, who took the term *public mail* literally. What looks had been exchanged between Astrid and Mrs. Bulin over the postcards, and had Mrs. Bulin really kept the secret the way she'd claimed? She'd lied to Astrid on her deathbed. How could she be trusted? Instantly, Lee is sure that everyone knew about the cards, everyone but him, and he tosses them to the floor again like a child having a tantrum.

Immediately sorry. The cards are precious. He picks them up carefully, one by one, thinking, *Winnipeg.* So his mother wasn't in California, or Norway. Winnipeg is not very far away at all, she might still be there, people live in the same place for twenty years, lots of people, most people. He could go there. He could find this Kelsey Hotel. Someone, an old front-desk clerk perhaps, might remember her, might remember a woman writing nursery rhymes on postcards and dropping them in the hotel mail. Or maybe she *is* the front-desk clerk, maybe she was an employee at the hotel and still is, that's possible too.

But why? Why would he want to go there and try to find her, for what purpose? A woman who abandoned him in the same way that Cracker's previous owner left him on the side of the road and drove away heartlessly, or perhaps not heartlessly, but drove away all the same. What good can possibly come of know-ing? Lee asks himself as he turns the postcards over in his hands, looking at the picture of the hotel, examining the neat handwrit-ing, the blue ink, the missing signatures.

As Lee sits on the edge of Astrid and Lester's bed flipping through the cards again and again, he thinks about Astrid sit-ting in this same room, thinking the same tangled thoughts and feeling the same confusion as the postcards arrived, one after another, with no clue as to the sender's intentions. She must have agonized about what to tell Lee, whether to tell him at all. Perhaps she hadn't told even Lester and had wondered, as Lee just did, *What good can possibly come of knowing?* And when the cards stopped coming she'd put them in the candy box and hidden them in the closet, and left the decision about what to do with them until later. And then she'd forgotten about them until she was on her deathbed and she remembered the cards in a fog of thinking about chores and responsibilities, and that's when she'd asked Mrs. Bulin to take care of the box so that Lee wouldn't find it and blame her for keeping the secret.

Which he would never do, blame Astrid for anything, the way she had cared for him so unconditionally, LOVING MOTHER, just as her headstone described her.

He puts the postcards back in the box, and then returns them to their place in the closet, under the pillowcases. He thinks of Astrid again, thinks about the trouble she must have felt as she added each new postcard to the others and wrapped them all up with an elastic band. Her fear that Lee's mother—whoever she was—would someday take back the child she'd left in the porch, the one Astrid had mistaken for a tomcat. How his life could have been different.

He can't imagine any other life. He doesn't want to. He wants only to be Lee Torgeson. He wants only to be here. Before he closes the closet door he runs his hand over the blue velvet box on the shelf above. The watch box. Together, the two boxes remind Lee of secrets, one he kept, and one that was kept from him. They seem, in a way that makes no real sense, to cancel each other out. He picks up the watch box, opens it and stares at the satiny lining. It was the worst thing he'd ever done in childhood, breaking the watch and throwing it in the sand and then lying about it. He takes the old watch he found on the trail out of his pocket and puts it in the box. Then he closes the lid and returns it to the closet shelf.

He goes back downstairs, hesitates briefly, and then calls Directory Assistance. Even though he knows it's too late and nothing will come of it. His heart beats normally. The operator tells him there's no listing for the Kelsey Hotel but there's a listing for the Kelsey Care Centre with the same address as the one on the postcards. Lee calls, and the person who answers tells him that the care centre is, in fact, on the site of the old hotel. The hotel itself was torn down fifteen years earlier.

So that's it, Lee thinks. The trail ends.

Lee is suddenly so tired that all he can think about is his bed. The horse will have to wait until tomorrow for his bath. He goes outside to fill Cracker's dish with kibble, and when he steps back into the porch his eye lands on the spot where Astrid found the laundry basket all those years ago, and he stares at it, but only for a second or two.

He doesn't bother with a bath for himself either, he's too tired, but when he goes to bed his mind won't stop working. It's still not completely dark outside, and even with the curtains drawn there's too much light in the room. When he closes his eyes he sees miles and miles of yellow sand passing beneath him, and old postcards scattering like a deck of cards. The dog barks and the sound seems to be coming from under his bed. Lee hears the cattle, the coyotes, every sound intensified, right in the room with him. His body aches and his saddle sores burn. He can't get comfortable.

For the second night in a row, he gives up on sleep and goes downstairs to the kitchen, and is faced once again with Astrid's tarnished teapot. The word *samovar* pops into his head, the image of a teapot in the sand, and the caption *The Persian samovar, whether simple or elaborate, is an essential item of hospitality and hot tea is enjoyed no matter how temporary a desert encampment might be.* He resolves to clean Astrid's tea service, take care of it, and in doing so, make it his. Surely he can figure out how to do this. He roots through the bottles of cleaning products in the cupboard under the sink, and he actually finds a jar that claims to be silver polish. He reads the instructions and goes to work.

Subtopia

"I broke my arm, Daddy," Daisy says from the couch as Blaine and Shiloh come through the door.

Shiloh is in front, and then Blaine, carrying the rifle. It's past the children's bedtime, that of the youngest ones at least, but Vicki has let them stay up for her own sake, frantic as she was about her absent husband and son. The house smells of Pizza Pops.

"Where did you find him?" Vicki asks Blaine. "He's been gone all day."

"Walking home" is all Blaine says.

Shiloh immediately goes downstairs to his room, and within minutes his CD player is blasting. Blaine leans the rifle against the wall and sits at the dining room table, the one that belonged to his mother, without saying anything more to Vicki, without acknowledging Daisy and her cast.

"Look, Daddy," Daisy says.

He still doesn't look. He takes the box of bullets out of his pocket and lays it on the table in front of him, and then he takes off his cap and lays that on the table too, and exhales a sigh that, to Vicki's mind, goes on forever, as though he's completely emptying his lungs of air. She'd been expecting anger, planning for it all day, ever since she loaded the kids in the car and went to town, but this is not anger, it's something else altogether, something more frightening. She doesn't like the way he's leaned the gun against the wall, so casually. Blaine is always careful with the guns, so careful to keep them in the locked cabinet.

"What is it, Blaine?" she asks. She can hear the caution in her voice. She doesn't like that either, caution in her own house. She's been feeling it for days, ever since she picked the beans. The beans that are now missing. She'd thought maybe Blaine had come home from work early and done them himself, but when she checked the freezer they weren't there. It was a ridiculous thought anyway. Blaine wouldn't know how to process beans.

"Look, Daddy," Daisy says again, this time getting off the couch and approaching Blaine, holding her arm with its white plaster casing out in front of her.

Blaine puts his index finger through the opening in the band of his cap and twirls it on the table. The peak spins around and around like a ceiling fan.

"Why won't Daddy look at my cast?" Daisy asks her mother, and Vicki shushes her.

She can't be sure what to do or say until she gets a better reading of Blaine and what is going through his mind. There's something in the drone of Shiloh's music that reminds her of the sound of a small plane spinning out of control toward the earth.

"Go sit on the couch for a minute," Vicki says to Daisy. "Let Daddy rest. He just got home."

"But I broke my arm," Daisy whines.

"I know," Vicki says. "We'll tell Daddy all about it. Just give him a minute."

Daisy returns to the couch, putting on her best pout. The other kids, all but Shiloh, have appeared from down the hall, having heard Blaine and Shiloh come in. Lucille, with her lopsided haircut, wraps herself around Vicki's leg. Of all the kids, Vicki thinks, she is the most sensitive to adult moods, gets upset when adult voices are raised. The kids wait to see what will happen. They want to know what Blaine will think about Daisy's broken arm, but they know better than to interrupt whatever is going on. They wait for Vicki's lead.

Blaine finally acknowledges that Vicki is looking at him.

She takes a first stab. "I'm sorry about the day, honey," she says. "Things started out so well, then one thing led to another."

Blaine still doesn't speak, just stares at her as though she's a stranger in his house, and the silence is so unnerving that she looks away.

"Well," she says, "I guess you two must be hungry."

She goes to the kitchen, which is open to the dining room, and takes the remaining Pizza Pops out of the freezer and finds a clean baking sheet. She keeps her eye on the situation and every once in a while she shoots the kids a look that says, *Wait. Be good. Just wait.* She puts the Pizza Pops in the oven and then she carefully breaks up the boxes they came in and sets them aside for recycling. She feels Blaine watching her. Shiloh shuts his droning music off, and then Vicki hears his footsteps coming up the stairs.

Finally, when she can stand Blaine's silence no longer, she asks, "What's wrong, Blaine? You'd better tell me." Even if the answer would best be spoken behind closed doors, without all the kids listening, she has to ask.

Blaine stops spinning his cap and says, "How did you pay for those Pizza Pops?"

Vicki opens the cutlery drawer and retrieves knives and forks for Blaine and Shiloh. "I wrote a cheque," she says, her back to him. She can smell the Pizza Pops now, their tomato sauce unlike anything she can create herself on the stove. She expects the anger will come soon, about the cheque, Daisy's arm, the Pizza Pops smell. And the beans, of course, although she has no idea what she'll say about that because she doesn't know where they are.

She tenses, gets ready, and then Blaine says, "This is not my fault, Vicki. I hope you know this is not my fault."

She turns around and the look on his face scares her half to death. There's not a trace of anger, just a terrible, terrible sadness. She remembers the long sigh when he first sat down at the table, like a dying man's last breath.

Shiloh appears on the landing from the basement.

"Where were you all day anyway?" Vicki asks Shiloh, fear creeping into her voice, disguising itself as annoyance.

"While you were looking for some stupid kitchen pot, I was looking for something else. What's wrong with that?"

"Just leave him be," says Blaine to Vicki.

"Buck's dead," Shiloh says to Vicki. "Did you know that?"

"What do you mean?" Vicki asks. "Bucko's out in the pen."

"No, he's not," Shiloh says. "He's dead. He colicked and died."

"Is this true, Blaine?" Vicki asks.

Shiloh says, "It's because of you, you know." He's in the room now, moving closer to the kitchen and Vicki.

"Me? How is it because of me?" Vicki is remembering the horse and the way he looked in the morning, how he was standing in the pen staring at his flank and she thought it was the flies bothering him.

"If you'd stayed home like Dad told you, we would have noticed."

"Never mind," Blaine says to him. "What's done is done."

"That was Dad's horse, the last one, the only damn horse left on the place." He is standing right next to Blaine now, waiting for him to tell Vicki she's useless. But he doesn't. He's too upset about the horse to talk, Shiloh thinks, and so he speaks for him, says what he knows Blaine wants to say. "It's all your fault that we're in this whole mess," Shiloh says to Vicki, "because you're so bloody useless." He lifts his chin, triumphant, and looks at his father.

Blaine stands up, towers over Shiloh. Shiloh hears his mother say, "Don't, Blaine. He doesn't mean it."

Don't, Blaine? What's she telling him not to do? Shiloh looks at his father's face and is confused when he sees that Blaine is not even looking at Vicki; he's looking at him. He grabs Shiloh by the shoulders as though he's going to shake him, and Shiloh has no idea what is going on. He shrinks back, tries to turn and run, but Blaine's grip is too solid, he can't get loose.

"Don't," he hears his mother say again, more quietly this time.

"Daddy," Lucille says with worry in her voice, and Vicki picks her up.

"Shush, baby," Shiloh hears Vicki say. "It's okay."

And then he feels his father's arms around him, and he struggles to get away, tries to push himself back, but he can't, he has to stand there because Blaine is holding him so tight. One of Blaine's big hands is on the back of Shiloh's head now, pressing his face into his chest, and Shiloh doesn't know what to do. He can see the kids and Vicki watching, their eyes wide. Vicki is smoothing Lucille's hair, that stupid haircut, and he can see that she is picking at something, a little piece of gum that Karla Norman missed. Then Shiloh closes his eyes and stops struggling to get away, and he lets himself sink into his father's chest and he's afraid he's going to cry, he won't be able to stop himself, and he leaves his face in Blaine's T-shirt so no one will notice if he cries. Leaves it there until the feeling goes away and he's sure he *won't* cry.

And then Blaine's arms loosen their grip and Shiloh steps back, and Blaine says to him, "It's not Vicki's fault, Shiloh. It's nobody's fault. Things happen. Don't ever call your mother useless again. I don't want to hear that. Not ever."

Then he feels ashamed, more ashamed now than he would have felt had his father yelled at him, smacked him even. His face burns with shame, but his father says, "Put that rifle away for me, will you. You know where the key is. Just make sure none of these kids sees where it's hidden." He remembers when Blaine showed him where the key was and said, *You're old enough to be responsible.*

Shiloh picks up the rifle from where it's leaning against the wall and asks, "The bullets too?"

Blaine nods and says, "You know where they go."

After Shiloh has gone down the hall to where the gun cabinet is, Vicki says, "I don't want to be too hard on him, but we have to say something about today. About him being gone all day."

Blaine thinks for a minute, and then he says, "Mostly I think you baby these kids, Vicki. But forget about today. Let's pretend today didn't happen. Let's pretend that it's yesterday. I'll eat the damned Pizza Pops and pretend they taste like food. How about that."

Daisy gets off the couch and holds out her cast. "But I really did break my arm," she says. "See?"

Blaine looks at the cast, then says, "Well, I guess you did. You'd better bring me a pen, then."

Daisy finds a pen by the phone and takes it to him and holds up her cast, and he writes something. Daisy can't read what it says, the writing is too messy.

"It says, 'Today you're the winner of the best kid contest,'" Blaine says. "Don't you know about that contest?"

Daisy shakes her head.

"Well, it's a contest, and today you won."

When Shiloh comes back, Vicki says to him, "You're off the hook. We've all got amnesia about the whole day."

Shiloh isn't sure what she means, but it's good enough. He can smell the Pizza Pops and realizes he's starving. Although this is something Vicki will not allow the kids to say—*I'm starving*— not as long as there really are starving kids in the world.

I'm hungry is the proper way to say it.

"I'm hungry," he says.

He goes to the fridge, looking for milk to go with the Pizza Pops, and there's Karla Norman's chocolate birthday cake sitting on a shelf under its plastic cover, only he doesn't know it's Karla's cake.

"Who's the cake for?" he asks.

Vicki looks at the kids, at Martin who held the cake on his lap most of the day. "We can't remember," she says. "I guess it must be for us."

Fire in the Hole

With the day's last light on the horizon and a can of no-name cola in his hand, Hank stands next to the buffalo stone—*his* buffalo stone, he thinks—and stares at the beer box of empties and the container of insect repellent that someone left behind. The same damned someone who left the gate open. Maybe even the same someone who covered the rock, once again, with graffiti and made him susceptible, once again, to the presence of the historical society and an art restorer in his pasture. Luckily, at this time of the evening his calves are by the slough to the west. It had been the last straw, though, the gate again, and then the beer box and his discovery of the new graffiti, the outlines of hands in pink and green and yellow as though his pasture were a public park. Hank had loaded into his truck box what he figured he needed to solve the problem once and for all, but now he scratches his head and stares at the stone and doesn't know what to do next. What seemed like a good idea an hour ago is starting to look like less of a good idea, due to his lack of expertise about what could be a hazardous venture. There's only one person Hank can think of who knows anything about blasting and that's old TNT Norman. He lives with his daughter now, Karla, and Hank figures he can't be calling her house at this hour, at least not without knowing that she stays up past ten.

He decides there's no harm in driving by the house to see if there's a light on since he can't very well just guess at this, and when he gets there the older daughter—Lou, the one who is so hard to get along with—is sitting out front in her car reading a magazine under the dome light with old man Norman in the back seat. Hank parks his truck behind the car and he can see Lou looking in the rear-view mirror to see who's pulling up behind her. Hank steps out of the truck and walks over to her open window.

"Howdy," he says. "Nice night. Hey there, Wally. How're you doing?"

"Nice night for sitting out here wasting time, waiting on that inconsiderate sister of mine," says Lou. "I missed a perfectly good candle party because of her. She's selfish, that's what she is."

Hank wonders why they're waiting in the car, but he doesn't ask. "Funny thing," he says, "but I need some advice. Mind if I climb in the back seat and ask your dad a few questions?"

"Go ahead," says Lou. "As you can see, we're not going any-where."

Hank opens the back door and gets in. He's still carrying his can of cola, which he drains, and then he isn't sure what to do with the can. If he were in his own vehicle he'd drop it on the floor. Old TNT is slumped against the far door, the ravages of the stroke showing in his flaccid face and the way his body looks loose, like he has no bones. Why Lou hasn't taken him in the house is beyond him, but then Lou has a reputation for being ornery. She had a husband once and it was no surprise to anyone when he took off with another woman.

"So, Wally," Hank says, "I seem to recall that you did a little blasting back in your pipeline days."

TNT Norman perks up considerably when he hears the word *blasting*, and shifts his weight awkwardly so that he's leaning toward Hank instead of against the car door.

"I was wondering if you could give me a few instructions on how to blast that old buffalo stone out of my pasture," Hank says. "Damned tired of the kids leaving the gate open and letting my cows out."

"Yup, yup," Walter Norman says, and Hank wonders if maybe his mind is too far gone for him to remember what Hank needs to know.

But then the old man asks what Hank has for blasting powder. Hank can't understand him at first, his voice is so quiet, and he leans closer and asks Walter to repeat what he said. This time Hank understands and he tells him dynamite. He's had it out in his shed for a while—thought he might need it for the new well, but then he didn't after all and it's been sitting around in the shed, probably should have found a safer place but no harm done. Hank lists what else he has in the truck, and Walter says quietly, "Good, good, good, that ought to do 'er."

Then Lou puts down her magazine and turns around and says, "I have a dandy idea."

And that's how Hank ends up heading back toward the pasture with old man Norman in his truck, his wheelchair in the box with the blasting supplies. Lou's instructions are to take him home to Karla when they're done, and if Karla isn't home, to deliver him to Lou's house. She'd asked the old man if he needed to go to the bathroom and he'd said no, and Hank hoped that he knew what he was saying.

When they get back to the pasture Hank opens the gate and drives the truck up to the stone and then he gets the old man out and into his wheelchair. The mosquitoes are bad, so Hank sprays himself and Walter with the can of repellent that's sitting on the stone's flat surface. The old man's eyes light up when he sees the box of beer on the stone but Hank disappoints him by telling him it's full of empties.

"Anyway," Hank says, "we're both as dried out as Methuselah these days and that's likely a good thing, eh."

The old man still looks disappointed.

With Walter Norman giving instructions, Hank grips the auger's handle and begins to twist it into the ground, leaning on it with his weight. Three blasting holes, the old man advises, six feet deep if Hank can manage that. His auger won't go down that far, but Hank figures he can go four and a bit. Good enough. He gets as close to the stone as he can, angles under as much as possible. The daylight is completely gone but the moon is bright and Hank can see what he's doing. A light breeze comes up, which makes things easier. It blows the mosquitoes off and cools Hank down. As he digs, old man Norman relates the story about blasting the dugout and the barn being blown all over the country. The old man speaks so softly that Hank has to listen hard to hear, but it doesn't matter because he's heard the story at least a dozen times before. It was one of the old man's favourite bar tales when he was still drinking. Hank was still drinking back then too, so he'd been in the Juliet Hotel bar on several occasions when it was told. Tonight, old TNT adds a part about the wife's laundry ending up full of holes and Hank hadn't heard that before.

Because the soil is so sandy, it takes Hank less than an hour to get the three holes dug, and then he lays the dynamite and lead-in line according to TNT's instructions and fills in the holes with gravel and soil and tamps it down. Once that's done, he loads his shovel and auger into the truck box and moves the truck back to the approach, and then he moves the old man, pushing him in the wheelchair across the rough pasture trail. He runs lead-in line from the blasting holes over to the truck and attaches the detonators. When Hank has everything ready he looks at old TNT in his wheelchair and sees that he can hardly contain his excitement. He's practically bouncing in his chair in spite of his paralysis, as though this is the most exciting thing that's happened to him in ages. Hank doesn't doubt that it is.

"Are we ready?" Hank asks.

"We sure as hell are," the old man says, and then he shouts something as loudly as he can, which isn't very loud. It comes out as an elongated grunt and Hank can't make out the words.

"What was that?" Hank asks, and this time he gets it. "Fire in the hole," the old man is saying, and Hank thinks that's so funny he laughs and then he shouts it himself, "Fire in the hole!" and Hank's voice is a good deal louder than old man Norman's. Then he detonates the blasts, one at a time.

Nothing much happens. They can hear the blasts all right, and dirt and gravel fly up out of the holes in the moonlight. But no big pieces of rock arc through the air, and once the dirt settles, the dark shape of the stone remains unchanged as far as Hank can see. The two men stare at the silhouette as though something might yet happen, another blast might rocket the whole massive stone, but it sits where it is and the night grows quiet again except for the mosquitoes and Hank's cows bawling off to the west.

"Should we have a look?" Hank asks, and then he wheels the old man through the pasture once again toward the stone. Pushing the wheelchair along the rough trail takes more effort than digging the holes did and Hank works up a good sweat.

When they get to the stone, they see the auger holes have expanded considerably in size, but other than that, the stone looks the same. The beer box is still sitting on top, just as it was before, not even disturbed, Hank thinks, but when he picks it up he sees that the bottles have disintegrated into a pile of glass in the bottom.

"How about that," Hank says, shaking the box and listening to the tinkle of the broken glass.

The old man looks puzzled. "I thought we had 'er," he says.

"That dynamite was sitting around for some time," Hank says. "Maybe it was past the best-before date." He puts the beer box on the old man's lap and says, "I don't think I'm good for another go tonight. Best get you home."

He pushes Walter back across the pasture to the truck, the glass tinkling whenever they hit a bump in the trail, and when they're just about to the gate they hear a crack, like river ice in the spring, and when Hank turns around he can see that the rock has split in two. Right up the middle, two near-perfect halves in the moonlight, and he turns the old man around so he can see it too.

"That's not really what I had in mind," Hank says.

"I figured we had 'er," the old man says again.

Hank would like to go back and have a look at the stone but he's had enough of wheeling old TNT around the pasture.

When he gets Walter into the truck and his wheelchair in the box, he goes back and pulls the wire gate tight to the fence post and latches it up. Then he gets into the cab and hauls the remains of his six-pack of cola into the front seat. He hands a can to Walter and cracks one for himself. It's warm, but it still tastes good. He sees Walter struggling with the tab, so he turns the dome light on, but even then Walter can't get it, doesn't have the strength to peel it back, and so Hank does it for him and then Walter shakily lifts the can to his lips and spills some down his front and Hank pretends he doesn't notice.

"Well, we did half a night's work anyway," Hank says, and old TNT says, "We sure did, we got 'er half done anyway," and then he says, "I want to thank you, Hank." Quietly, but Hank hears it.

"Hell," Hank says. "You don't have to thank me. I should be thanking you. Wouldn't have got anywhere without a foreman. Likely would have blown myself up."

And they leave it at that.

When Hank gets to Karla's house, there are no lights on. Hank is going to take the old man over to Lou's, but then Walter tells him to just take him inside.

"I don't know," Hank says. "I'm a little scared of that Lou. Maybe I should do what I was told, eh." He tries to make a joke out if it and cajole the old man into agreeing to go to Lou's, but TNT insists that he wants to stay at Karla's and he says that Karla will be home sooner or later. He's just going to go to bed. He'll be okay on his own.

When they get inside Hank finds out that he has to help the old man onto and off of the toilet, and then out of his clothes and into a pair of cotton pyjamas. He doesn't mind. Fair trade, he figures, for the help with the blasting. He gets Walter a glass of water, just like you would a child, and then he helps him into bed. He turns out the lights, all but a lamp by the couch in the living room. He sees the little pile of sheets and blankets on the floor by the couch and supposes that this is where Karla sleeps.

Lucky man, he thinks, to have a daughter who'll take care of him like that. He wonders what it is he can smell in the air and then remembers that Karla does hair. He thinks she's done Lynn's hair a time or two. He hears a rooster crow from someplace close by and wonders what a rooster is doing in town, and crowing at this time of the night. Must be lost, a country rooster lost in town.

When he gets outside, the rooster is sitting on the hood of his truck. It looks at him and crow-hops a bit, up and down on the hood, but it doesn't scramble off, so Hank makes a grab for it and catches it by the legs. He holds it squawking upside down, not sure what to do with it now that he has it. It's a bantam rooster, too scrawny for the stewpot, but kind of pretty. He can see the green and rusty colours under the street lamp. He decides any rooster that is found hopping around on the hood of his truck belongs to him, finders keepers, and he opens the door and tosses the rooster into the cab. Lynn has a few chickens. He'll add this one to her flock. The rooster settles right down on the seat of the cab like it's used to riding around in trucks.

On the way home Hank decides to stop and have another look at the stone, and when he's walking up to it he sees that his year-lings have made their way around to this corner of the pasture and the way they're standing makes him think of buffalo, and he can almost see the giant beasts wallowing in the dust and scratching up against the stone to rid themselves of their winter coats. And when he thinks of the buffalo he almost feels bad that he's split the stone in two instead of leaving it up to nature to decide when it's time for change. He walks around the stone, taking care not to stumble in a hole, and he leans in and runs his hand against the clean hard split. There's a V between the two pieces, and the way the moonlight shines through, it looks like a gorge or a canyon, or perhaps the Red Sea parting. Hank steps through the opening and when he emerges on the other side he sees a white-faced steer staring at him. The moonlight shines on a pink fluorescent hand painting, and he places his own hand over the outline but his hand is much bigger, so he walks around the stone and tries a few more until he finds a lime green one that fits. He thinks about the compulsion humans seem to have for leaving their mark, the kids are no different, and maybe the art restorer would be kind of interesting with her white gloves and fancy tools and little jars of chemicals, like a scientist. Although her tools wouldn't help her repair this latest assault on the stone, the split down the middle.

He decides to leave the stone the way it is, not to try again to blast it to pieces. Maybe the split will be enough to keep the kids out of his pasture, since the stone no longer looks like a tabletop. He comes up with an official story: *What next? If it's not beer, it's blasting caps. Just lucky they didn't hurt themselves, or start a grass fire.* If you stick to your story, who's going to argue? Two people already know the truth—Lou and old TNT—but it's his pasture, he can say what he likes.

Hank walks back to his truck and cracks the last can in his six-pack of cola. He heads home, taking a shortcut across the pasture to the west, the truck bumping over the rocks and the gopher holes. He hopes Lynn is there. She stays in the restaurant as late as midnight if there are customers, but if it's dead she closes up early. Won't she be surprised, he thinks, looking at the rooster on the seat beside him. The fine-feathered present for his wife has settled in like a lapdog.

The Oasis

Offerings

It's late, almost midnight, when the owner of the lost horse pulls into the Oasis Café for a bite to eat. The parking lot is pretty much empty, just two semi-trailers and a half-ton, a car parked close to the door, a motorcycle in front of the Petro-Can. For a moment Joni worries that the restaurant might be closed but then she sees the lights on inside and she picks out two men—probably the truckers—sitting at a table by the window. She steps into the foyer between the Petro-Can and the restaurant and stops to look at the bulletin board, which is plastered with notices and ads: livestock sales, sports days, farm auctions, equipment for sale. There's an ad for taxidermy services, a plea for hay from someone in Alberta. She finds a pen in her purse but no paper, so she takes the hay notice and flips it over and writes: *Missing. Grey Arab gelding. Call Joni.* And then her cell phone number. As she looks for a good place to stick her note, her eye lands on a small, plain poster in black and white, with photographs of children who are missing. Several of the photos are identified as being computer-aged. She thinks about her grandchildren—the ones she's never met—as she studies the photos, and wonders if these posters do any good, if any of these children are ever found. Would she recognize a child from the poster, she wonders, if a car pulled up right now and the child got out and spoke to her, said hello, or asked for directions to the washroom or a pay phone? She wonders if she'd recognize her grandchildren from their pictures if they walked up to her on the street. Probably not.

There's a bare spot on the board next to the drive-in movie listings. Joni pins her missing horse notice there and then reaches into her purse and turns her phone back on, thinking it must be safe to do so by now. She sees a pink highlighter pen among the gum boxes and gas receipts and other detritus in her purse, and she decides to highlight her notice to make it stand out. At that moment, a woman with an apron comes from the restaurant and passes her on her way to the washroom, a middle-aged woman with roots in need of a touch-up. She's wearing pointed leather shoes that look like cowboy boots and Joni wonders how her feet can stand them.

"Hello there," the woman says, but she's all business, so Joni doesn't bother to answer.

Joni draws a pink circle around *Grey Arab gelding,* and then enters the restaurant. She's looking around, trying to decide where to sit, when her phone rings. She curses under her breath, then she reaches into her purse and turns the phone off again.

When she looks up, she notices an older man in a plaid shirt watching her from where he sits alone at a table. He sees he's been caught staring and says, "Damned phones, eh. A person could be up there in the Arctic, sitting on an iceberg, and someone would be trying to get him on the phone."

"No hiding from the phone," she agrees. She's been trying all day.

This restaurant is like an iceberg, she thinks, thanks to the air conditioning, and she wishes she'd brought a sweater in with her. She chooses a table by the window and sits, thinking about what she should order to ease her hunger this late at night. She has sandwich fixings in a cooler in the truck but it's too much trouble to get everything out in the dark. There's a menu on the table and she studies it, trying to decide between something reasonably light (soup du jour and a bun) and the full meal deal (a burger with fries and coleslaw).

The cold air makes her shiver, and it hits her how tired she is. She wishes she were in Peace River, or at least Edmonton, instead of freezing in an over air-conditioned restaurant in a town she's never heard of. *If it weren't for that damned horse*, she thinks, although it had been her own rash act that had put the horse in her possession in the first place, and she should have known that it would sprout feathers and turn into an albatross. As she searched the countryside around Juliet, she'd been tempted by the idea of leaving without the horse, selling the trailer cheap to the first dealer she could find, stopping somewhere to buy appropriate gifts for the children—LEGO, books, video games— and then carrying on unencumbered. But she was worried about the horse, that he'd been chased by coyotes or whatever chases horses, or got tangled in a fence, and she couldn't just leave, so she'd driven the grid roads and had somehow ended up at a surprising stretch of yellow sand that rose in dunes as far she could see. She remembered the old cowboy in the campground mentioning the sand hills, and then the woman in the post office had waxed on about them as though they were a wonder of the world that shouldn't be missed. Joni hadn't paid much attention. She'd passed several such promises on her way through Saskatchewan, aimed at making people stop on their way to somewhere else: mysterious tunnels under Main Street, country mansions built and abandoned by old-world gentry, the longest bridge over the shortest span of water.

Still, the sight of the dunes had tempted her enough that she'd parked her truck in the yard of an old schoolhouse and found a faint trail to follow on foot. It was mostly covered over by sand, but she could make out the two vehicle tracks worn into the surface and it was enough of a trail that she could stick to it and not risk getting lost. When she left the trail to climb one of the dunes and looked to the west where the sun was shining hot on the waves of sand, she'd thought, *The woman in the post office was right, these hills are a wonder.* The landscape was so vast and simple, reduced to sky and grass and sand. Yet in the surface at her feet, she saw patterns as intricate and complicated as the veins in an insect's wings. The discovery of this spot was almost worth the aggravation of the missing horse.

A rogue gust blew sand in her eyes and she had to turn away, blinking, her eyes watering. When they cleared, she slid back down the dune, and when she got to the bottom she saw something at her feet, mostly buried in the sand, a leather strap, so she reached down and pulled on it and it came loose. It looked like an old halter. The leather was warm in her hand from the sun and cracked and dry as toast, but it was in one piece, still buckled as though whatever had been wearing it had sloughed it off and wandered on without it. She wondered what else was buried under all this sand. She thought of taking the halter with her, but then she laid it back down to be covered up again.

She'd returned to her truck then and driven more miles around the countryside, checking herds of horses in pastures, stopping at farmhouses to inquire. She came to a Catholic church out in the middle of nowhere, and across the road, an old woman named Anna working in her flower bed. When Joni asked her about the horse, she nodded and said, "You talk to that boy, Lee Torgeson. He might know something about your horse." Joni had imagined a ten-year-old. Then Anna had insisted she come into the house for coffee, and Joni couldn't say no and ended up telling Anna about her grandchildren and showing her the school pictures, and Anna had gushed appropriately over them. When Joni finished her coffee Anna had provided directions to the Torgeson place, back the way she'd come, but when Joni got to the farm there was no one there. Just a black-and-white dog that barked a few times and then came and rolled at her feet. More driving around until after dark and the hunger pangs got to her, and she'd seen the Oasis sign and pulled in.

Joni makes up her mind to stick with the soup du jour, whatever it turns out to be, because it's too late to be eating a big meal. Potato soup would hit the spot. She could hope for potato. When the woman in the apron comes back into the restaurant—the waitress, Joni assumes—she closes the menu to indicate she's ready to order. She should maybe ask what kind of soup the du jour is just in case it's clam chowder. Seafood that's been sitting on a warming plate for hours is not likely a good idea.

The waitress doesn't make a move toward her table and Joni begins to wonder if this is the kind of place where you help yourself, like a cafeteria, or maybe go to the counter to place your order. She looks around and doesn't see any kind of buffet table. She holds up her menu. The waitress just stares at her, or perhaps *glares* would be a better word. Joni wonders if maybe she missed seeing a CLOSED sign hanging on the door, and is about to get up and ask if she's too late to get a bite to eat, when the woman strides over to her table and says, "What can I get you?"

"Just soup. Du jour. And a bun. What is the soup? I guess I should ask that."

"Beef barley."

She wants to ask about potato but is afraid to, the way the waitress is looking at her. "Beef barley's good," she says. "I'll have that. And a bun."

"A bun. So you said. You can help yourself to coffee." The waitress turns and goes through the swinging doors to the kitchen.

Before Joni can get up to help herself to coffee, the man in the plaid shirt says, "I'll get that. You just sit." He gets a mug and the pot from the burner and carries them to Joni's table, where he sets the mug down and fills it without saying anything else.

"Thanks," she says.

He responds with a nod. Then he fills his own cup before he puts the pot back on the burner.

Joni shivers and wraps her hands around the hot mug, wishing again that she'd put on a sweater or even a jacket. The waitress comes back through the kitchen doors and slaps Joni's soup down in front of her. The broth slops over the edge of the bowl and splashes the bun.

"Thanks," Joni says. She's thinking how strange this is, this bitchy waitress, but the soup smells good and she would have dipped the bun anyway.

The two truckers stand up from their table and make their way to the cash register.

"Sorry," one of them says to the waitress, "nothing smaller than a twenty."

"I thought you were a big tipper," she says, following them.

"Not that big."

After they leave, Joni can see the waitress is watching her again from behind the till. It's unnerving.

When the man in the plaid shirt says, "I wouldn't mind another slice of that pie," the waitress goes through the swinging doors and returns with a plate of something lime green.

"This is the last piece for you, Willard," she says to him. "You'll be turning green." She sets the plate on the table in front of him and asks, "So how's the movie business treating you?"

"Marian's doing the movie tonight," he says.

The waitress goes back behind the till counter and begins replacing the menu inserts with new ones for the next day. Joni finishes her soup and pushes the plate and bowl aside. She watches as the man Willard eats the pie, wondering if she should maybe try a piece. As soon as he's done he slides away from his table and stands, searching through his pockets. He checks one pocket, and the next, and the next, and then an expression crosses his face that clearly means he's realized he has no money with him.

"I left the house in such a hurry," he says.

"Don't worry about it," the waitress says. "If I can't trust you, I might as well pack it in right now and give up on humanity."

Still, he stands there.

"Everything okay?" the waitress asks.

Willard licks his lips. "That pie was good all right," he says. And still he stands.

"Willard," the waitress says, looking alarmed. "If there's something wrong . . ."

And then he quickly turns on his heel and leaves, muttering something about Marian and the drive-in and all those kids who need a man to keep them in line. Through the restaurant window Joni can see him hurrying across the parking lot. He backs his truck out and onto the highway so quickly he hardly looks to see if another vehicle is approaching.

Joni is now alone with the waitress in the restaurant and she decides it's time for her to leave too. She reaches for her purse, but then the waitress approaches Joni's table, stops right next to it and says, "Just turn your damned phone on."

"Excuse me?" Joni says.

"Your cell phone," the waitress says. "Turn it on."

Joni would love to tell this rude woman to go to hell, she can keep her green pie, it's probably not real food anyway, but then the waitress sighs deeply, and when Joni looks at her face she sees that the glare is gone and the woman looks very tired, just the way she feels herself. Joni reaches into her purse, takes out her phone and switches the power on. The waitress takes her own phone out of her apron pocket and dials a number. Joni's ring-tone sounds. Once. Twice. The waitress switches her own phone off and the ring-tone stops.

"What the hell," Joni says.

"Yeah. What the hell." The waitress turns to walk away.

"Wait a minute," Joni says. "You're the one who's been calling me all day?"

"Looks that way."

"Why? And how did you get my number?"

"I got your number out of my husband's back pocket."

"Well, frankly," Joni says, "that doesn't make sense. I'm not in the habit of handing out my phone number. . . ." She stops, remembering that she gave her number to a cowboy in the campground that morning. "Wait a minute."

"Never mind," the waitress says. "No explanation needed. I read your notice out there. The mistake was mine. I thought I had a missing husband, turns out you had a missing horse. So sorry about all the calls. I went nuts for a while. There's a story but you don't want to hear it."

"I might," says Joni.

"Well, I don't want to tell it."

The waitress goes through the doors to the kitchen again and Joni thinks, *That's that*, but then the woman returns with a slice of the green pie.

"On the house," she says.

Joni isn't altogether sure she should eat the pie given the waitress's suspicion about her cheating husband, but the woman says, "Don't worry, I'm not planning to poison you. It's a new recipe. I've been trying it out on my preferred customers all day. I figure I owe you at least a slice of pie. Like I said, I don't know what got into me."

Joni takes a tentative bite. The lime flavour dances on her tongue. "Wow," she says. "Very tasty."

"That seems to be the general opinion," the waitress says. "It's going on the menu. Anyway, I'll leave you to your coffee. I've got some cleaning up to do in the kitchen."

She looks so tired and depressed that Joni says, "Hey, don't worry about the phone calls. It doesn't matter. Really."

"You're not about to run off with my husband, are you," the woman says. It's not even a question.

"No," Joni says, "definitely not."

"Christ, I don't know what's the matter with me. Well, for one thing, my feet hurt. I do know that."

Joni looks down at the woman's feet, the pointed leather shoes, and then sticks one of her own feet out from under the table, shows off her new green cross-trainers.

"Running shoes," she says. "I never wear anything else any more."

"Just one more sign that you're on the downward slope. Practical footwear. Not that those are especially practical, not the colour anyway. No offence."

"Why don't you sit down?" Joni says. "Take a load off." She should probably just leave and let the poor woman go home to bed, but the way she's standing by the table, she looks as though she would dearly love to get off her feet.

Joni's assessment is right because the waitress, Lynn is her name, pours herself a cup of coffee, refills Joni's cup and sits across from her.

And then Joni can't stop herself. She asks Lynn if she has any grandkids, and when Lynn says no, Joni takes out the pictures of her own grandchildren. In spite of the fact that Lynn harassed her with phone calls all day long and behaved so rudely before revealing her motive, Joni tells her reunion story. She knows there's no reason for Lynn to be interested, but she just can't help talking about her newfound family, proudly showing off the school pictures when she doesn't know yet whether she has a reason to be proud. But these children are her offspring. Whatever is in the past between her and her daughter, she tells Joni, whatever happens when they meet again, maybe she can help in some way. She wishes she had more money. That's likely what her daughter needs more than anything.

Lynn expresses the opinion that the boys are fine-looking kids, and Joni agrees and puts the pictures away. Lynn looks out the window, at the truck and trailer under the light in the parking lot.

"That must be your rig out there," she says.

"Unfortunately," Joni says. And she tells Lynn the rest of the story—the foolish purchase of the now-missing horse.

And then, a development Joni could not possibly have predicted when she walked through the restaurant door: Lynn says, "Tell you what. I'll buy that horse from you, and when I track him down, I'll find him a good home. Someone around here will want him."

Joni is stunned. "Why would you do that?" she asks. "For a stranger?"

Lynn says, "I'd like to say it's because I'm a good old-fashioned nice person. But I'm not. I'm hard to get along with—just ask the girls who work for me—and most of the time I can't be bothered doing favours for people." She looks out the window again and nods at the truck and trailer. "What I really want is your trailer. If I buy the horse, I assume you won't need the trailer any more and you'll be open to offers."

Such a relief, Joni can't believe it, horse trouble dissipating just like that. Lynn goes for her cheque book, and Joni is free of the burden she's been dragging around since the auctioneer said SOLD and pointed in her direction. And then Lynn surprises Joni again by laughing. At the circumstance that put the trailer

in her possession—the phone calls, the ridiculousness of it all—
and Joni thinks how Lynn looks like a different person when she
laughs, how laughing makes everyone look better and she should
remember to do it herself, often, when she's with her daughter
again, because there hadn't been much laughing in those last
ugly years before the girl left to live with her father. And she
should laugh right off when she meets her grandsons, she thinks,
to make a good impression.

"Well," Lynn says, looking at the clock on the wall. "It's been
nice doing business, but I suppose it's time to get this placed closed
up." She asks Joni if she has an e-mail address so she can let her
know about the horse, one way or the other, but Joni doesn't have
one. She says, "You've got my cell number," and they both have
a good laugh about that. Lynn walks out to the lot with Joni and
helps her with the trailer hitch, and then Joni pulls away, free of
the trailer, and heads back to the campground for the night.

Once she's gone, Lynn goes inside and carries the last remaining plates and coffee cups to the kitchen and washes them and
wipes down the tables and, finally, turns out the lights. As she
leaves the dark restaurant and looks across the lot at the trailer,
she's pleased that she has a surprise for her husband. A present—
a little rusty but good enough—to make up for the fact that she
had, briefly, lost faith.

Cowboy

Sometime after midnight Lila hears Kyle's truck on the street in
front of the house. It's unmistakable. The truck stops, and a door
slams, and Kyle's boots sound on the step. The doorbell.

Lila quickly goes to the door before the bell wakes Rachelle.

When she opens it, Kyle teeters on the top step. She can see that he's left the lights on in his truck.

Kyle looks terrible, worse than she does, Lila thinks. She'd like to believe that when Rachelle told him she wasn't going to marry him—she assumes Rachelle was the one who broke it off—Kyle drank himself into this state out of hurt and heartache, but then she remembers the night before, Kyle passed out in the backyard, and a few other times that she was pretty sure he'd been drinking, even though she'd argued with Norval that Kyle was a responsible boy who wouldn't dream of getting behind the wheel of a car with alcohol in his veins. Maybe Norval was right, the wedding had been a mistake from the beginning. She is suddenly so very sick of the soap opera of her daughter's love life.

"You can't drive home in that state," Lila says. "You just can't."

Kyle asks if he can see Rachelle, and Lila thinks he is saying something about sorry but she can't make it out, his words are so slurred.

"How could you allow yourself to drive?" Lila says. "You could have killed someone. No one would forgive you for that, Kyle. No one. It would haunt you for the rest of your life."

He stares at her, as though he just can't process what she's said.

"Get in here," Lila says.

Kyle steps inside and the smell of alcohol fills the foyer. Kyle struggles to get his boots off without falling, and when he finally does, he starts for the stairs to where the bedrooms are.

"No," Lila says. "Not that way."

Kyle stops and looks at her. She points down, to where there's a basement recreation room with a pool table, a pullout couch and a bathroom. "You can talk to Rachelle in the morning. She's going to need you then, Kyle, if that means anything to you at all."

Kyle obediently turns and stumbles past Lila and goes down the carpeted stairs to the basement. She thinks about leaving his truck lights on all night to teach him a lesson, but then she thinks again about morning and how she and Rachelle will need all the strength they have to get through the day, and Kyle's truck with a dead battery will be just one more impossible detail. She goes outside and switches off the lights, and on her way back up the walk she notices again Norval's lawn. It's a dense, green, beautiful lawn, even if it is overgrown. She's been lobbying for some kind for xeriscaping, which she read about in a garden magazine. This would entail getting rid of the grass entirely and installing in its stead materials that require no watering. And, of course, no mowing. She wonders why this had seemed like a good idea when Norval had so loved his lawn, and the act of mowing. She doesn't understand herself.

She steps back into the house and locks the door, then decides she'd better go downstairs and check on Kyle. She finds him passed out on the pool table, curled into a fetal position like a little boy, although he is far from little. These children, Lila thinks. These foolish, ignorant children. How in the world will she deal with them without Norval? She flicks off the light and climbs heavily up the stairs to the living room, where she sits once again in the armchair and takes up her box of Kleenex, knowing that she must be brave, she must tell Rachelle, she cannot put it off much longer. She turns on the television, which is on Norval's favourite channel, and watches the weather forecasts for the Atlantic provinces and the Far North and Mexico and Russia and the south of France.

For the first time she understands the appeal of the Weather Channel, the lulling monotony of weather. She will let it soothe her for a time, she decides, a short time, and then she will wake Rachelle and lead her—or drag her, if need be—through the door to adulthood.

Your father loved you very much is how she will begin.

Wreckage

When Vicki hears the plane this time, she is positive she's awake. She hears a hiccup, and another one, and then silence, a long awful silence, and the sound of a crash. Close by. It had to be, or she wouldn't have heard it.

She shakes Blaine, switches on the bedside lamp, shakes him again.

"Blaine," she says, "I just heard a plane go down. I'm not sure where, but close."

Blaine stares at her, uncomprehending. His eyelids flutter, then close.

"I'm sure, Blaine," she says, shaking him awake. "We have to look."

"Not the damned beans again," Blaine says, rolling away from her.

"Not beans," Vicki says, poking him with her foot. "An airplane."

"You look for it. And turn that light out."

Vicki slides her bare feet into the easiest things, her worn old plastic flip-flops. She switches off the light and leaves the bedroom, slips through the kitchen and out the door, from one darkness to another, and stands in the yard looking, trying to decide which way to go. She can't believe that this has really happened after all the years of dreaming, that she is really heading out to look for a downed plane and its pilot, passengers if there are any. She has no idea where to turn. The sound had been overhead. Right *inside* her head, in fact, directionless. She scans the horizon, looking for lights or fire. Nothing. She listens. Nothing but silence. She takes a step toward the pasture fence, thinking she will try that way.

But before she is across the yard it all fades—the sound over-head, the crash, the dread. She can feel it fading, becoming less and less real, and in no time at all it's turned into the same pleas-ant sensation she felt in her old dream about paddling across the lake in a canoe. No droning sound of a falling plane, just the splash of her paddles. She stops. She's aware now of dew in the grass; she can feel it through the plastic straps of her flip-flops. She listens to the sound of a cricket, leaves rustling in the stiff breeze that's come up, an owl somewhere to the east. Not the sounds of mayhem. Perhaps she just doesn't want to go looking, she thinks. She doesn't want to find burning debris, or worse, human remains. But in no time even these thoughts are gone and she's left standing in the yard, feeling foolish.

She returns to the house in a sleepy stupor, shakes the san-dals from her feet and crawls back into bed. She rolls up against Blaine's warm back, but he mumbles "too hot" and gently pushes her away. She knows, because Blaine told her, that he poured kerosene on the beans and burned them, and the thought of all those beans reduced to ash makes her want to whisper in his ear: *Thank you, sweetheart.* Which she does before she obediently rolls back to her own side of the bed.

Beneath Vicki and Blaine, in his second night in his own room, Shiloh lies awake, his light shining on the rodeo poster of the bull rider with the purple-and-gold chaps. He imagines the bull rider flying off the bull and landing hard on a hip or a shoulder, can just feel him flying through the air, feel the pain as he hits the dirt. Or maybe he gets hung up in the well as the bull spins, struggling to get his hand free from the bull rope, his life depending on his ability to stay on his feet, his arm practically pulled from its socket, until he's free from the rope, the suicide wrap, then an adrenalin-fuelled dash to the chutes to grab a rail and hoist himself up and out of the bull's way. Dropping down onto his feet again once the bull is heading for the gate, a tip of his hat, now feeling the hurt, on his knees in front of all those people, the breath sucked right out of him, until he's helped to his feet by another pair of cowboys. *Let's make this young cowboy feel a little better about bein' bucked off,* the announcer says, *show him that you appreciate his effort.* And the fans applaud.

He, Shiloh Dolson, got bucked off a horse today. His hip hurts where he landed and he's already got a huge black bruise that he won't be showing to his mother, not to anyone. He's proud of that bruise, though. He hopes it lasts for a few days at least, a secret that he alone knows about. He rolls over onto his sore hip just so he can feel the bruise. It's the first time in his life he's been bucked off a horse. He's fallen off a couple of times, soft landings in the dirt, but Blaine never put a kid on a horse that he didn't trust. He wouldn't let the kids, not even Shiloh, ride Buck.

Shiloh's hip hurts too much and he has to roll over again and take his weight off the bruise. He wonders if any other parts of his body will hurt tomorrow. He imagines himself walking up the alley behind Brittney Vass's house wearing chaps—maybe not purple, though—bruised and limping and dragging a bull rope, the cowbell clanging as he walks. Brittney watching him over her backyard fence. But he won't look her way, not even a glance, won't let on that he knows she's there. It's pleasing, this vision of himself. He closes his eyes.

He's almost asleep but the light is bothering him. He can see it through his eyelids. He reaches over to switch it off and sees the bull rider's face.

The face is his, and he's not dreaming.

Ghost

There's just enough light from the moon that Willard thinks he sees Marian put her finger to her lips, and then she crosses the linoleum floor and when she's halfway between the door and his bed he can see that, yes, she does have her finger to her lips and she's whispering, *shhhh,* as though there's someone else besides Willard who might hear.

When Marian lifts Willard's covers, lifts her nightgown, *removes* her nightgown, he couldn't be more astonished. It takes a minute and the warmth of Marian's body for him to realize that she hasn't come to talk, that words aren't, in fact, needed. Marian kneels over him, and Willard isn't sure what to do. He should say something—*Christ, woman, stop whatever it is that you're doing*—but he doesn't want her to stop, feels all his pent-up love for her rushing to that one mysterious organ. His hands rise and he places them on her white thighs. *Shhhh,* she says again, now lowering herself to meet his naked body—there's that word, *body,* he wonders if he said it out loud, but *shhhh* is the only sound he hears—and he's ready for her—another surprise—and he closes his eyes and surrenders until a shudder passes through him and he moans, he can't help it. He's embarrassed at the guttural sound. The warmth he feels makes him want to talk, makes him want to say things, but there are no words in his head. Only fragments, nine years' worth of words and phrases and truncations. He *has* to say something, for her sake, but what? All they've ever spoken about is business (the drive-in) and household appliances (the dishwasher with its tendency to leak) and who's going to pick up the mail (usually Willard). *Her name,* he thinks, *I could say her name,* and he's about to utter it, or try to, when Marian moves her finger from her lips to his, touches him gently, then lifts herself off him, out of the bed. She picks up her nightgown from where it has fallen and she turns, and her bare feet carry her across the floor, away from him, and she disappears.

Silence. The vapoury stillness of night almost unbearable. Willard wants the dog to bark, a truck to pass, a crack of thunder, anything to bring him back to what is familiar. But why? The last few minutes were perhaps the most pleasurable he's experienced since childhood. He closes his eyes and tries to hang on to the feeling but it fades and then a truck does pass and the dog barks, and he's no longer sure if Marian really came to him or if he spilled his own warmth in a dark dream.

He can't sleep. In fact, he doesn't want to sleep. He lies awake, listening to the dog bark but not registering that *his dog is barking,* and wonders what is ahead. He tingles with expectation, although he has no idea where this night is going to take him. Perhaps nowhere. He knows that in the darkness the edges of things are blurred—the past and the present, dreams and memory and time. He doesn't try to understand Marian's ghostly visit. One word rolls around in his head, over and over, the word *lovers.*

Even as the dog barks and a teenage boy lights the wick of a crude Molotov cocktail, his friends hanging back, not as brave, and throws it as hard as he can toward the dark shadow of the movie screen.

Even as the fire catches in the dry grass, flames licking at the looming wooden structure, the dog barking furiously now, and Marian returns to Willard's doorway and says, "Willard, the dog. I think the kids are out there again."

The two of them, Willard pulling on a pair of pants and Marian in her nightgown, out the door to be greeted by the sight of fire, a real fire this time. Marian gasps, is ready to run with a bucket of water, but Willard holds her back and says, "Too late. Let it go." Then, "Don't go, Marian. Don't leave me. I love you."

Surprising the absolute hell out of himself.

And then he quickly goes back inside to the phone and calls the volunteer fire department to keep the fire from spreading through the grass, it's too late for the movie screen.

And Marian stands in the open doorway as though she's on fire with the flames behind her, watching him, and she says, "I'm not going anywhere, Willard. Where in the world did you get that idea?"

Sand

When Lee was a boy he dreamed of living in the desert, a student of sand, the protege of a Bedouin camel driver, learning from a master how to find his way through endless miles of dunes with no landmarks because the landscape keeps shifting and reinventing itself. Lee would lie in his bed with a flashlight late into the night and look at the soft, hand-coloured photographs in Lester's old books—pictures of smiling nomad wives in front of their tents wearing heavy and elaborate jewellery. The caption under one such photograph informed Lee, *A Bedouin woman wears a large part of her husband's capital, and as his wealth increases, so will the number of silver chains supporting coins or charms.* He had no idea what that meant. He didn't know what capital was, unless the word was used as an adjective, as in capital city. He knew all the capital cities of North America.

He would try to talk Astrid into letting him camp out in the sand hills up the road, but she would never agree. He didn't know why. "You're not old enough to stay out there alone, pretending to be the Sheik of Araby," she would tell him, and he would argue that he wouldn't be alone, Rip would be there too, and Astrid would say, "Yes, but for how long? That old horse has a dinner bell in his head and he's going to set off for home the second he hears the first ring." Lee started to say something about hobbles and Astrid nipped that in the bud. "Oh no you don't," she said. "You're going to get yourself in big trouble if you try hobbling a horse and you don't know what you're doing. There'll be none of that nonsense." And when she told Lester what he had planned, Lester backed her up in his usual laconic way. "Tomfoolery," he said. He could have said malarkey. That was another word Lester used to put an end to things.

So Lee lay in his bed at night and imagined himself in a home-made tent with its back to the west wind. Lester had a tanned hide in a shed—his father's first purebred Hereford bull, named Lucky, shipped from Ontario and the foundation of his herd— and Lee planned how he could load Lucky's hide onto Rip's back somehow and take it into the sand and then drape it over a frame of fresh-cut poplar boughs, creating a tent that he could leave open on one side, like the ones in the photographs. He'd build a fire in front and cook for himself—beans and cheese (preferably goat cheese but he didn't know where he would get that)—and he'd have dates from Astrid's baking supplies for dessert. When the wind came up he would lie under a single blanket inside the tent and listen to the sand battering the hide, and his tent would be sturdy, and Rip would close his eyes and turn his back to the wind just outside the tent and stand still as a statue until the storm was past. Maybe Lee would even find Antoinette out there somewhere and increase his standing, as Lester's book said, by the animals he possessed. Capital. Maybe that's what capital was.

Once Lee hit puberty, his interest in Lester's obsolete books waned, and eventually he quit looking at them altogether. While

other kids outgrew Saturday morning television, Lee outgrew
the naive descriptions of a simple nomadic life with a small
herd of animals and a wife laden with charms. He couldn't picture himself any more as a hospitable nomad draped in layers
of flowing garments, who invited strangers into his tent and
served tea from a Persian samovar. And one day he looked in
Lester's shed and Lucky's hide was gone—he supposed Lester
had thrown it out, taken it to the dump—and then Rip and Tom
died, and Lee discovered Saturday night and the joy of back
roads in a car driven by someone a few years older until he was
old enough himself to be the driver, a case of beer on the floor,
thinking about girls from the next town but never doing much
about it because he was too shy. Even though a couple of the girls
tried to snap him up. Whenever they phoned he told Astrid to say
he would call them back, but he never did—except for that one
girl who was serious and smart and couldn't wait to get to the
city. Then after grade twelve graduation, full-time farming with
Lester, all the work of the different seasons, and Lee tried to be
an able hand and learn the job well, and then Lester died when
Lee was twenty-two, and then Astrid.

And now, here he is, the sole owner of their capital. *His* capital.

He stretches out on one of Astrid's webbed plastic lounge
chairs in the yard. A wind has come up—the old trees are creaking—and the air feels good. He's wearing a pair of worn grey
sweatpants pulled up to his knees so the breeze can cool the saddle burns on his calves. Cracker is lying in the grass beside him,
no unusual sounds keeping him alert and awake tonight. Lee is
envious of the dog's ability to sleep.

He closes his eyes, but it's no use. He can't stop the sand from
passing. The same sand, he keeps thinking, that was there when
the Perry cowboys rode the hundred miles, just blown around and
rearranged the way he'd shuffled and rearranged the postcards

earlier. And then the postcards are in his mind again, the certainty that the messages are from his mother, the handwriting not quite a picture of her face, but evidence of her existence. He thinks of the box in the closet and is satisfied now with its place there, even though Astrid had wanted it burned. He feels as though the postcards belong in the house, since the words written on them were spoken aloud and recited time and time again until they were part of the walls. He wonders whether their discovery will cause him to ask new questions, but for now he's content that one question has been answered. Did she, his mother, ever think about him once she'd placed him in Astrid and Lester's porch and driven away into the night? Yes. She had.

Lee drops the back of the webbed lounger down farther so that he's lying almost flat. He wishes he'd brought a pillow outside with him. He longs for sleep but it won't come. Instead, the day replays itself over and over: the miles horseback, the heat of the sun, Mrs. Bulin in his kitchen, the postcards. And always the sand passing beneath the horse's hooves.

He recalls again how he'd never been able to talk Astrid into letting him sleep in the sand hills overnight. He thinks, *I could now, why not?* He's on his own, the master of this spread—surprisingly, the idea of that does not scare him at this moment. He gets up from the chair, pulling down his pant legs, and goes into the house and down to the basement, where there's an old nylon pup tent packed away, purchased for a school camping trip. He finds a lightweight sleeping bag, not that he'll need a sleeping bag on such a warm summer night.

Already thinking about what else he should take with him—a bit of firewood, water, an old pot for coffee—but the list gets too long and makes the whole venture seem like too much trouble. He settles on just the tent and a blanket and a flashlight, and his desert scrapbook, kept in a drawer in his childhood desk. He'll look through it one last time and then put it away forever, maybe in Astrid's closet. As he's going out the door he decides that a hot drink would be good after all, so he takes the time to boil the kettle and make tea, which he puts in a beat-up metal travel mug from the Oasis, a poor excuse for a samovar but there's only him and he doesn't have to bestow hospitality on himself. He thinks briefly about riding the horse into the dunes again, but immediately dismisses that idea because the thought of getting back on is much too painful.

When he gets outside, Cracker is at the doorstep, wagging his tail, ready again for whatever might unfold. Normally, Lee would leave him behind but this time he says, "What the hell," and motions for Cracker to jump in the truck box, then he changes his mind again and lets him ride in the cab, which Lester would never have done. He takes a loop through the yard so he can check on the horse. The truck's headlights shine on the grey coat and the horse barely lifts his head. He's standing up against the side of the barn, relaxed, resting one hind foot, the breeze keeping the mosquitoes away.

As Lee leaves the yard, a gust of wind hits the side of the truck and he wonders if maybe something is moving in. He drives north, the lights of Juliet in the rear-view mirror, heading once again for the big dunes up near Lindstroms' and the Hundred Mile School. He rolls down the window so he can feel the night air, and watches the dark shapes pass: the familiar rolling landscape, the cemetery, the bins and sheds and farm machinery, and rows of fence posts and telephone poles. A white-tailed deer jumps out of the ditch onto the road in front of him and he has to slam on the brakes to avoid hitting her, but she flashes off to the east while Cracker struggles to keep his balance on the seat.

Lee parks the truck across the road from the old school. With the rolled-up tent and its poles and pegs in a nylon bag under one arm, his blanket and the scrapbook under the other, and the travel mug and flashlight in his two hands, he sets off across the sand, Cracker sticking close to his side in this new territory.

Lee doesn't go far. Walking in the sand is difficult and he's packing his gear awkwardly. As soon as he's at the foot of a dune, he drops everything in the sand. The pages of the scrapbook rustle and flap in the wind as he unpacks the nylon tent. He pieces together the cross-poles and threads them through, and the breeze fills the tent like a sail, the gusts threatening to carry it off. He tries to stake it down but the pegs are useless in the sand. The only thing to do is sit inside and use his body weight on the floor to hold it in place. He manages to get it set with the door facing east and throws his blanket and the scrapbook and flashlight inside. Then he crawls in himself with his travel mug and ties the door open. He spreads the blanket out and sits on it just inside the door. Cracker sits in the sand staring at him and Lee says, "You stay put there, no wandering off," and Cracker immediately lies in the sand with his head on his paws so close to the tent he's almost inside. Lee takes a sip of tea and feels sand all along the rim of the plastic lid.

He opens the scrapbook and sees photographs cut from old magazines and brochures, captions written in a boy's earnest hand. He knows it's his own handwriting, but he feels as if he's looking at the work of another boy, a stranger, although one he wouldn't mind knowing. The school glue he used on the clippings has dried and cracked, and as he shines the flashlight on an aerial photograph of an oasis in Morocco, a gust of wind grabs it from the page and carries it out into the night. He slides the scrapbook closer to the door, flips the page and watches the wind take a map of the Sahara. Another page and a marketplace in Cairo flies away. As he turns the pages, one picture after another is caught by the wind.

Lee closes the scrapbook. Its demise is no real loss, and then he wonders if maybe that's what Lester and Astrid had concluded when they spoke about the watch behind closed doors: no loss, just a keepsake, nothing on which life and death rest. He sets the scrapbook outside the tent. The pages flap and paper blows off into the darkness. Then the whole scrapbook slides across the sand until it's out of range of the flashlight beam.

Lee brushes the grit away from the rim of his cup and sips his tea. The wind is getting stronger. He shines the flashlight beam outside again and he can see fine, loose sand drifting from west to east along the surface. He leans out the tent door, aims the beam in a half-circle around the opening, and he can see that the whole surface is drifting, beginning to lift. A veil of sand hovers a few inches above the ground. A gust hits the back of the tent and the veil rises into a cloud. Cracker whines and inches forward until his front paws are inside and his nose is on Lee's blanket. Lee slides back into the tent and sets the flashlight in the doorway with its beam outward, so he can watch the drifting sand. Wind gusts under the edges of the tent and causes the floor to lift around the weight of Lee's body. He can hear sand hitting the taut nylon.

He remembers a poem about sand from high school: "Look on my works, ye Mighty, and despair," and then the irony of the words referring to a lost and buried empire. He'd been captivated by that poem—its setting in the desert, its meaning unmistakable—but it strikes him that he and his classmates studied it without thinking about the sand in their own backyard, or the inevitable end of their own empires. As much as he'd liked the poem, he hadn't thought it was especially significant. In general, that's what he thought about school. Although he'd been a good student, never wanting to let Astrid down, he'd had no desire for higher education. When he passed on the scholarship, he'd worried that Astrid and Lester would think he'd done so just to help them on the farm. That hadn't been the case.

He lies on top of the blanket and listens. He tries to hear himself breathing, but he can't. It's too noisy with the wind blowing and the nylon flapping. Periodically, something larger than a grain of sand slaps up against the side of the tent and he wonders what it is. He imagines things blowing around outside—clumps of tumbleweed, empty cigarette packs, plastic water bottles. The wind exposing objects from the past. A deerskin pouch, perhaps. The dipper from a water pail. A worn leather boot cracked and missing the lace, a coffee can blown from the windowsill of a one-room shack.

And a camel bone, polished smooth and white by the wind and sand. Antoinette. He wonders what happened to Antoinette. Maybe Willard knew and never told him.

He retrieves the flashlight from the door of the tent and lies back down and shines it on his own chest, rising and falling, then switches it off. He listens for the hoof beats over the noise of the wind, but he knows they won't come. He waits for the voices of Astrid and Lester—*get yourself a good map . . . use the silver tea service*—but their words don't come either. Maybe they won't ever come again. He has a map, drawn carefully for him by Lester, as assuring as any map can be. And he'd offered Mrs. Bulin a cup of tea tonight, hadn't he. He'd used her well enough.

He closes his eyes and listens to the wind, the flapping of nylon, sand against the tent walls. As sleep finally comes, he thinks, *The very same sand that has been in these hills for centuries.*

The wind blows until dawn, releasing the past, howling at the boundaries of the present.

The land forever changing shape.

To the east, the pale pink of early morning.